✔ KU-765-786

ALSO BY MORGAN MATSON

Amy & Roger's Epic Detour

Second Chance Summer

Since You've Been Gone

The Unexpected Everything

Save the Date

TAKE
ME
HOME
Tonight

WALTHAM FOREST LIBRARIES

904 000 00702677

MORGAN MATSON

TAKE ME HOME
Tonight

SIMON & SCHUSTER

First published in Great Britain in 2021 by Simon & Schuster UK Ltd

First published in the USA in 2021 by Simon & Schuster Books for Young Readers

Copyright © 2021 Morgan Matson

This book is copyright under the Berne Convention.
No reproduction without permission.
All rights reserved.

The right of Morgan Matson to be identified as the author of this work
has been asserted by her in accordance with sections 77 and 78 of
the Copyright, Design and Patent Act, 1988.

1 3 5 7 9 10 8 6 4 2

Simon & Schuster UK Ltd
1st Floor, 222 Gray's Inn Road
London
WC1X 8HB

www.simonandschuster.co.uk
www.simonandschuster.com.au
www.simonandschuster.co.in

Simon & Schuster Australia, Sydney
Simon & Schuster India, New Delhi

A CIP catalogue record for this book is available from the British Library.

PB ISBN 978-1-4711-6390-6
eBook ISBN 978-1-4711-6391-3

This book is a work of fiction. Names, characters, places and incidents are either the
product of the author's imagination or are used fictitiously. Any resemblance to actual
people living or dead, events or locales is entirely coincidental.

Printed and bound by CPI Group (UK) Ltd, Croydon, CR0 4YY

WALTHAM FOREST LIBRARIES	
904 000 00702677	
Askews & Holts	06-Aug-2021
JF TEE	
	L

For Maux, Sarah, and Derick
TCMC forever

ACKNOWLEDGMENTS

Justin!*

Thank you to Emily van Beek, my brilliant agent. And many thanks to the entire Folio team—Elissa Alves, Melissa Sarver White, Katherine Odom-Tomchin, and Madeline Froyd.

I'm beyond grateful to get to work with the best of the best at Simon & Schuster, my home for the last decade. Thank you to Chrissy Noh, Alyza Liu, Anne Zafian, Anna Jarzab, Lisa Moraleda, Jenica Nasworthy, Devin MacDonald, Chava Wolin, Christina Pecorale, Michelle Leo, and Jon Anderson. And thank you to Lucy Ruth Cummins, the genius cover designer I'm so lucky to work with. You knocked it out of the park again!

Thank you so much to Anna Carey, Jennifer E. Smith, Jenny Han, Adele Griffin, and Diya Mishra. And a big hug to Rebecca Serle, my write or die, who kept me on track during the first draft.

This book exists because of a conversation I had with my brilliant friend Siobhan Vivian, as we drove across Western Pennsylvania. Thank you for your early encouragement, brainstorming help, and fifteen years of friendship.

Thank you to my family—Jane Finn, Jason Matson, Katie Genereux, and Catherine Matson.

And finally, I would not have been able to write this book—or get through this year—without Maurene Goo, Sarah Enni, and Derick Tsai. Thank you for the text thread that is my lifeline, the conversations, the boba and fried chicken deliveries, the pizza and rosé nights, the movies and the hangs. You're the best, fronds.

---

* Jus-tin Chan-da! (Clap, clap, clap, clap.) What can I even say? As ever, there is no book without you. I would be lost without your patience and brilliance and good humor during the hardest time. Let's not revise books in a pandemic ever again, deal? Thank you for everything—I'm the luckiest author ever to get to work with you. (Also, you were right about the footnotes but I couldn't leave the book without just one, mwahahahaha.)

TAKE
ME
HOME
Tonight

PART ONE
1:30 p.m. – 4:15 p.m.

All those theater kids
With bigger dreams than this auditorium can hold
Kiss me after curtain call
I'll wait for you backstage.
—The Henry Gales

CHAPTER 1

*B*y the time the bell rang, I was already halfway out the door.

I didn't look behind me as I hustled down the hallway of Stanwich High School, knowing I was missing last-minute assignments and instructions, but at the moment, not caring.

I had honestly not been paying the slightest bit of attention in the second half of AP US History. I'd spent the last twenty minutes of class with my eyes fixed to the clock on the wall, willing it to go faster, not taking in a word of what Mr. Batcheler was saying about the Continental Congress. Because the sooner class ended, the sooner I could get to Advanced Acting ... and the sooner I'd find out the casting for *King Lear*.

And that cast list—seeing that piece of paper—would answer the question that had been keeping me up nights. It would let me know if I'd gotten the part that would determine the rest of my year, college acceptances, and, potentially, my entire life going forward.

I had been so fast out the door that the hallways weren't too full yet, but even so, I was surrounded by people walking just as fast as I was, and not because they had life-changing news they needed to get. (I mean, as far as I knew. Maybe the kids who were really into forensic science or coding were also waiting on big news. I didn't know their lives.) Stanwich High was huge—over two thousand kids—and as a result the building had been expanded over the years to try and accommodate everyone, sprouting wings and annexes and ad hoc trailer classrooms. But even though the school had gotten bigger, the time allotted to get from one class to another had not gotten longer, which meant that everyone just tended to hustle in the hallways, like this particular public school in suburban Connecticut was home to a surprising number of speed walkers.

And today, I was among them as I beelined for my locker.

It wasn't *technically* mine. I shared the locker of my best friend, Stevie Sinclair. I'd misplaced my combination the first week of school, and rather than go through the hassle of dealing with the front office, I'd just started using Stevie's. It worked out, since we could drop off and pick up things for each other, and leave notes on the occasions our phones got confiscated.

I grabbed my coat, tossed three books in my bag, then after a moment's hesitation, grabbed Stevie's coat for her too. The first play meeting was always right after school, after the cast list was posted. And since we had Advanced Acting as our last class of the day, this way we could just stay in the theater and Stevie wouldn't have to come trekking back over here to get her long black puffer.

I slammed the locker shut and gave the dial a spin. I wanted to get over to the theater as soon as I could, to be in the building where it happened. I couldn't help but think that the next time I saw this door—the next time I opened this locker—I would know. About the cast list, and everything after.

I would know if I'd gotten Cordelia.

"Kat!" I looked over to see Zach Ellison speed-walking toward me. Stevie had been mentioning lately that she thought he was cute, and Zach always seemed to be hanging around the locker when she was here too, so I was subtly trying to nudge them together. Stevie hadn't expressed any interest in anyone since her boyfriend of a year had dumped her at the end of the summer. As it was now early November, it was well past time for her to be crushing on someone new, and Zach seemed like a promising rebound.

"Hey," I said. "What's up?"

"Can you give this to Stevie for me?" he asked, digging in his messenger bag and coming up with a marine biology textbook. He held it out and I took it with a silent sigh. Why were boys so stupid? Why didn't he realize that he could have used this opportunity to give it back to Stevie himself?

"Sure," I said, tucking it under my arm, since my bag was getting pretty full. It wasn't surprising that he'd given something of Stevie's to me. Since we were always together, people tended to treat us like we ran an old-timey post office or something, knowing we could get whatever it was—clothes, books, messages, veiled threats, and one time an oversized teddy bear—to the other one. "But you could also give it to her yourself," I said, raising an eyebrow.

Zach just blinked at me. "But you're right here."

"Okay," I said, giving up. I didn't have time to give Zach Ellison instructions on flirting opportunities. I had to get to the theater building. "See you." I headed down the hall, which was now more crowded than before. I made it to the end of the hall, then pushed out of the doors of Lansing House and joined the crowd going down the stairs to the student center. Stanwich High was divided into four houses, like a fancy British boarding school, but with less cricket and more AXE body spray.

I crossed my fingers as I took the curving staircase down to the student center. It felt like maybe—*hopefully*—everything was lining up. In my experience, you didn't get many moments like this, and I wanted to savor it. It was a Friday, my favorite day, in November—my favorite month. It wasn't freezing yet, but there had been a bite in the air all week, the good kind of cold, the kind that made you dig for your thicker sweaters in the cedar closet and search for last year's gloves, the kind that let you know that winter really was on its way.

The first semester of senior year hadn't been quite as hard as we'd all been led to believe, which was a huge relief, since junior year had come close to doing me in. My bangs had *finally* grown out enough that I could tuck them behind my ears (never, ever get breakup bangs. You will regret them. Stevie and my stylist and all the people who answered my Insta poll had told me this, but I hadn't listened), and I was wearing my new purple cashmere turtleneck sweater, the one with little puffs at the top of the sleeves.

And I was potentially less than an hour away from finding out if I'd gotten my dream role.

Cordelia, King Lear's youngest daughter, was a great part, and I already had most of her lines memorized. I'd gotten chills the first time I'd read her speech to her father—the inciting incident that kicks off the whole play. Lear is dividing up his kingdom between his three daughters and demands they all pay homage to him, something her older sisters Goneril and Regan are only too happy to do, promptly telling the king what he wants to hear. But when it comes to Cordelia, she can't do it. She can't suddenly profess emotion on command. She has one of my favorite lines in the whole play: "I cannot heave my heart into my mouth." As soon as I'd read that, I knew it was the role I wanted.

And it was a real possibility I could get it—I was a senior, after all, and I'd been regularly getting leads since the end of my sophomore year. Nothing was guaranteed—I knew that—but I was still allowing myself to hope.

I'd been a part of Stanwich High School's drama department since the first month of my freshman year. I had never acted before—never been in any of the plays in middle school—because I'd been dancing.

I'd taken ballet since I was three, and had spent all my time after school—and every summer, at sleepaway ballet camps—dancing. My life was a blur of leotards and convertible tights, bobby pins and hairnets, breaking in pointe shoes and comparing calluses and bloody blisters after class like war wounds, like battle scars. I had fully believed that it was what I was going to do with my life. I wasn't going to go to college—I was going to dance professionally.

And it wasn't like it was out of the realm of possibility to think that I could do it. Gelsey Edwards, two years older than me and the star of our dance school, became an apprentice at the New York City Ballet when she was fifteen and joined the company the following year. But right before my freshman year started, my teacher sat down with me and my parents and told me she didn't think I'd be able to make it. That while I was technically proficient, she didn't "anticipate" I'd get an offer from a company. I still auditioned for the School of American Ballet—but didn't get in. And suddenly, all my plans—all I'd thought my life would be—were thrown up in the air. I wasn't going to SAB and Professional Children's, in the city. I was going to Stanwich High and would have to figure out something else to do with my life.

At fourteen, I was all washed up.

But during the second week of school, there was an announcement about auditions for the fall play. I dragged myself there, not expecting anything, just to have something to do. But there in line behind me had been Stevie Sinclair. We were both cast as maids in *The Cherry Orchard*, and I fell in love. With all of it. With my new best friend, with the camaraderie, with the long rehearsals, punchy tech run-throughs, sitzprobes and opening nights, striking the sets and cast parties. I loved it all. Joining the theater department turned what had been the lowest moment in my life into something better than I ever could have imagined. I was all in, 100 percent. And I'd barely danced since.

"Kat, wait up!" I stopped crossing the student center and turned around, seeing my friend Teri running toward me, her brown hair flying behind her.

"Hey," I said, giving her a smile. "Where are you coming from?"

Teri (short for Teresa) Tsai had been in middle school with me, but we'd never really gotten to know each other until we were in theater—and a surprising number of classes—together as freshmen. Teri was my closest friend who wasn't Stevie, and I think this was mostly because Teri's best friend was always whoever she was dating. She usually had a boyfriend, and they usually seemed to live out of state. Stevie and I had never pressed the issue, but we honestly weren't sure these boyfriends of Teri actually existed. At any rate, we'd never managed to meet any of them.

"Just had French," she said, pausing to catch her breath and then straightening up again. She frowned. "Why do you have two coats?"

"This one's Stevie's," I said, trying to squish it down over the arm that was carrying her textbook. We fell into step together as we headed toward the north exit.

"Heard anything about the list?"

"It won't be up yet," I said with confidence, even though hearing her say *the list* sent an excited, nervous thrum through me. There was an order to this, one we had never, in four years, deviated from. Mr. Campbell, the head of the theater department, had a routine.

Auditions and callbacks started on Monday and went all week, and the cast lists were always posted on Friday just after classes let out—typed up and taped to the front door of the theater building. You were supposed to initial next to your name to indicate that you were accepting the part, and then the first meeting was held right after—just a quick one, everyone getting their scripts and either celebrating or pretending they were okay with being the butler who's only in two scenes. It was the first time we all sat around together, as a cast, and even when I was a freshman, with silent walk-on roles, I'd loved it. The sense of possibility that came with that first day—the beginning of the adventure.

The Stanwich High theater department, to put it plainly, was a big effing deal. We'd won tons of awards, including a few national ones.

We had a tech and costume shop that did near-professional work, and everyone on the crew side took things just as seriously as we did. All our productions got reviewed in the *Stanwich Sentinel*, and we had at least one famous, nearly movie-star alumna. And our shows were *good*.

It wasn't like the theater programs at the schools my cousins went to, where they did one musical at the end of the year, and that was it. We did three main-stage productions a year: a play, a Shakespeare, and a musical. This didn't include the musical revue or the improv shows or the Shakespeare Competition or the volunteering we did at senior centers and elementary schools. Auditions for the next production started the week after we'd closed the last one, rehearsals were every day after school, and weekends too as we got closer to tech. It was a full-time commitment, something my parents frequently complained about. But I never did. There was nowhere else I ever wanted to be.

"Erik and Jayson were heading over early to see if it was up," Teri said, sliding the *R* charm on her necklace back and forth, her expression worried.

I shook my head. "It's not going to be. Mr. Campbell isn't going to do that before we all have to be in class together. Can you imagine?"

Teri sighed deeply. "I'm just bracing myself," she said, "to see the whole cast and then at the bottom, 'Teri, see me about assistant directing.'"

I bit my lip as we negotiated around a group of sophomore girls walking five across, which was not good student center etiquette. The truth was, while Teri was good, she wasn't one of the best actors in the department. And so twice, when he couldn't cast her, Mr. Campbell had asked her to assistant direct. I understood why you might be disappointed by this, since you wouldn't have all that much to do. But it meant that Mr. Campbell still wanted you to be a part of the show. You'd still get to come to the rehearsals and be a member of the team. You just had to do it from the sidelines. Sometimes when he offered assistant director to people, they turned it down—and then they never got cast in anything again. Some people thought this was harsh; I thought it was completely understandable. You didn't get to decide when you were going to be a part of this department—you were either all in or out, and that was just how it was.

But it was senior year, and Teri had been dedicated—I was sure she'd get cast. "I don't think you need to worry about it," I said, and Teri brightened.

"So what are you thinking?" she asked. "Jayson will be Lear, Stevie will be Goneril . . ."

"Erik will be Gloucester," I said. We all paid incredibly close attention at the callbacks, since it was our best window into Mr. Campbell's thought process. Who he paired up, who he read multiple times, and who got told they could head home early—the worst thing of all.

"Not Kent?"

"I don't think so. He read Perry more for it."

"You'll be Cordelia—"

"Don't jinx it," I said, even as butterflies swooped in my stomach. "He read Emery for her too."

"Yeah, but not as much. I think you're a lock." The first bell—which meant *hurry up and get to class*—rang. We picked up our pace as we left the student center and headed down the long hallway that would lead us to the north exit.

We were only a few steps in when I saw Stevie walking toward us. I grinned at her, throwing my arms up in an exaggerated *what the heck* gesture. "You're going the wrong way!" I yelled, and saw her smile even though she widened her eyes at me, and I knew she thought I was being too loud. Stevie often thought I was being too loud; I usually thought she was being too quiet. And I was certain that I was always at the exact right volume.

"Was going to pick up my coat," Stevie called, as she closed the distance between us. I held it up for her and she grinned. "Thanks, frand."

"I've got you, frond."

She caught up with us, tucking her long, dark hair behind her ears. I was incredibly jealous of her hair, which was so thick she could legitimately hide behind it, like she was a character in a Victorian novel, and she regularly popped her ponytail holders and sent them flying. And despite the fact that I'd been taking prenatal vitamins for years in an attempt to get my hair to grow thicker (pro tip: don't leave these sitting out unless you want to have a very uncomfortable talk with your mother), it was to no avail.

Stevie Sinclair and I looked nothing alike—in fact, it was almost like we were opposites of each other. I was pale and freckled, she had olive skin that tanned perfectly; I was tall, she was petite; I had fine blond hair, Stevie's was dark and wavy; I was lanky, she was curvy. But despite all this, when we were walking around together, or shopping, or hanging out at Paradise Ice Cream, people would ask us if we were sisters. This delighted us to no end, because it meant that they weren't seeing that we didn't look *anything* alike. It meant that whoever had asked this was asking because of how we were together. An energy, a sameness, a kinship that had been there from the very first day.

I had never had a best friend before I met Stevie. I'd had ballet friends, and a different "best friend" every year in my class in elementary school, and in middle school, I was part of a group of four girls and we wore lots of Best Friend jewelry and accessories. But when I met Stevie, everything that had come before suddenly seemed so trivial. It was like Stevie and I saw each other, and recognized something. *You,* we both seemed to say. *You're my person.* And that had been that.

"I'll take that," Stevie said as we all started down the hallway together. She reached for her coat, but I shook my head.

"I've got it."

"What do you mean, you've got it? There's no need for you to carry my coat."

"Why not? It's not like it weighs much."

"Kat—"

"We were just debating the list," Teri interrupted as Stevie reached for her coat again and I sidestepped her, nearly crashing into a very tiny freshman boy. "Jayson for Lear, Kat for Cordelia—"

"Don't jinx me!" I cried. I passed one of the benches that lined the hallway and ran a few steps over to knock on it, accidentally waking up the girl who'd been napping there. She glared at me; I shrugged and saw Stevie mouth, *Sorry!* to her as we hustled past.

"You for Goneril . . . ," Teri continued, ticking roles off on her fingers.

"Well, that's a given," I said, joining them again. "Though I think Stevie should probably be Lear. *Queen* Lear." Even though I knew Mr. Campbell wasn't going that way—he'd only read guys for Lear—if anyone could pull it off, it was Stevie. She was more talented than me—she was more talented than basically everyone else in the department, except maybe Jayson, who was so good he got cast as Othello when he was only a sophomore.

Stevie and I didn't compete for the same roles. I was usually cast in the more comedic, ingenue-y roles, and Stevie tended to play older characters, and she could handle meaty dramatic stuff better than anyone else. She could disappear into roles in a way I really didn't even understand, and sometimes during rehearsals I'd be so captivated, watching what she was able to do, that I'd miss my own cues.

More than that, she made it look effortless. I knew the hours of work I put into every part, the time I spent drilling my lines, the rehearsals where I could feel the gap between where I wanted my performance to go and where it currently was. But with Stevie, it was like watching someone do the thing they've always known how to do. She could casually toss off something that would have taken me months of preparation, and not even seem to realize what she'd just done.

"I mean, if he'd been open to it, I would have gone for it," Stevie said with a grin. "Glenda Jackson did it, after all." I looked at her blankly. "On the West End and then Broadway, a couple of years ago," she explained. "It was supposed to be amazing." She reached out for her coat again, and I dodged her again. "I can carry my own coat, you know."

"Let me do nice things for you!"

"Kat!"

"Stevie!" I replied, matching her tone, laughing.

"Katrina."

"Stephanie." I raised an eyebrow at her. "Should we do middle names now too?" Teri, as usual, was watching us with a patient, bemused expression on her face, like she was waiting for this to stop so she could continue the conversation again.

Stevie started to answer just as the second bell rang. The second bell meant *you should really get a move on*, and in the hallway all around us, flirting and conversations stopped and people picked up the pace as one, like this was a musical and the dance captain had just snapped out a tempo change.

"Here," Stevie said, turning to me. As we walked, she twisted her long, thick hair around in a knot she pulled through on itself—and then it just stayed, like magic. I'd been seeing Stevie do this for years now, but it still impressed me every time. She reached into her bag and pulled out a bag of Doritos—Cool Ranch—and a can of Diet Coke. "Got you a snack."

"Bless you," I said, then looked around, realizing my hands were full with Stevie's coat and textbook. *"Fine,"* I huffed, like I was giving her some big concession, and handed her back her stuff.

"Where did this come from?" she asked, holding up the textbook.

"Zach Ellison was at the locker." I gave her a look. "I think he was disappointed you weren't there."

"Ooh," Teri said, her face lighting up. "He's cute! Stevie, you like him?"

Stevie shrugged one shoulder. "He's okay."

"You need a rebound," I said firmly as I opened up the bag of chips and my stomach grumbled on cue. I hadn't realized how hungry I was until I'd seen them. I crunched into the first chip. "Thank you for this. You're the best."

"I'm purely self-interested. I know how you get when you're hangry."

"What does *that* mean?" I snapped, then looked over to see her smiling at me. "Ah. Point made." I tipped the bag toward her. Stevie preferred regular Ruffles but would eat Doritos if presented with them. She reached for the bag, concentration written all over her face. Stevie had big feelings about proper Dorito dust ratio and wasn't about to leave this up to chance. She carefully selected one, and then I held the bag out to Teri, who took two at random—Teri had no strong feelings about Doritos—and crunched down on them.

"If you need a rebound," Teri said, brushing her Dorito dust off on her jeans, "I could ask Ryan if he has any cute single friends."

I frowned. "Ryan?"

"Ryan Camper," Teri said, shaking her head. "My boyfriend."

"Oh right," Stevie said, glancing over at me and then immediately away again. "Your boyfriend from—camp. I thought he lived in Maine?"

"He does," Teri said, smiling as she spun the *R* charm on her necklace. "But he still might have some friends around here. Remember, I told you how he comes into the city sometimes to do his modeling?"

"You should absolutely set Stevie up with one of Ryan Camper's friends," I said, widening my eyes very slightly at Stevie. "Especially if they're models."

"Um . . . I don't know . . . ," Stevie murmured. I popped the top on my Diet Coke and offered her the first sip, but she shook her head. I took a grateful gulp—was there anything better than cold Diet Coke? Stevie knew my hierarchy: fountain was ideal, then cans, and then if you had no other option whatsoever, bottled.

"Hey, how'd the project go?" I said, turning to both Stevie and Teri, both of whom shook their heads in unison. Stevie and Teri were in AP English together, which I was very jealous of. The only non-theater class Stevie and I had ever had together was sophomore year PE, in which we'd both almost failed because we'd spent the whole time talking and almost no time memorizing the rules of volleyball. "That bad?" I asked. I held out the Dorito bag to them again, feeling like they both could use a snack.

This group project had seemed doomed from the start. Teri never wanted to be the one in charge, or the one making any decisions, and Stevie avoided confrontation at all costs—so, fairly predictably, their terrible third partner, Bryce, had taken over and was counting on them to do all the work, despite the fact that he hadn't even read the book, and still seemed to believe *The Mill on the Floss* had something to do with dental hygiene.

"Well, the two of us had *planned* on doing the class presentation," Teri said.

"You know, since we don't think George Eliot is a man," Stevie continued, annoyance creeping into her tone.

Teri nodded. "We'd practiced and everything. But then Bryce jumped up and just started talking. . . ."

"You should have told Bryce to knock it off! And also that he might want to try, you know, *reading the book*," I said, and Stevie snort-laughed, my favorite kind of her laughs, since it meant that she'd been caught by surprise. "Did you?" I asked, looking at my best friend, who just shook her head.

I wasn't surprised. Stevie didn't like drama, or arguments, or yelling—at least, not offstage. It had shocked me to see she was always the one volunteering for any scene where you got to scream and cry and rage—her hand was always the first in the air in Scene Study when we were doing Mamet. Offstage, though, she liked things quiet and calm, everyone getting along, whereas I never minded a little volume.

But even as I would nudge her about it, I understood that was just who she was—it was who her whole family was. Stevie had grown up as an only child in a house filled with priceless art, with thick woven carpets on the floor that seemed to muffle everything. Whenever I was in Stevie's house, I automatically started speaking more quietly. You couldn't imagine anyone yelling in her house—not in front of the Rothkos.

"Want me to have a word with him?"

"No," said Stevie and Teri together, and I tried not to be insulted by that as we took the four steps down to the north exit together, three sets of feet falling at the same time.

We pushed open the door and walked outside, heading across campus, past the faculty parking lot and the dumpsters people were always vaping behind. The theater building was separate from the rest of the school, and big—two stories, with a main stage, a black box theater, a tech shop, a costume shop, and classrooms.

I drew in a breath—there was a dampness in the air that meant snow later, I was sure of it. "It's going to be cold tonight," I said, glancing at Stevie. "Might be even colder in the city, since you'll be walking around."

Stanwich was forty-five minutes outside Manhattan by train, an hour by car. It was a commuter town, which meant you never ever needed to specify which city you meant. You *always* meant New York—nobody was ever talking about Hartford or Boston or New Haven.

Stevie pulled her coat on without breaking her stride, switching her purse expertly from shoulder to shoulder as she did. "I don't think I'm going to be spending a lot of time walking, but thanks for the tip."

I pulled my coat over my shoulders without actually putting it on and turned to Teri. "Are you busy tonight? Stevie's going into the city and abandoning me."

"Ooh, fun," Teri said, clapping her hands together. "Well—the city part. Not the abandoning part."

"I'm not *abandoning* you," Stevie said, rolling her eyes.

"I'm just kidding."

"I know you are."

"What are you doing? Seeing a show?" Teri asked.

"My dad's taking me to dinner at Josephine's." Stevie's tone was offhand, but she wasn't fooling me. She'd been looking forward to this for a month.

Stevie had turned eighteen last week, and like always, she didn't want a big fuss made for her birthday. I had never understood this—I *loved* when a big fuss was made. To mark the occasion, she'd done a high tea with her mom at the nicest hotel in town, and then she and Teri and I had gone to the movies and had pizza afterward. But I did arrange for cupcakes and candles post-pizza—you can't celebrate a birthday, especially not one as big as eighteen, without a little sparkle.

She was celebrating with her dad tonight—he had somehow gotten a reservation at Josephine's, the tiny fancy restaurant in the West Village that celebrities were always being photographed at.

Stevie's parents had gotten divorced two years ago. I wasn't totally surprised when it was finally official—Stevie had been spending more time at my house after rehearsals, and always wanting to sleep over at my house, not hers. It was still hard to watch her go through it, and it made me realize how little I'd considered my own parents' marriage.

It was boring and steady, like background music, a TV left on in the other room, nothing I had to worry about.

Stevie's dad moved into the city and got an apartment in a doorman building on Central Park West; her mom stayed in their house and went back to using her maiden name, Pearce. It seemed like this was just the new normal, but a year ago, Stevie's dad got remarried. Joy Lampitoc was an accountant at Stevie's dad's law firm. She had three children from a previous marriage, which meant that Stevie suddenly had three stepsiblings. They were all older than us, and they all lived in New York City. Stevie had never said anything outright—all she would say was that they were fine, that she didn't know them well. But it was clear to me that all three of them—Mallory, Margaux, and Mateo—were mean jerks. Anyone who wouldn't make Stevie feel welcomed and included couldn't be anything but. I assumed they had gotten this from their mother—Joy had, as far as we'd been able to tell, never once smiled.

"It's just you guys, right?" I asked. "Not the stepmonster?"

"Yes, and don't call her that," Stevie said automatically, even though I could tell she was trying not to smile. "Joy's not so bad." I made a *hrm* noise that meant *oh really*, but Stevie continued on. "When my dad called to make sure I was free, before getting the reservation, he said that he wanted it to be just the two of us. So that he could 'see me off on the path to adulthood.'"

"Well, I'm glad you're getting to celebrate with him," I said, giving her a smile, even though it pained me to see how her whole face had lit up. I exchanged a glance with Teri, who shot me a look that clearly said *we'll see*.

Ever since the divorce, Mr. Sinclair had a habit of flaking on Stevie that filled me with an incandescent rage. In moments where I could manage to give him the benefit of the doubt, I could see he wasn't being cruel on purpose. But he would invariably get busy and cancel plans, and Stevie, being Stevie, would tell him it was fine, even when it clearly wasn't. And he would, for some reason, choose to *believe* this, and the cycle would start all over again.

Because it *wasn't* fine, and I knew it bothered her. She never came out and said this, but then, being best friends with Stevie was sometimes like being in a Pinter play: you had to learn what was happening by what wasn't being said.

But there had been too many instances in the past for me to forgive him, or trust now that he'd come through for her. I'd picked Stevie up late on too many occasions, going to the diner just to try and salvage a night she'd spent waiting for her dad, who'd invariable cancelled; tried to comfort her when she was red-faced and shaking and blinking back tears after he'd missed the final performance of the fall play *Arcadia*—his last chance to see it; tried not to see the look on her face when she would see my dad waiting for me after the curtain call with flowers that always made him sneeze.

"Joy shouldn't be allowed to go by that name," I pronounced as we passed the dumpsters—not a single vaper to be found. "Like, people's names need to be somehow indicative of their personality or they're just misleading."

"Should there be a rule?" Stevie grinned at me.

"There *should* be a rule!"

"Like people named Sunny are required to be happy, at least some of the time."

"You can't be named Saylor if you hate the water."

"And at least you're safe," Stevie said. "Since you like cats."

"This is true," I said, "for all the good it did me." We didn't have any pets, despite the fact that I'd begged for one for most of my childhood.

"Well, Ryan Camper's in the clear," Teri said. "He *loves* camping."

Stevie smiled. "That's great."

"Wait, so do you have plans?" I asked, slightly annoyed that we'd gotten derailed before remembering that I was the one who derailed us. "I heard there's going to be a party at the Orchard. . . ."

"I do have plans," Teri said, shooting me an apologetic smile. "Ryan and I are going to Netflix and chill."

Stevie just frowned; I jumped in. "You're going to what now?"

"We're going to watch movies together! I call him—or he calls me—and then we start the movie at the same time, so that we can talk about it as we watch."

"I think you should call it a different name then," I said, shaking my head. "That—means something else."

"But you're welcome to come Netflix and chill with us," Teri went on, clearly not getting this. "I have a great lineup of movies tonight and all the best snacks. . . ."

I slowed down as we approached the theater building, my heart starting to pound again.

"What?" Stevie asked.

"Just," I said, taking a deep, shaky breath, "about to go and meet my destiny."

"I'm really glad that you're keeping this in perspective," Stevie said, raising an eyebrow.

"Don't you want to find out the casting?"

"Of course," Stevie said a little too quickly. "Of course I do."

I gave her a look as we started walking again. From the beginning, I'd been more focused on these auditions. I was the one suggesting we prepare our monologues and scene work; I was the one who'd wanted to debrief every night after each callback, speculating and theorizing for hours about what Mr. Campbell was thinking, which way he might be leaning. I'd just put it down to Stevie being sure she'd get Goneril and not even having to worry about it, but now I wasn't so sure.

Emery Townshend was hurrying up behind us, doing that walk that's almost running but not quite. "Well," I said, letting out a long breath and nodding at Emery, "at least we'll know soon. T minus forty-five minutes until the list."

"Oh," Emery said, turning to look at me, her eyebrows flying up. "Did you not *hear*?" We all just stared at her blankly and she smiled— Emery loved to be the one to break news. "I heard it from Erik. The list isn't going up today."

I grabbed Stevie's arm and felt my stomach plunge as I stared at Emery. "Wait, *what*?"

CHAPTER 2

O kay, don't panic," Stevie said as we stepped inside the theater building.

"I'm not panicking. *Who's panicking?*" I said this louder than I intended to, and Eric (with a *c*) looked up from where he was sitting on the couch next to Jayson and Erik (with a *k*).

"Um—you?" he ventured.

"Do we know for sure the list isn't going up today?" Stevie asked, her voice calm and reasonable. Stevie, for reasons passing understanding, didn't want to keep acting in college or try to do it professionally. She had it planned out—she wanted to go to Northwestern for undergrad and then Harvard for law school, just like her dad had done. She intended to be a lawyer, also like her dad. And while I disagreed with this career path entirely, since she would be throwing her talent away—it would be like Simone Biles going into taxidermy—I had to admit that there were times when I could see it, Future Stevie methodically working through some contract, taking the legalese point by point.

"Well, that's what *I* heard," Emery said. The thought that the list wouldn't be up today had honestly not occurred to me. It would be like the sun rising in the west—it just wasn't what was supposed to happen.

I crossed the lobby and sat on the floor, trying to steady myself, my back against the side of the couch.

Mr. Campbell would sometimes complain, when he was passing through the lobby and we were all lounging around, eating (or throwing) snacks, that this building wasn't even ten years old and we'd turned it into a rec room. He wasn't wrong—I'd probably spent more time in the theater department lobby than anywhere else in the school over the last four years. If I had an open and wasn't going off campus, I'd always hang out here. Even if I was just doing homework while curled in one of the overstuffed armchairs, I still preferred to be over there than anywhere else. It was our headquarters, our hideaway, our clubhouse. The theater building was home. All the rest was just a school.

Stevie shot me a look as she came over and sat on the couch behind me, and Teri joined me on the floor. "I don't think you should worry," Stevie said in a half whisper, widening her eyes toward Emery, across the room on the opposite couch. "You know how she is." She pulled at her hair, and it tumbled down from her makeshift bun in one long sheet, like she was a cartoon princess.

I nodded, telling myself to calm down. Emery *did* love to stir the pot—I should have remembered that. Also, why wouldn't Mr. Campbell be posting the casting today like normal? It didn't make any sense.

I held out my Dorito bag once again to Stevie and Teri, and Stevie reached for a chip, then froze. I figured she was just choosing carefully like always, until I looked up and saw why.

Beckett Hughes was walking through the lobby.

He had a two-by-four over his shoulder and was walking toward the shop, big over-ear headphones on. He nodded at all of us, but then locked eyes with Stevie and gave her a half smile. "Hey," he said as he pulled his headphones off, draping them over the back of his neck. "Can we talk for a second?"

Stevie just blinked at him, looking stunned, and I jumped in. "We have class," I said, my tone cool.

"Yeah," Beckett said flatly as he looked around at everyone lounging in the lobby. "Clearly."

I narrowed my eyes, about to say something when Stevie got up. "It's fine," she said, looking from me to Beckett, and I wasn't sure which one of us she was talking to. "Just for a second." Beckett smiled at her as they walked toward the shop hallway, her long hair swishing behind her, before they disappeared from view.

"I thought they broke up," Erik said, frowning, also looking in their direction.

I exchanged a glance with Teri, who knew this saga all too well. "They did."

Stevie and Beckett had dated almost all of last year—her junior year, his sophomore. They'd been flirting and circling each other all throughout *Noises Off* rehearsals, and they finally got together at the cast party. Beckett had been part of the theater department since his freshman year—not surprising, considering that his parents were award-winning Broadway playwrights. But he'd always been on the tech side of things. He had absolutely no fear of heights, and Mr. Ruiz, who ran the technical theater program, quickly realized this and Beckett became an expert at running the tension grid, the lighting floor at the very top of the theater.

I'd had a handful of boyfriends: Glenn, the cause of my breakup bangs; Eric; and Beau, who'd graduated last year and who'd played opposite me in *City of Angels*. Stevie had had a few short-lived relationships, but her relationship with Beckett, right from the outset, had been different. This wasn't us exchanging phones to analyze text messages and figure out what some guy we were crushing on could possibly be thinking. This was *real*.

As they got more serious, it was like Stevie pulled a curtain across their relationship. I was always happy to talk about what was happening with her and Beckett, but at some point, she wasn't. I didn't get this at all—I still wanted to tell her everything, and sometimes for me, it was almost like what happened wasn't as important as her reaction to it. The first time I slept with anyone (Beau), I drove to Stevie's afterward, even though it was past midnight, and we stayed up for hours in her kitchen, eating whatever we could find in the fridge and talking about every detail. But the first time Stevie and Beckett slept together, she didn't even tell me for three days, and even then, she didn't want to go over every moment like I had. Which was fine—Stevie had always been a little more private than me, and it always took her a while to sort out her feelings. But it was also why, when she told me they'd broken up, I was so thrown for a loop—I hadn't seen it coming.

The night before school started, Stevie showed up at my house, sobbing. I'd been in the middle of clearing the table, but my mom took one look at the situation and had relieved me of my chore—and what's more, ten minutes later, knocked on my door bearing ice cream.

We'd gone up to my room, Stevie still hysterically crying, telling me that it was over with Beckett. She didn't go into specifics, just told me that he'd broken up with her at the Boxcar Cantina, which had up until that moment been her favorite restaurant, but that I now understood was a place we'd never go again. I'd asked gently for details, trying to figure out what had happened: Had he given a reason? Did it have anything to do with Annabel, Beckett's best friend, who I'd long suspected had a crush on him?

She didn't answer any of this. All Stevie would say was that Beckett had broken up with her, and that it was over.

I had always liked Beckett a lot, but just like that, all my good friendship feelings toward him curdled. He was clearly the asshole here. He thought he could just dump my best friend out of the blue and suffer no consequences? Expect me to still be friends with him?

That was *not* going to happen. I was cool and aloof when I saw him, just so he would know whose side I was really on. Stevie and Beckett managed to be cordial to each other in the halls and when we all hung out in the lobby together. When *Arcadia* rehearsals started, it was clear they were going to be able to work together, which was a relief—you did *not* want to make an enemy of someone on the tech crew. (When Erik and Marco, who ran the lights, had a terrible breakup, Marco took it out on Erik onstage, the follow spot always *just* managing to miss him.)

Stevie never brought Beckett up or talked about him, but even so, I'd been worried she still wasn't quite over him. This was why I had been so excited about the Zach Ellison development—and why I wasn't thrilled that Beckett and Stevie were now having a random private conversation.

Mr. Campbell pushed through the lobby door, a stack of papers tucked under his arm. "Are you telling me your teacher isn't even here yet?" he asked, grinning, as he took the stairs up to the second level two at a time. "What kind of operation is this? Class is starting, chop-chop!"

Everyone jumped to their feet, and I looked over at the shop hallway, wondering if I should go get Stevie, not really minding the fact that I'd have to break up whatever was going on with them. A second later, though, the hallway door swung open. She headed out, and I saw Beckett walking toward the shop, lumber back over his shoulder. I grabbed her stuff from the couch and walked over. "What did he want?"

"Thanks," she said, taking her bag from me. "It was about tonight. His parents' new play is in previews, and he wanted to know if I wanted to see it. He got an extra comp ticket."

"Seriously?" I'd been hearing online speculation about Andrea and Scott Hughes's new play for months now as anticipation had built. Their last play, about Edison and Tesla, had won the Tony, so interest had been high from the start. Stevie had told me about seeing Beckett's parents—who she'd gotten to know, of course, over a year, along with his older sister, Emily—working on the play, the two of them sequestered in their dining room, sitting opposite each other, laptops open and mugs of coffee at the ready. When they had made the casting announcements—a mix of movie stars and veteran theater actors—I'd gotten even more excited, despite the fact that nobody knew what this play was about. Even the title, *George & Suzi*, didn't provide much information. I lobbied my parents to get tickets, which had started selling out, but my mother had a policy of not wanting to get tickets to a show until it had been reviewed—despite the fact that if the reviews were good, then getting tickets got a lot harder.

"Yeah," Stevie said with a shrug. "Since when . . . when we were together was when they were writing it. I guess they asked Beckett to offer me the ticket? But I have the dinner with my dad at nine thirty, which would be right in the middle of the second act, so . . ."

"Right," I said, relieved that I didn't have to get into it with Stevie about how hanging out with your ex who dumped you was never a good idea. "Ah well. Too bad."

"The timing is crazy," Stevie said, shaking her head. "Have you noticed that, how everything always seems to land on the same day?"

"I have!" Teri, who was walking ahead of Stevie, chimed in. "It's weird, right?"

We hustled into class, dropped our bags along the wall, and then, like usual, took our seats on the floor. The acting classrooms were practically bare—there was a table pushed off to the side, some chairs, and a couch that we were only supposed to use for scene work but that, over the years, we'd all used for naps. Mr. Campbell was sitting in a chair he'd placed in the front of the room, just looking at us, and everyone quieted down in a hurry and sat on the floor in a loose semicircle as we looked up at him and waited.

As soon as I sat down, and the silence fell, I looked closely at Mr. Campbell, trying to read something in his expression. Did Emery know what she was talking about? Or were things decided already, the answer tucked somewhere in his pile of papers? But his expression revealed nothing—he was as impassive and hard to read as usual.

Mr. Campbell was thirty-eight, divorced, no kids. He hadn't volunteered any of this information, but we knew how to google. He was an actor, too—when he was younger, he'd done lots of commercials, guest spots on long-cancelled TV shows, roles on all the Laws & Order. But at some point, he'd clearly switched his focus to theater—teaching, running the entire department, and directing. He did a reverse commute every day into the suburbs, returning after school was over to New York City, where things were much more exciting.

He always wore button-downs and dark pants, and never a tie except on show nights. He had a beard, dark hair he kept short, and black-framed glasses he was always perching on top of his head and forgetting about. "Don't you think he looks like Paul Rudd?" I'd asked Stevie freshman year. "Young Paul Rudd or old Paul Rudd?" she had clarified, then had withdrawn the question when she realized it was redundant. We all spent a lot of time speculating about Mr. Campbell—about his acting career, about his personal life, about what his life in the city was like.

"You guys are obsessed with him," Beckett had told us once at lunch last year, when Stevie and I had spent most of the time debating what, exactly, Mr. Campbell had meant when he'd said something cryptic, leaving rehearsal the night before. Stevie and I had looked at each other, a little guiltily, as Beckett had pushed back from the table to get some fries—but, more likely, a break from us. And he wasn't wrong. We all spent a lot of time talking about Mr. Campbell. But Mr. Campbell *was* the theater department.

He cast and directed both plays every year, and taught the advanced theater classes. The musical theater department was run by Ms. Wallace, who cast the spring musical and taught the musical theater classes. But most of the leads in the musicals went to the people who got leads in the plays, even if there were technically better singers for the parts—it was common knowledge she consulted with Mr. Campbell before casting. And anyway, it wasn't like the choir kids who always auditioned were getting any leads—and they should have known better than to expect them. None of us were suddenly walking into the choir room expecting to get an aria, or whatever it was they did in choir.

Stanwich High was just so big that the competition for everything was intense—but especially in the theater department. I'd always liked to write, and at some point freshman year I'd thought about joining the paper or the literary magazine—but that was before I got cast in my first play and realized that wasn't how it worked. You couldn't do anything else if you did theater. Whenever I saw a television show set in a high school where characters were on the football team one week and then in the school play the next, I'd roll my eyes and then invariably find something else to watch.

"So," Mr. Campbell said softly, crossing one ankle over his knee and settling back in his chair. He almost never raised his voice—we were always quieting down and leaning in closer to hear him. "We need to talk about the *Lear* casting."

I twisted my hands together. The room was totally silent, like my fellow thespians had stopped breathing.

"I am sorry to disappoint you," Mr. Campbell said, his brow furrowed. "But the list isn't going up today."

There was a pause, and then everyone started talking at once, but I just sat there, a roaring in my ears. This was *not* how things were supposed to go. I was supposed to *know* today. I was supposed to return home after school cloaked in glory, able to tell my parents that I'd gotten the part, able to start to see the rest of my year and how everything would fit together. I'd prepared myself to get only as far as seeing the list—it was like my imagination ran out after that. I had no idea what things looked like now, like my brain couldn't adjust to this new reality.

"What?"

"But you said—"

"You always—"

"What's the problem? Is it Erik?"

"Shut *up*, Jayson!"

"You always post it on Friday—"

"Are you going to switch plays? Do we need to prepare another monologue?"

"Mr. Campbell," I said, raising a shaking hand, "I just think—"

"Guys!" We all quieted down immediately. "I get that you're disappointed, and I'm sorry. But it's just taking me . . . a little longer than I thought to cast this one. Things aren't as clear as I thought they'd be."

I swallowed hard. What did this *mean*?

"Do you . . . want to do another day of callbacks?" Eric asked, a tentative note in his voice, and I drew in a sharp breath. We'd never done that before.

"I don't . . . think so," Mr. Campbell said slowly, like he was turning over the words in his head as he said them. "I'm just . . ." He looked around the room, then leaned forward. "I can't say that recent events haven't shaken my faith in this department. I'd thought we were all on the same page, that we valued the same things. Loyalty. Commitment. Dedication. And honestly, even having to wonder these things . . . it's just making this decision harder."

I looked over and caught Stevie's eye, and then we both looked away, but it had been enough to let me know we were both thinking the same thing—that this was about Dara Chapman.

My stomach was in knots, because what were we supposed to *do* about this? If he'd just said he was having trouble casting the ensemble, or the guys, it would have been different. But this was all of us.

And then an even more terrible thought occurred to me—what if it *wasn't* all of us? What if it was *me*?

"How long are you thinking?" Jayson asked. "I mean—when do you think we'll know?"

"I'd say . . . Monday."

"Monday?" I hadn't even realized I was going to speak this out loud before it was already happening. I bit my lip and Mr. Campbell raised an eyebrow at me.

"Kat? You have a problem with that?"

"Just . . ." I took a breath. "It just seems like kind of a long time, that's all. Maybe you could email it when you make the decision and that way we wouldn't have to wait?"

"The list has to be posted," Teri said, sounding scandalized. "It's tradition."

"Tradition," Jayson, Emery, and Stevie sang together, throwing their hands up in the choreography from when we were all in *Fiddler* freshman year.

"Tell you what," Mr. Campbell said, smiling at me as he shook his head. "If I finalize the casting tonight, I'll email it to the office and have them print it out and post it sometime over the weekend. But no promises—I'm busy tonight."

"Are you going to the premiere?" Aminah asked breathlessly. "The new Amy Curry movie?"

Amy Curry was the department's most famous alumnus. I hadn't believed it the first time I'd walked through the theater lobby, looking at the framed pictures from past productions, but there she was, at eighteen, with the lead in *Hedda Gabler*—the person that I'd seen in big blockbusters and small prestige movies and a few memorable episodes of a medical drama that ended in a summer-ruining cliff-hanger. If she wasn't a star yet, she was getting there, and the fact that she was kind of from Stanwich (she'd transferred from California her senior year) and had gone to Stanwich High, had been a part of the Stanwich drama department like me . . . it somehow made it all seem more possible. Mr. Campbell had taught her when she'd gone here—his second year teaching in the theater program, and if we begged enough, he would sometimes tell us Amy Curry stories. He'd tell us about what a scandal it was when she got a lead role straightaway, since she hadn't paid any of the dues that you usually had to—but her talent was just that undeniable.

And while Stevie thought the Amy Curry trivia was cool, I didn't get the sense she spent a huge amount of time thinking about this fledgling movie star she'd never met. But I'd gone deep down the rabbit hole, reading articles online and features in magazines, practically memorizing some of them, staring at the glossy images—her red hair, her big smile, her off-duty casual wardrobe of vintage T-shirts and high-waisted jeans. I knew all about how she lived in Los Angeles with her landscape architect boyfriend, how they had two rescue dogs, how she took a long road trip once a year. I wasn't even entirely sure why I sought out all these articles and stories—but every time I read one, it was like the jump from here to there got smaller. That maybe this thing I wanted to do wasn't that impossible, because Amy Curry had acted on this stage and walked these same halls and was now being interviewed for *Vanity Fair*. It was like if I looked at the pictures long enough, I could conjure the same kind of path for me.

"It's a Ghost Robot movie, not an Amy Curry movie," Erik said to Aminah with a roll of his eyes. "Isn't she, like, the fifth-billed?"

"And how many movies have *you* been in, Erik?" I asked, raising an eyebrow.

"Yeah," Teri chimed in.

"I didn't say I had!" Erik yelped. "Jeez."

"It's premiering in the city?" Jayson asked.

"Yeah," I said—I was as up on this information as Aminah was.

"The premiere in LA was last week. New York premiere tonight, and then an after-party at the Gansevoort." I wasn't sure exactly what the Gansevoort *was*, but it was a word I very much enjoyed saying.

"Are you going?" Aminah asked again. Mr. Campbell just smiled. Even though Amy had graduated over eight years ago, she'd kept in touch with Mr. Campbell—he would occasionally drop references to notes and emails she'd sent him, and one time she had him give feedback on a self-tape she was submitting to a casting director.

"Let's just say I have plans tonight," Mr. Campbell said enigmatically. "Plans you guys do not necessarily need to know about."

I quickly looked down at my hands. I was pretty sure that out of everyone in the class, I was the only one who *did* know what Mr. Campbell was doing tonight.

I had found out about it by accident last year, late one night when I'd been procrastinating writing my history essay and I'd gone down a Google rabbit hole about Mr. Campbell. His name, Brett Campbell, was common enough that you had to be willing to wade through a lot of pages that weren't about him, and figure out how to pair the best keywords with your search. I hadn't even been looking for anything in particular—just idly searching and avoiding writing about the Stamp Act (my working title was "Who Cares About the Stamp Act," but obviously I was planning on changing it)—when I found the website.

It was for a theater company in New York, the Echo Theater Company. I'd had to go several pages into the website to confirm it was really him, onto a page with pictures of the members of the group. But there he was, in a black-and-white headshot that looked a few years old, under the name B. L. Campbell. He was the founding director of the company, and it seemed like he wrote and acted in a lot of their plays as well.

I'd just stared at my laptop for a few moments, heart hammering, not able to believe how cool this was. It was like finding out Mr. Campbell was a superhero, with a whole other life and a secret identity.

But a second later, I realized that he'd never mentioned this at all—and that I probably shouldn't let him know that I'd found it. The last thing I wanted was for him to be mad, or feel that I had crossed some line. Because if everyone knew, we all would have shown up to see his plays—that was just a given. Which was maybe why, I'd realized as I clicked through the website, he hadn't. He probably wanted something that was separate from us, from his job in Connecticut. Probably the other members of his company were cool New York City people and wouldn't have appreciated a whole bunch of suburban teenagers suddenly showing up.

But even though I'd never been to see any of the shows—or told anyone but Stevie about my Echo Theater discovery—I still checked the website occasionally. Which was how that I knew that a new play—*Navel Gazing*, written and directed by Mr. Campbell—was premiering at the Echo Theater tonight.

"Anyway," Mr. Campbell said, shaking his head. "I'm really sorry about the list, guys. I know you were expecting it. But I promise it'll be soon." He gave us all a smile that crinkled his eyes at the corners, then glanced at his watch. "And somehow class is now half over. On your feet, everyone! Warm-ups!"

We all jumped to our feet, Mr. Campbell moved his chair out of the way, and with only twenty minutes left, class officially began.

STARBUCKS COFFEE COMPANY
11/5
2:15 PM

CAT
Hot
Grande
Mocha

ASK ME
One pump white mocha

STEVE
Iced
Venti
Sugar-free vanilla
Soy
Latte
ASK ME
Only two shots espresso
Only four pumps sugar-free vanilla
Less ice
Still ice, but just less than normal
Like half the amount of ice
(guest seems overly concerned about the
ice)

PAID
Starbucks card account XXXXXXXXXXXX1981

I frowned at Stevie's Starbucks cup. "Is there enough ice in there?" I had ordered for both of us—I had long since memorized Stevie's far-too-complicated latte order—and I wanted to make sure it was right.

"It's perfect," Stevie assured me with a laugh. She took a sip and then made a face.

"What?"

"It's fine," she said hurriedly. "I think maybe they put three shots of espresso in, not two. But it comes with three, so maybe they got confused. It's okay—"

I shook my head and took the drink from her, walking back to the place where you pick up drinks. "Hi again," I said, smiling at the barista, who raised an eyebrow at me. "This was just supposed to have just two shots in it?"

"It's fine," Stevie whispered, coming to join me. "We don't need to make a thing. I can just ask for more soy milk."

"I've seen three-shot Stevie," I reminded her. "Three-shot Stevie is not a good idea."

"I'll remake it," the barista said with a sigh. I took off Stevie's lid and straw, and she took the cup from me.

"Thank you!" I called, and took a sip of my mocha. There were three Starbucks in Stanwich, in addition to Stubbs Coffee, one town over in Putnam, and Flask's Coffee, which Stevie preferred. But since my ex Glenn preferred it too, we'd switched to Starbucks after running into him three days straight—the last thing I wanted was for him to think that I was going there hoping to see him. It was bad enough that our relationship had landed me with bangs.

Because we hadn't had our first *Lear* meeting after school, Stevie and I had found ourselves at loose ends once the final bell rang. We'd hung out in the lobby with Teri for a while, until she had to get home to get ready for her phone date, which was when we both realized that we could use some bux.

"What are you going to wear tonight?" I asked as the barista started to pull two more shots, the espresso machine hissing steam. "I feel like you want to look good, but not like you're trying too hard. You want to look . . ." I searched for the words and finally just waved my hand expansively. "New York."

She laughed. "That's very helpful."

"Want to get ready at mine? You can borrow anything you want."

"Could I? That would be great, actually."

"Of course." Since I wouldn't be at Josephine's tonight, if Stevie was wearing something of mine or if I helped her get ready, it would feel a little more like I was there with her.

"Iced *double* soy latte with sugar-free vanilla," the barista called, sliding the drink across the counter.

"Thank you," we chorused together.

"So," I said, taking another sip of my drink, ready to get back to the only thing I'd been thinking about since we'd left school. "What do you think Mr. Campbell meant when he was talking about loyalty? He meant Dara, right?"

"Probably," Stevie said with a barely audible sigh and a shrug as she snapped her lid back on with a little too much force and headed over to the sweetener station. I beat her there and handed her some napkins. "Thanks," she said, wiping off her cup.

I tipped my head to the side, studying her. "What's going on with you?"

Stevie turned to me, sweeping back her hair and frowning. "What do you mean?"

"Do you not care about this? About what Mr. Campbell is thinking? About the *Lear* casting?"

"Of course I do," she said, maybe too fast. "Of course. I care. I just . . ." She looked down and dropped her napkins into the trash. "Kat, I actually should—"

The door to the Starbucks opened and my eyes widened. "Look," I said quietly, grabbing Stevie's arm and nodding toward the door. "Speaking of."

Dara Chapman was walking up to the counter, pulling off her beanie as she went. She turned her head and our eyes met across the bux. Both Stevie and I gave her *hey* nods—tipping your chin up first rather than down. Dara raised a hand in an awkward wave, then turned back to the counter, looking up intently, like she was studying the board of drinks. Stevie and I exchanged a glance, and I knew right away we were thinking the same thing: *let's go*. When we'd stepped out into the chilly afternoon, I turned to my best friend. "Weird."

"So weird."

Until the start of the school year, Dara had been one of the stars of the theater program—and she and I found ourselves up for the same parts more often than not. I'd assumed this fall's auditions for *Arcadia* would be no different. I really wanted Thomasina, but I was worried Dara would get it, and I was prepared for a marathon of callbacks, both of us duking it out. But Dara didn't show up. We were all worried about her that first day, thinking that something awful must have happened. You weren't supposed to be eligible for callbacks if you didn't make the first day of auditions, but everyone knew that Mr. Campbell would make an exception for one of us if something had gone wrong. But the next day, at callbacks, we found out the truth—Dara was fine. Nothing had happened. *She just hadn't auditioned.* She'd essentially left the theater program for no reason whatsoever, just in time for senior year, right when you get to the mountaintop.

When we'd asked Dara why she hadn't auditioned, she'd just shrugged and said she wanted to try something else, which nobody believed. And as we started working on *Arcadia*, it became clear to all of us how hard it was to reconcile hanging out with the theater kids when you weren't in the play. Dara didn't know any of the inside jokes, she couldn't chime in when we talked about rehearsals, and with every week, we all just seemed to have less to say to each other. Dara stopped sitting at the theater table at lunch as much. I'd heard she'd even joined mock trial as an alternate, and I saw her hanging out in the halls with people I didn't know.

She came to the opening night of *Arcadia*, and I remembered looking out to the audience and feeling a jolt as I saw her there. And the whole performance, in the back of my mind I was wondering what it felt like for her to be sitting out there, not onstage with the rest of us.

What it must have been like to see me playing Thomasina, wearing the costume and saying the lines that at one point, she must have thought were going to be hers.

None of us had known what would happen with *Lear*. I didn't think she would even audition—but she'd shown up at general auditions on Monday with the rest of us, her monologue prepared, just like nothing had happened.

But she didn't get a callback.

On one hand it was shocking—Dara Chapman, a former star of the department, not even making it to the second round! But on the other hand, it was completely understandable. You didn't get to pick and choose when you were going to be part of this department, like you went to one of those TV high schools. And Dara should have known that.

I was thinking about this, and what Mr. Campbell had said, as Stevie and I crossed the bux parking lot to Nikola, her electric car. Of course it was about Dara—but what did that mean for us? How were we supposed to prove that we were nothing like her? Was he worried about our loyalty to the department? About *my* loyalty?

I was almost to Stevie's car when I passed a truly adorable dog tied up outside. "Hi, buddy," I said, bending down, trying to see if he'd be okay with me petting him. He looked like a yellow Lab, round and happy. He thumped his tail on the ground, and I gave him a scratch behind the ears. I looked over to see that Stevie had walked a few steps away and was looking fixedly down at her phone. "He's friendly," I called to her, and she nodded, but didn't make any move to come closer.

"He really was fine," I said as we reached her car, with its Pearce Museum of Art bumper sticker.

"I'm sure," she said, shooting me an unconvincing smile as we both got into the car. For someone who was such a good actress, she really was terrible at lying in real life. "I just had to check my texts."

"Totally," I said as Stevie started the car and I buckled my seat belt. "And also, you're afraid of dogs."

"I'm not!" Stevie said, but I could see a dull flush was starting to creep into her cheeks. "I just don't love them, that's all. I don't like how they jump up on you."

"Uh-huh," I said, raising my eyebrows, deciding to let that be for the moment. "Want me to DJ? Any new playlists on Ophelia?" Stevie had gotten at least two phones since I'd known her, but even as she upgraded, her phone was always named Ophelia. I hadn't asked why this was until we'd been working on homework together sophomore year, both of us backstage with our laptops, Stevie's phone plugged into her computer. *OPHELIA IS SYNCHING* flashed across the screen, and I laughed so loudly that some of the upperclassmen told us to be quiet.

"I made one last night," she said, and I picked up her phone, pointed it at her face to unlock it—Stevie smiled wide for me—and scrolled to her streaming app. The top mix didn't even have a title, just the emoji with hearts around it, and I selected it. I scrolled down, looking for what I knew would be there—Billy Joel songs. All of Stevie's mixes had at least two; this one had *four*. Her dad loved Billy Joel, and when he still lived here and would drive us around, he'd only ever have the Billy Joel station playing. His songs had filtered into Stevie's playlists too, and now, without hesitation, I picked "Only the Good Die Young." Stevie smiled without looking away from the road, turned up the volume, and as soon as the second verse kicked in, like we'd planned it, we both started singing along.

CHAPTER 3

What about this one? " I walked out of my closet with a short black strapless dress and held it out to Stevie, who was sprawled on my bed, a bag of candy on my comforter next to her—on the drive home, we'd stopped by Ada's, the candy store/mini-mart that was a Stanwich institution.

"That looks supercute on you," Stevie said, sitting back against my pillows and picking out a sour belt. "But you know I can't do strapless."

"What, because you have boobs and I don't?" I called as I put the dress back on the rack and contemplated other options.

"Well . . . yeah," Stevie said, and I laughed. "You've got that ballerina body. And ballerinas can't have boobs, or they'd get unbalanced and fall over during pirouettes."

I grabbed a velvet blazer and headed back out. "Oh, is that how it works?"

Stevie laughed. "Don't get mad at me. It's just physics. Ooh, that's cute."

"Right?" I tossed it to her on the bed. "Like over a tank, with skinny pants?"

"Totally." She shucked off her cardigan and tried it on over her T-shirt.

I hopped up onto the bed and grabbed a peanut butter cup. "What train are you taking in?"

Stevie picked up her phone and pulled up the Metro-North app. "Probably the six-ten. I'm meeting my dad at his office, and we'll go down to the Village together. The reservation's not until nine thirty, so we'll have time to hang out."

Growing up so close to Manhattan meant that we'd both spent a lot of time in the city. I'd go in with my parents and my little brother for dinners and Broadway, to see the Christmas lights, to go to museums. Or we'd go in on school trips—theater department excursions to see matinees, science and history class trips to the Hayden Planetarium or exhibits at the Historical Society. I'd never gone in without my parents or a school group, though. Stevie took the train by herself on the occasions when she went in to meet her dad, because he almost never came back to Connecticut now. Since the divorce, it was like he'd lost custody of the state as well.

"Why is your reservation so late?" I picked up my bux from the bedside table.

Stevie shrugged. "I think it was all he could get. But he told me that we're just going to pretend we're in Spain, since you never eat there before ten." She smoothed down the lapels of the blazer. "I'm not sure about this."

"What about that maroon dress you like?" I asked as I started to get off the bed again. "You know, the prairie one?"

"I'll check," she said, sliding off the blazer, carefully laying it over her arm and getting off the bed. "And I'll hang this back up while I'm in there."

I took a sip of my mocha and unlocked my phone. Nothing new on the group thread, barely any new Stories, but I scrolled through them anyway. "Did you find the prairie dress?"

"No," Stevie said, walking out, still holding the blazer. "But I did find this." She held up the long blue-and-white dress that I'd borrowed from her at the beginning of the summer.

"I can explain," I said immediately.

"Have you had this the whole time?"

"It's not my fault," I said automatically, trying not to laugh at Stevie's outraged expression. "I put it with my mom's dry cleaning, and then it ended up in her closet by mistake. She only found it, like, last week when she was packing up the last of her summer things."

"Hmm." Stevie shot me a look as she took it off the hanger and placed it on her bag.

"I'm not making it up," I said, throwing a pillow in her direction. "Blame my mother."

"Blame your mother for what?" I looked over to see my dad standing in the doorway. "Hi, kid. Hello, Miss Stephanie."

"Hi, Mr. Thompson," Stevie said, giving my dad a smile.

"Please, call me Mr. Thompson," my dad said. It was his favorite joke, despite the fact that I'd begged him to stop telling it. My dad was a journalist who worked from his office at home—so when he was dressed for work, it meant he was wearing what he wore now—an ancient cardigan over a Red Sox T-shirt, jeans, and slippers.

"What's up?" I asked. I held up my candy bag. "Candy?"

"Don't mind if I do," he said, crossing over toward me and picking out some sour watermelon slices. "Just wanted to say hi . . . see how you're doing . . ."

"That's nice," Stevie said with a smile, a slightly wistful expression on her face.

"Don't buy that," I said, taking the candy back from him. "He wants to use us for research." Since my dad was freelance, he covered a pretty wide beat, with the freedom to focus on subjects that interested him. Sometimes it meant that he was in Montana for a month, talking to fly-fishers. But unfortunately, at the moment, it meant that he was here and judging my behavior.

"Actually," my dad said, sounding affronted, "I just wanted to see how the casting turned out. And only after that, possibly, ask you some questions for my article."

"It's not up yet," Stevie said, coming back to sit on the bed.

"Monday," I said. And then a second later, crossed my fingers on both hands, just in case.

"Well, good luck," my dad said. "Not that you two have anything to worry about."

"Dad!" I cried, leaning over to knock on the wood of my headboard. "Don't jinx us."

"What's the article?" Stevie asked.

"It's about technology," he said as I sighed and scrolled through my phone again. I'd heard this spiel far more than I wanted to. "And our addiction to it, and how some of us are unprepared to deal with the world without it."

"And apparently it's also about shaming your daughter for her perfectly normal behavior."

"Oh no," Stevie said immediately, looking from me to my dad. "I'm sure he didn't mean you, right? Just technology in general?"

"No, I was actually thinking about Kat specifically," my dad said, reaching in for more candy. I yanked the bag away from him. "And how she's never without that phone."

"You're never without *your* phone," I pointed out. "Everyone everywhere always has their phones. Why single me out?"

"It is interesting," Stevie said loudly, and I could tell that she was trying to shift the conversation, move it to something less contentious. I'd told her, over and over again, that we *liked* to argue in my family— but she never seemed to believe that this wasn't stressful for me like it was for her. "Because I was reading this article about how the things that used to be there to help in the olden days from when people didn't have phones have all disappeared because of technology. Like there's no more pay phones, or maps, or anything."

"I don't know if I would call them the *olden* days," my dad said, looking pained. "I mean, there are still maps . . . and some pay phones . . .

probably . . ." His voice trailed off, and he looked so consternated, I relented and held out the candy bag to him.

"Thanks," he said, a little grudgingly, helping himself to some sour cherries. "So how are you, Stevie? How's the museum?"

She smiled. "It's good, thanks."

Stevie's grandmother, Mary Anne Pearce, was a legendary art collector. She'd donated her art collection to the town, along with a grant to build a museum—the Pearce, which I'd been going to since I was little for drawing classes and craft workshops. The museum had kept acquiring since her death, and Stevie's mom was now the curator.

"Good afternoon." I looked over and saw Grady, my ten-year-old brother, standing in the doorway, a book tucked under his arm. Grady tended to dress—and act—like he was a middle-aged stockbroker, and not a fifth grader, for no reason we'd ever been able to figure out. His eyes went wide behind his round-framed glasses. "Kat, what are you doing here? Shouldn't you be at rehearsal?"

"List isn't up yet," my dad said, reaching over to ruffle Grady's hair, but Grady quickly sidestepped him. He carefully combed it every morning, in his preferred look of *divorced bank manager*.

"What are you reading?" Stevie asked, nodding toward Grady's book. "What day are we diving into now?"

"April 14, 1912," he said, and Stevie squinted at the cover. My brother was obsessed with a book series, Today's the Day, that all took place over a single day during different historical time periods. I didn't get the appeal. How exciting could a single day really be? He'd insisted that I just hadn't read the right one yet; I very much doubted this.

"What happened then?" Stevie asked.

"*Titanic* sank," Grady and I said at the same time. He looked at me with raised eyebrows, and I raised mine back at him. Honestly, if our teachers really wanted dates to stick with us, they should just make epic action-romance movies about all major world events.

"Yeah," Grady said, running his hand over the book's dust jacket. "It's okay. Not as good as some of the other ones I've read, like the ones about Leopold and Loeb or the assassination of Franz Ferdinand, or the Manson murders."

"Wait, *what*?" my dad asked, pulling the book out of Grady's hand and flipping through it. "You've been reading about what now?"

"But it's one of the days that's incredibly impactful, but nobody living through it realized it at the time. It was only later that we could understand it."

"Sounds cool," Stevie said with a smile. "I'll have to check it out."

"Can I have a snack?" Grady asked my dad.

"Sure," my dad said, brightening. He always used getting us snacks as an excuse to partake too. "Want some chips?"

"I'd prefer plain almonds."

My dad sighed and turned to go, then stopped, like he'd just remembered something. "Oh, Stevie, I just wanted to say I got the kindest note from your mother. Please tell her thanks for me—and that I loved working with her, too."

"I will," Stevie said, her voice polite, but we exchanged a quick look. This summer, my dad had written an article for the *Times* Sunday magazine, about incomplete art collections—either by theft or just circumstance. He discussed the famous heist at the Isabella Stewart Gardner Museum in Boston, and the empty frames that still hang there; and a Russian billionaire who'd spent decades and untold sums of money trying to track down one Basquiat, without ever getting it. And he'd also featured Stevie's mom, who'd taken over her mother's hunt for one particular painting.

Neither one of us had liked the few weeks when my dad was spending so much time talking to Stevie's mom. We were fine with our parents chatting postshow or at school events, or when we were all taking prom pictures, or whatever. But this regular contact had unnerved us both, just because it was in an environment we couldn't control. Over the years there had been a *lot* of times that I'd been "sleeping over" at Stevie's house when we both went out to a party, and when Stevie was "staying the weekend" at my house, but was actually at Beckett's while his parents were at a play festival in Scotland. What we really didn't need was our parents starting to compare notes and stories.

"Why were you working with Stevie's mother?" Grady asked as he adjusted his glasses.

"It was an article about a painting Stevie's mom has been trying to find," my dad explained, his face lighting up the way it did whenever he was about to go into detail about one of his articles. "By Hugo LaSalle." He frowned at my brother. "You know who that is, right?"

"I'm guessing a painter?"

My dad sighed. "We need to get you into a museum."

"I like museums. Like the one in the stock exchange."

"An *art* museum."

"Oh. In that case, no thank you."

"Stevie's mom," my dad said, taking a deep breath like he was trying to will himself to find patience, "has been trying to find one particular painting for a long time now."

"Starting with my grandmother," Stevie said, giving Grady a smile. "It's a multigenerational art search."

Mary Anne Pearce was an avid collector of Hugo LaSalle, the Pittsburgh street artist turned world-renowned painter. There was a series, *New York Night*, that the Pearce had three of. But it was a four-canvas series, buildings and colors stretching across an interconnected tableau in a horizontal line, blue turning to purple to black. At the Pearce, *New York Night* one, two, and four hung on the wall, with an empty space where three was supposed to go. Hugo LaSalle died twenty years ago, and Mary Anne Pearce had assumed that at some point, she'd be able to buy number three and complete her collection. But she hadn't been able to find it anywhere.

My dad's piece had gone into the blind alleys and rabbit holes that Mary Anne—and then her daughter, after her death—had gone into trying to track it down. Apparently, it was an art world anomaly that there was not even a record of a sale. There were rumors, of course—that LaSalle had it stashed somewhere in a storage unit, or had destroyed it because he wasn't happy with it, or even that he'd given it to his mover when he had admired it—but these were unsubstantiated.

"So did she ever find it?" Grady asked.

"Not yet," my dad said.

"Wow," my brother said in a deadpan he didn't often use, but was nevertheless quite skilled at. He turned to leave. "That sounds like a riveting story, Dad."

"Watch your attitude, young man," my dad called after him. "Or no plain almonds for you!" He headed for the door. "I'll leave you to it." A second later, though, he stuck his head back in my room. "Just let me know if you'll be staying for dinner—we're getting pizza. GRADY!" he yelled as I heard him walk down the stairs.

I shook my head and closed the door behind him. "Sorry about that. Want me to take another look in the closet?"

"It's okay," Stevie said, shaking her head. "I can just wear something of mine. It's not a big deal."

"But it's a special night!" I said. "Let me think what else might work." I had just started to walk to the closet when I heard Stevie's phone ring.

"Hey!" Stevie said, answering her phone with a smile. *My dad*, she mouthed to me. "So I was thinking I'd take the six-ten—" She stopped talking and her expression changed, slowly morphing from excited to confused. I sighed as I walked over to the bed to join her. I knew what this meant; I'd basically been waiting for this shoe to drop since Stevie first told me her plans. "But I thought . . . ," she started, then bit her lip. I sat on the bed next to her, watching her face, silently cursing her dad in my head.

She caught my eye and placed her phone on my comforter, then pressed the button to put it on speaker. She didn't have to tell me not to be quiet; we'd done this before.

". . . just came up," Mr. Sinclair was saying, talking fast, his words clipped. "I have to close this deal tonight and I can't take the time. And I am sorry, but I'll make it up to you." Somewhere in the background of Mr. Sinclair's call, I could hear people talking, phones ringing, beeps of incoming emails.

I closed my eyes for a minute, trying to calm myself down so I wouldn't start screaming at Stevie's father. But just for *once* he couldn't have come through for her? To celebrate her eighteenth birthday?

"I get it," Stevie said, voice determinedly cheerful as she swung her legs up underneath her. "These things happen—but why don't I come in anyway? We can skip the reservation, and I can hang out in the office! We can get takeout and I'll help you file. I'm great at filing, remember?"

Filing?! I mouthed at Stevie. She grinned back at me, clearly still thinking her night was going to happen.

"That's nice of you to offer, hon," said Mr. Sinclair, a little louder now, since a phone in his office had started to ring again. "But that wouldn't be any fun for you."

"It would, though," Stevie said, her grin fading slowly, like someone had hit a dimmer switch. "It's just been a while, and this way—"

"No!" Mr. Sinclair snapped, his voice loud through the phone, and we both froze. "If that goes out without me reviewing it, you can clear out your desk. I need to see this stuff, especially after the last time. . . ." There was a pause; Stevie stared down at the phone, waiting for her dad to return.

"I think . . . ," I started, but she waved me off.

"Sorry," Mr. Sinclair said after a moment. "Why do they keep saddling me with these idiots?"

"So I'll just take the train in," Stevie said, talking fast, like she could outrun what was clearly going to happen. She sat up straighter and tucked her hair behind her ears. "And I'll help or just stay out of the way. . . ."

"No, no, that's not going to work, honey. You're sweet to offer, though." Stevie took a breath like she was going to say something, then bit her lip, staying silent. "Look," Mr. Sinclair said, his voice rising since the phone was ringing again, "why don't you keep the reservation? You and your mother can use it. I'll have Carla call the restaurant and give them my card number. It'll be on me. You can still get to go."

"But," Stevie said, so quietly now that I even I could barely hear her, "I wanted to go with you. . . ." She took a shaky breath. "I just . . ." I reached out and grabbed her hand and squeezed it. She squeezed back.

"What?" her dad asked, sounding more harried than ever. "Look, I know you're upset—"

"I'm not," Stevie said immediately. I shot her a look, but she avoided my eye. "It's fine, Dad. Really."

"No," I whispered to her. "Stevie!"

"It's fine," she hissed at me, picking up the phone and moving it away from me.

"It's *not*. Tell him—"

"There's my girl," Mr. Sinclair said, and you could practically hear it in his voice; he was already checking this off and moving past it. "And I'll call you soon and we'll make another plan, okay?"

"Sure, Dad," Stevie said, a bright, false note in her voice. I wondered if her dad could tell she was faking this—or if he even cared that she was, since it was making his life easier. "Sounds great. Good luck with the deal, okay?"

"Thanks, pumpkin," Mr. Sinclair said. "Talk soon." And then he was gone, and Stevie's phone changed back to her lock screen—a picture Teri took of the two of us sophomore year, in our *Doll's House* costumes, sitting backstage with Diet Cokes and sharing a bag of fries, deep in conversation.

"I'm so sorry," I said after Stevie had just stared down at her lock screen for a moment, swallowing hard, like she was waiting for her dad to call back, say that it was a mistake, that he was going to be there for her birthday dinner after all. "That really sucks."

"It's okay," Stevie said with a one-shouldered shrug. "I mean, he's in the middle of a deal. He has to work. He can't, like, leave because he has to have dinner with his kid." She flopped back on the bed, and I did too. When you feel the need to flop back on a bed, it's no fun to do it alone.

I looked over at Stevie. There was a lot more I wanted to say about her dad and how he wasn't showing up for her when he needed to, but I knew I couldn't. If your friend was complaining about their parent, you could agree and sympathize, but you could never criticize their parent without it being initiated. It was just one of the rules of friendship. "Do you think maybe," I said, after a moment of silence, "you should have told him that you were upset?"

Stevie shook her head, still looking up at the ceiling. I looked up too—at all those glow-in-the-dark stars that I'd stuck there in constellations I'd invented. They were still hanging on, even though they now only emitted the faintest glow. "There's no point. He couldn't just stop working. And then he'd be feeling guilty."

"But then at least he'd know how you felt?"

"It's not like it would change anything."

I wasn't so sure about that, but I also knew when to stop pushing her. We lay there in silence for a few moments together. I knew she was working through it, doing a dive into her feelings, which she always, for whatever reason, seemed to keep buried five fathoms deep. Finally, she turned her head and gave me a quavery smile. "I was really looking forward to it. How stupid is that? Just me and him, and actually getting some time together. No Joy. No Mallory or Margaux or Mateo. Just us. And I wanted to tell him that I'd started my application to Northwestern . . ." Her voice trailed off.

"You know what else Northwestern has? A really great theater program!" Stevie gave me a look. I held up my hands. "Sorry. Not the time."

"And it was nice of him to offer the reservation to me and my mom, but she has plans with my aunt tonight." She sighed deeply. "So you said there's a party at the Orchard?" she asked after a moment, sounding like someone who was trying very hard to look on the bright side, and not entirely succeeding.

"Don't forget, we can always hang out with Teri and Ryan Camper."

"How could I?"

"Hey," I said, making a decision and sitting up, "let's have a really fun night, okay? We have to shake this off. Maybe a movie? Your pick. And then we could see if maybe they'd let us back into Café Asiago."

Stevie sat up as well. "They were pretty mad about the mint thing."

"I thought they were free!"

"There was literally a sign that said twenty-five cents."

"Which, clearly, I didn't see!"

She laughed. "What's even playing now?" She pushed herself off the bed, grabbing the blazer. "I'll just put this away."

"It's really okay."

"I don't mind."

I watched her go, feeling like it wasn't really about the blazer and more about taking a moment to adjust to the new reality. I picked up my phone again, opening up my browser to look up movie times. As I did, I saw among my open windows the Echo Theater website. I clicked on it now, looking at the poster showing tonight's premiere of *Navel Gazing*—a woman in a bikini, an orange held over her belly button.

I looked at the show information and was starting to scroll through the website when suddenly an idea—a *possibility*—occurred to me. I sat up straighter, my heart pounding, my thoughts racing.

It was a *great* idea.

We probably shouldn't do it.

But it would be a lot of fun.

It would save Stevie's night and make up for the fact that her dad wasn't coming though for her. She'd have a birthday celebration to remember, as opposed to just feeling disappointed.

And also . . . it would give me a way to solve the problem that had been haunting me ever since Advanced Acting, about what I could do about the casting. It would fix things, and not just for me—for Stevie, too.

It was high risk . . . but also really, *really* high reward.

Stevie returned from my closet and stopped short. "Okay, what's going on?"

"What do you mean?"

"You look like you did that morning you kidnapped me and we went to Six Flags."

"I didn't *kidnap* you," I said automatically. It was last spring, on a perfect bright and sunny day, and Stevie thought we were just going for coffee when I'd gotten on I-95 and headed for New Jersey. I knew if I'd told her at the time what we were doing she wouldn't have agreed, but once we got there, we had a fantastic time, our parents never found out, and it was one of our top five best days.

"You kind of did."

"I was just thinking . . . ," I said slowly, trying to figure out in real time what to say and what to leave out, "that we should go."

"Go where? Teri's house?"

"No. Well—kind of. Why don't we go into the city?"

"To New York?" Stevie stared at me. "By ourselves?"

"We can still do your dinner. We have the reservation, your dad left his card . . ."

"My mom is not going to let me go into the city alone. Not at night."

"You were *planning* on going in alone," I pointed out, helping myself to a sour gummy peach slice.

"Yeah, to meet my father at his office. Not to go gallivanting around Manhattan."

"I can assure you we won't gallivant. It will be a gallivanting-free zone."

"You know what I mean. I don't think your parents would be okay with it either."

I knew they wouldn't, but I didn't want to focus on that right now. "So we won't tell them. We'll tell them we're sleeping over at Teri's. And we *will* sleep over there—we'll just go into the city first."

Stevie frowned, and I could practically hear her thoughts whirring, looking for the hole in the case. "What if my dad mentions something to my mom about the dinner?" she finally asked.

"Do they ever really talk that much anymore?" I asked, as gently as possible. Stevie shook her head. "I just think," I said, leaning forward, "that we shouldn't let our Friday be wrecked like this. Your dad has to work and Mr. Campbell is rethinking the casting, but so what? We can still have a great night, right?"

"You would do that for me?" she asked, her eyes a bit brighter than usual. "Go into the city with me to celebrate my birthday?"

I smiled at her. There was more to it, of course, but Stevie didn't need to know it this very minute. Like with Six Flags, when she was asking things like why we weren't getting coffee, why we were getting on the highway, where we were going, I'd just said *New Jersey*. Stevie handled things best in steps, and in the end, she'd loved Six Flags. We'd returned home happy and sunburned, Stevie's new gigantic stuffed unicorn (she'd named it Travis) taking up most of the backseat. And I knew eventually she'd love this plan too. "Of course! We need to give you a proper celebration. It's going to be great."

"And you really, *really* think we should do this?" Stevie asked, and I looked her straight in the eye. It was like I could see her teetering between caution and excitement, and I knew all she would need was a tiny nudge to bring her over to my side.

I smiled, and when I spoke, my voice was full of confidence. "Absolutely."

CHAPTER 4

*T*here were several *ironclad, unimpeachable* rules you had to follow when lying to your parents.

Rule #1: Cover your bases. *All* the bases. The reason that neither Stevie or I had ever been caught was that we planned. We thought ahead. We tied up loose ends. We had learned long ago from *Friends* that you always had to think about the trail, and we always did. So the first thing we did was get Teri onboard, before my dad could call her parents, who would have no idea what he was talking about and would blow the whole operation.

Which led me to Rule #2: Never look like you've counted your chickens. So before I packed anything, I asked my dad for permission. He was on the phone, but he nodded distractedly at me. "I can stay the night at Teri's?" I asked slowly and loudly, to make sure he'd remember. The last thing you wanted was to get in trouble because your parents weren't paying attention to your alibi if you were going to the trouble to set one up.

But saying that also allowed me to hew close to Rule #3: Stick to things that are technically the truth. I *was* going to be staying the night at Teri's. I was just going to be doing a lot of other stuff before then, but since he hadn't asked me for specifics, that was on him.

So when I came downstairs with my duffel packed with what I'd need for a night in the city and then a sleepover—my favorite dress, a pair of ankle boots, my makeup bag and magic curling iron, sweatpants and a show shirt (*Anything Goes*) to wear as pajamas, and an extra sweater to wear on Saturday—it was knowing I'd done my due diligence, dotted my i's and crossed my t's.

I stepped into the kitchen and saw, to my surprise, that my mother was there. My mom worked in finance, at a hedge fund in Putnam, one town over. She was with a company named Blackpool, which *sounded* interesting, and like something out of a fantasy novel, but was actually just an office filled with people in zip-up sweaters moving money around. But she usually wasn't home until at least seven, and it was now only a little after three—this was *very* early for her. I wondered if maybe the FBI had raided the offices again, and that was why she was here. She and my dad were standing around the kitchen island, having what sounded like a kind of intense discussion, while Grady sat at the kitchen table with his book, seemingly oblivious to all of it.

"We didn't RSVP yes, right?" my dad asked. "We said we'd try."

"I know," my mother said with a sigh as she ran her hand through her hair. "But then I got an email from Sarah this afternoon saying she was looking forward to seeing us tonight."

"What's tonight?" I asked as I walked through the kitchen, heading for the fridge. "Also, Mom, why are you here?"

"That's nice," my mother said, shaking her head at me even though she was smiling.

"I just meant it's early."

"I had an off-site with a client and they cancelled last-minute, so I just came home. You dad and I need to figure out this invitation."

"To what?" I asked as I pulled open the fridge.

"Engagement party at some hotel in the city," my dad said. "For one of your mother's colleagues' daughters."

"Are you going to go?"

"No," my dad said, looking at my mom. "Right?"

My mother picked up her phone again and scrolled through it. "I would rather skip it," she said. "I like Sarah, but I don't know her well.

I've never met her daughter . . . it feels like we would be encroaching."

"That settles it," my dad said, looking relieved. He nodded at my duffel. "You're off to Teri's?"

"Don't stay up too late," my mom said, smoothing my hair back, and I nodded, trying not to grin, aka Rule #4: Don't look too happy when your parents believe your cover story. "And I'm sorry about the list—your dad told me."

"At least this is the last time we'll have to live through this," my dad said.

"No—there's still the musical."

"Oh right," my dad said. "The musical."

I closed my eyes for a moment, mostly so I wouldn't start yelling. Even though my parents had told me, from the time I could remember, that I could grow up to be anything I wanted, I knew they didn't really take me seriously when I told them that what I wanted to do— *all* I wanted to do—was act.

And no matter how hard I'd tried, I couldn't seem to get through to them that *Lear* wasn't just any play. It wasn't just some *after-school activity*. It might actually determine the course of the rest of my life. I was set on auditioning for colleges with conservatory acting programs, so I could get my BFA and start doing this for real. And what would it say to those schools—to those cream-of-the-crop, best-of-the-best acting programs—if I couldn't even get the part I wanted in my high school play?

"You guys know this won't be the last play I'll ever audition for," I said, wondering why we had to keep doing this. "You know that's what I'm going to be doing at college."

"We're fine with that," my mother said, but I noticed she was speaking carefully now, like when I'd heard her on work calls where she weighed every word for its potential repercussions. "At the liberal arts college of your choice, where you'll get a BA—"

"It is *so unfair* you won't let me go to a conservatory!" I exploded. This was a fight we'd had over and over, to the point where it was like a well-rehearsed scene. Ever since we'd started talking about my college options, I'd only been looking at the ones that would let me focus on acting— Tisch at NYU, BU, Carnegie Mellon, University of Michigan, USC. My parents told me I could study whatever I wanted—and they were okay with me being a theater major—but they'd drawn a hard line at conservatories, saying I was not under any circumstances going to a BFA program. "I want to act, you guys know how important it is to me, and—"

"And we're not saying you can't act," my dad said, his voice soothing. "But act while taking all kinds of other classes, not so focused on one thing that you might not even like in two years."

"After all, just a few years ago, you were going to be a professional dancer," Grady said, putting a bookmark in place and turning toward us, apparently deciding he was going to join the conversation.

"You were six," I pointed out. "What do you remember?"

"Oh, I remember," he said darkly.

"What's that supposed to mean?"

"Like when you were dancing in the kitchen and kicked me?" My brother gave me a long look. "It's not something you forget."

"Look," I said, turning back to my parents, "I don't know how you can doubt I'm serious about this. The theater department has been my life for the last four years—"

"And maybe that hasn't been such a good thing," my mother interjected, causing me to stop short. This was a deviation from our previous fights—it was like she'd suddenly gone off-script on me.

"What does that mean?"

"It means," she said, "that, yes, you've been very focused the last few years. And while we admire the commitment, it means that you didn't give yourself the chance to expand your interests."

"You can't," I said, my voice rising at the unfairness of this. I hadn't set up the Stanwich High theater department, after all. Also, why was it that parents always wanted you to be involved and disciplined and dedicated to something, but then as soon as you were, they started complaining that you were limiting yourself? "I've told you guys how it is—"

"But maybe it shouldn't be," my mom said, shaking her head. "You guys are in high school. You're *kids*. Why should you have to commit to doing only one thing? You should be trying as much as you can, figuring out what you like."

"Um," I said, just staring at her. "That's not what it's like. What am I supposed to do about it?"

"Change it," she said simply.

I opened my mouth and then closed it when I realized I didn't have a response.

"And if you can't," she continued, "you could at least take the opportunity to broaden your horizons in college. That's all we're saying."

"Anyway," my dad said, "we don't need to get this all figured out right now. We can talk about it when you're back from Teri's, okay?"

"Yeah," I said after a moment, trying to get my priorities back in line, remembering a beat too late that I shouldn't be annoying my parents right now. I needed to go into the city tonight—that was what was important, and I shouldn't have lost track of that.

"Sounds good," my mother said. She gave me a small smile, and I gave her one back.

"Okay," I said, grabbing my keys. "See you guys tomorrow. Two?"

"Noon," my mom said, raising an eyebrow at me.

I just nodded and gave her a smile, all too aware of Rule #5: Don't push your luck.

"You guys look great," Teri said from where she was sprawled on the couch.

I smiled and flounced out the skirt of my dress. It was my current favorite, a mid-length dress with a fitted bodice and a bright pink skirt that billowed out and spun around me if I turned quickly, which I did constantly when I wore it, of course. I had paired it with ankle boots—I figured it was going to be too cold in the city for flats tonight, and there was practically nothing I hated more than my feet being cold. I had used my magic curling iron on my hair. I'd found it online and it was amazing: it did all the work for you and gave you perfect beachy waves every time. It was way better than what I'd been doing before that, which was watching YouTube tutorials and then completely failing to re-create the results. My hair was now in soft waves that I knew would fall out in a few hours, no matter how much hair spray I used.

Stevie was wearing a gorgeous jade-colored jumpsuit with long sleeves and a cinched waist, and pointy-toed heels. Whenever I wore flats and Stevie wore heels, I felt that it threw off our whole dynamic, because suddenly she wasn't where I expected her to be, but instead was a few inches higher. Stevie always liked to add to her height whenever possible, whereas I avoided heels if I could. I'd tortured my feet enough over my dancing years and figured that they really deserved a break.

Stevie had straightened her hair so that it hung long down her back and moved in a glossy curtain. We were both wearing more makeup than usual. Teri, who was the best of us at it, had done a cat-eye on me and a smoky eye on Stevie, and as I glanced down at myself, and then at Stevie, I was startled to see just how unlike our usual selves we looked. We looked older, more pulled together. Like we were heading somewhere exciting, off to have an adventure—which, I reminded myself as I patted my waves, was exactly what was going to happen.

"I think we're passable," I said. "I don't think they'll kick us out of Josephine's."

"I wish I could come," Teri sighed as she crossed to the kitchenette and pulled a Sprite out of the fridge. "You'll give me updates?"

"It's so cool you have your own fridge," I said. It honestly seemed like the dream to me—your own fridge, your own snacks.

The Tsai house was huge and modern, all right angles and glass. It was a smart house, and Teri's parents were constantly updating it, so that oftentimes when we were there, it took us hours to figure out how to do things like turn on lights or heat or the television. Teri had moved out back to the non-smart guesthouse at the beginning of the year and seemed much happier now that she could turn on lights by hitting a switch.

The guesthouse was two stories, with a kitchenette, two bedrooms, and a living area with a couch and a huge television. The second bedroom had two beds, and Stevie and I had each claimed one before we'd started getting ready. But the best part about Teri living in the guesthouse was that we would be able to come and go without her parents seeing and asking pesky questions like *why are you here* or *where have you been* or *do you have any idea what time it is?*

Teri sat back on the couch with her soda, then placed it carefully next to her phone and the remote, which were lined up just so— making me wonder if maybe Ryan Camper *was* real. This seemed like an awful lot of effort to go to for a figment of your imagination.

"Okay," Stevie said, picking up her clutch. It was a medium-size black bag and I'd last seen it at the prom. "We good to go?" She glanced at her watch. Stevie was the only person I knew who wore a real, non-Apple one, with ticking and hands and dials and everything. I'd had a plastic Swatch when I was little, but around the time I outgrew it was when I got my first phone, and then I always knew what the time was without having to wear it on my wrist. "If we're trying to make the four-ten, we need to leave now."

"Can I put my stuff in your bag?" I asked, my tone wheedling, as I crossed to my bigger purse. I took out what I thought I might need—

license, cash, emergency credit card tied to my parents' account, lipstick. "You know I hate carrying one." Stevie rolled her eyes good-naturedly and held her bag out to me. "Thank you!" I said as I tucked my things into the zippered pocket.

"Don't forget your phone," Teri reminded me.

I met Stevie's eye and smiled. This was Rule #6 of lying to your parents: Let them occasionally think they're smarter than you. I'd learned from Eric's mistake. He'd been grounded for two straight months when his parents tracked his phone and realized that he wasn't at a study group, like he'd told them, but at Jones Beach at a concert. I'd checked my parents' phones—both of them had the same password, it was honestly embarrassing—and found they had tracking apps installed so they could make sure I was where I said I was. As soon as I'd seen that, I realized I had to think one step ahead, and was now always careful to leave my phone where I told them I'd be, so that if they did track it, all they would see was that I had been telling them the truth. It was sad, this lack of trust. I mean *really*.

"I'm actually going to leave it with you," I said, holding it and saying a silent goodbye for just a moment before setting it down on the coffee table. Even though I knew I had to do this, it was always hard to part with my phone. And despite the fact that I could use Ophelia, it just wasn't the same. "Would you mind posting a Story or two? Just so that there's incontrovertible proof I was here. And if my mom or anyone texts, just call Stevie and I'll tell you what to text back. My lock code is 1717."

"No problem," Teri said. She clapped her hands together. "Have the best, best time. And if you think you see a celebrity, take a picture!"

"For sure," I assured her. "Say hi to Ryan for us."

"And you have a good time too," Stevie said, grabbing her long black puffer and tucking her clutch under her arm.

"Oh, it'll be a quiet night in for me," Teri said, waving at us as she curled up on the couch. "I'll see you guys in a few hours."

"We'll probably be back by midnight," Stevie said.

"Or one," I said as I put on my navy coat with its wooden toggles and faux-fur-lined hood. Stevie raised an eyebrow at me and I just shrugged. "It's New York!" I said, trying for breezy. "Who can say what's going to happen?"

We waved to Teri, then left the guesthouse and darted across the back lawn of the Tsai house. Stevie had parked a ways up the street, better to deflect attention.

As though we'd discussed it, neither one of us spoke as we ran across the lawn and then out to the street—it would have been the actual worst to be busted before we even had a chance to do anything.

It was like I could practically see our night stretched out ahead of me, and just the anticipation of it was making me smile. We were going into New York City, at night, all dressed up, just the two of us. We were going to celebrate Stevie in style. I was going to give her a great birthday dinner. And I was also going to make sure that for both of us, the rest of the year was going to work out. It was going to be an adventure, and it had been far too long since we'd had one of those.

We got into Stevie's car and slammed our doors at the same time. Stevie looked over at me and grinned as the interior lights started to fade down. "Are we really doing this?"

I smiled back at her. "We really are."

"Here we go then," she said as she signaled and pulled out onto the road.

"And anyway," I said as I reached for my seat belt and snapped it in, "we're just going into the city for a few hours. What's the worst that could happen?"

PART TWO
4:15 p.m.–5:25 p.m.

This cold night will turn us all to fools and madmen.

—William Shakespeare, King Lear

The stops along the Metro-North New Haven line were the familiar background noise of all my train rides into the city. The list of stops was kind of like the list of state capitals—I knew them all but could only get the order right when I recited them. Putnam, Winthrop, Old Stanwich, Stanwich, University, Waterside, Hartfield, Port Chester, Rye . . . and on and on until 125th Street and then the tunnel into Grand Central, which was always the sign that it was time to get your things together, put on your coat, and grab your bag, because the train would be making its last and final stop, at Grand Central Station.

There were five train stations dotted around Stanwich, and the trains ran into Grand Central and back again, multiple times an hour during the morning and evening and then tapering off to once an hour during the less-peak times, finally stopping service for good at two a.m. The Old Stanwich station was closest to Teri's, and Stevie and I had arrived there early enough to get actual paper tickets from the machine. The platform wasn't that crowded yet, but it was still early. I knew from other trips that in a few hours, both sides of the platform would be packed—with people going into the city for the night on one side and commuters returning back home for the weekend on the other.

It was the same train as ever: maroon-and-white leather seats, two-seaters running along one side, three-seaters on the other, an aisle in between. There were posters by the doors, advertising an online MBA program and a condo development going up in Hartfield.

We'd gotten seats a few rows back from the door. The train wasn't that full—the car we were in was just half-occupied, with lots of empty seats. Stevie sat by the window, and I was in the aisle seat, and as the doors slid shut and the conductor announced the next station—Stanwich—I let out a long breath.

We were doing this.

I'd been so focused on convincing Stevie that it would be no big deal—and then getting my parents to believe that we were just staying at Teri's—that the enormity of what we were embarking on was just now hitting me. I was going to go into New York City by myself for the first time ever. I tried to keep my face impassive—if Stevie saw that I was even a little bit anxious, I knew she'd start to get nervous, maybe even change her mind, and I needed this all to work out.

I looked around for my purse to take out my phone until I remembered I didn't have one—all my essentials were in Stevie's clutch. "Can I see your phone?"

Stevie nodded and reached for her bag, but I was already unsnapping it. "Just . . . ," she said, keeping her eyes on Ophelia, looking concerned as I held the phone up to her to unlock it.

"I'll be careful," I promised. I didn't have the *best* track record with my own phones. In the last year I'd dropped two, shattering both screens, and accidentally sent a third through the wash cycle, resulting in a waterlogged phone that was beyond the reach of even the biggest bag of rice. My parents had told me if anything happened to this one, I was on my own in terms of replacing it.

As the train slowed down for the East Randolph stop, I scrolled through Stevie's Stories, even though there wasn't anything new since the last time I checked—just one that Teri had posted from my account. It was a picture of snacks out on the coffee table, and her TV in the background, with a blurry picture on it—it looked like a girl climbing the side of a building. Teri had captioned it *Just a quiet night in with my fronds! Snacks and movies!♥!—Kat.* I knew I shouldn't be picky when she was doing me a favor, but I thought it might be good to mention that she didn't need to sign my Stories, since that wasn't something I normally did, or that any sane person would do.

I'd just pulled up Stevie's messages and was starting to write to Teri when three texts came in, one right after the other. And it wasn't like I *wanted* to read them, but I also couldn't help myself, since they were right there in front of me.

Beckett

Hey—nice to chat today

Hope you have a great time in NYC

And happy belated birthday—hope it's the best one yet.

"Kat?" Stevie asked, and I glanced up from her phone to see her looking at me. "What is it?"

"Beckett," I said, holding out her phone to her. "He texted." I watched Stevie's face as she read the texts. A smile flashed across her face quickly and then was gone, like someone flicking a light switch on and then off again. I rolled my eyes and sighed.

"What's that look about?" Stevie asked with a half laugh, tucking her hair behind one ear. I could see the *S* and star earrings I'd bought her for her birthday in her double-pierce.

"I just don't like how he seems to want to pretend he didn't do anything wrong. Like he thinks he can invite you to plays like everything's forgiven?"

"I . . . ," Stevie started. "I think it was just a gesture—"

"I mean, it's not like he gave you any sort of explanation." It had been over two months, but I was still annoyed about this. You did *not* get to dump my best friend in a mid-priced Mexican restaurant without any explanation. You just didn't.

"I'm not going to the play," Stevie said, glancing out the window, a note of finality in her voice. "So it's a nonissue."

"Good," I said. I was heartened by how definitive she sounded. It had been clear to me recently that she was finally getting over being broken up with, and I didn't think it would be the best call to start hanging out with Beckett again. "I don't like that he's suddenly doing this now. Do you think he's having second thoughts?"

"I . . . ," Stevie started, then looked down, her hair falling over her face like a curtain and blocking it from view. "I don't know."

As I took a breath to reply, I happened to glance up and felt my heart stop. Kathie Alden, one of my mother's friends, was stepping onto the train and looking around for a seat.

I turned away and ducked down, heart thumping, pretending to be pulling on my ankle boots, praying to any deity currently available that she hadn't seen me.

"What is it?" Stevie asked at a normal volume. "Kat? What's—"

"Shh!" I hissed at her. Stevie ducked down too so that our faces were level.

"What's going on?" she whispered. "Are we about to get whacked?"

I turned my head slightly and saw Kathie stop at a two-seater halfway down the car and take her coat off. I straightened up and sat back against the seat, slouching down so that my head couldn't be seen. "My mom's friend," I murmured, and Stevie's eyes went wide and she slouched down too.

"Oh *noooooo*."

"Exactly."

I swallowed hard, trying to get my heart rate to return to normal. I was suddenly aware that I was sweating in really awkward places, like the top of my lip and in between my shoulder blades.

"Did she see you?" Stevie asked, still talking just above a murmur.

"I don't think so," I said with more confidence than I currently felt. I closed my eyes for a second, trying to marshal my thoughts, but it was proving difficult. All I could think was that if Kathie

Alden saw me—and told my mother—I would be in *such* trouble.

The reality of what might actually happen if my parents found out made me feel dizzy and slightly vertigo-y, like I'd just looked over the edge of a canyon and seen how far the drop was. If they found out I'd lied to them—and then went into the city, alone, at night, with Stevie . . . I shuddered even thinking about it.

The conductor announced that the Hartfield stop was upcoming, and Stevie nudged my foot with hers. "Let's move cars," she said, her lips barely moving.

"You don't think it's better to stay put?"

Stevie shook her head. "Safer this way," she said. "Just move slowly and don't look back."

I was tempted to make a joke about Lot's wife—or Oasis—but knew it wasn't the time. As the train slowed to a stop and the station was announced, I got up, gathering my coat and looking resolutely straight ahead. Knowing that Stevie was behind me, I stepped out of the train onto the Hartfield platform. We ran for the next car up, stepping back onto the train again just as the doors were sliding shut.

I let out a sigh of relief as the train started to move again, grateful that nobody had collected our tickets yet, since it was pretty much impossible to change seats once that happened.

This car was a little more crowded than the one we'd just left, and we ended up in a two-seater with a toddler's face peeking over the back of the seat in front of ours. As soon as we got close, she ducked down, and I just hoped she'd be quiet for the next forty minutes or so.

It wasn't that I didn't like kids—I was just burned out on them. I'd babysat for years, starting as a mother's helper when I was twelve, until this fall, when I'd quit. I told my parents that it was just too much to take on senior year. But truthfully, I had hit my limit. My former clients still called—and some even called my mom, which felt extra sneaky—but even though I missed the money, I'd held the line. I was retired.

Stevie took the window again and I dropped into my seat next to her as the conductor moved through our car, calling, "Tickets!" Most people just held out their phones, but we held out our paper tickets to be punched, and then she handed them back to us—we'd gotten round trips and would need them to get home again at the end of the night.

It wasn't until she walked away that I realized I'd been half expecting the conductor to look at us and ask what we were doing there, somehow suss out that we were doing something we weren't supposed to. And even though next year at this time we'd both be on our own, in college and probably allowed to take whatever trains we wanted—it didn't change the feeling that right now, we were doing something we shouldn't, and it seemed to me like it would be obvious to everyone around us.

"It was a good call to change seats," I said, handing my ticket back to Stevie. She zipped both of ours into the inside pocket of her clutch. "Way better than spending the entire ride hiding and panicking."

Stevie laughed. "Well, I thought so." She glanced toward the car we'd just left—we could see just a little of it through the swaying window at the back of our car. She turned to me again. "Do you think she saw you?"

"I don't think so." I shook my head, trying to get rid of the lingering canyon-vertigo feeling. "Thank god. I would have been in so much trouble." I squashed my coat down next to me, wishing that we could have found a three-seater in this car too, since the two-seaters were tight if you needed to turn and talk to someone.

"Would they have pulled the nuclear option?"

The nuclear option was what my parents had held over me but never ever followed through on. And because I was aware that it was in their arsenal, I had made sure never to go too far over the line—which meant, I suppose, that it had been a successful deterrent. It was the worst consequence they could come up with, the one floated in those times when they'd found out I'd gone off campus when I was supposed to be in class, or lied about not having any work when I had a massive essay due, or forgot the fender bender I'd gotten into until they got the insurance claim.

It was simple but devastating: I couldn't be in the plays. I didn't think they would have made me drop out of a current production, but I'd never wanted to test it.

"They might have," I said, knowing full well as I said it that there was no *might* about it. If my parents found out I'd lied to them and gone into the city alone, I wouldn't be allowed to be in *King Lear*—and possibly not the musical, either. "It would be really ironic," I mused, leaning back against the seats that were never as comfortable as I wanted them to be, "that I'd go into the city to save my part and then not be allowed to play it because I went into the city." I shook my head. "That would be like 'Gift of the Magi'–level irony."

Stevie's brow furrowed. "What do you mean?"

"You know, the O. Henry story. The girl sells her hair for a pocket-watch thing for a Christmas present—"

"No, not that," Stevie said. "I meant, what did you mean about going into the city to save your part?"

My eyes went wide as I realized what I'd just done. I'd been intending to tell Stevie the plan just as we were pulling into the tunnel to lead us into Grand Central, well past the point of no return. But there was no time like the present, I figured as I turned to face her more fully. "So okay, here's the thing," I said, giving her a smile. "What if we—"

"Kat." Stevie's eyes narrowed. "What did you do?"

"I didn't do anything," I said, talking fast, just wanting to get to the point where she was fine with this. "Here's my idea. Mr. Campbell has the premiere of his play tonight at eight. And so I thought we could go and see it, since the reservation is so late!"

Stevie folded her arms, her face impassive. "You just now thought that?"

I decided to drop any pretense—I hated lying to Stevie, and it wasn't like she was buying it anyway. "Okay, fine. I thought it back at home. But listen, it'll fix everything," I said, my voice rising. The guy sitting across the aisle, reading a thick fantasy novel, frowned at me, and I leaned closer to Stevie and dropped my voice a little. "Just think about it. Mr. Campbell is concerned about our dedication, and he can't cast the play because of it. But! If he sees that we've shown up, gone out of our way to support his art, he'll realize how dedicated we are. He'll see how serious we are. It'll help us for the *Lear* casting, and the musical, too." I smiled at Stevie and leaned back, but she wasn't looking at me.

Stevie was looking down at her clutch, snapping and unsnapping the closure. "I thought . . . ," she said, then shook her head and took a breath. "I thought that you wanted to go into the city to celebrate my birthday."

"I do," I said firmly. "And we will! We get to do both! We'll get to see the premiere of a play and go to Josephine's. Best night ever, right?"

"We aren't going to have time—"

"We are," I said, speaking over her. "That's the best part. The reservation's not until nine thirty, and the show starts at eight. It might be a super-short play, in which case, no problem. But if it's not, maybe you duck out a little early, go down to Josephine's, and I'll be right behind you after I put in a good word for both of us with Mr. Campbell. Perfect, right?" Stevie nodded, but she still wasn't looking at me, and I felt a tiny, guilty pull in my stomach. "Don't be mad."

"I'm not mad," Stevie said immediately. I could sense that she wanted to say something else, and sure enough, after a moment of silence, she took a breath. "I just—why you didn't just tell me this back home?"

"I'm telling you now!"

Stevie gave me a look. "Come on."

"I mean . . ." I hesitated. "It's kind of Six Flags all over again, you know?"

"How is it Six Flags?"

"You didn't want to go when I told you where we were going—"

"You mean after you'd kidnapped me, you always forget to mention that part—"

"And if I'd asked, you would have said no, but once we were there, we had the best time. Right?" Stevie nodded slowly. The toddler's head started to creep back up over the seat again—I could see straight-across bangs, then wide blue eyes. I made a funny face at her and she dropped down immediately. "I just think that sometimes . . . you stand in the way of things that would make you happy." It was something I'd been feeling for a while but never said out loud to my best friend.

Stevie drew back slightly, frowning. "What's *that* supposed to mean?"

"It's not a bad thing," I said quickly, "just that sometimes you say no initially to stuff that's really fun. Like Six Flags."

"I don't . . ." Stevie shook her head and snapped her clutch open and closed a few more times. "I don't do that," she said, her voice quiet.

"Okay." I figured we had lots of time in the future to talk about the fact that Stevie did, in fact, do this. "So . . . you're good with going to the play?"

Stevie looked out the window and let out a long breath, like she was preparing to say something. But when she turned back to me, she was smiling ruefully. "I mean, do I have a choice?"

"It'll be great," I said quickly, relief flooding through me. "It'll be so great. We'll get to see it, and then go to Josephine's, and it's just going to be the best night ever." I nudged her with my shoulder and settled back into my seat, smiling.

We rode in silence for a few stops, and I was on the verge of asking

Stevie for Ophelia again—it was *hard* to be without your phone—when she turned to me. "Just don't put everything on this, okay, Kat? I don't think Mr. Campbell is going cast you based on your showing up to his play or not."

"I know that," I said, trying not to feel stung by this, "obviously. But it can't hurt."

"I just think he's going to decide what he's going to decide," Stevie said, shaking her head, "and that you don't need to, like, make a pilgrimage to show your *devotion*...."

"It's not that," I said, starting to get annoyed. "And it's not just for me. It might help you, too, not that you need it."

"Wait, what does that mean?" Stevie asked, frowning.

"Come on," I said, rolling my eyes at her. "You know you're the best actress in the department."

"It's not true. You're—"

"Not as good as you, and I know that, and it's fine. It is," I said firmly, knowing she was about to start arguing this. "But it can't hurt, right? For *Lear*, for the musical ..."

"Yeah," Stevie said. She looked at me for a moment, almost like she was deciding something, then took a breath. "That might not actually ... matter as much."

My head whipped around to stare at her. "What do you mean?"

"I mean," she said, turning her clutch over on her lap, end over end, "that I'm thinking about ... not auditioning for the musical."

"What are you talking about, not auditioning for the musical?" I asked, hoping this was just a really weird joke I didn't get yet. "We *always* do the musical. The musical's the whole spring." It was, too—because there were songs to learn and choreography to memorize, and because the orchestra and band were involved (sometimes *too* involved, like when we did *City of Angels* last year and the band had gotten way too into the jazz element of it all and Ms. Wallace had had constant fights with the band director about saxophone volume), the rehearsal time was longer. As soon as we struck the set for the Shakespeare play in February, the rest of the year was the musical. I had a serviceable soprano, but Stevie had a brassy alto with a belt—which meant while I was stuck singing love duets, she was usually getting fun, showstopping numbers, and sometimes I'd see her face as her applause just kept coming after she'd killed it, just waves of it rolling in as she kept trying to start the scene again but the audience wouldn't let her. It was like seeing someone's unfiltered happiness. "You love the musical."

"I know," Stevie said, but like she was trying to brush this aside. "It's just—"

"It's our *senior year*. And didn't you hear we might do *Follies*?" Stevie was a fool for Sondheim, and I saw her flinch slightly as I said this.

"I might apply for this internship at my dad's firm," she said, in a voice that was trying for casual but not pulling it off. "I just think . . . since I'm going to be prelaw at college, I might as well start, you know?"

A cold, clammy fear gripped my insides. I couldn't shake the visions of Dara Chapman, sitting at the lunch table but not getting any of the jokes, then not showing up at our parties, just slowly fading out. What if that happened to Stevie and me? Right when it was supposed to be our senior-year swan song, the celebration of all we'd worked so hard for? The thought of it was making me feel ill. I couldn't let it happen.

"Why didn't you tell me earlier?"

"I'm telling you now," Stevie said. She raised an eyebrow at me and I knew, in that moment, that whatever she said, she was not 100 percent okay with the switch I'd pulled on her.

"Are you mad at me?"

"I'm not mad."

"It's okay if you are. Just tell me."

Stevie looked out the window, taking a halting breath. "I don't, like, need your *permission* . . ." She stopped and looked back at me.

"I'm not mad," she said again. "I just—you didn't need to lie to me."

"I didn't!"

Stevie gave me a look that said *come on*.

"I didn't," I insisted. "I just didn't tell you all the facts at that exact moment. What's the legal term? Omission something?"

"It's a *lie* of omission," Stevie said, now looking like she was trying hard not to laugh. "'Lie' is literally right there in its name!"

"Oh," I said, momentarily stymied, and Stevie laughed, which made me laugh too. "I am sorry, you know. I just . . . really need this to all work out."

"I know." She gave me a smile. "I really hope it does, Kat."

"It will," I said, in case *The Secret* was an actual thing and the universe was listening. And to be on the safe side, I crossed my fingers and toes and leaned over Stevie to knock on the fake wood paneling by the window. "So, what is this internship? Besides being a terrible idea?"

"Hello." We both looked over to see that the toddler was back, her whole head now above the seat, looking between the two of us. She extended a chubby fist and opened it to reveal a T. rex figurine. "I have a dino."

This was such an objectively true statement that I smiled. "You sure do," I said, leaning closer to look.

"Her name is Lulu."

I saw Stevie's mouth twitch in a smile. "Lulu the dinosaur," she said, giving the kid a nod. "Very cool."

The little girl dropped out of sight again—apparently this was what she'd wanted to tell us—and Stevie turned to me. "Look, nothing's decided about the internship," she said. "We've got lots of time to figure it out."

"Right," I said, nodding. It was true, after all, even if when Stevie said *figure it out*, what I meant was *talk her out of this bananas idea*. But she was right—we had lots of time to sort it through.

Twenty minutes later, we'd had three more dinosaur updates, we'd seen one of Erik's Stories in which his whole search history was accidentally visible in the background and now we had lots of questions about Erik, and Stevie had gone though all potential casting possibilities with me, even when I knew I was repeating myself and just needing reassurance. Just as we were debating whether to message Erik and let him know, the train loudspeaker crackled. "We are approaching Grand Central Station, our final stop. Please collect all your belongings when exiting the train."

I glanced out the window just in time to see the outside world disappear as we went into the tunnel that would take us into the heart of the city. I sat up straight against the leather seat as everything else began to fade away in importance. Tonight was about *Lear*, and making sure I would get my part, and Stevie would get her part, and celebrating Stevie's birthday. And now that I knew she was thinking of doing something as crazy as not auditioning for our final musical, the whole night seemed to take on even more importance. We'd go to this play and it would be amazing and Stevie would realize she had been crazy to think about quitting.

The train slowed, and then came to a stop, and all around us, people jumped to their feet, gathering up coats and bags (and, in the case of the little girl ahead of us, dinosaurs). I looked at Stevie. "Ready to do this, frond?"

She grinned at me. "You know it, frand." She nodded toward the train doors, which had slid open. "Lead the way."

CHAPTER 6

*W*e *waited on the train* until everyone else in our car had gotten off, and then a few minutes more—I wanted to put as much distance between myself and Kathie Alden as possible. When the conductor walked through, saying, "Last stop!" very loudly, we figured it was our cue to go.

We pulled on our coats and headed out of the train. The first view of the station wasn't particularly glamorous—a little overheated, and not much to see beyond the round trash and recycling bins in the center of the walkway. But I'd never minded, because up ahead, literally the light at the end of tunnel, was Grand Central.

Stevie and I stepped out of the entrance to track eighteen, on the upper level, and walked a few steps out of the way. But then, we both stood still for a second and just looked up.

Because that was what Grand Central did to you. It made you draw in a breath and look around, taking it all in. The expanse of it, how *big* it was. The vaulted ceiling with the constellations painted on it, the way they seemed to catch the light and twinkle. The massive American flag hanging vertically by the south entrance. The digital time boards along the right side, above the ticket windows, where you could still buy tickets from an actual person, like you were Ginger Rogers in a movie from the 1940s. The people, bustling through and walking, like all New Yorkers seemed to, a beat faster than anyone else.

There were the marble stairways on either end of the building— with the Apple Store and restaurants on the top story, and on the bottom level, bathrooms and more restaurants and the lower-level trains. There were the Metro-North ticket kiosks, the Hudson News with its overpriced gum, and the Starbucks on the first level that was almost a secret, tucked away over by track thirty.

But best of all was the clock in the center. The clock was brass, and it sat atop a round marble information desk, so big that you couldn't see all the way around it. Someone sat in the middle and answered questions, and there were pamphlets all around it, with information about New York City and train timetables. The clock had always been my favorite part of Grand Central, and I had vague memories of getting chased around it by my parents when I was little, and then clearer memories of chasing Grady around it, until he turned six and got much too mature for such things.

I stood there for a moment, just taking it all in: the squeak of people's shoes on the floor, the snatches of conversation as people passed by—"So I told him that he needed to call first. I told him!"—the maintenance workers in their orange vests, two besuited men running flat out for a train, their long coats streaming behind them, a little kid spinning around in the center, looking up.

As I stood there, occasionally getting jostled by someone in a hurry, I suddenly felt very clearly that I was seventeen, and in from the suburbs for the night. Everyone else seemed to know exactly where they were going, and I hoped it wasn't painfully obvious that I had never once been here on my own, without someone to lead the way and tell me where to go.

"Okay," Stevie said, shaking me out of these thoughts. She looked down at her watch. I saw some tourists with suitcases walk by us, then pause, also stopping to look up at the ceiling. "So we have—what, three hours? Maybe a little less, since we need to get to this play. Where's Mr. Campbell's theater?"

"In the theater district," I said confidently, even though I realized as

I said it that I'd left the exact address in my phone, which was currently on Teri's coffee table. But it would be fine—I could always google it on Stevie's. "On Tenth Avenue."

"So we'll have some time. What do you want to do?"

I looked around at the people passing by me, heading off for their own New York night, and thought about it. Suddenly, I could see the bright side to being here for the first time without supervision—I was *in the city alone*. With no parents and no agenda . . .

"We could just wander and see where the night takes us!" I suggested. Stevie frowned, and I wasn't able to stop myself from laughing. My best friend always preferred when there was a plan. "Or . . ." I thought for a second. "We could go to the *Ghost Robot* premiere? We could line up and see if we could see Amy Curry."

"The one at the Gansevoort?"

"That's where the after-party is," I said. "But I'm sure we could find out where the premiere is." I reached for my phone, only to realize a second later, once again, that I still didn't have it. "Could you look it up?"

"I'm not sure I want to stand outside in the cold on the chance that *maybe* we'll see a glimpse of a movie star." Stevie shook her head. "How about we go to the Drama Book Shop? That's in the theater district, so we'll be close."

"Oh, let's go there," I said. "Mr. Campbell will love that we went."

"It's also a really cool store."

"I mean, that too."

"Awesome," Stevie said with a nod, looking happier about the whole situation now that we had a destination. "Just let me figure out what train we should take. . . ."

"And we should have the clock as a meeting place," I said, nodding toward it. "If we get separated for any reason, meet there."

Stevie looked up from her phone, her brow furrowing. "Separated?" she echoed. "Why would we get separated?"

"It's what my mom always used to say," I explained. "When we'd all go into the city, and she and I would be going to the American Girl store or the Frick and my dad would be taking Grady to the Natural History Museum or the Morgan Library or whatever."

"The Morgan Library?"

"It was, like, Grady's favorite place. I don't even know. But we'd always have it as an in-case-of-emergency meeting place. Not that we'll need it. But just to be on the safe side."

"Well, we need a meeting time then too," Stevie said, in her practical voice. "Otherwise one of us might be hanging out by the clock for hours."

"Eleven-eleven?" I suggested with a grin. I was always pointing out when it was 11:11 and insisting we make wishes on it, which Stevie was always was telling me was ridiculous but went along with anyway.

Stevie laughed. "Of course you'd pick that. Sure. Eleven-eleven at the clock if for whatever reason we get separated. Which we won't."

"Of course we won't. This is just in case."

"Okay," Stevie said, scrolling through her phone, "it looks like we'll take the shuttle across to Times Square, and we can walk from there."

We headed over to where the subways were, crossing the huge expanse, which seemed more crowded than usual. Everyone was walking fast, like they all had somewhere they needed to be *right now*.

Stevie had her own MetroCard from the last time she was in with her mom, and she took it out of her wallet and tucked it in her coat pocket. She'd told me when we got our tickets on the platform that she was pretty sure there was enough on it so that I could use it too.

"Do you think we should get something to eat on the way?" I asked, falling into step next to Stevie as we made our way through the crowds. "Like a pretzel or a slice or something? Since dinner's not until late—"

"Stephanie?" We both stopped and looked over. There was a woman standing next to us, sunglasses perched on top of her head even though the sun was going down depressingly early now. She was squinting at Stevie, head cocked to the side. "Is that you?"

I glanced at Stevie, wondering if she knew this woman. She was in her late twenties, with long, blown-out dark hair and perfectly applied makeup. She was dressed all in black, with boots, also black, that had spike heels that had to be at least five inches. She was carrying a big black leather bag and a duffel from a luxury brand, its logo printed on it over and over again.

She didn't look familiar to me at all, but Stevie was giving her a wan smile and a half wave. "Hi, Mallory," she said. I stared at her, realizing that this must be Stevie's stepsister. I had never met any of Stevie's siblings, and the only pictures I'd seen had been from the wedding, in which Stevie's smile was bright and fake, and hurt me a little to look at. Mallory was the oldest, and in publicity; Margaux was the middle child, and though apparently she did something in fashion, her job mostly seemed to be traveling the world and taking gauzy selfies; and Mateo was the youngest, in college, just a year older than us. And even though I knew these three people existed, it was still strange to be confronted with this whole other part of Stevie's life that I knew very little about, and wasn't a part of.

"I thought it was you!" Mallory said, giving Stevie a kiss on each cheek, like we were in France. "What are you doing here?"

"Well, we—that's my friend Kat," Stevie said, gesturing to me, and I waved, hoping I wouldn't get kissed. "We just got off the—"

"This is such a coincidence!" Mallory interrupted. "But like the good kind! What's that called? Kismet?" She looked from me to Stevie, but just when I took a breath to answer, she was speaking again. "How are you? How's your boyfriend?"

"Oh," Stevie said, looking uncomfortable. From everything Stevie had said—or not said, but let me infer—her stepsiblings had never wanted anything to do with her, so I wondered why Mallory was doing this, double-kissing her cheeks and being fake-chummy, even if she was getting massive details wrong. "We—um—broke up...."

"That's great," Mallory said, clearly not listening at all. "Listen, I'm so happy to run into you, because I'm dealing with this thing and I do *not* have time to handle it because I have to get this train—I'm going upstate, to Bear Mountain. Have you been? There's like a lodge, and a spa, and I need it, let me tell you." She started to run her hand through her hair, but it got stuck on her sunglasses. She plucked them from her head like she was surprised to see them there, then dropped them into her purse.

"What's the thing?" I asked, curious, but regretted it a second later when Stevie shot me a look.

"It's really annoying, and it's not even my fault! So my roommate left her wallet out on the counter, and when I was packing to go, I accidentally knocked it into my purse." She shook her head. "And I *told* her that I could bring it back with me next week, but apparently she wants her credit cards and, like, needs her license to 'get on a plane on Tuesday.'" Mallory made air quotes with one hand as she rolled her eyes. "So I was going to go home and get the later train and totally miss my welcome massage, but now I don't have to!"

"Um," I said, trying to follow all this. "And why is that?"

The (all-black) watch on her wrist lit up and she frowned at it for a second, before tapping it again and turning the screen back off. "God! My train's in like ten minutes. Okay," she said, like she was trying to get herself to focus. "If you guys wouldn't mind running it back over to my apartment? You would help me out so, so, so much." She smiled hopefully at us.

"Sorry," Stevie said, shaking her head, her voice firm. "We're seeing a show tonight, actually, so we can't." I smiled, glad to see that Stevie was as excited about the show as I was. I knew she would be—just that she might need a minute to get there.

"What time's the show?" Mallory asked, not missing a beat, eyes locked with Stevie's.

"Eight," Stevie said with real reluctance. "But—"

"That's perfect!" Mallory said, clapping her hands together. "Because I promise that it won't take long, like fifteen to twenty, tops, and you'll still have plenty of time before your show and you'd be helping me out *so* much." She motioned for us to follow her over to the side, out of the way of people passing, where there was an optical shop that had closed for the night.

"I just . . ." Stevie's voice trailed off.

"I know it's in here." Mallory dropped her duffel to the ground, and then started going through her enormous purse, handing things to Stevie as she searched for something in its depths. "So all you need to do is bring the wallet back to my apartment. And you can even do it after your show—my roommate is working tonight. She acts like working in the mayor's office is so important, I swear. . . ."

"Well," I said as Mallory piled an iPad, a planner, a scarf, and an oversized pair of headphones into Stevie's arms, "isn't it?"

But Mallory rolled right over me like I hadn't spoken. "And apparently, they have to do the budget or something, so she'll be working late. Aha!" She retrieved from the depths of her bag a small red leather wallet. Her phone beeped again and she groaned. "Okay, I've got like five minutes and I'm not going to have time to get a Starbucks apparently. God! Can you believe today? I cannot even. So here's the wallet. Just drop it off on the kitchen counter, since that's apparently where Flora thinks a great place to leave wallets is." She took all the things she'd put into Stevie's arms back and swept them into her purse. "My keys," she said, holding them out to Stevie along with the wallet. Stevie took both with what looked like extreme reluctance. "I'll text you my address—I have your number, right?" She pulled out her phone, scrolled through it, then nodded. "I do. Great."

"How should I get the keys back to you?" Stevie asked, putting the wallet and keys in her clutch with a sigh.

"You can just leave them in the apartment—the door locks when you close it."

Stevie widened her eyes at me, basically an eye roll that she was too polite to do in front of Mallory, and I could tell that she was getting very annoyed by this. "So do you live far?" I asked, trying to wrap this up.

"No, super close." Mallory glanced at her watch again, then started to walk in the direction of the trains, and Stevie and I followed after her. "But I'll give you cab fare." She pulled out her own wallet as she walked and looked through it. "Ugh, all I have is a hundred. Well, it's your thanks for helping me out," she said, pulling out a crisp one-hundred-dollar bill and handing it to me. "Thank you so much!" She swooped down on Stevie and kissed her cheeks again. "You're just the best. You're saving my life!"

She'd only walked a few steps toward track twenty-one before she jogged back toward us. "Oh—Brad will be there, but just ignore him. He's so spoiled it's unbelievable. And he might cry when you leave, but don't let it worry you. It's all just for show."

"Wait, *what*?" I asked, but Mallory was now running in her heels toward her train, duffel bumping against her hip.

"You're the best! Thank you!" she called with a wave over her shoulder. Then she started running even faster—which was honestly impressive, in those shoes—and then a second later, disappeared.

Stevie and I looked at each other for a moment. "Okay, what just happened?" she asked.

"I know," I said, starting to laugh. "She seemed . . . interesting."

"Yeah, that's one word for it."

"But it is cool that we bumped into someone! I feel like that's always happening in New York movies and shows but I never believed it was real." I held up the hundred-dollar bill. "And we made some money off it too!"

Stevie laughed and shook her head. "Let's just get this over with." As if on cue, her phone beeped from inside her bag, and she pulled it out. "Mallory just texted her address," she said. "Somewhere called Murray Hill? It's on Thirty-Seventh Street, at any rate."

"So that's probably pretty close to the theater district," I reasoned. "Since that's around Forty-Second. We're not going too far out of our way, and we'll still have more than enough time before the play."

"Great," Stevie said, looking relieved. "Let's get this done and then we can be back on track. Just let me figure out trains."

"No need!" I said, flashing the hundred again, and then a second later, worrying that maybe I shouldn't do that. "We've got cab fare!" I started to walk toward the nearest exit I saw, Stevie following behind me. I heaved open the heavy door, with its brass handle, then held it for her.

I stepped outside and there it was—*New York*. Horns were honking, crowds of pedestrians were surging forward into the intersection as they crossed against the light, and a man, his guitar case open, was singing an enthusiastic but off-key rendition of "Dancing in the Dark." The light changed and blurs of yellow cabs sped forward, as all around us, crowds of people streamed past, scrolling through their phones, walking fast and frowning, talking to people they were with, or grooving along to the music only they could hear in their earbuds.

I looked up—at the sliver of sky you could see in between all the tall buildings, the way the whole world seemed to have been stretched higher than anyone had ever thought to make it back home.

It was cold out, with that damp bite in the air that had always, always meant snow—like a promise for later, if only you were patient. I zipped up my coat as I took it all in, the two police officers in blue on the corner, the flashing ads on top of the taxis, the bus stopping across the street and lowering itself with a hiss to let people on.

I turned to Stevie and gave her a spontaneous hug, squeezing her tight.

"What?" she asked, even as she hugged me back.

"New York!" I said, gesturing to everything around us, not caring if it made me look like a tourist. "We're here!" I felt like doing a spin—if I'd had a hat, I might well have thrown it into the air. I strode forward, full of confidence, and stepped off the curb, putting my hand out. "Taxi!" I yelled, even though I knew real New Yorkers didn't actually do this.

"Taxi line's back there," a passing woman in a suit said without stopping, nodding toward the corner. I could now see that there was a line of people with suitcases and a sign that read TAXIS.

"Thanks," I called after her, but she'd already crossed the street and was out of earshot.

"We can just take the subway," Stevie said as she got into the taxi line and I hurried over to join her.

"It's more fun this way," I insisted. And it was—as long as we made it to Mr. Campbell's play with more than enough time to spare, having a mini adventure—even if it was only to return a lost wallet—sounded good to me.

"But will they take the hundred, though? Don't people hate to change them?"

"I think they have to," I said with confidence as we moved up a step. "It's currency, after all. It won't be a problem."

"No hundreds," the cabdriver said, shaking his head and pushing the bill back through the plexiglass partition.

We had arrived at Mallory's. It hadn't taken long—Murray Hill was a few blocks from Grand Central—but traffic had been almost bumper to bumper. Our fare came to eight dollars, and the driver sighed audibly when he saw what I was trying to pay him with.

"Don't you have to take it?" I asked, trying to remember where I'd heard this. "Because it's, you know, legal tender?"

"Read the sign," he said. I looked all over the back of the seat in front of me and saw Stevie doing it too. She spotted it before I did, and tapped on it—NO BILLS LARGER THAN $20 ACCEPTED.

"Oh," Stevie said. "Sorry." She reached for her clutch and I took back the C-note.

"I have some cash in there," I said, nodding toward her clutch. "Or I have my card—wait." I shook my head. "I can't use that, because it's linked to my parents'."

"I can use my card," Stevie said, pulling it out. "It's tied to my dad's, but he expects me to be in the city." She paid using her card, and after a whispered consultation, we decided to give the driver a 15 percent tip. We told him we didn't need a receipt, and then got out and slammed the door. He sped away, and I looked up at the row of apartment buildings in front of us.

I had been expecting more like a high-rise building with a doorman, the kind that I knew Stevie's dad had moved to. But these were redbrick buildings in a row next to each other, with moldings at the top, only about four or five stories high. It was quieter on this street— not as many cars rushing past, fewer people.

The entrance to the building was down three steps behind a wrought-iron black gate, with a call box mounted to the wall outside the black-painted door. "Do we have a key for the outside?" I asked, realizing that Mallory hadn't said anything about that—just about Brad, who I wasn't thrilled to meet, because he sounded pretty troubled, honestly.

Stevie pulled the keys out of her clutch. There were two on the ring, along with a number of brightly colored membership fobs. "I guess we try them?"

The first key didn't work, but the second one did, and Stevie pulled open the door, holding it for me. The lobby was small—the mailboxes and a small noticeboard took up almost all the space. I could see steps leading down to the basement unit, with SUPERINTENDENT on a sign attached to the door. There did not seem to be an elevator anywhere. "Which number is she?"

Stevie pulled out her phone again. "Five B," she said, and shook her head. "She's really not making any of this easy, is she?"

"I guess that explains why she gave us a hundred."

"Speaking of, want me to hold it for you?" Stevie asked as she started climbing the stairs. I followed behind her, secretly glad that I'd worn flats tonight, even though I wasn't about to share that with her. She glanced over her shoulder at me as she rounded the first story. "Just . . . in case."

"I can be trusted to hold on to a hundred dollars," I protested, trying to figure out if I was annoyed by this or not.

"I know," Stevie said quickly. "I was just . . . putting it out there."

"What should we do with it? Go crazy at the Drama Book Shop?"

Stevie laughed, sounding slightly out of breath. "We're really lucking out tonight," she said. "Dinner's on my dad, Mallory gives us a hundred. . . ."

"We could bring Teri back a thank-you," I suggested. "Do you think that Mallory will mention to your dad that she saw me with you?" I knew that Stevie's dad wasn't as on top of her whereabouts as my parents were with me, but the fact remained—you always had to think about the trail.

"I doubt it," she said, pausing and leaning on the railing for just a moment before starting to climb again. "And I could always say that you came in with me and then I met my mom later. I think we're fine."

By the time we reached the fifth floor, we were both out of breath, and I was resolving to start doing more cardio, because this was embarrassing.

"Should we start running or something?" Stevie asked, turning to me, brushing her hair back, and I smiled.

"I was just thinking that," I said. "Ooh! We could use the hundred dollars to buy some spin classes."

"We've got big plans for this hundred," Stevie said, raising an eyebrow at me as she pulled out the keys again. She started to turn the key in the lock when I thought of something.

"Wait! Should we knock first, do you think?"

"Why? Mallory gave us the keys."

"What if that Brad guy is in there? I don't want to startle him or whatever."

"You'd think *he* could have come and gotten the wallet."

"Seriously." She nodded at me and I knocked on the door. We both listened, but I couldn't hear the sound of anyone coming, and after a minute, I shrugged. "Maybe he's out."

Stevie turned the key in the lock and stepped inside, and I followed behind her. It was dark, and I hit the light that was right by the door and looked around. We had walked into the living area—the small kitchen was in front of us, and to the side, a couch and two chairs were positioned in front of the television. Down a hallway, I could see three doors, one cracked open, presumably the bedrooms and bathroom. It was *small*, and I knew New York apartments were, in theory, but it was something else seeing one up close. Compared to this, Teri's guesthouse was a mansion.

"It's so small," I whispered to Stevie.

"I know," she whispered back. "My dad's is a little bigger, but not that much."

"Um, hi," I called into the empty, quiet space, just in case there was someone there who wasn't expecting two teenagers from Connecticut to barge in and start judging their apartment. "We're . . . friends of Mallory's? We're here to drop something off?" We both waited in silence for another minute, but still, nobody emerged and Brad seemed to be MIA, so I walked farther into the apartment, Stevie following me, the door slamming shut behind us.

"Okay," I said, as Stevie put the red wallet on the kitchen counter and set the keys next to it. "Do you think we need to leave a note or something?"

"Probably not," Stevie said. "I mean, it's not like Mallory's roommate won't be looking for it." She set her clutch down on the counter and took a step farther into the kitchen, peering around.

"What?"

"I was just wondering. You know that stereotype about people who live in New York turning their ovens into closets?"

"They what?"

"To save space, and because they don't cook. I was just curious. . . ." She pulled open the oven door and seemed disappointed when it was just an oven and not filled with shoes or sweaters. She turned to me, looking affronted. "It appears that *Sex and the City* has been *lying* to me."

I laughed. "Well, maybe Brad is a big cook or something." A second later I heard a scrabbling sound, and my blood ran cold. "Did you hear that?"

Stevie had also turned pale. "Do you think it's a mouse?"

I would sometimes see mice darting across our yard back home, but we lived in the woods, practically. You didn't mind seeing or hearing critters there, because it was their territory. But now, I wanted to crawl out of my skin, and I understood why in movies, when people saw mice, they were always shrieking and jumping on chairs. "Or maybe a rat," I said, my voice barely above a whisper. "It sounded loud."

Stevie shuddered. "Oh my god." She froze as the sound got louder—and a second later, a white-and-tan blur ran out of the room with the door cracked open. "What is that?" Stevie asked, her voice panicky.

"It's a dog," I said as I realized it was. I laughed with relief as I understood that the scrabbling sound was just the dog's nails on the apartment floors. The dog was small, definitely not more than ten pounds, and low to the ground. It was running around the apartment, only stopping to jump up and spin in a circle, and then start running again. It was very fluffy—it looked like a Pomeranian, though it was moving a little too fast for me to tell.

"Oh," Stevie said, now backing up against the kitchen counters, not looking thrilled by this information. "That's—good."

"Come here, bud," I said, bending down to try and pet it. The dog stopped mid-twirl and ran up to me. It did not seem to mind at all that it had never seen us before, and practically threw itself at me, licking my face aggressively along with happy little yipping sounds. "Hi," I said, scratching him—I could see it was a him—behind his ears. This dog seemed to be 90 percent fluff, like if he got wet he would be a fraction of the size. I looked at the tag swinging from his blue leather collar. BRAD was engraved on one side, with a phone number on the back. "Well, that's one mystery solved," I said, straightening up, as the dog—Brad—started running in circles around my legs.

"What?" Stevie asked, not moving from where she was still pressed against the counter. For someone who really tried to pretend she wasn't afraid of dogs, she wasn't doing a great job of it.

"That's Brad," I said, pointing to the dog. He immediately stopped running and sat, like he was showing us just how well he knew his name.

"That's Brad?" Stevie said, then frowned. "I guess now that does make a little more sense—that he would cry when we left."

"You might want to tell Mallory that she should use a few more specifics when talking about her dog."

"Seriously," Stevie said. "Also, Brad? For a dog's name?"

"And this dog really doesn't look like a Brad." Maybe unable to contain himself after hearing his name so many times, Brad jumped up and ran over to Stevie, who cautiously put her hand down.

"Nice doggie," she said, giving Brad a very unconvincing head pat. "Good . . . boy." She straightened up and brushed her hands off. "We should probably get going."

I glanced at the clock on the microwave. It was only a little after five, so I had a feeling this was more about getting away from the dog and less about our timeline. But we still wanted to go to the Drama Book Shop and get something to eat—and getting to the Echo Theater early might be a good idea. There hadn't been online ticketing for the show, and what if it sold out?

"Good call," I said. I bent down and smooshed Brad's fluff down, giving him a back and neck scratch—it was honestly hard to tell where any of his body actually was, as the floof was all-encompassing. "And you're a good boy, aren't you? Hmm?" I must have hit a good spot under his collar, because his back leg started thumping. "Yes, you are!"

"All right," Stevie said, looking down at her phone. "So, weirdly, because of traffic, to get to the bookstore, it's like a twenty-minute car ride, a twenty-minute subway ride, or twenty minutes on foot."

"So maybe we should just walk?"

"I think we should walk."

Brad suddenly bolted, running full speed back into the bedroom where he'd come from. "Okay, bye," I called, trying not to be hurt. Clearly, what Mallory had said about him crying when we left was not true.

"Ready?"

"Yep," I said. Stevie opened the door, just as Brad returned, but now carrying a leash in his mouth that dragged on the floor behind him. "What's—" I started, but didn't get to finish, because the dog kept going, running straight out the open door.

"Oh my god," Stevie said, and then we both ran after him.

"Brad," I called, and I looked down the stairs to see, in a panic, that he was already two floors down, on a step looking up at me. "Stay, okay, buddy? Just—stay."

"Do you think it's because we said 'walk'?" Stevie asked. The second she said this, Brad leaped up and started running down the stairs again, the leash thumping down the steps behind him. "Sorry!" she yelled as we both chased after him.

"C'mere, pup," I said, and Brad stopped on the third-floor landing and looked at me, his whole back half waggling from side to side, the long blue leash clenched in his teeth. "Here, bud," I said, making my voice sound as excited as possible as I edged toward him, just trying not to make any sudden movements that would get him to take off again. The last thing I wanted was for the front door to somehow be open and for this tiny dog to go running out into the streets of Manhattan. The thought of it was actually making me feel sick. "That's right," I said, moving closer to the dog, and closer still. "We'll just be . . . very gentle . . . and . . ." I reached out and grabbed his collar, then let out a long breath, now that I had the dog again.

"You've got him?" Stevie said from a few stairs above me, sounding as panicked as I'd felt.

"Yes," I said. I still held him tightly as I reached out and took the leash from him and snapped it onto the ring of his collar. I felt better, just having this dog on a leash, feeling like he wasn't out of my control. "Thank god."

We turned around and started to walk up the stairs, Stevie ahead of me, Brad trotting along, not seeming to care that he was going back to his apartment, now that he was on his leash. Maybe he didn't mind where he walked—just that he was walking. "Seriously," I said, shaking my head as we reached the fifth floor. "That was almost a total disaster."

"Kat," Stevie said, her voice strangled.

"What?" I asked. I came to stand next to her on the landing, then looked where she was staring, and understood. The door to the apartment must have slammed behind us when we ran out—because the door was closed.

Which meant the door was locked.

Which meant that we were screwed.

Meanwhile, back in Connecticut . . .

TERI'S NIGHT WAS NOT OFF TO A GREAT START.

She'd been all set to Netflix and chill with Ryan Camper—she had thought the phrase was self-explanatory, and didn't know why Kat had been confused about what that meant. She had the movies queued, the snacks out, her phone charged. But just as she was about to call Ryan in Maine, Kat's phone beeped with a text. And then another. And then another still.

They were all from a woman named Bobbie Stone. She was texting Kat because she needed a babysitter. Right away.

Teri had stared, frozen, as more messages had come in. With each *beep*, her panic increased. Bobbie Stone apologized for the late notice, but said that it was an emergency and she needed to hear back from Kat as soon as possible.

Teri called Stevie immediately.

No answer.

This sent her heart racing. She did *not* like to be the one in charge, the one deciding things. It always made her nervous. She was always sure she was making the wrong choice. But with nobody telling her what to do, it seemed she had no option—she would agree to babysit. Because what if she said no, and then Bobbie Stone reached out to Kat's mom? And then Kat's mom called Kat's phone?

It was too risky.

So Teri had texted Bobbie Stone back, pretending to be Kat. She told her that she could come a little later, but for the moment, she would send her friend Teri to the house ASAP.

Teri had called Ryan Camper on the drive over, to cancel their Netflix-and-chill date. She explained the situation, but Ryan had not been understanding. He'd accused her of lying, then hung up on her—which was *not* the Camp Ogilvie Way! Had they just broken up? She called him back, but the call went to voice mail. So typical of him. Teri was honestly exhausted by the games Ryan Camper played. He never just said how he felt.

But she tried to put these thoughts behind her as she drove. It seemed like the only benefit to this was that it would distract her both from wondering if Ryan was going to call back and thinking about the cast list. She was hoping to be cast as one of Lear's daughters, but all she truly wanted was not to see the dreaded words at the bottom of the cast list: *Teri, please see me about assistant directing.*

As she drove, she tried Stevie again. No answer.

There was a dented yellow car in the driveway of the Stone house, with a Hertz sticker on the back. This seemed out of place—it was a big house, all glass and (ironically) wood with a three-car garage. Teri was ushered inside by Mr. Stone, who wore a tuxedo and looked about her dad's age.

"Sorry for the late notice." He led Teri down the hall. "We completely forgot about this event. I had to fly back from DC early and didn't even wait for a ride at the airport, just grabbed a rental car. I told them not to even bother cleaning it, just took the first one they had. . . ."

They reached the kitchen and Bobbie Stone, dressed in a long gown, introduced herself, keeping an eye on the clock in the kitchen as she pointed out the list of emergency numbers and allergies. Teri told her, lying through her teeth, that Kat would be along shortly, and that they babysat together a lot. She figured the Stones didn't need to know this wasn't true. After all, she'd been a camp counselor. It wasn't like she had no experience with kids.

"Here they are," Bobbie Stone said, and Teri turned to see three children standing in front of her. She blinked. She'd been expecting one, maybe two. What were the Stones thinking, having three kids? In this economy?

"This is Chris, Daryl, and Parker," Bobbie Stone said, resting her hands in turn on the heads of a girl who looked around eleven, a boy who looked seven or eight, and a toddler who was maybe three.

"Who are you?" Chris asked. "Where's Kat?"

"She's coming any minute now," Teri lied. The girl narrowed her eyes at Teri.

"So we have to be going," Mr. Stone said, pushing back his sleeve like he was looking at a watch—but there was no watch there. "Parker!" He turned to the toddler. He knelt down in front of her, frowning. "Did you take Daddy's watch?"

The toddler folded her arms and stuck her lower lip out, but a moment later lost her bravado. She sighed, reached into the front pocket of her overalls, and produced a diamond-studded Rolex.

"You'll have to watch out for her," Bobbie Stone said, shaking her head. "She steals anything that glitters. Our little magpie."

The Stones kissed their kids goodbye. They thanked Teri again for coming on such short notice. Then they departed in an SUV, leaving the rental car in the driveway. Teri shut the door behind them. When she turned around, all the kids were staring at her.

"Why were you lying about Kat?" Chris asked. Her arms folded, her gaze direct.

"What do you mean?" Teri frowned. How did this girl know that? Unless she was a little medium, like she'd seen on *Little Medium*.

"It's obvious," Daryl said, folding his arms too. The toddler, Parker, also folded her arms but didn't say anything.

"We watch a lot of cop shows." Chris arched an eyebrow.

Teri relented. She'd learned the hard way at Camp Ogilvie not to lie to kids once they were onto you. "Fine. Kat's in New York City tonight and isn't going to make it."

"Told you," Chris said to Daryl.

"You were right."

Teri looked at Parker, who stared silently back. "Does she not say much?"

"She's a late talker," Chris explained, turning red. "It happens to some kids."

"Maybe she doesn't have much to say yet," Teri said, smiling at Parker, who gave her a small smile back.

"So what are you going to give us?" Daryl asked. "To keep quiet?"

Teri raised her own eyebrow, trying not to show that she was a bit impressed. A heated negotiation followed. It was finally agreed that the Stone children wouldn't tell their parents that Kat never showed. They'd pretend she came but had to leave before their parents returned home. Daryl even offered to Photoshop her into pictures for evidence. Teri was surprised by this but Chris, with evident pride, told Teri that her brother was great with Photoshop. And in return, they would get to stay up an hour past their bedtimes and Teri would take them all out for ice cream immediately.

The kids bundled up, and as they walked outside and Teri locked up the house, she reflected that it might not be the worst way to spend her night—eating ice cream and watching Pixar movies. It was going to be no sweat.

She'd taken only a few steps toward the car when she heard the noise.

It was coming from the trunk of the yellow rental car.

A banging, scratching sound.

The kids heard it too, and they all clustered around the car, looking to Teri for answers. "What is it?" Chris asked, her eyes wide.

Teri stared at the trunk. "Maybe an animal got trapped in there?"

The kids looked at her, and she knew she had to do something. She also knew that she couldn't just take them for ice cream now without worrying that an animal was slowly suffocating. She squared her shoulders and reached for the trunk latch, bracing herself for the worst—an angry squirrel or bat flying out at her.

But what came out was not at all what she'd been expecting.

A man clambered out of the trunk. He whirled around. His eyes were wild. He wore a crumpled suit and looked like he was in his thirties. He had a bruise on his cheek and a gash on his forehead, and he was wielding a tire iron like a weapon.

His gaze fell on Teri and the kids, and his eyes narrowed. "Where the hell am I?"

CHAPTER 7

Do you see anything?" Stevie asked as I stood on my tiptoes, feeling around on top of the light fixtures and the moldings, trying to find a spare key. We'd spent a few minutes desperately trying the knob, like if we turned it hard enough, somehow it might just open. There was a blue-and-white-striped mat in front of the door, but the only things under it were a squashed spider and a desiccated leaf. Which really wasn't that surprising—we didn't even keep a spare key under our mat, and we lived in one of the safest towns in America. This was New York City; of course people weren't going to leave their keys sitting out.

Stevie was holding Brad's leash, but as far away from her body as possible, and every time the dog turned to her, rose on his back legs, and waved his paws—which really was ridiculously cute—Stevie just gave him half a pat on the head and then looked away. "Nothing?"

"Nothing," I confirmed, brushing the dust off my hands.

"I'll call Mallory," Stevie said, pulling out her phone with a deep sigh. She shook her head. "I can't believe this. She's . . ." But Stevie didn't finish her sentence, just turned the speaker on Ophelia on as it started to ring.

"Hello?" The connection was *bad*—scratchy and staticky—but it was there.

"Mallory!" Stevie gripped the phone tighter and raised her voice. "We got locked out of your apartment! We're here with Brad. Do you have an extra key?"

"What—" Whatever she said next was swallowed by a patch of static.

"We have the dog!" Stevie practically yelled into the phone. "We can't get into the apartment! What should we do?"

"Ugh, that's so annoying." This came through clearly, and more loudly than I had been expecting. I drew back from the phone slightly. "The super has extra keys, he can let you—" This was broken up by a wave of static, and when Mallory started speaking again, she clearly hadn't realized she'd been cut off. "...close Brad in the bedroom, okay?"

"So we just . . . ask the super for keys?" Stevie asked, leaning closer to the phone.

"Yeah, he's—*static*—basement—*static*—tell him you're my *static static static*. Okay?"

"What?" Stevie and I said together, but a second later, the line went dead.

"I'll try and get her back," Stevie said. She pressed the button to call Mallory, but now it was going right to an automated voice mail. "I guess she lost reception?" Stevie asked, looking down at her screen. "Or her phone died."

"So it sounds like we find the super," I said. "I saw the apartment when we came in, back on the first floor." Stevie sighed as she looked down the stairs. "I can go get him if you want."

"No, it's okay," she said, holding out the leash to me. I took it, and she leaned against the railing for a second as she eased her heels off, leaving them in front of 5B. "Just tell me if you see any, like, broken glass."

"I will absolutely be your John Cusack in this situation."

"Just no stalker-y boom boxes."

"Never." We headed back down the stairs—Brad seemed thrilled that his walk was recommencing and started to spin in circles again. When he got tangled up in the leash, I picked him up and carried him.

He didn't seem to mind this, taking in the view from the raised height and looking around, then resting his head against my chest.

When we reached the lobby, Brad started squirming, and when I set him down, he lunged for the glass door with more force than I would have expected from such a tiny dog. "No," I said, pulling him toward the basement unit. Clearly the dog, no fool, saw the front door and assumed that meant a walk was in the cards. "Sorry, bud." I knocked twice on the superintendent's door. A second later, it swung open.

I had been led to believe, by movies and TV, that building super-intendents were guys in their fifties who often had mustaches, some-times wore undershirts with overalls, and usually walked around carrying a wrench or a plunger. So I was very surprised to see, stand-ing on the other side of the door, a guy who looked around my age, with nary a wrench in sight. He was almost my same height—I got to look straight at him, which was honestly a little jarring, because his eyes were a light brownish-green, a true hazel, with lashes that seemed almost criminally unfair for a boy to have. He had tan skin and thick dark hair, cut short and pushed back from his forehead so that it stood up slightly. He was, in short, *very* cute.

"Hi," he said, looking from me to Stevie with a quick smile that flashed bright, slightly crooked teeth. "Can I help you?"

"Hi there," I said, giving him a smile of my own. Stevie cleared her throat, and it brought me back to the moment, and the situation we were dealing with. "Right. Hello. Are you . . . the super?"

"That's my uncle," he said. He took a step closer and I could see that he was wearing an NYU sweatshirt with a checked collared shirt under it, skinny jeans, and Converse. "But he got called away suddenly and I'm holding down the fort. You're not . . ." He looked from me to Stevie, his brow creasing slightly. "You're not residents, right?"

"We're not," Stevie said, coming to stand next to me. Brad also seemed to take this as his cue to come forward as well, launching himself at the guy, dancing back and forth, his curved tail wagging furiously.

"Brad!" the guy said with a smile as he picked him up. Brad's front paws flew up and down as he tried to get close enough to lick this guy's face. "Hey, buddy. How's tricks?"

"You know the dog?" Stevie asked.

"Sure," he said, settling Brad in the crook of his arm and scratching underneath his neck. "I help my uncle out a lot, and sometimes will do walks if people are working late, that kind of thing. Are you guys friends with Mallory and Flora?"

"Mallory's my stepsister," Stevie said. "And she gave us her key to drop something back at the apartment for her, but when we were in there, Brad ran for the door, we ran after him, and—"

"The door locked behind you?" the guy finished for her. "Yeah. I've been trying to get my uncle to install different locks. People are always getting locked out."

"So we just need to get back in the apartment," I said, relieved that this was going to be so easy, and glad we had the dog for proof that we weren't just grifters trying to talk our way in so we could case the joint. "And then we can put the dog back and get our stuff."

"This is really bad timing," the guy said, "because my uncle had to head out of town this afternoon. He was supposed to be back by now, but it sounds like he and my aunt are having car trouble. And he didn't realize it until he left, but he accidentally took the extra apartment keys with him. We've already had one lockout today, in 3C, but luckily, Mr. Gibson's husband had an extra set."

"You mean the extra keys are just *gone*?" I asked, needing this not to be true.

The guy winced. "I know," he said, shaking his head. "My uncle's been talking about wanting to retire for a while now, and this just seems like proof that maybe he should."

"So . . . how do we get back into the apartment?" Stevie asked, her voice high and stressed. I felt exactly the same. This was *not good*. I'd expected that once we talked to the super, this would just be a tiny blip—we'd put the dog back, Stevie would get her bag, and this would just fade into a funny anecdote to tell Teri about when we got back. I'd practically started rehearsing it in my head—*and then we got locked out, with a dog!* What were we supposed to do with him? How was I supposed to go see Mr. Campbell's play with a Pomeranian in tow?

"I mean," the guy said, shifting his weight from foot to foot, "I can try my uncle again and see what his ETA is. But the only reason we're supposed to call the fire department to break down the doors is if there's a gas leak, or like someone in peril, that kind of thing. Emergencies only."

"Yeah, let's not do that," Stevie said quickly. "It's just my bag, really. . . ."

"And the dog," I pointed out. Brad looked over at me, with what I could have sworn was a smile, even though realistically I knew he was probably just panting.

"Right, the dog."

"Oh no—did you lock your shoes inside?" the guy asked, looking down at Stevie's feet, then up at us.

"No," Stevie said, shaking her head. "I just left them on the fifth floor. They're heels."

The guy nodded. "Gotcha. I'm really sorry about this. . . ." He ran his hand through his hair, and it stuck up even farther. It was maybe even thicker than Stevie's, and shining with faint highlights under the fluorescent hallway lights.

"It's not your fault," Stevie said.

"Not at all," I murmured, looking at her, and understanding that she wanted to have a talk so that we could figure out what we were going to do now. "Can you—give us just a second?"

"Sure," he said easily. "I actually have some treats in here, if I can give them to Brad?" He looked from me to Stevie, like we had any say over Brad's diet.

"It's fine with me," I said, and he gave me a quick smile as he backed into the apartment, taking the dog with him.

"Oh my god," Stevie said, staring at me, her eyes wide. "We're locked out, and we have a Pomeranian."

"It's not ideal," I acknowledged.

"What are we supposed to do? Our train tickets home are in there, my money, your money, our IDs, my car keys. . . ." Stevie shook her head. "Why couldn't you have brought your own bag?"

I drew back at her tone. "How is this *my* fault? She's your sister—"

"She's *not* my sister—"

"Fine, stepsister, sorry. But what does my bag have to do with anything?"

"Because maybe if you hadn't made me carry all your stuff, at least one of our bags would still be on the right side of the door."

"Or both of them would be gone. And I asked if I could put my stuff in your bag. I didn't *make* you. If you didn't want me to, you should have told me no!" My voice had risen, and it bounced off the wall of the lobby. Stevie took a breath, like she was going to say something, then just shook her head.

"Sorry," she said, running a hand over her face. "This just . . ."

"It's okay," I said quickly, wanting to put this behind us. "Let's regroup. What do you have on you?"

"My phone," Stevie said, holding it up. "Thank god."

"Seriously."

"Um . . ." She dug in her coat pockets. "The MetroCard, nineteen dollars and thirty-seven cents, and half a pack of gum." She looked up at me and held it out. "Gum?"

"Thanks," I said, taking a piece, despite the fact that Stevie only ever chewed bubble-gum-flavored gum, like we were still in elementary school. "Okay, so we have a little bit of cash, we have your phone. . . ." I reached into my right coat pocket and pulled out three quarters and a dime. "Eighty-five cents . . ." I reached into my other pocket, and when I realized what I had, I smiled.

"What?"

"Look." I held up the hundred-dollar bill, beyond relieved—this would surely be enough to buy our tickets for the performance and get us around. "We have more than enough cash. We have your phone. I'm sure we can leave the dog with that guy. It'll be okay." I unwrapped the gum and popped it into my mouth, hoping that if I said this with enough conviction, it would turn out to be true.

"Okay," Stevie said, nodding. "Great. So . . . do you think we should just wait here until his uncle comes back?"

"Wait *here*?" What was she talking about? We had to go see Mr. Campbell's play at eight.

The door swung open again, and Brad came trotting out on his leash, the guy walking behind him. "Any word from your uncle?" I asked hopefully. I was happy to see that the dog looked so comfortable with him—it would mean I wouldn't feel too guilty leaving Brad behind with this guy when we had to go.

He shook his head. "No updates," he said. "I'm really sorry. But I can give you my number. And I can take yours, and that way when I do hear from him, I can call you right away and let you know."

"That sounds great." It really seemed like it was the best we were going to do for the moment.

"Yes, thank you," Stevie said, giving him a quick smile. "That's really nice. I know this isn't actually your job." She unlocked Ophelia. "What's your number?"

He told us an area code I didn't recognize, then added, "I Cruise." Stevie and I both stared at him. I wondered if maybe he'd just had a tiny stroke and this was how it was manifesting.

"What?" I asked, after a moment.

"Sorry—that's what the numbers spell out. It's usually easier than just giving them to you."

Stevie typed his number into her phone, widening her eyes a fraction of an inch at me.

"How did you figure that out?" I asked because I knew Stevie wouldn't. She truly would have made the world's worst detective. Murderers and bandits would have been wandering around free because asking a follow-up question might have made someone momentarily uncomfortable.

"No," he said with a laugh. "I only know it because Paradise Cruises has been trying to buy my number for years. They're trying to get all the numbers that spell out that phrase, with all potential area codes, and apparently, I'm one of the only holdouts. They call me constantly, trying to talk me into it. But so far, I've held out."

"Because you care deeply about your number? Or because you hate Paradise Cruises?" I arched an eyebrow at him. I knew I was flirting, just a little bit. Obviously, there were bigger things to deal with here, but he was seriously cute, and my hair was not going to be holding these waves for much longer.

"No, I'm actually doing this for purely mercenary reasons. Hoping if I wait them out a little longer, they'll up their offer. College isn't going to pay for itself."

I nodded, but my smile froze. For me and for Stevie, college *was* going to pay for itself, in that I'd always known I had a college fund waiting for me, and that I could go wherever I wanted (the caveat about no conservatories was new). Loans and grants and how people actually paid for college was not something I'd ever had to concern myself with.

Hearing this guy say it, so matter-of-factly, was making me feel ashamed of myself—and at the way I'd yelled at my parents about college just a few hours earlier.

"Sounds like a plan," Stevie said, shaking me out of these thoughts. "And—what's your name? I could save this as 'I Cruise,' but ..."

"Let's not do that," he said, giving us a smile that crinkled the corners of his eyes. "I'm Cary."

"Like Grant?" I asked.

"Or Fukunaga," he replied. "But I'm Cary Tasso."

"I'm Kat," I said with a smile. "And that's Stevie."

"Nice to meet you both," he said as Stevie pressed a button on her phone. A second later his phone rang, a jazzy, upbeat guitar sound, and he looked down at it. "I assume you're the 203 area code?"

Stevie nodded. "We're in from Connecticut for the night."

"Number saved," he said, typing in his phone. "So I'll let you know as soon as I hear something." He started to put his phone in his pocket just as it rang again. I stared at it, hope flaring in my chest that it was his uncle, saying he was just around the corner and would be there any second, the answer to all our problems.

"Is that him?" I asked, crossing the fingers on one hand.

Cary looked at the screen, then shook his head, pressing the button to silence the phone. "Paradise Cruises," he said. "They've started calling from creative area codes recently, trying to get me to answer. That one was Alaska."

Brad must have decided he'd had enough of all this standing around and talking without getting any closer to a walk, and he lunged in the direction of the door. "I think he's getting antsy," I said, as though I'd had a lot of experience with Brad's various moods. "So we can leave him with you, right? Since you guys already get along so well?"

"Normally I would totally take him," he said, leaning down to stroke Brad's fluff. "But I actually have to get ready for work—I won't be back until late. And I don't want to leave him in a strange apartment alone. But I've left a message with my uncle that there's a lockout happening here, and I'll leave him a note too. . . ." He held out the leash to us, and Stevie and I exchanged a look.

I knew she wasn't going to reach for it, so I finally did, wondering as I did so what we were supposed to do now. How were we going to see the play—or then, after, go to a restaurant—if we had a dog with us?

"Okay," I finally said, because what else was I supposed to say? "I guess we'll just look after him until we can get him back in the apartment." I really wasn't sure what other choice we had—it wasn't like we could just tie the dog to the doorknob of 5B and leave him there.

"Great. I'll head out with you. Just give me a sec," Cary said, and he disappeared back into the basement unit.

"Head out?" Stevie echoed, frowning. "Does he think we're going to leave?"

"Maybe he doesn't want us to hang around the lobby."

"Should we risk leaving? What if his uncle comes back in the next few minutes?"

"But what if he doesn't?"

"Also a good point."

We stood there in silence for a minute, during which I started to feel distinctly panicky as all our options to solve this problem seemed to be disappearing. "Can you try Mallory again?"

"Yeah," Stevie said, putting the phone on speaker. It went right to voice mail, without even ringing—which seemed to me to mean that Mallory's phone had either died or was out of range, neither of which were helpful for us right now.

"Who else can we call?" I asked, closing my eyes and trying to think. "Ooh, maybe a locksmith?"

"I'm pretty sure you have to have ID proving you live in the place to get someone to unlock it. Otherwise, wouldn't burglars just do that?"

"Yeah, that makes sense." I racked my brain, trying to think about who else could get us back in. "Should we try and find Mallory's roommate? What was her name? We know she works for the mayor, right?"

"Yeah, Flora," Stevie said slowly. After a second, she shook her head. "What, we're supposed to go to City Hall, somehow they'll let us in, and she's going to give her keys to two girls she's never seen before?"

"Well, do *you* have an idea?" I snapped at her. I regretted it immediately. "I'm sorry. I'm being an asshole."

"You're not, and it's okay," Stevie said. "I wish I did have some kind of plan. I just . . ." She shrugged helplessly as she looked down at the dog, then around the lobby.

I was wondering if she was feeling what I was feeling—like she was waiting for someone to show up and tell us what to do. We spent most of our lives that way, after all, whether it was parents or teachers or Mr. Campbell literally telling us where to go, what to say, and how to say it, our every move onstage blocked out. "If it wasn't for the dog," she said, shaking her head, and I nodded. I felt the same way. If it wasn't for the dog, we could just leave now, and trust that at some point tonight, we'd be able to get back into the apartment to get our stuff. We had enough cash to get around. But the Pomeranian was complicating things.

Like he knew we were talking about him, Brad looked up at us. He let out what could only be described as a disappointed whine before flopping down on the ground, head on his paws, looking longingly toward the door.

"What about Mateo?" I asked, getting an inspiration. "Would he have an extra set of keys?"

"Maybe," said Stevie, her tone reluctant. She stared down at her phone. "I just—it was bad enough to have to see Mallory, you know? I don't really want to have to deal with him, too."

"I know," I said, even though in that moment, I really didn't. Who cared if her stepsiblings had never been friendly? We had an emergency here! "Want me to call?" I asked after a minute in which Stevie continued to stare down at her phone but didn't actually dial it.

"No, I'll do it," she said with a sigh as she scrolled through her contacts and stopped on Mateo, putting the phone on speaker.

"Hey! Howzit, Stephanie?" a cheerful-sounding guy's voice said, picking up after the second ring.

"Hello, Mateo," said Stevie, her tone polite.

"What's going on?"

"Um—so we're at Mallory's apartment—" Stevie took a breath and filled him in (I jumped in too, and then introduced myself when he got confused) about our situation. "We were hoping that you might have an extra key to her apartment?" Stevie locked eyes with me, and I crossed my first two fingers on both hands.

"You know . . . ," Mateo said slowly. "I am pretty sure I do." My eyebrows flew up and I looked at Stevie, who looked as happy and surprised by this news as I was.

"That's—amazing," Stevie said. She was starting to lose the pinched, stressed look she'd had ever since the door had slammed behind us.

"Yeah," Mateo said. "Listen, can you come up here to Columbia to get them? I'm finishing up a study session."

"Sure," I said immediately, even as I glanced at the screen to see what time it was. We still had more than two hours before Mr. Campbell's play, so we would have enough time to get there and back. I was pretty sure. "That would be great."

Mateo promised to text Stevie the address to his dorm, and then cheerfully told us he'd see us soon.

She hung up and I looked at her, happy and surprised. "Oh my god."

"I know." She nodded. "Bullet dodged."

"He seemed . . . nice," I ventured, still trying to square the guy on the other end of the phone with the one Stevie had described to me. Before she could reply, the super's door swung open.

Cary emerged from the basement unit. He was still wearing jeans, but they looked different from the skinny jeans he'd had on before, and he was wearing a tan leather bomber jacket, zipped up, and a messenger bag. It was a look that reminded me of something, but I wasn't sure what it was, exactly. "Everything okay?" he asked. He looked from me to Stevie as he locked the super's apartment behind him.

I nodded. "We think Stevie's stepbrother might have an extra set of keys. We're going to Columbia to get them."

Cary smiled, looking relieved. "That's great news. So sorry that this derailed your night."

"It wasn't your fault," I said, smiling back at him.

Stevie cleared her throat. "But just in case—could you still let me know when your uncle gets back?"

"Absolutely," Cary said. Brad leapt to his feet and shook himself all over, a shake that moved over his body like a wave, starting at his head and moving back toward his tail. He bent down to pat Brad. "You be good, pal, okay? Oh," he said, straightening up, "you have to watch this one around rollerbladers."

"Around what now?" Stevie asked.

Cary nodded. "Yeah, he's good with everything else, but for some reason, rollerbladers freak him out."

"Maybe he's fed up with all these nineties trends coming back," I suggested, and Cary laughed.

"I hadn't considered that. But just watch out for people on wheels, and you should be fine with him."

"All right," Stevie said as she looked up toward the fifth floor. She squared her shoulders, like she was preparing herself. "I just need my shoes, and then we'll head out."

"I'll go," I said, turning to the staircase.

"I've got them," Cary said. And before we could protest, he dropped his messenger bag and jogged up the stairs, taking them two at a time, and disappearing from view.

In what felt like a very short amount of time—considering just how long it took us—Cary was thundering down the stairs again, carrying Stevie's heels by their straps. He jumped the last three steps and stuck the landing easily, like he'd been doing this for years—which maybe he had. He held out the shoes to Stevie. "Here you are."

"Thanks for that," she said, and I automatically moved a step closer so that she could lean on me as she put them on.

"Ready to go?" Cary asked as he walked toward the lobby door. He pulled his messenger bag over his head, so that it was a cross-body.

Stevie met my eye and I nodded. This had not been the quick and easy errand we'd been promised—we had lost a purse, but gained a Pomeranian. And now, it seemed, we were heading to Columbia. "Yeah," I said after a minute. "Let's do it."

CHAPTER 8

*I*t wasn't until we'd reached the entrance to the Bryant Park station that I thought to ask the crucial question. "You can bring dogs on the subway, right?" I looked down at Brad, as though he could answer this, but he just scratched his ear.

Stevie had walked down the first step, then paused and turned around and walked up, to the consternation of the woman who'd been behind her.

"Make up your mind, hon," she snapped as she dodged around Stevie and into the station. Stevie came up to join me, and we stepped out of the way of the flow of people entering and exiting the subway. Everyone seemed to know exactly where they were going, and I was sure they could tell that we most certainly didn't. From what I could see, it didn't look like anyone else had a dog with them. Brad, who was on his leash, sat down and looked around. He just seemed happy to be out and about, not really caring where we were going as long as there were things to sniff.

Stevie had looked up the directions for how to get to Mateo's dorm at Columbia—we'd take the B or D to Columbus Circle, then transfer to the 1, and ride uptown to 116th Street—and since his dorm was on 113th, it didn't seem like it would be that far a walk. And best of all, her phone had estimated it would take us forty minutes round trip. So even if this took us an hour round trip, we'd still be more than on time for an eight o'clock curtain.

"I don't know," Stevie said, also looking at the people coming and going. We were right by the main branch of the library, the one with the two lions outside.

"I guess we could take a cab?" I asked, though even as I said it, I worried it might actually take longer. If I had my own phone, I could have checked the traffic, but now I was reduced to squinting at the line of cars going past and trying to predict the future, like I was an old-timey sailor looking out at the waves.

"What if they won't break the hundred either, though?"

"Good point," I said, figuring that it might be a taxi policy, and not just the one car we'd happened to get. "Can you call an Uber?"

Stevie shook her head. "It's tied to my mom's card."

We stood there in silence for a moment, and I could practically see the time ticking away, time we really didn't have to waste. And though I was trying not to, I was starting to get annoyed at the fact that Stevie was just shooting down all my ideas and not coming up with any of her own. "Maybe I should just carry Brad?" I suggested after it became clear Stevie wasn't going to contribute. "And if anyone asks, we could say he's my emotional support animal."

Stevie nodded. "Sounds good." I scooped up Brad, who took the opportunity to lick my face as we walked down the subway steps, Stevie holding on to the railing carefully as she navigated the steps in her heels. "What is he emotionally supporting?"

I laughed as I scratched his head. "I have a crippling fear of being without a dog," I said. "He fixes that."

Once we got down the steps into the station, it was suddenly much too hot, like the heat had been turned up full blast and then not turned off again. I held Brad close to me as I looked around, but there didn't seem to be anyone working in the glassed-off booth, and the two police officers stationed by the entrance didn't say anything, so I figured we were okay on the dog front.

Stevie pulled out her MetroCard and swiped it. It didn't work the first time, and I could see her getting anxious, looking behind her like she was worried about other people waiting, as people in the next two turnstiles zipped through with no problem. She finally got it to work, and I could see the relief in her eyes as she pushed her way through the turnstile and handed the card to me. I swiped it through, pushed through the turnstile, and handed it back to her.

There was the *whoosh* of trains coming and going, announcements about what was arriving, reminders about keeping your belongings close to you, and the intermittent *Stand clear of the closing doors* echoing throughout the station as various trains departed. There was also a man with an alto sax, his case open in front of him, playing "New York State of Mind" very loudly.

I tipped my head toward him and Stevie smiled. She tossed her change into the man's case—he nodded at her without stopping playing—and pulled out her phone, recording a video for a few seconds. "I'll send that to my dad," she said. "He'll love it."

"So what now?" I asked as I looked around at the signs for the different trains.

"We need the B or D uptown, which is . . . there." Stevie pointed, letting out a small groan when she saw getting to the train meant going down more stairs.

"Should we buy you some flats?" I asked as we descended and she gripped the railing again. "We could break my hundred dollars."

"You mean *our* hundred dollars."

"Sure, *our* hundred dollars. Think of the shoes we could get with it!"

Stevie laughed as we reached the platform, which, in contrast to the station, was cold again, and drafty. I pulled Brad a little closer to me in case he was cold too. "There," she said, pointing up at the B and D sign, "that's what we want." We walked up to the edge of the platform, standing just behind the yellow safety line.

I looked around the station. Most everyone was looking at their phones; a few people were reading as they waited. There were advertisements along the tiled back wall of the subway for movies that came out last month, now scribbled over excessively.

I glanced up at the electronic sign, trying to see how long it would take for the train to arrive, but it was flashing an error message, *00:00* where the arrival time of the train should be. "Apparently, the train is coming never," I said, shifting Brad to my other arm.

"I don't know about that," Stevie said, nodding at it. "It's coming at zero, apparently."

"Maybe it's a fancy New York way of saying midnight."

The couple standing next to us on the platform, who'd been having one of those whisper-hissing arguments, suddenly both started to get a little bit louder. Apparently, Richard was always pulling this shit and his—boyfriend? husband?—was over it. Without discussing it, we walked a few feet down the platform to give them some space. That must be the hard part about being in New York—you had to live your life in public, no cars to duck into when you needed to cry or yell at someone.

"So I don't know anything about Mateo," I pointed out after a few more minutes of silence, mostly to distract myself. The train still hadn't arrived, which was beginning to worry me. We still had a lot of time, but I was realizing that when I'd done the time math, I'd planned on things like trains arriving immediately. "Besides the fact that he's a freshman at Columbia."

Stevie brushed her hair back from her face and shrugged. "I don't know much more than that either."

I let my eyes drift over the platform and gave Brad's head a scratch. "Why do you think they're acting like this now? Mateo and Mallory, I mean." Stevie never talked much about her stepsiblings, but I'd now met one and was about to meet another, and I was having trouble squaring their behavior—Mallory's cheek-kissing and effusiveness and Mateo's immediate offer to help—with the people who seemed to want nothing to do with her.

"Like what?"

"Like suddenly they're being nice after acting so unfriendly to you." Stevie looked fixedly at the train tracks, and I shook my head. "Not unfriendly," I corrected. "I mean, I know they were never outright rude or anything. Just . . . unwelcoming, right? But *now* he's willing to help?"

"I don't know," Stevie said, still looking at the train tracks littered with trash. I was about to ask a follow-up, but something in her tone stopped me. It was the same tone I heard whenever the subject of the divorce or her dad came up. Like there was suddenly caution tape around a subject, a blinking neon NO TRESPASSING sign. And I didn't feel like it was just there to keep me out—it was like Stevie didn't even want to go there herself.

"Well, we're getting to know a lot more about Mallory tonight," I said, trying to lighten the mood. "She has a dog named Brad and a super with a cute nephew."

"I *knew* you were flirting with him!" Stevie said, finally looking at me and doing a tiny victorious hop. "I can always tell. But don't you mean he's *super*cute?"

I groaned. Stevie laughed. "Do *you* think he's cute, though?"

Stevie shrugged one shoulder. "He's too short for me."

"*You're* short!"

She gasped theatrically, and I laughed. "How *dare* you. I am not short," she said, drawing herself up to her full height—which, in her heels, was admittedly almost the same height as me. "I'm shorter than you, but that doesn't mean I'm short."

"You do have a thing for tall guys, though," I pointed out. "Beckett was, like, six feet."

"Six-two."

"I rest my case."

"Seriously, Cary's all yours," Stevie said, arching an eyebrow at me.

"I don't want him to be all mine. I don't even know the guy! I was just saying that I appreciated his . . . aesthetic qualities. And I wanted to flirt with him before my hair totally fell."

"It still looks good," Stevie assured me as she pulled out her phone.

"You've got pretty good reception down here," I said as I reached for Ophelia.

"Wait—" Stevie said, trying to pull her phone back from me.

"What?"

"Just let me—Teri's calling." Her screen was buzzing and lighting up, and I let go of the phone just as Stevie tried to yank it away, and then everything went wrong, all at once.

The phone flew up, turning end over end in the air. Stevie grabbed for it, but her fingers closed around nothing, and as I watched, helpless, the phone hit the platform, bounced off, and then fell straight down, until it landed with a muted *thud* on the subway tracks.

Stevie and I looked at each other in horror. I set Brad down as I leaned forward to look. There was Ophelia, faceup next to a crumpled pack of cigarettes and a Skittles wrapper. This was Stevie's *phone* and it was lying on a subway track. It was so awful, and so not what was supposed to be happening, that I couldn't even get my head around it.

"Oh *no*," I breathed.

"My phone," Stevie said, her voice high and panicky. "I can't—what are we supposed to *do*?"

I held out Brad's leash to her and she took it. I leaned over more, looking down onto the subway tracks. It wasn't that far, really—and weren't track workers always jumping up and down and fixing things? They had to be, right?

"Kat," Stevie said, her voice sharp, like she'd just read my mind. "Get back here."

"But—" I started, just as I felt a *whoosh* of air and heard a rumbling sound. We both looked to the left. There were lights coming around the curve of the tunnel, and a moment later, a train was barreling down the track—but it looked like a maintenance train; it didn't even stop. And now that it was moving fast enough to blow my hair back over my shoulders, I realized just how stupid and reckless it was to think I could hop down and back up again safely.

The train disappeared into the tunnel and I made myself lean forward to look, half-afraid of what I was going to see. There, on the tracks, were some shards of glass and metal—what was left of Stevie's phone.

Ophelia was no longer synching. She had finally drowned.

"Oh my god," I said, staring, stunned, at what was left of Stevie's phone. "It wasn't my fault—it was an accident. I can't . . ."

"My phone," Stevie said, her voice sounding strangled as she also stared down into the subway tracks. "My phone is in pieces—my purse is locked in an apartment we can't get into. . . ."

"It'll be okay," I said, because I felt like someone should say this, even though I really didn't think that it was going to be.

"*How* is it going to be *okay*?" Stevie asked, wheeling around on me, her cheeks flushed. "How are we supposed to get around? How are we supposed to find anything or anyone?" She stopped and her eyes widened. "Oh god. How are we going to hear from Cary when his uncle comes back?"

"We can still find Mateo, right?" I asked. If we couldn't, what were we supposed to do with the dog? We couldn't show up to a theater with a dog in tow. "Do you remember his address?"

"Why is that my responsibility?"

"Um." I stared at her, wondering why this needed to be spelled out.

"Because he's *your* stepbrother, and I don't have a phone."

"Well, I don't have one either now, thanks to you!"

"How is it my fault? It was an accident—"

"You were the one who said we should come into the city tonight—and now my phone is destroyed. And yet somehow, it's still, magically, not your fault. Because nothing *ever* is!"

"What does *that* mean?" I snapped back. Why was Stevie acting like we weren't in this together?

"Nothing," she said, but in the way that meant she wasn't going to tell you, not that there was actually nothing to tell.

There was a charged, awkward silence between us, one that I could practically see, like it was a living organism. I didn't know how we'd gotten here. I could understand that Stevie was upset about her phone, but that didn't mean she got to take it out on me. We didn't usually fight like this—when we fought, it usually felt like we were saying what we needed to say to clear the air, and then we could hug and put it behind us. This felt different, dangerous and spiky and not at all done with us yet.

"But you do remember Mateo's address, right?" Stevie hadn't answered me before, and we needed to focus on this and not just stand around with no plan. "And the trains we're supposed to take to get there?"

"Why is *this* what you care about?" Stevie raised her voice, and I saw a few people glance at us and then walk a few steps away down the platform. Clearly, we were the new Richard and his boyfriend/husband.

"Because he's our best chance to get back into the apartment!" Brad shrank back slightly, pressing himself against Stevie's legs. "Losing your phone doesn't change our time frame, right?"

"What time frame are you even talking about?"

"Us going to Columbia, getting the keys, dropping the dog off, and being in the theater district before eight."

Stevie narrowed her eyes. "You still want to see Mr. Campbell's play? After all this?"

"Of course." I stared at her. "Don't you?"

"I never wanted to see it in the first place! I know you won't understand this, but I don't care about Mr. Campbell and his precious opinions and getting in his good graces. It doesn't *matter* to me. I didn't even—" Stevie stopped herself.

I folded my arms, trying not to look as stung as I felt. "You didn't even what?"

She took a big, shaking breath. "I didn't even want to audition for *Lear*. I just did it because I knew you'd freak out if I didn't."

I took a step back from her. It was like she'd just pulled the solid ground out from under my feet. "You—*what*?"

"This!" Stevie said, pointing from her to me and back again. "I didn't want to do this. And it seemed easier—"

"How is it not important to you? Our senior year, being in the shows together? You would throw that all away?"

"I'm not going to keep acting!" Stevie burst out. "It was just a fun thing I did in high school, but I'm not delusional enough to think—" She broke off.

"So," I said. I was on the verge of tears but didn't want to show it; my voice came out high-pitched and shaky. It was like she'd just reached right into my chest and yanked at my heart. "You think I'm delusional—"

"I think you can do whatever you want, but we don't have to do the same stuff all the time, and you don't seem to get that."

"No," I said, shaking my head. "You're trying to turn this around on me, but you're not being honest. You love acting and you're pretending like you don't and this is—"

"I swear to god." Stevie was staring daggers at me. Brad was looking between the two of us, his ears back. "If you say Six Flags—"

"It *is* Six Flags! You're standing in your own way and not actually giving it a shot, even though you're amazing. I don't understand how you can just throw all your talent away. Do you know what I'd give to be as good as you are?" My voice broke on the last word, but I made myself push through. "Do you even care? You never just go for anything, give it a chance—"

"It's better than what you do."

"What do you mean, what I do?" It suddenly felt like we were on a roller coaster, the moment you truly realize that there's no way off—you just have to strap in.

"I mean the way it's always all or nothing with you. You drop things when you're done and move onto the next thing like it never even happened. You run full-out toward something, and never even think about if it's what you really want."

"I don't—"

"You do, Kat. Beckett always said—"

"*Beckett.*" I rolled my eyes, my anger flying to the surface. "Please, enlighten me. I'm dying to know what the guy who dumped you said."

"He didn't dump me!"

This brought me up short. "What are you talking about?"

"The only reason Beckett broke up with me was because I gave him no choice," Stevie snapped, then blinked, like she was surprised she'd just said this out loud.

"*What?*" I was now more confused than anything else. "What does that mean? And why wouldn't you tell me?"

"Because sometimes it's easier not to go into things. It can be exhausting, with you. You have to know that, Kat. You're a *lot*. And you need so much reassurance. You want to go over everything a million times—"

"That's better than you!" I swallowed hard, trying not to show how hurt I was that Stevie—my best friend—was saying this to me. "I might tell you too much, but you never want to talk about *anything*! You never say how you feel, ever. And at least I don't keep things from you for months—"

"Don't pull that. You lied to me tonight, to get me on the train! And now look—"

"And least I'm going for something that's important to me, not just convincing myself I want to be a lawyer to get my dad to pay attention to me!" Stevie drew in a sharp breath, and I knew I'd crossed a line.

"Stop—" Stevie said, her eyes bright, but I was already talking over her.

"And I'm sorry that I had the idea to come into the city. It would have been way better to just lie around and be depressed, right? If it wasn't for me, we'd never do anything fun, or have any adventures—"

"Going to see Mr. Campbell's play is not my idea of an adventure, and I can't believe you still want—"

"Of course I want to see it! This play is the only reason I even came into the city!" A second later, I realized what I'd just said, like the words were reverberating around the subway station. I felt the blood drain from my face. "Stevie—"

"That's great," Stevie said, her face pale and shocked, her eyes brimming with tears. "Well, thanks for finally telling me the truth. You didn't want to celebrate my birthday. You weren't going to be there for me when my dad bailed on me. I was just the excuse you needed because you were too afraid to do this alone."

"No." I shook my head, trying to fight back the tears that were threatening to spill over. "I didn't—"

"Well I'm *done*," Stevie said, and angrily wiped a tear off her cheek. "We can get the keys and drop the dog off, but then I'm going home."

"But Stevie—"

"And you can do whatever you want—not that you weren't going

to do that anyway. God forbid someone get in the way of you getting to do whatever you want, at the precise moment you want to
do it."

I tried to think of something to say just as I felt a rumble and heard
the whine of a train.

The B train pulled up, and unlike the other train, it slowed down
as it reached us. It came to a somewhat jerky stop and the doors slid
open, the automated subway voice telling everyone to please let all
passengers off before boarding.

When the exiting crowd thinned out, Stevie stepped onto the
train with Brad, and I went to follow—but crashed right into a
man in a hoodie, who was barreling off the train and not looking
where he was going. I fell backward, hitting the platform hard. The
man didn't even stop, just kept on running up the stairs, not looking
back at me.

"You okay there?" A woman who looked like she was in her thirties held out a hand to me and I took it as I hoisted myself up, tried
to get my bearings. She shook her head as she glared in the direction
the guy had gone. "What an asshole, probably some brogrammer
who thinks he can just—"

"Stand clear of the closing doors," the automated MTA voice said.
I rushed toward the train, but the subway doors slid closed in my face
before I could make it on. I looked around, wondering if there was a
conductor I could signal to, someone who could help—but there didn't
seem to be anyone.

Through the window, I could see Stevie looking around like she was
wondering where I was. Then she looked out, and our eyes locked. I
could always tell what Stevie was thinking, but right now, her expression was unreadable as she looked back at me.

And before I could say anything, or do anything else, the train started to move and a few seconds later it had sped away, leaving me standing on the platform.

With no best friend, and no phone.

At night, in New York City.

By myself.

PART THREE
5:25 p.m.–9:25 p.m.

Yet, as only New Yorkers know, if you can get through the
twilight, you'll live through the night.
—Dorothy Parker

For a moment, I didn't understand what had happened.

Like how they say that in trauma, your brain blocks the pain receptors. As though something in your mind understands you're not up for knowing the full story just yet. That was what it felt like for a few seconds, like I was getting a little mini vacation from reality.

I could see my reflection in the subway window, my eyes with way more eye makeup than I normally wore staring back at me. Nobody else on the train seemed to be aware that the world had just ended. People were hunched over their phones or books, yawning and reading magazines, or staring up at the ads that ran along the top of the subway—Dr. Zizmor, Arecibo Car Service, 1-800-BANKRUPTCY, period underwear, meal-delivery kits.

For a second, I was just like all those people. But then, at my feet, Brad whined, and everything came flooding back. There's only so long, after all, that your brain can block the reality of your situation. And mine was hitting me, full force.

I was in New York City with no phone, practically no money, and no friend.

And somehow I was the one who had ended up with the dog.

I closed my eyes, trying to fight down the waves of panic.

You don't have a phone! You don't have a phone! What are you going to dooooo? This was the fun chant my brain had come up with, and it was going round and round in my head to the tune of something that sounded a lot like "Baby Shark."

Rather than actually face my situation, I decided instead to let myself feel just how mad I was at Kat.

Like it was an instant replay in sports, I saw it playing out in my head—Kat grabbing my phone like she always did, not even asking first, me for once trying to take what was mine back from her, and Ophelia flying up into the air, my grab that wasn't close enough—and then the phone crashing down on the tracks.

And then our fight.

We'd never had a fight like that before—so vicious, so raw. I couldn't believe the things I'd said to her, the ones I wished I could take back. And the things she'd said to me. I closed my eyes for a second, like this could stop me remembering, because replaying it was making me feel like I was about to burst into tears, right there on the B train.

And even after all that, she hadn't even followed me onto the train. She'd left me behind. I spent my whole life following three steps behind her, and the *one time* I went first, she couldn't even do a small thing like follow me, just *once* in four years.

Then a thought hit me that was so awful it made me feel shaky— what if Kat had done this on purpose? Was she that upset about what I'd said to her? I couldn't block out the way her face had looked when I'd told her she was a lot. She *was*—but usually it was a good thing, one of the reasons I loved her. I wished I could take it back. I'd hit below the belt—we both had—but had she been upset enough to leave me behind?

Or—and this thought slithered into my mind like an insidious snake—had she done this to solve her problem? Had she left me to take care of the dog, even though she knew I didn't like them, so that she could go ahead and see Mr. Campbell's play unencumbered?

No, I decided, shaking my head, even though it probably made me look crazy. Kat wouldn't have done that. We'd just gotten separated accidentally. . . .

Brad whined and I looked down at him, my dog panic replacing friend and phone and general situation panic.

What was wrong with him? Why was he making that sound? Was I supposed to do something? What if he needed to go to the bathroom and had an accident on the train? How was I going to clean it up? What if everyone saw me with this dog—that I probably wasn't even supposed to have on the subway in the first place—and he made a mess and everyone was looking at me and getting mad? I could practically see it playing out in front of me.

WHAT ARE YOU GOING TO DO-DO-DO-DO-DO-DO?

I reached down warily to pat him on the head, wondering what he wanted and how anyone ever lived with a dog. Was your whole life just a long game of charades without ever getting an answer? A Lab had knocked me over when I was three, and it was one of my first memories. I'd never quite gotten over my fear of the unknown with dogs—that this was an animal that you couldn't control, and at any moment they could jump up, or lunge, or bite you.

Brad rose up on his back legs and waved his paws again, which wasn't any answer I could translate. He seemed to want something, so I picked him up, holding him away from my body, wondering what happened now. He'd stopped whimpering, though, which I counted as a positive. The train lurched suddenly, and for one heart-stopping moment I thought I was going to drop the dog. But I managed to pull him against my body and brace myself on the pole with my back, and when the train—and I—had achieved some equilibrium, I shifted him so that I was holding him with one arm against my chest, the other holding tightly to the pole.

I wasn't exactly thrilled to have a dog this close to me. His nose was twitching as he looked around, making a little snuffling sound. I could feel his heart pounding hard through his fluff, and he was panting. I seemed to remember from some nature documentary (or more likely, *Psychic Vet Tech: Off the Leash*) that when dogs did this when it wasn't hot out, it was because they were stressed. I suddenly realized that he might be scared. He didn't know me or Kat, after all, and we'd taken him out of his home and brought him to a loud place he didn't understand. He no doubt could sense that the person holding him didn't know what to do with dogs, and didn't particularly like them.

For whatever reason, knowing that the dog was possibly as freaked out as I was actually made me feel better—like I wasn't in this entirely alone. "Okay," I said quietly to him, rubbing my thumb over his fluff. We'd already stopped at one station, and I didn't want another one to pass before I figured out what to do here. "Okay, let's figure this out."

I had to do this in bite-size chunks. If I thought about everything that was happening, it would be too much. I'd learned this from my dad, before I could even remember learning it. My favorite place to do my homework—even in kindergarten, when we really didn't have any—had always been wherever my dad was working. I'd pull up a chair next to him at the kitchen table or sprawl on the floor under his desk in his office. I'd tell him about my book report/science project/social studies paper, and he'd discuss what he was working on too. He'd tell me about how you had to build a legal case piece by piece, and how everything had to be airtight or the whole thing fell apart.

When I was particularly stressed about whatever homework I had, he'd calm me down by talking about how you just had to take everything one step at a time. That if he thought about his entire case at once—how much was at stake, how much he had to correctly argue—he'd never get past the first motion.

So he just took it step by step, only trying to control what he could. "How do you eat a whale, pumpkin?" he'd ask me, looking over his glasses.

"One bite at a time," I'd always reply.

"Atta girl," he'd say, giving me a wink.

"One bite at a time," I murmured to the dog, who panted at me. "Okay." I glanced around, worried that someone had heard me talking to myself—then realized that Brad's presence was probably insulating me from that. Because while muttering to yourself was a surefire way to have people not want to stand next to you on the train, it was perfectly acceptable to talk to a dog. Maybe this was why people had them.

The biggest problem was that *I didn't have a phone*. I could barely remember the last time I'd been without one—not since I was a kid. I was in New York City, and I didn't know how to get anywhere, or how I was going to get in touch with anyone—

It suddenly hit me—*Kat didn't have a phone either*. So even if I could somehow get ahold of someone else's, there was no way to contact her. Did I even know Kat's number?

This was enough to startle me out of my panic.

Did I?

She'd been saved in my phone, first in my favorites, for the last four years, so I'd never had to actually punch in her numbers. But it was moot anyway, because even if I managed to remember her number, all it would do was ring on Teri's coffee table.

It was now becoming clear to me that maybe I didn't know *anybody's* phone number. Maybe Beckett's . . .

And he was in the city tonight. I remembered his text that I'd gotten on the train. But immediately after I thought about him, the shame that I felt whenever Beckett came up crashed over me once again. How I'd wrecked things with us, there in the dining room of the Boxcar Cantina. And then I hadn't been brave enough, or honest enough, to tell Kat what had actually happened. . . .

All of which meant that I probably shouldn't call Beckett, even if

I remembered his number, which I wasn't sure that I did.

I glanced up at the 1-800-BANKRUPTCY ad and realized that I at least knew Cary's number: I Cruise. I knew my home number, my dad's work number, and—I was almost positive—both my parents' cell phones. Realizing that made me feel a little better. But then I thought about Kat once again and remembered I had no way to contact her—and she had no way to contact me—and I was back to panic again.

What. Are You Going. TO DO?!

"Seventh Avenue," the announcer said, and I looked out the window as the train started to slow down. I rubbed the dog's fur with my thumb again as I tried to think about my next steps. Just a tiny bite of the whale—not everything, just what I needed to do right now. And what I needed to do right now was find Kat. Even though I was still furious, even though I was reeling from the loss of Ophelia, we still needed to find each other.

If I got off at this station, I could just switch back to go downtown two stops, and hopefully Kat would still be there on the platform. It was what I'd always been taught growing up: if I got separated from my parents, wait. Don't go looking for them, they would find me. I had to believe that Kat was following the same advice. Because otherwise . . . I couldn't think about that. That was eating the whole whale, and nobody could do that.

So Kat would be there, and we'd move past our fight somehow, and I'd get us up to Columbia. I'd been annoyed when Kat just expected me to have the answer, but I did, in fact, remember where we were supposed to be going. Ever since my phone had gotten wrecked, I'd been repeating it on a low loop in the back of my head so I wouldn't lose it—*B or D to Columbus Circle, transfer to the 1. Take the 1 train to 116th, and Mateo is in the dorm at 600 West 113th.*

The train came to a stop, and I got off, looking around the station.

Brad looked around too—his panting seemed to have lessened a little. There were pockets of Manhattan I felt I could navigate, mostly the blocks directly around West 72nd Street, where my dad's apartment was, and East Fifty-Third, where his office was. But aside from that, the city was just so big, so fast, so intimidating. Did real New Yorkers get a sense of home when they got out at their particular subway stop, know all their favorite spots, feel that they could walk astride the city like it was theirs? I wasn't sure—I had certainly never felt like that. I was just scurrying around it, head down, hoping I wouldn't be found out, an interloper with a scarlet *S*—for suburbs—that everyone could see.

Unlike the previous station, this one was practically deserted, and less well-lit. As I looked around to try and find the downtown track, I could see that the pillars, the walls, and practically every available surface were plastered with papers that detailed all the track changes and delays at this particular station.

I walked closer to a series of the papers to try and understand what they were saying. There were the circles with the subway letters and numbers in them, and I tried to make sense of it as Brad nudged my hand with his head, like he was trying to tell me he wanted to be scratched. I hesitated—what if he had fleas and that was why he was itchy?—then gave him a quick scratch behind the ears. When I stopped, he nudged my hand with his head again, more aggressively this time, and I tried not to laugh as I scratched him again. The papers made no sense to me—the leaflet on top seemed to contradict the one below it—and I took a breath, then tried to read them calmly, without emotion, the way my dad told me he always had to break down briefs and court decisions. I was starting to read them again when I looked over and saw a guy heading toward me. He had pale skin and bleached-blond hair and looked like he was in his early twenties. I gave him a half wave, figuring that easier than trying to decode the MTA's flyers would just be to ask someone what was happening with the trains.

"Hi," I said, with an apologetic smile. "Do you know—" But I never got to finish, because the guy was suddenly much closer to me than I'd anticipated, and I could see the flash of a blade in his hand.

"Gimme your phone," he said, his voice low and menacing. "Now."

CHAPTER 10
Kat

In last year's production of A Midsummer Night's Dream, *I'd had a stage fight with Dara Chapman.*

I'd played Helena, even though I really wanted Hermia, which Dara got, despite the fact that I was shorter than her. Stevie was Titania, and the whole thing had been set at a Coachella-esque music festival; the critic in the local paper had hated it. We'd worked through the fight choreography for weeks, but in the tech rehearsal, when we were just supposed to be marking, one of the punches that she was supposed to have pulled went wide and hit me, hard, right in the stomach.

A gut punch.

It had left me gasping and fighting to get my breath back, but even more than that—it had been the shock of it all, the unexpectedness of it. And that was exactly what I felt as I stood on the subway platform, watching Stevie disappear uptown in the B train without me.

It's okay, it's okay, it's okay, I repeated to myself like a mantra. Stevie had seen me not get on the train. She was going to come right back.

And when she did, everything was going to be okay. Because Stevie was turning around to come to me, because she would know that I was staying put. That was what you did, after all. If you got separated, you waited in place for the person you were separated from to come and find you, you didn't go off chasing them. It was basic elementary-school logic.

I swallowed hard as I shifted my weight from foot to foot. I didn't even want to move. I didn't want to sit on one of the wooden benches along the back wall, next to a pay phone. I didn't want to go anywhere that might prevent Stevie from finding me the second she got off the other train. Which was coming soon now. It had to be. Any minute. Any minute.

I forced myself to look out at the tracks, trying to stay in the moment, but everything that had just happened was pushing its way through in my thoughts. The fight we'd just had—the things she'd said to me—*the things you said to* her, the quiet, honest voice in my head piped up. We'd never had a fight like that, ever. But it wasn't my fault that Stevie held on to things so tight that when she finally said how she felt, her face practically melted off. And I was just responding to her. . . .

It hit me a second later that I was doing just what she said I did, not taking responsibility. But whatever. We would sort it all out when she got off the train. As soon as she got here. Any minute now.

The B train pulled into the station on the downtown track and I scanned over all the passengers getting off, looking for any hint of Stevie and Brad. I could practically see her, stepping off the train onto the platform, throwing up her arms in comedic frustration, coming over to join me. Any second now.

But then the train doors closed and the train moved on—and she wasn't there.

My heart thudded harder, and my *it's going to be okay* mantra suddenly sounded to my own ears like a question. Because if she didn't come—which of course she would—but if she didn't—

I made myself keep breathing so I wouldn't panic. Big breaths, from my diaphragm, the way Mr. Campbell had taught us. Pre-monologue, high-note breaths. And while I felt a little calmer, it didn't change the fact that I was alone in New York—a place I was not supposed to be—which was *not good*.

Because that was Rule #7 of lying to your parents: Everything had to go exactly right.

And if it didn't, you were screwed. If anything went wrong, and you needed help or to call home, you would now be in twice the trouble, because you'd have to admit to all the lies and subterfuge that came before. I'd never had to do this, but I'd heard the stories, and they were always awful. Like, I imagined it was bad enough to have to call home and wake your parents up and tell them that you crashed the car. But to have to do it while admitting that you'd lied about where you were going that night, that there was no study group, and that you were, in fact, in New Jersey (just to take an example from Emery's life) was *so much worse*.

But it would all be okay! Because Stevie was coming back. Any second now.

Any second.

My feet started to hurt. I felt the cold *whoosh* of air that accompanied the trains through my long coat.

Well aware that I was grasping at straws, I wondered if there was any chance I'd misread this. Was it possible that Stevie was somewhere waiting for *me*, getting upset that I wasn't finding her? But even as I thought this, I dismissed it. She'd been the one with the directions. Stevie wouldn't have expected me to find her.

And the more time that went by and the longer I stood there, as trains departed and arrived, and as people came and went all around me, the louder a terrible thought in my mind became.

Stevie wasn't coming back.

She'd left me on purpose.

Too much time had passed. She could have easily changed trains and come back by now. And she hadn't. Which meant she'd chosen not to.

All of a sudden, it seemed painfully obvious that I'd been waiting for someone who wasn't going to show up. Her unreadable expression through the train window was haunting me. Had she been saying I was on my own? That she didn't care what happened to me? She'd told me she was going home, after all. She'd told me she was done and she was going back to Connecticut. She'd taken the subway straight to Columbia to get the keys, and was probably halfway to Mallory's by now, without a single thought for me, standing alone on the cold platform and trying not to cry.

Had she been *that* mad about our fight? Mad enough to go off and leave me alone? Mad enough to abandon me?

Clearly, she had been. Which meant I was on my own.

The enormity of this situation was hitting me in waves that just kept on getting bigger, like a terrible version of that old car game about going to grandma's house.

I was alone in New York City. I was alone in New York City and my best friend had abandoned me. I was alone in New York City and my best friend had abandoned me and *I didn't have a phone.*

I looked around, like there was someone who could tell me what to do, suddenly feeling like my fancy dress and curled hair looked like a bad costume, fine onstage but tacky and gaudy in the light of day. I was all too aware of how much younger I was than everyone around me, and how much I wasn't up to this. Why had I thought I could do this? I felt a sob catch somewhere in my throat.

I needed to talk to my parents. I wanted to go home.

I didn't care if I would get in trouble, or that this was admitting I couldn't hack it in the big bad city, even for a couple of hours. Everything in me was on high alert, telling me that I needed to touch base, go back to where it was safe, get out of this situation. But how was I supposed to do that? I turned in a circle on the platform, my hands shaking—and then saw, back by the benches, the pay phone.

I practically ran over to it. Would it even still work? It looked like it had seen better days—the phone was battered and scratched, and covered in what looked like decades' worth of graffiti and scrawls. I picked up the receiver hesitantly.

A dial tone sounded in my ear—so this phone was working, which was a huge relief. But now what? At the bottom, under the keypad, was a series of instructions, white letters on a bright blue background. Since I was outside the calling area, I had to press one, then our home number. Luckily, I could do that—our landline was one of the very few numbers I had memorized.

I dialed, and an automated operator voice rang through, very loud, making me jump, telling me the call I was trying to complete cost seventy-five cents. I reached in my pocket for my change and slid three quarters through the coin slot. "Thank you," the automated voice said, and I gripped the receiver, willing the phone to hurry up.

The phone rang twice, and at the start of the third ring, I got nervous. This was the last of my change—what if my parents didn't answer? What was I supposed to do then?

"Hello?" a girl's voice, one I didn't recognize, answered. I frowned, wondering what was happening. Had the phone somehow connected me to whoever lived in my house back when there *were* pay phones? Or, more realistically, had I dialed the number wrong?

"Hi," I said. "Um—I was calling for the Steinberger-Thompson house?"

"This is it," the voice on the other end said cheerfully. "Can I help you?" I narrowed my eyes. Were we being robbed? By someone very polite?

"This is Kat Thompson," I said. "I live there and I need to talk to my parents. Who is this?"

"Oh, gotcha," the voice said. "This is Willa, I go to the high school? I'm babysitting for Grady tonight, you want to talk to him?"

"No," I said quickly, since I was on the clock here and Grady would probably just tell me the day the first pay phone had been invented. Why had my parents gotten a babysitter? When I'd left them, everyone had been talking about getting pizza and staying in for the night.

"I need to talk to—" I started, but Willa was talking over me, her words coming out in a rush.

"I'm actually—I don't know if you remember me? I auditioned last year for *Noises Off*? I actually read with you in a scene? I didn't get cast, but I ended up helping out with concessions during the show. You guys all did such a good job."

"Oh. Okay. Um—"

"And I auditioned for *Lear*, too, and I'm hoping to just get ensemble. But I'm sure you'll get a big part. You're one of the stars—you're *Kat Thompson*!" I couldn't help but notice she said my name the way I said Amy Curry's. "Anyway, I guess we'll find out on Monday?"

All at once, it was like my fog of panic vanished and I could suddenly see myself clearly. What was I *doing*? If I told my parents where I was—and what I had done—I wouldn't be allowed to be in *Lear*, even if I did get Cordelia. And I'd have to tell Mr. Campbell the reason why. And he'd be so disappointed in me. . . .

My mind was racing, now that I'd moved beyond *run to my parents for help*. Maybe I could still make this work. Yes, I'd panicked, but finding out that your best friend has just abandoned you in a subway station can do that to a person.

"So, want me to tell them that you called?"

I blinked, trying to focus. "Oh—um. No. Where are they, anyway? Did they go get dinner?"

"No, they went into New York for the night," Willa said cheerfully, clearly not realizing that she'd just given me terrible news on multiple fronts, like it was suddenly the Napoleonic war over here.

"They—what?"

"I think they said they were going to an engagement party? They gave me the address where they'll be . . . just hold on a second." There was a pause, then three beeps sounded through the phone. What did that mean? Was the phone about to explode or something? Or, even worse, was I running out of time?

"They're at 18 Ninth Avenue," Willa said, and my heart started hammering.

My parents were in New York? They were *here*, in the city? What if I ran into them? Then I wouldn't just be able to not be in *Lear*. I might find myself going to Stanwich College in the fall, still living at home.

"There is an uptown D train arriving," the loudspeaker voice intoned. "Stand clear of the closing doors."

"Where are you?" Willa asked curiously.

"Um—nowhere," I babbled. "Just—don't tell them I called. And good luck with the casting, and—what's that, Teri? Gotta go!"

I hung up the phone like it was hot and stepped back from it, trying to think.

I still had a hundred dollars. I would be able to find *someone* who could break it for me. Yes, I was still alone in Manhattan. But Mr. Campbell's play was still happening.

What was I supposed to do—*not* see this play? Not try and do everything I could to get this part? The more I thought about it, the angrier at Stevie I got. Yes, we'd had a fight. I hadn't thought it was a fight that was worth abandoning me over, but apparently it was.

So fine.

Fine.

If Stevie wanted to go back home and leave me to figure out the city on my own, that was her choice. I had wanted to help her, since going to Mr. Campbell's play was going to be good for both of us. But since she was apparently giving up on theater forever, it was no longer my problem.

And if she didn't care what happened to me, I didn't care what happened to her. She could go back home, but I was going to do what I came in for and go see Mr. Campbell's play. I was pretty sure that I could walk there from this subway station—that this train wouldn't help me get any closer. Manhattan was a grid, right? That was what everyone said. I'd be able to find the Echo Theater.

Armed with my plan, I turned toward the exit just as the phone rang again. I hesitated, then crossed back to it. What if it was Willa calling again? Because the number of the pay phone would have shown up on our caller ID when I'd called. Maybe she'd heard from my parents—either way, I needed to make sure she didn't report anything suspicious to them. I walked back and picked up on the third ring.

It was then that I noticed two people, dressed excessively cool, who looked like they were in their mid-twenties, walking up to stand behind me. Were they waiting to use the phone? That didn't make sense—they were both *holding* phones.

"Hello?"

"Hello," a voice said—a voice that was not Willa's. It was a woman, her timbre low. "Tonight. At eleven. The night to end all nights." The voice was speaking carefully, like every one of her words was italicized, like she was sharing some fabulous secret with me. "See you in the elephant's house. Alaska. Pilgrim. One thirteen. Password is Daedalus. Good luck . . . and good night." The dial tone sounded in my ear, and I set the phone down in the cradle. I had no idea what that was about—maybe a prank or a clue for some escape room.

I walked a few steps away, and the couple swept past me to the phone. "Look how cute," the girl cooed. She posed against it and turned to the guy. "Take a picture first."

"We don't have much time," he said, even as he started to frame the shot.

I headed up the stairs, then walked back through the turnstile again. It was something that would have been unimaginable half an hour ago—me, leaving without Stevie. But here we were. I zipped up my coat and buttoned the toggles before I started on the last set of stairs that would take me back out onto the street. I paused for one more moment in the station. When I left, it would really, truly mean admitting that Stevie and I had had a fight so big that she'd left to go home and I was now on my own. The second I stepped out into the cold night, this would be real.

And as much as I might have wanted it to be otherwise ... there was nothing left to do but go.

I took a deep breath and started climbing.

W hat?" I asked. Suddenly, a thousand openings to a thousand *Law & Order*s were flashing through my head—and I was the person it was never good to be. I stared at the blade in the guy's hand, the one catching the flickering overhead fluorescent light. Was I being mugged? Like, for real? I glanced around, my heart pounding, but somehow the only other people around were the ones across the platform. And even if I yelled for help, what were they going to do about it?

"Your *phone*," the guy said, taking another step toward me.

"Um," I said. I took a stumbling step back but didn't get any farther than that, because that was when Brad started to growl.

I was still holding him, so the dog was pretty close to eye level with the guy. I looked down in shock at the tiny, fluffy dog, who no longer looked so cute and helpless. His eyes were narrowed and locked on the guy's, his top lip was drawn back, and he was baring tiny teeth that suddenly looked very sharp. And there was a low, steady, menacing growl coming from his throat. This dog may have weighed less than ten pounds, but he wasn't messing around.

"Call off your dog," the guy said, frowning at Brad, but I noticed he took a step back.

"He's not my dog," I said, rubbing Brad's fur with the hand that was holding him.

"Look, I don't want to hurt you," the guy said, flashing the blade again but keeping his eyes on Brad. "Just give me your phone!"

"I don't have a phone," I blurted.

"Everyone has a phone. Give it to me and I'll be out of here."

"I *don't*," I said, and my voice broke on the last word. It was maybe not surprising, considering that I was actively being mugged at the moment, but a second later, I burst into tears. It was suddenly all too much, all at once. "I—don't—have—a—phone," I sobbed. "I had one but then my best friend and I—had—had a fi-fi-fight," I managed to get out, feeling hot tears hit my cheeks. I hated that I was crying, but that was only making me cry harder, because it's embarrassing to cry in front of strangers. Even if they are trying to rob you. "And my phone f-fell on the tracks and then we got separated and I don't know where she is and I have to find her or I'm just . . . just . . ." I wiped my non-Pomeranian hand across my face and remembered my eye makeup a second later, which made me cry harder. "And now you're here and you don't believe me and I don't even have my wallet and you have a *knife*. . . ."

"Um," the guy said, looking exceedingly freaked out. "Look, it's okay, all right? See?" He pressed the blade down onto his hand and I gasped—and then saw that the blade had disappeared. He pulled it away and the blade popped out again. "It's fake, okay? I got it at Tannen's. This way, if I get caught, I can't get in trouble, because it's not a real knife." He raised an eyebrow proudly.

"No," I said, shaking my head. The surprise of the fake knife had given me a moment to pull myself together, and I wasn't actively crying anymore. I took a sniffly breath. "That's not—you'll still get in trouble. Like when people rob banks pretending their fingers in their pockets are guns—they still get arrested."

"They pretend their fingers are guns?" The guy looked interested. "Does that work?"

"No," I said, feeling like he'd taken the wrong thing from this conversation. "That wasn't—"

"You really lost your *phone*?" He sounded horrified.

I nodded and wiped the back of my hand across my cheek again. "It got run over."

"That *sucks*." Then he smiled, like he'd just gotten an idea. "Do you want one of these?" He slid his backpack off his shoulder and put it down at his feet. He opened it and I could see there was a pile of cell phones—and what looked like a laptop—inside.

"Oh," I said, taking a step away from all the stolen goods. "Um, that's really—nice—of you, but I'm okay."

"All right," he said with a shrug, zipping up his bag. "Suit yourself."

Brad looked up at me, and I ran my hand over his head, pushing his ears back, and he closed his eyes when I did it, as though he liked that. He was no longer baring his teeth and growling, like he'd picked up on the vibe change.

The guy stood up and slung his backpack onto his back. A man who looked like he was in his thirties walked past, texting on his phone. My would-be mugger's eyes lit up. "I gotta go," he said. "Good luck."

"You too," I said, then regretted it a second later, because I had just said it automatically. I hadn't meant, *Good luck taking that guy's phone.* He started to walk away, and I decided I might as well ask rather than stand around trying to read these signs and make myself a target for someone *else* to mug me. "Do you know where I get the downtown train?"

"You have to cross the platform," the guy said, pointing across the tracks. "It says uptown, but with the construction, they're running downtown."

"Thanks," I called, giving him a quick wave. He may have been a phone bandit, but there was no need to be rude.

I could hear the sound of a train coming and I knew I needed to make this one—from my little experience, it seemed like the more of these paper track service flyers there were in a station, the less frequently the trains ran.

I pulled Brad closer to me as I ran up the staircase, crossed to the other side, and started to run down the other staircase just as the train was stopping. I hurried down the steps, cursing my heels with every step, and Brad and I squeezed onto the half-empty car a second before the "stand clear of the closing doors" announcement sounded.

I took the nearest seat and flopped down on it, settling Brad on my lap. He spun around to face me, sitting up very straight and getting hair all over my coat. His mouth was half-open, and even though I knew that dogs didn't really smile—that this was the anthropomorphizing that we projected onto them—I could have sworn that he was grinning at me.

I reached out and ran my hand over his head. He immediately scooted closer and nudged at it the second I stopped. I smiled and gave him a scratch behind the ears. "Good boy, Brad," I said as he tilted his head to the side, really leaning into the scratch. I still couldn't believe that I'd survived an attempted mugging, and that this tiny, fluffy dog had been trying to protect me the whole time. I leaned down slightly toward him and scratched the other ear, whispering to him like we were sharing a secret, no longer caring at all what the other random strangers on this train thought. "That was such a good boy."

Every now and then, I would get a feeling about something. It wasn't even anything close to psychic powers—which I wasn't entirely certain I believed in, despite the fact that I'd watched a *lot* of *Little Medium* marathons with Teri and Kat. It was more like, the phone would ring, and before my mom answered it, I knew it would be my aunt. Or as we walked up to the cast list for *Midsummer*, I knew suddenly that I was going to be Titania despite the fact that I'd only read for it once. Just very occasionally, and probably completely explained by lucky guesses and coincidences. But they still happened. And even before the doors opened at the Bryant Park station, I had a feeling that Kat wasn't there.

It didn't stop me from looking. I walked up and down the platform, even switched to the other side and back again, hoping against hope that every person I saw in a coat with a hood—and there were a lot of them—would be my best friend. But it never was.

She was gone, just like I somehow knew she'd be.

Meanwhile, back in Connecticut . . .

ERI STARED AT THE MAN WITH THE TIRE IRON. IN THAT MOMENT, she wished she'd never agreed to let Kat leave her phone at her house. She could be watching eighties movies with Ryan Camper right now.

"Where am I?" he repeated, his voice louder. He took a step closer, and Teri took a step back, motioning for the kids to get behind her.

"You're . . . at the Stone house," she said. Her voice came out shaky. "In Stanwich." He just stared at her. "Connecticut?"

"Why were you in the trunk?" Chris asked.

"Yeah," Daryl added.

"Connecticut," the man repeated. He closed his eyes for a long moment.

"Uh-huh," Teri said, taking a step toward the house. She wasn't sure what was going on here, but it didn't seem like anything she wanted to be a part of. This wasn't a Hertz employee who'd fallen asleep in the trunk by accident. This was something else. The sooner she could get the kids inside, the better.

"Stop right there," the guy said, his voice coming out sharp. They all froze. He nodded toward the yellow car. "Get in."

"Oh," Teri said, grabbing Parker's hand and taking another step toward the house. "We'd rather not, actually."

The guy sighed and set down the tire iron. Teri started to breathe a little easier, but then he reached behind him and pulled a gun out of his waistband.

"Cool," Daryl said.

"*Not* cool," Chris snapped. Parker whimpered and gripped Teri's hand hard.

"I'm not asking," the guy said, pointing the barrel of the gun at the yellow car. "Let's go. *Now.*"

CHAPTER 12

Kat

I *walked out onto the* street and fell into step with the crowd, heading away from the subway station. I needed to get to Tenth Avenue, and the street in front of me was Fifth. I was already on Forty-Second, and I knew that was the right street for the theater district, so I figured I'd just stay on this street until I got to Tenth.

Buoyed by this plan, I crossed with the rest of the crowd at the crosswalk, even though the light hadn't changed. None of those people seemed to care, though, so I just put my shoulders back like I was one of them and hurried across the street.

As I walked, I stuck my hands in my pockets, wishing that my gloves had made it into the city with me. When Stevie and I were together and only one of us had gloves, we always split the pair and put the other hand in our pockets. . . .

I pushed aside thoughts of Stevie. I didn't want to think about her right now, or I'd get filled with rage all over again. Who cared that Stevie had left me alone? I was going to get to Tenth Avenue, and once I was there, if I didn't see the theater, I'd just ask someone to google it for me. I'd hoped that this night could have been about the two of us—making sure we'd both get good parts, getting to celebrate Stevie's birthday at Josephine's. But if she was only thinking about herself, then so was I. I was going to look out for myself, just like the song in *City of Angels* told me to. I'd go see Mr. Campbell's play and we'd talk afterward, and when he realized that I'd come all the way into the city to see it, he'd see how committed I was, and there was no way he couldn't cast me as Cordelia. It was all going to work out.

I was walking faster than usual, picking up the rhythm of everyone around me. Since I was now alone, it was like I could take it all in a little more—the relentless *thrum* of the construction drills, the smoke rising up from the taped-off construction zones in the middle of the road. The cacophony of honking that soon became just like background noise, the distant wail of sirens a few streets over.

I had expected the next intersection to say Sixth Avenue, but instead, it said Madison. I hesitated for a moment, then crossed the street with everyone else as the light changed from the red hand to the white outlined figure of a guy. I knew that there were streets in Manhattan that weren't numbered—and then when they were over, the numbers came back again. So I just had to get past these named streets and then I'd be back on track.

I stepped onto the curb just in time to avoid a Sea Food delivery guy on a bike zooming around the corner. Pedestrians and drivers yelled at him as one, then immediately moved on.

I passed by the façade of a grand-looking hotel, flags out front flapping in the breeze, black town cars idling at the curb, and then had to jump back when a car zoomed out of the attached parking garage and out onto the street. The guy next to me, AirPods in his ears, met my eye and shook his head and I rolled my eyes in solidarity, before we both walked on. But as I did so, it was with a secret bounce in my step. I'd just been taken for a New Yorker! Someone who'd also reached the end of their rope with these parking-lot car shenanigans. I quickly reached the next street—this one was Park. As I waited for the light to change—I didn't yet feel confident to cross against the light unless there were also a lot of other people doing it—I looked up and my breath caught in my throat.

There was a stunning building ahead of me, silver and Art Deco and stretching high above the rest. My first thought was that it was the Empire State Building, but a moment later I realized that wasn't right, and that I was looking at the Chrysler Building. Humming the line about it from *Annie*, I smiled as I crossed the street.

It wasn't until I'd passed Lexington that I realized something was wrong. Not only had I not seen any sign of the theater district, but the buildings seemed to be getting smaller, not bigger. And when I reached the next intersection, and it said Third Avenue, I understood, with a sinking feeling in my stomach, that I'd just walked three avenues in the wrong direction.

I sighed as I turned around, bitterly aware that this wouldn't have happened if I'd had access to Google Maps like a civilized person. But because I didn't—because Stevie had gone home and left me behind— I'd just wasted time going in the exact opposite direction, and now I needed to retrace my steps all over again.

I looked around, and when I saw MURRAY HILL BAGELS on an awning, I realized that I'd ended up back in Mallory's neighborhood. I'd never even heard of Murray Hill an hour ago, and now I'd been here twice.

I rubbed my hands together as I started walking back where I'd just come from, feeling the cold seeping into them. I really needed to have prepared better for this. Gloves, scarf, maybe even earmuffs—a hat would truly mean the end of my waves. But I was only now realizing that when I'd been to the city in winter in the past, it had involved going from train to cab to restaurant to theater, then back again. My parents had always figured out which trains to take, and if it was far, they usually just decided to get a cab or an Uber. Or we'd drive into the city—we had certain garages we always used in the theater district, and my dad would duck out when the curtain call started, so that by the time we got to the car it was warmed up, seats heated and ready to go as we drove home across the bridge to Connecticut.

As I headed in what I now knew was the right way, I passed a fruit vendor on the corner—BANANAS 75 CENTS—and wished I hadn't used all my change to call home. But just seeing the fruit was enough to make my stomach rumble, and I realized how hungry I was. I remembered there was a bodega I'd passed on this street, and suddenly a soda and a bag of chips sounded not just good but necessary. And surely they would take my hundred. Because at some point, it wasn't even like your change would be so much that it would be a problem to take it. Like if I was buying eighty dollars' worth of stuff, they wouldn't have an issue with it then, right? I also wasn't entirely sure it was possible to spend that much at a bodega—it wasn't like it was a Target. But surely it would be okay.

"No hundreds," the bored-looking guy behind the counter said. He looked like he was a few years older than me, maybe in college. He had been highlighting a textbook and only set down his highlighter with real reluctance when I'd approached with my armful of stuff.

"Oh," I said, looking at what I'd set down—a bottle of Diet Dr Pepper, Cool Ranch Doritos, peanut butter M&Ms, and a pack of gum. "Um, this is all I have," I said, nudging the hundred a little closer to him. If I never saw Ben Franklin's face again after tonight, I would honestly not be upset about it. "Can you make an exception?" I smiled at him, trying my best not to look like a counterfeiter.

"No. Hundreds," he said more slowly this time, tapping on a paper underneath the glass counter: NO BILLS OVER $20 ACCEPTED.

"Right," I said, nodding. I pulled the bill back, looking with real reluctance at my snacks. "Would it help if I bought more stuff?"

"How would that help?" the guy asked, and I took a breath to answer with my Target-change theory.

"Causing trouble?" I turned around, annoyed, ready to glare at whoever had said this—but then stopped when I saw, to my surprise, that it was Cary. He was standing behind me, leaning on the

ATM, one eyebrow raised. "Of all the bodegas in all of Manhattan."

I rolled my eyes at that even as I held back a smile. I put my gum back, took my armful of stuff off the counter, and walked toward him. I was thrilled to see Cary—not only because he was still very cute, but because surely *he* wouldn't mind googling an address for me. I wouldn't have to ask a stranger after all—and I wasn't sure the bodega guy would have googled it for me, since he visibly brightened as I departed. "What are you doing here?" I asked, trying not to smile too wide at him. After everything that had happened, I hadn't realized how nice it would be to see a familiar face, even if it was only someone I'd only met an hour earlier. He was still wearing his jeans and brown leather jacket, his thick dark-brown hair standing up a little bit more, like it had gotten windblown. Again, the outfit was ringing some faint bell, I just couldn't bring it to mind at the moment.

"Getting a grape soda," he said, holding up the bottle in his hand.

"Who drinks grape soda?"

He brandished it at me. "Excuse me, grape soda is delicious."

"I don't think I've drunk grape soda since I was ten."

"Well, it hasn't changed," he said, and I had to press my lips together not to laugh at his outraged expression. "Why do people see a benefit in disowning the things we loved when we were little? Why are we always casting everything aside?"

I just looked at him for a moment, then walked over to put back my candy. "That's very deep."

He laughed. "Well, I also really like grape soda, and everyone is always giving me shit about it."

"Fair enough."

A jazzy song started, one that sounded familiar. I realized why when Cary pulled out his phone—it was the same ringtone I'd heard in the lobby. He frowned at the screen, then pressed a button to silence his phone.

"Paradise Cruises?" I guessed.

"Calling from South Dakota this time," he said. "But I am much too intelligent to be fooled by them changing location. Wait, what are you doing here?" he asked, falling into step behind me as I put back the M&Ms. "Where's Brad? And where's your friend? Stevie, right?"

I busied myself for a moment, straightening the bags of candy. I wasn't quite ready, I realized, to tell him what had happened, say the words out loud—that would make it more true than I felt prepared to handle. "We, um, decided to go our separate ways tonight." My voice threatened to break and I bit the inside of my cheek, hard, to bring me back to the moment. It was a trick I learned during *Winter's Tale*, whenever I would get so caught up watching Stevie's monologue that I would start to get teary too. "But anyway," I said, making my voice bright as I turned around again. "That's why I'm not with Stevie. Or Brad, because she took the dog."

"Got it," Cary said, his forehead furrowed, like he could somehow tell there was more to this story. It was disconcerting, looking almost directly into his eyes like this. I was always choosing to date people taller than me, people I had to look up at, and this was new. Not necessarily bad—just new. I wasn't used to having someone right on my level like this. "That's a lot to deal with tonight. On top of getting locked out."

"Yeah," I said with a shrug that I didn't feel at all as I put my Diet Dr Pepper back in the refrigerated section, pushing my hand through the plastic strips. "Wait," I said, thinking of something and turning to face him more fully. "Did you hear from your uncle? Is he back with the keys?"

Cary shook his head, looking abashed. "He's still stuck on the side of a highway in Pennsylvania. Apparently the tow truck they called missed them, so another one's being sent. . . . I'm really sorry."

I nodded as I walked over to where the chips were and set down my bag of Cool Ranch Doritos. With everything else that had gone wrong tonight, this probably shouldn't have been surprising. "It's not your fault," I said, turning back to him. I remembered that the last time I'd seen him, he'd told me he was going to work—but I realized now I didn't know what that was. "I thought you were going to work."

"I did go to work," he said. "I water plants at three buildings in the neighborhood, so I took care of it. Excuse me." He reached around me for a bag of Cool Ranch Doritos—as he did this, his arm brushed against my back. This gave me an excited shiver—which was ridiculous, since we were both wearing layers of clothing. "And now I actually have to go to another job." He headed to the cooler and reached in, took out a Diet Dr Pepper.

"How many jobs do you have?" I followed behind him as he walked to the candy aisle and picked up a bag of Skittles and a bag of M&Ms—peanut butter.

He paused and tilted his head to the side, like he was thinking. "Right now? Six. Six if you count helping my uncle out, even though it doesn't pay in money."

He made his way up toward the counter, and I glanced at the crooked clock on the wall. I was relieved to see that there was still just over two hours before I had to be at the Echo Theater—I was still good on time. "What does it pay in, then?" I asked, turning to him. "Gold bars? Experience?"

"Ha," Cary said with a smile, but without actually laughing. "No, I just meant—I live with my aunt and uncle, so it pays in room and board."

"Oh, right," I said. My cheeks get hot, and wished I'd never tried to make a stupid joke. "Sorry."

"Nothing to be sorry about," he said cheerfully. "And—fun fact—do you know where the expression 'room and board' comes from?"

"I don't," I said, hoping that my tone conveyed that I was actually okay with keeping it this way. "But wait—what are the other jobs?"

"I water plants," Cary said, setting his things down on the counter, "help my uncle—"

"Elwes!" the counter guy said, smiling wide at Cary. He and Cary did a multistep handshake that ended with bumping shoulders—Cary jumped up slightly to reach him over the counter. "How's it going? How's the scrivening?"

"Hey, Pete," Cary said, rolling his eyes. "You know, I've been in here for, like, ten minutes. I'm kind of worried that someone could be robbing you and you wouldn't notice because you'd be focused on your Kant."

"Wittgenstein," the guy—Pete—said, sounding disdainful. "We covered Kant practically the first week. And these classes are no joke. If I'm not studying, I'm falling behind. You'll find out next year."

"No way I'm taking moral philosophy," Cary said as he set a pack of gum down on the counter too. "Or any kind of philosophy, for that matter."

"You don't want to learn how to be a better person and understand your place in the universe?"

"I'm covered with horoscopes, fortune cookies, and Lord and Miller," Cary said with a smile. "Thanks, though." He nodded toward me. "Oh, this is Kat," he said, and I gave Pete a wave, even though we'd very much met already.

"No hundreds," Pete said immediately.

"I know!" I said, slightly offended, since I wasn't even trying to use my apparently radioactive bill. Maybe that was why Mallory had been so eager to give it away. Maybe she was—literally—trying to pass the buck.

"Since when do you eat peanut butter?" Pete asked as he rang up Cary's items. "I thought you were allergic."

"I am," Cary said. "They're not for me." I looked down at the items on the counter and realized—probably much too late—that in addition to Cary's grape soda and Skittles, all the items he was buying were the ones I'd put back. The Doritos, the Diet Dr Pepper, the M&Ms, the gum. It was such a small, sweet gesture that it took me fully by surprise. And I realized, with a pit in my stomach, that it was the kind of thing that Stevie would have done. She was always buying me snacks and not letting me pay her back. This had culminated in the Great Venmo War of last year. It had led to us both being banned for a month; I'd worn it like a badge of honor.

"Thank you," I said, as Pete scanned the rest. "But you didn't have to—"

"It's my pleasure," Cary said simply. "Consider it repayment for my uncle going missing."

"Uncle Georgios is *missing*?" Pete asked, his jaw falling open. "Since when?"

"Not like *missing* missing," Cary said quickly. "Just having car trouble in the Keystone State. Not the best day for it, since Kat got locked out and needed to be let into an apartment."

"Got it," Pete said, looking relieved. "Bag for ten cents?"

Cary nodded, and Pete swept the items into a white plastic bag with I ♥ NY printed on it in red, over and over again. He handed it to Cary, along with his change, and picked up his highlighter.

"You around later?" he asked.

Cary shook his head. "Working."

"Sunday then," Pete said.

Cary grinned. "See you on the field." Pete gave us a nod before going back to his book, and it was like you could somehow feel that even though he was still physically here, he had actually left and was elsewhere, probably in Austria or Switzerland or wherever Wittgenstein was from.

"Field?" I asked, following Cary as he made his way toward the door. He paused to scratch the head of the orange cat who was lounging in the window. I figured this must be a bodega cat—I'd heard about them, of course, but had never seen one in real life. My parents weren't really ones for ducking into delis when we were in the city to see a play. I reached for my phone to take a picture, already debating the caption—*meowdega!*—before I remembered. I settled for also scratching the top of the cat's head and was rewarded when it gave a low purr that seemed to rumble through its body.

"Yeah," Cary said as he held open the door for me and I stepped outside, drawing in a breath against the cold air. "We play kickball on Sundays, then get brunch."

"Kickball?" I raised an eyebrow. "I haven't played that since third grade. At least."

"And yet," Cary said, smiling, with an overly patient air, "it's still just as much fun. Maybe even more so, because you're no longer constrained by the time frame of either recess or PE. Things don't stop being fun just because you get older."

"Is this like the grape soda thing?"

Cary laughed. "Possibly." He pulled out his soda and candy, then handed the bag to me. "For you."

"Thank you again," I said, my stomach growling in anticipation. "Here," I said, pulling out my hundred. "Please let me pay you back." I was suddenly hopeful that maybe Cary could break it—maybe his plant-watering clients paid him in cash and he kept a lot of it on him for some reason.

"No," Cary said firmly, even as he smiled. "It's on me. But thank you."

"Okay," I said, putting the hundred back in my pocket.

"So what now?" he asked. A group of girls who looked like they were in their twenties hurried up the street toward us. They were dressed for a night out, you could see, even with their coats on—heels and makeup, a certain swaggery confidence in the way they strode down the sidewalk in a group. They were laughing and yelling as they walked, and Cary and I took a simultaneous big step back to let them pass. I watched them go for just a second, thinking with a fierce jealousy that that should have been me and Stevie right now, together, walking and laughing, cutting our way across New York City in triumph.

"Oh," I said, when I realized that Cary had asked me a question I still hadn't answered. "I'm actually going to see a play. My drama teacher wrote it." I tried to say this like it was no big deal, but even I could hear I didn't pull it off.

"Are you an actor?"

I nodded, not able to stop myself from smiling. "I am. And he teaches us in Connecticut, but he has his own company here in the city." I felt a flush of pride as I said this. "The show starts at eight, and I have to get up to the theater district. And—would you actually mind googling the address for me? I don't have a phone."

"Of course," Cary said, pulling his phone out of his back pocket. He shook his head. "I honestly don't know how you're even managing without one. It's like you're living in 1984."

"Yeah," I said, not wanting to admit my phonelessness was because I didn't want my parents to track me. That would probably seem super juvenile to someone who lived in New York and was friends with deli guys and worked six jobs. "Luckily, cute guys in bodegas are helping me out," I said. I saw Cary's cheeks flush, but he had a small, pleased smile on his face as he unlocked the phone and handed it to me.

"Google away."

I pulled up the address, but as soon as I did, another problem presented itself. Was I just supposed to memorize the address and hope I wouldn't forget it? "You don't have a piece of paper, do you?" I asked, feeling like I'd already asked him for too much. "And . . . a pen? Sorry about this."

"It's fine," he said. He started to set his grape soda on the ground, but I reached out and took it from him. "Thanks," he said as he slung his messenger bag off his shoulder and pulled out a black sketchbook, covered in stickers. He flipped through it—most of the pages were covered in drawings—before ripping out a blank page. He pulled out a pen and handed both to me.

"Thanks," I said, scrawling down the address to the Echo Theater, which, it turned out, was on Tenth Avenue and Fifty-First Street. The paper was thick vellum, and the pen was much nicer than the ones I normally used; this felt like the kind you bought in art supply stores. While I was at it—because who knew when I would have access to another pen—I wrote down the address that Willa had told me. I needed to remember where to avoid. Just the fact that my parents were currently in the city was *not good*, and I knew I would feel better giving wherever they were a wide berth. *18 9th Avenue*, I wrote quickly, then capped the pen and handed it back to him. "Thanks a lot."

"Anytime," he said, with a smile that crinkled the corners of his eyes. A second later, though, his expression turned worried. "Why don't I give you some cash?" he asked, starting to reach into his messenger bag again. "I've got some smaller bills. . . ."

"No," I said quickly. "I'm sure it'll be fine." Cary straightened up, but I could still see a question in his eyes, and I nodded firmly. "Really. But thank you. And for the snacks, too. It's really nice of you."

"Well, okay," he said, slinging his messenger bag across his chest again. "It was nice to run into you. And I guess I'll see Stevie when she comes for the keys."

"Oh no, wait," I said, suddenly remembering. With all the snacks and talk of moral philosophers, I'd forgotten that he needed to be updated on the current state of play. "Stevie's phone . . . got broken." I shook my head angrily, thinking about how all of this—our fight, Stevie leaving me behind and going back home—might not be happening if she hadn't tried to grab her phone back from me.

"Oh *no*."

"Yeah, it fell on the subway tracks . . . and then the subway kind of ran over it. So, to make a long story short . . ."

"Too late."

I smiled at that; I'd seen *Clue* way too many times to be offended. "Nicely done. Anyway, Stevie doesn't have a working phone. But she's going to get the keys from her stepbrother, so she'll be able to get back in on her own anyway."

"Gotcha." Cary walked over to a moped—or was it a Vespa? It wasn't a full-fledged motorcycle, at any rate—that was wedged in between two cars on the street. He took keys from his pocket, unlocked the compartment over the back wheel, and took out a helmet.

"Nice ride," I said, looking at it, a little surprised. Cary seemed like he was around my age, but then certain things—like riding a motor scooter around New York City—made him seem suddenly older, and like he was living a life outside of anything I'd experienced.

"Beats the subway," he said with a grin as he pulled the helmet on.

"I bet." I waved with my free hand. "See you around." I turned and headed up the street. A moment later, Cary was standing in front of me—a little out of breath, as if he'd run around to be there. "Hey," he said, glancing at his phone. "Listen. You still have a while before you have to be at the theater, right? When's the show?"

"Eight," I said slowly. "Why?"

"Well," Cary said, "I mean, you could walk all the way up there and then . . . just wait around for two hours." He arched an eyebrow. *"Or."*

I laughed at his expression. "Or what?"

"Or you could hang out with me while I make deliveries, and then I'll drive you right to the theater in plenty of time." He gave me a hopeful, nervous smile.

"Oh," I said, mostly to give myself some stalling time. Riding around on a scooter sounded like fun—and better than killing time in a pizza place or something that might not even sell me pizza because my bill was too big. But I had to keep my eye on the prize. I had to get to the theater in plenty of time. I didn't want to be running in late. But I also didn't want to be hanging around the theater in the cold for hours like a stalker. . . .

"What do you say?"

"I can't be late," I said firmly, and Cary's smile became happier, the nerves washed away. "Like, I should probably be there at seven forty-five. Or even seven thirty. To be on the safe side."

"Seven forty? Compromise?" he asked, and I nodded. "Okay," he said, taking out his phone. "I'll even set an alarm, so we don't lose track of time."

He showed me the alarm on his phone. "Good?"

I smiled at him. "Good."

He walked back to his bike, unlocked the back compartment, and pulled out another helmet. He held it out to me and raised an eyebrow. "Want to take a ride, Kat?"

*H*alf an hour later, as I limped toward Mateo's dorm on 113th Street, I'd learned several things I hadn't known before.

For one, heels were an evil, patriarchal invention, and I was never wearing them ever again. With Brad as my witness, I would spend all future dressy occasions in flats or boots and everyone would just have to deal with it. A blister had started forming on my right heel when I'd changed trains at Columbus Circle, and it was soon joined by a friend on my left toe that was throbbing and incredibly painful by the time I got off the subway. There were Duane Reades everywhere, and I was well aware they sold Band-Aids and blister pads, but I hadn't wanted to break into my nineteen dollars. I needed to stay pretty frugal, in case I couldn't get back into Mallory's apartment. It would take me ten dollars to get a train ticket back home, and then I figured I could get a Stanwich Taxi with the rest. It would cost more than nine dollars to get to Teri's, but I was sure I could borrow the rest from her to pay the driver. Of course, Kat had the hundred dollars, but Kat had left the subway, probably as soon as my train had pulled away, clearly not caring about what happened to me or how I was going to get home. So I'd just walked past the brightly lit drugstores, cursing the very invention of heels and also wishing that I'd done a better job of breaking these shoes in.

The second thing I'd learned was that everyone was friendlier if you had a dog with you. As soon as we emerged onto the street on the Upper West Side, random strangers were smiling at us as we passed, or pointing out Brad and saying how cute he was. And like he understood, he started strutting. When two girls who looked college-aged saw Brad, they immediately started cooing over him, and I took the opportunity to ask for directions to Mateo's dorm. They told me where to go, and after they'd both taken selfies with Brad (he seemed pretty skilled at it, giving strong looks right to camera), I'd been able to find it, only getting turned around one other time.

There were fewer big buildings here, more sky, and Columbia gear in store windows and on people passing me on the street—the school's name visible on hats and sweatshirts under open coats.

And the third was that if you look vaguely college-aged, you can, apparently, get into a dorm in New York City. Mateo's dorm was pretty intimidating—the building was white sandstone with columns, and when I pulled the door open and stepped inside, I could see there were chandeliers hanging from the ceiling and a round desk in the center. But the desk was empty, a handwritten note on the top that read *Gone for dinner back in 5*.

Since asking some kind of official person to call Mateo for me—and at least tell me where in this building he lived—had been my plan, I was a little bit at a loss.

But then the door opened again, and two guys walked in, both wearing COLUMBIA CREW sweatshirts under open jackets. They walked over to the elevators, and I followed, hoping that maybe they could help me.

"Um," I said, taking a deep breath and trying to tell myself that even though these were cute college guys who rowed crew, there was no reason to be nervous about talking to them. (Kat had a theory that the cutest college guys rowed crew, and when I tried to tell her this was entirely based on *The Social Network* and not even college guys who rowed crew looked like Armie Hammer, she would not be dissuaded. Also, who knows, they could have been *tech* crew. The sweatshirts were not very specific.) But I tried to tell myself that they at least would probably not try and rob me, so I could count whatever came next as a net win. "Do you guys know Mateo Lampitoc? He lives in this dorm?" My voice went up at the end, and I mentally rolled my eyes at myself. I was trying to break the habit—if I was going to clerk someday for a Supreme Court justice, I couldn't be using upspeak. "He lives in this *dorm*," I said again, dropping my voice lower than I probably needed to on the last word.

"Matty? Sure," one of the guys said as the elevator doors slid open and I lifted Brad a little higher and hobbled in. I'd noticed he'd started panting a little, like he'd been doing on the train, so I was thinking that maybe different forms of transportation in general just made him nervous. Which was nothing to be ashamed of, really, I reasoned as I rubbed my hand over his head, pushing his ears down again the way he seemed to like. He was a very small dog, and there were fully grown humans who didn't like elevators or trains. "He's on the fifth floor. Five . . . C?"

"Five D," the other guy corrected as he pressed the button for the ninth floor.

"Cool," I said, pressing the button for five. "Thank you."

"You'd better keep the dog out of sight," the first guy said to me as the doors slid closed again and we started to move upward. "The Raptor's on the warpath."

"Ugh, really?" the other guy asked with a deep sigh. "Do you think he'll make me get rid of my pizza box collection again?"

"He should," the first guy said, shaking his head. "Because it's disgusting, and there's no way it can be hygienic."

"The Raptor?" I repeated, but that was when the elevator doors slid open on the fifth floor, and I stepped out.

"Five D," the pizza box guy said, pointing. "Just down to the left."

"Thank you," I called as the doors slid closed again. I headed down the hall, unzipping my coat as I walked and tucking Brad inside, not sure what someone who was called the Raptor looked like, and also not particularly sure I wanted to know.

I made it to the front of the door . . . but couldn't quite bring myself to knock.

I did not want to do this.

You don't really have a choice, a small voice in my head reminded me.

I closed my eyes for a second, wrestling with myself. It had been easier when I was concentrating on getting here—the trains I needed to take, counting the stops, making sure Brad didn't go chasing after any rollerbladers (we hadn't seen any, though, so he'd been fine so far). But now that I was here—and there was nothing left to do but knock—I didn't want to do it.

The truth—the one I had never admitted to Kat, or Beckett, and barely liked to admit to myself—was that my stepsiblings were nice to me. They always had been.

But I wasn't nice to them.

When my dad married Joy, upending my life right as I'd started to get adjusted to the postdivorce landscape, I suddenly had three stepsiblings I was expected to have a relationship with. And I didn't want to. If I bonded with Mallory, Margaux, or Mateo—joined in on the text chain, started hanging out with them like they were always inviting me to—it would be like saying I was okay with any of this. And I was going to college next year anyway, so what was the point?

Occasionally, I'd feel my resolve start to crack. They'd be kind and funny and inviting, and it was like it was hovering right there like a mirage—the relationship that we could be having. But all it would take was seeing a Story of everyone watching a movie at my dad and Joy's, with a big bowl of popcorn to share. A picture on one of their feeds of everyone out to dinner, appetizers for the table. Hearing one of them in the background when I was talking to my dad on the phone.

A world I was not a part of, my dad smiling and relaxed with his new kids, his new wife. All of them getting so easily what it felt like I was fighting so hard for—and I'd slam the door on them again.

Except for tonight, apparently.

Knowing there was nothing else to do, I took a breath, flexed my poor beat-up toes, and knocked on the door of 5D.

There was no answer. After all of this—after psyching myself up to do something I really didn't want to do, after dragging myself and Brad uptown, after all the pain my feet were in—Mateo wasn't even here? It wasn't beyond the realm of possibility. In the reality he was living in, people still had their phones and it wasn't necessary to show up in person to contact them like we were in the 1850s. And it was a Friday night—he might have decided he had lots of better things to do than wait around for his stepsister, who he didn't really even know and had never been particularly nice to him.

I knocked again, and this time I was pretty sure I heard something inside—sounds of scuffling and loud whispering. I pressed my ear closer to the door and knocked a third time.

"Um, can you come back later?" a voice called from inside. It was hard to tell through a door, but I didn't think it was Mateo. This voice was high and stressed and—I was pretty sure—British.

"I'm looking for my . . . for Mateo Lampitoc?" I called, suddenly worried that the crew guys had gotten it wrong and this wasn't actually the right room after all.

The door creaked open a few inches, and I saw brown eyes behind thick black glasses look at me. "Hi," I said, wondering just what exactly was going on, as the door closed again. A second later, though, it swung open, wider, and I was yanked inside.

I stumbled in and looked around, trying to get my bearings. It was a suite, I realized—I was in what seemed to be a common room, with two mismatched couches facing each other, and two doors off either side of the common area, where I assumed the bedrooms were.

"Apologies about that," said the guy who'd yanked me in. He was around my height and was, in fact, British. He looked like a less-cute Dev Patel—though in fairness, that is a *very* high bar to clear—and seemed very nervous about something. "Were you followed? Did you see anyone in the hall?"

"I . . . don't think so."

"It's safe!" he yelled out behind him. "You can come out!"

"Is Mateo here?" I asked as one of the doors opened and two people emerged—a petite girl wearing a flowing black dress, and my stepbrother.

He smiled when he saw me, though he looked confused. Mateo didn't really look like Mallory—though when all three of the siblings stood together, you could see a family resemblance, the same nose and smiles repeated. Mateo had dark, straight hair that he kept short, tan skin, and brown eyes. He was probably around Kat's height, but broader—I'd heard him complain once that his friends were always asking him to help them move. But I didn't think it was just about the fact that he looked like he was in good shape. There was just something about him that seemed steady, like the kind of person you'd trust with your couch or refrigerator.

He was by far the most stylish person in the room. Not that there was much competition—in addition to the girl wearing the dress, the British guy was wearing a knitted sweater and plaid pajama bottoms. But Mateo was wearing a gray Dodgers hooded sweatshirt, with a fitted jean jacket over that and the hood hung over the collar. He had olive-colored pants that were just a little bit cropped, brown boots that laced up, and a black beanie. It shouldn't have worked, but it absolutely did.

"Hey, Stephanie," he said. "What's—"

Whatever he was going to say was drowned out by the girl, who shrieked. "A puppy!" she said, running straight up to Brad. "Who's my woofer? Who's a pupster?"

"That's Brad," Mateo said, coming closer.

"Brad!" This seemed to send the girl into paroxysms of joy. "That is the best name for a dog ever. May I hold him?" She didn't give me a chance to answer, just scooped him up and headed over to the couch with him. Brad did not seem to mind this in the slightest, and I could see he was already doing his paw-waving trick for her.

"That's Alyssa," Mateo said, looking over at the couch. "She, um . . . likes animals."

"Welcome to the Brandenburg Suite," the guy who'd opened the door for me said, gesturing around grandly. "Sorry about the delay. We thought you were the Raptor."

I took a breath to ask who that was—and if it meant raptor in terms of the bird, the mascot for Canadian basketball players, or the dinosaur that could open doors—but Mateo was already crossing over to me. "Archie, please stop calling our suite that. It's not going to catch on."

The British guy—Archie—shook his head. "It just hasn't been given a chance yet."

"Nobody even gets the joke!"

I raised my hand, then realized what I was doing and quickly put it down again. "I did."

Archie pointed at me in triumph. "See!" Then he frowned. "Wait a minute, who are you?"

"That's Stephanie," Mateo said. "My stepsister." We looked at each other for a moment, and it seemed like he was, like me, trying to figure out what we did in this situation. I didn't hug any of my stepsiblings—Mallory kissed everyone on two cheeks, but she'd apparently been doing that since she was little, even when they were growing up on Kauai, where people really didn't stand on ceremony. The rest of us, in the handful of interactions I'd had with them, had just kind of waved or nodded at each other across various restaurant tables. But somehow, in his dorm room, it felt like it would be really bad to shake Mateo's hand—adding a level of formality that would just be depressing, like we'd be highlighting the fact that we barely knew each other. Finally, just as the moment was starting to turn awkward, he gave me a double pat on my shoulder. "Hi," he said, taking a step back, seeming as relieved as I was now that we'd gotten that out of the way. "Um—what are you doing here? Didn't you get my text?"

It was like my stomach plunged into my shoes. "No," I said. I felt beyond foolish and very much wished that I could somehow just disappear from the Brandenburg Suite. "No, I—"

"I texted you," Mateo said, "when I looked but realized I didn't have Mallory's keys after all. I was trying to stop you from making the trip. I'm so sorry you trekked all the way up here for nothing."

"Right," I said, beyond embarrassed. These college students were probably wondering what was wrong with me. "It's just that I kind of . . . lost my phone." It was like I'd just said something unspeakable—there was a collective gasp, and I could feel all the heads in the room, with the exception of Brad's, whip over to me. "I mean, I know where it is," I added quickly. "It's just that it's on the subway tracks at Bryant Park. And a train kind of . . . ran over it."

The girl holding Brad—Alyssa—was staring at me in horror. "That's the worst thing I've ever heard," she said, her voice barely above a whisper. "And I've heard Archie's a cappella group."

"Wot!" Archie sputtered.

"God, I'm sorry," Mateo said. "Are you . . . okay?"

Their horrified expressions were, paradoxically, making me feel better about the whole thing—like I wasn't crazy for being this shaken up about losing my phone. "I'll be okay," I said, almost starting to believe it. "Thanks, though."

"So tell me what happened," Mateo said, gesturing to me, then

Brad on the couch. "You got locked out of Mallory's apartment?"

I took a breath to explain when three text messages sounded, one right after the other. Mateo, Archie, and Alyssa all pulled out their phones and then looked at each other, eyes wide. "It's on the move," Alyssa said, her voice a low whisper.

"What's going on?" I asked as I watched everyone in this suite jump to their feet and start running around.

"It's the Raptor," Mateo called, as he ran toward one of the bedrooms. "That's what we call our RA."

"Why?" I called, though I wasn't sure who exactly I was talking to, as all of them were now moving triple-time and nobody was in the common room for more than a few seconds before disappearing into one of the bedrooms again, bongs and beer and armfuls of scented candles appearing and then disappearing a second later. Brad was watching everyone move back and forth, and I crossed to the couch where Alyssa had left him and sat down next to him. Maybe seeing something of mine that he hadn't shed all over yet, Brad immediately climbed onto my lap and gave himself a good shake. "Thanks for that," I whispered to him.

"We call him that because he's the worst," Alyssa said, stopping and shaking her head.

"Truly," Archie agreed, hurrying through the common room. "He's had it out for us all year for no good reason."

"Well," Mateo said, passing through carrying a tequila bottle, "there was the whole thing with the fires."

"Fires, plural?" I asked, but Alyssa waved this away.

"We put them out, didn't we?"

"And the thing where Chester lived here for a month," Mateo added. "There was that."

"Yes, wasn't that fun," Archie muttered as he returned to the common room and looked around. "Are we sorted? Contraband hidden?"

"I think we're good," Mateo said with a nod, just as there was a double knock on the door.

"Dog," Alyssa said in a strangled voice, and everyone looked over at Brad.

"Oh hell," Archie said, his whole body seeming to sink.

"RA spot inspection," came a voice from the other side of the door. "Either open the door or I will open it in thirty seconds."

"Um . . . ," Mateo said, looking around wildly for a place to hide a small, fluffy dog.

"Is it illegal to have dogs in the dorm?" I whispered, even though it seemed, from the looks on everyone's faces, that the answer was clearly yes.

"If it's like a service animal, or emotional support," Archie said, just as the doorknob started to turn. "But clearly he's not. I'm knocked for six here." Everyone stared at him. "Cricket!" he said, sounding exasperated. "How many times must we go through this?"

The door swung open, and an annoyed-looking guy, who seemed a little bit older than everyone else in the Brandenburg Suite, stepped in and looked around. "RA spot inspection," he said, adjusting his round-framed glasses.

"You said that already," Mateo said, taking two big steps so that he was standing directly in front of me. And while I appreciated the gesture, we weren't in a cartoon—he wasn't going to be able to block me from view.

"I am required to make my presence known before entering a room," the RA said, his tone pompous.

"Like, just when you're on duty?" Alyssa asked. "Or all the time?"

"Maybe don't antagonize the person who can get us kicked off campus," Archie said to her in a whisper that I nonetheless heard perfectly.

"Well, as you can see, we're totally in compliance," Mateo said, trying to move the Raptor toward the door. "Thanks for stopping in, though—"

"I don't think so," he said, and I realized that when Mateo had moved, the Raptor now had a clear view of me—and of Brad. "What is *that*?"

There was a long pause as everyone looked at each other, clearly trying to figure out the best way to play this. I held Brad tightly with both hands, and I could feel his heart beating fast, like even he'd picked up on the tension in the room. I suddenly felt the absence of Kat so strongly it made my breath catch in my throat.

She would have stood up to this guy. She would have created a scene, spun a story, told whatever lie she needed to. It might not have *worked*, but she would have gone in swinging. It wasn't like *I* was going to argue with the Raptor. Even the thought of it made me feel panicky, the way confrontations always did—palms sweating, heart racing, like everything in my body was screaming at me to get out, that this was dangerous. And especially tonight, after I'd fought with my best friend and cried in front of a pickpocket, it was like I'd used up my quota of confrontations, maybe for the year. The only time I'd ever been able to really fight with anyone was in a play.

So pretend it's a play, I could practically hear Kat whispering to me.

I took a deep breath, preparing myself. I had, after all, run around the stage in what was essentially my underwear (*Noises Off*), sung an incredibly difficult score (*City of Angels*), and had to convincingly utter the lines, "Torvald, we may be a wee bit more reckless now, mayn't we? Just a tiny wee bit!" (*A Doll's House*) before hundreds of people. This was just in front of four college students and a Pomeranian. I could do this.

"Excuse me?" I asked. I stood up, taking Brad with me. This character was getting sketched out in real time, but it seemed like her voice was a little lower than mine, and her posture much better. I tossed my hair over my shoulder. "What did you just say?"

Mateo gaped at me, and I wished there was some way I could

silently let him know what I was doing, but I knew from experience that if I broke character, it would be that much harder to get it back—like looking down for a second on a balance beam.

"The *dog*," the Raptor said. "Having it in a residence hall is a clear violation. Who are you, by the way? Did you sign in?"

"That's my stepsister," Mateo said quickly. "I'm sure she did."

"I didn't," I said as I strode a few steps closer to the Raptor, still holding Brad up by my chest. If he had any idea that he'd found himself in the middle of a drama, he gave no indication, just tried to lick my face. "There was no one behind the desk—apparently they'd gone out for dinner. Is that the kind of operation you're running?"

"Whoa," Alyssa murmured to Archie.

"I know," he murmured back. "Can we keep her?"

"I'm not running any operation," the Raptor sputtered. "But you can't have a dog in here, and this is well beyond three strikes for this particular suite—"

"This is my emotional support dog," I said, holding Brad up even higher. He panted at the Raptor. "He goes everywhere with me. I am, um, emotionally unsupported without him." I said a silent apology for all the people who actually relied on emotional support animals, since I was about to besmirch their good names and actual needs.

"Really," the Raptor said, raising his eyebrows.

"Yah," I said, then a second later wondered where that had come from. Did this person have an accent? I decided just to go with it.

"It's true," Mateo jumped in.

"So true," Archie added.

"The truest," chimed in Alyssa. She and Archie had taken seats next to each other on the couch, settling in like they were watching a movie.

"I've heard that kind of thing before," the Raptor said, shaking his head. "Down the hall, in Five A, they were trying to convince me they needed an emotional support *goldfish*. I mean, come on."

"This is very real," I said, running my hand over Brad's head. "Do you want to see what happens when I'm without him?"

"Uh," the Raptor said, looking around. "Not really . . ."

"Here," I said, thrusting Brad toward him. I saw the Raptor recoil and I immediately liked him less, not that he was starting with a huge surplus, because Brad was clearly a *very* good boy.

"I'll take him," Mateo said, jumping in and taking the dog from me. He settled him in the crook of his arm and started scratching Brad's belly, all the while looking at me like he was trying to figure out what was currently happening and why his normally silent stepsister was apparently losing her mind.

"Look," the Raptor said, "I don't have time for this—"

I burst into tears. Not quiet crying, with a single tear running down my cheek. Big, ugly, heaving sobs. I'd always been able to start crying at a moment's notice. It was like there was an untapped reservoir of emotion just behind a door, and all I had to do was give it a nudge. "My *puppy*," I sobbed.

"Oh my god," the Raptor said, looking horrified.

"This is the best thing I've ever seen," Alyssa whispered to Archie.

"I know. I wish we had popcorn."

"Give her the dog back," the Raptor said, sounding panicked.

I took a deep breath and then screamed for all I was worth, trying not to smile as I did so. You get to yell all the time when you're acting, and there was just something so cathartic about it.

"Stop that!" the Raptor said, covering his ears as I started to cry again, this time in little shaky breathless sobs.

"I . . . need . . . my . . . emotional support animal . . . ," I gasped. Mateo widened his eyes at me as he handed me Brad, and the second that I had him in my arms, I stopped immediately, like a switch had just been flipped. I let out a breath, then smiled calmly at the Raptor, totally composed. "Thank you," I said to Mateo, who was covering his mouth with both hands like he was trying to prevent himself from bursting into laughter.

"So are we good?" Archie called from the couch. "Inspection sorted?"

"Yeah," the Raptor said, backing out of the room, looking horrified. He fumbled with the door handle, which seemed particularly ironic, given his nickname, and practically sprinted into the hall. "You guys are all set, just keep the noise down."

He slammed the door behind him, and in the silence that followed, I suddenly started to feel embarrassed as I came back to myself again. This was why in plays, there was a curtain call—a moment to transition from pretending to being a regular person again.

"That was amazing," Alyssa said as Archie started clapping. "Truly. How did you do that?" She frowned. "Wait, *is* that your emotional support animal?"

"No," Mateo said with a laugh. "It's my sister Mallory's dog." He looked at me and shook his head. "Impressive."

"Thanks," I said, brushing off my tears and hoping my eye makeup hadn't smudged too much, very much wishing we could all go back to talking about something else. "So—"

"Oh, so you're the actress," Archie said. "That was brilliant."

"I'm not an actress," I said quickly. "I just do high school theater, that's all."

"Your dad's always talking about how talented you are, but I figured that was just, you know, parent pride stuff," Mateo said. "Clearly, he meant it."

"What?" I asked, the word catching somewhere in my throat. My dad had never said anything of the sort to me, ever. And he'd never even made it to any of the *Arcadia* performances. Which was fine, I knew he was busy . . . but he always used to come. Somehow, since he moved, he couldn't seem to travel the forty-five minutes back to Connecticut. And I'd given him the DVD of the performance, but if he'd watched it, he'd never told me what he thought.

"Right, now that that's out of the way," Alyssa said, jumping to her feet again, "what are we doing tonight? And does Brad live here now?"

"I'm afraid not," Mateo said, and Alyssa's face fell. "We might have been able to get away with that for the moment, but we can't keep a dog. Stephanie here only got stuck with him because she got locked out of my sister's apartment."

"Right," I said. Now that the Raptor was gone, the reality of the situation was returning to me—I'd barged in on Mateo's Friday night for no reason and was still no closer to getting into the apartment. "Actually, would you mind if I made a call from your phone? Maybe Mallory's super is back."

"Sure," he said, handing it over.

I pressed in Cary's area code, then I CRUISE, but he didn't answer— after four rings, the call went to voice mail. "Hey, Cary," I said. "It's, um, Stevie, Mallory's stepsister? We met earlier. Just checking to see if you had an ETA on your uncle. Thanks!" I hung up, then realized that when Cary heard my voice mail, he might call me back at my old number—which would not be helpful at all. I pressed his number again—it went to voice mail after only two rings this time, and as soon as it did, I said quickly, "Hi, Cary, it's Stevie again. Sorry. But can you call *this* number when you hear anything? Not the other one. Okay. Thanks. Bye." I hung up and handed the phone back to Mateo, who looked thoughtful.

"Be right back," he said, taking his phone and heading into one of the bedrooms. I watched him go, not sure what I was supposed to do now.

"If you're free later," Archie said, "you should come out with us! We've got big plans, with Ukrainian food on the Lower East Side, and then an infused vodka bar in Soho that's Russian themed. It's a real Iron Curtain kind of evening."

"Yeah, you should come!" Alyssa said, settling into the couch with her phone and glancing up at me over the screen. "And you should bring the dog!"

They both started to sell me on the night, even reading out pieces of Yelp reviews for the Ukrainian place—which really wasn't necessary, just hearing the word "pierogi" was enough to remind me that I was getting hungry—when Mateo came back in.

"Okay," he said, holding up his phone. "I just talked to Margaux. She has Mallory's keys."

"Really?" I asked, hope flaring in my chest. Margaux, the middle of my stepsiblings, was the one I knew the least—she traveled a lot, always seemingly on a trip or just having returned from one. "She's sure?"

"I asked her to double-check—you know what she's like—and she swore they were labeled and everything."

"Oh my god," I said, starting to smile. For the first time all night, it felt like there was a light at the end of this tunnel—that I could actually get the keys, get back into the apartment, drop off Brad, get my stuff, and go home. "That's amazing."

"She told me she has them with her—they're on her key ring. The only thing is, she's at work right now."

"Ah," I said. I wasn't entirely sure what this meant. Margaux was a freelance stylist/designer/photographer, bouncing from one thing to the next with seemingly no larger plan. Even hearing second-hand about Margaux's freewheeling career and utter lack of structure was enough to make me feel like I was going to break out in hives.

"She's on a shoot," Mateo said, maybe sensing I needed more clarification. "She gave me the address, though."

"Great," I said, giving him a quick, tight smile. I certainly hadn't planned on seeing all my stepsiblings in one night, but that was apparently what was going to happen. "Well, if you could just write down the address? And maybe text her I'm coming?"

Mateo gave me a skeptical look that plainly said *Come on*, then got to his feet and headed into one of the bedrooms, emerging a second later with a black motorcycle jacket. "Of course I'm coming with you," he said, like it was the most obvious thing in the world. "You're only in this situation because of my sister. I'm not going to leave you to figure this out with no phone."

"Oh," I said, feeling a wave of relief wash over me. It wasn't that I wanted to do this with Mateo, exactly, but the fact I wouldn't have to do it all alone, and stand outside another door hoping someone would let me in, was hitting me harder than I realized it would. I knew I didn't deserve this—not at all—and the fact that he was willing to help me took my breath away for a moment. "Thank you."

Alyssa jumped up and cuddled Brad's face in her hands. "Goodbye, my love," she said to him seriously. "You're the cutest and goodest boy that there ever was, and I want to make sure you know that." Brad licked her hand, and she beamed, then looked at Mateo. "We're still going out later, right?"

"Of course," Mateo said. "In Russia, bar crawls *you*."

"Exactly," she agreed with a nod.

"Nice to meet you," I said, waving at Archie and Alyssa.

"You as well," Archie said. "I think you've saved us from any more inspections for the rest of the year, so we are eternally in your debt."

"'Thanks' works too," Mateo said, rolling his eyes at him. I picked my coat up off the couch, gave it a shake, and followed Mateo out the door and into the hallway.

"So where is the shoot?" I asked, setting Brad down on the carpet and pulling on my coat.

"She just gave me the address," he said, squinting down at his phone. "1000 Fifth Avenue."

I raised an eyebrow. "Sounds swanky."

Mateo smiled. "It's a good thing I wore my fancy boots," he said, zipping up his jacket. "Looks like we're going to the Upper East Side."

THEY'D BEEN DRIVING IN SILENCE FOR TWENTY MINUTES BEFORE THE guy slowed the car down. Teri was sitting shotgun, Parker on her lap, Chris and Daryl in the backseat. When the man told them to get into the car, Chris pointed out that the rental didn't have any of the car seats they'd need, but the man with the gun hadn't seemed to care about that. He'd pointed with the gun once more, and she'd stopped telling him about children's vehicular safety.

Teri held on to Parker tight as they drove. She stared out the window, wishing that someone would tell her what to do, feeling very strongly that twenty bucks an hour was *not* enough to make up for having to deal with this.

The man pulled the car off to the shoulder of I-95 and killed the engine. Teri's heart pounded. What did this mean? "Look," she said, already edging toward the door handle, glancing to the backseat. "We'll just get out here, how 'bout that? And call an Uber, and we won't mention this to anyone. Right?"

"Never," Chris agreed.

"Mention what?" Daryl asked.

Parker shook her head emphatically.

"Oh no," the guy said. His eyes went wide as he looked around the car, illuminated by the flickering roadside light above them. "I'm sorry—I didn't mean to scare you kids. I just had to get you out of there for your own safety. I wasn't sure if I was being followed. If I was, it would have been dangerous to leave you there. Let's start over. I'm Damon Gilroy, but call me Gilroy. CIA."

"CIA?" Chris echoed from the backseat, impressed.

"If you're CIA, what were you doing in a trunk?" Daryl asked.

Parker raised a skeptical eyebrow.

"I can't tell you everything." Gilroy lowered his voice. Everyone in the car leaned closer. "But I've been deep undercover for the last year with the Bulgarian mob. Today—somehow—I was burned."

Teri winced. "Where?"

Daryl scoffed. "It's what it's called when a spy's cover is blown."

"Impressive." Gilroy gave a ghost of a smile, then his troubled expression returned. "I don't know how they found out. But they drove me away, and I knew I was about to get . . ." He hesitated.

"Whacked?" Chris supplied.

Gilroy nodded, looking disconcerted. "Well—yes. I was trying to figure out my exit strategy the whole drive. When we stopped for gas, I knew it was my opportunity. I fought my way out of the car. I knew I needed to get away. To hide. There was a yellow rental car filling up. I saw my chance. I got into the trunk. And was trapped in there until you let me out."

"So what now?" Teri asked. She hoped the answer was *now you go home and never mention this to the Stones.*

"I have to get my go bag."

"Your what?" Teri asked.

"It's what all spies have stashed somewhere," Chris explained, her voice patient. "Money, passports, a change of clothes."

"I'm impressed," Gilroy said. "But yes. If I have even a chance of surviving, I have to get it and go to ground. Because if I was made . . . it means there might be a mole in the department. That I don't know who I can trust." Gilroy shook his head, laughing quietly to himself. "You know, it seems like the only people I can trust right now . . . are you four."

"We can help," Chris piped up. Teri shot her a look. "Isn't it what our teachers are always telling us to do? Be helpful?"

"Well," Teri started. She wasn't sure Chris's teachers actually meant things like *help a spy start a new life in Mexico.*

"I'm so sorry to ask this of you," Gilroy said. "If I had any other choice . . ."

His words hung heavy in the car—the fear and desperation behind them.

"We can help," Teri said, making a decision but still feeling uneasy. "We'll drive with you to get your go bag, but it can't be too late. These three have a bedtime."

"Teri," Chris whined.

"You're embarrassing us in front of the secret agent," Daryl hissed.

Parker dropped her head in her hands.

"I'll get you back in plenty of time, don't worry." He looked at all of them in turn, emotion visible in his dark eyes. "Thank you all, so much. And your country thanks you too."

He started the car and Teri released her vise grip on Parker. "So— where are we going?"

Gilroy signaled, then pulled back onto the highway. His jaw was set. The expression in his eyes far was away. "North."

CHAPTER 14
Kat

After a few minutes, I could decisively say that by far the best way to get around New York City was to ride on the back of a scooter driven by a cute boy.

It was my first experience with this particular mode of transportation, but it was already easily outpacing cars or taxis or buses or the subway, and I had decided I never wanted to get around New York any other way.

I'd hesitated only a moment before taking the helmet he'd offered to me, then said a silent farewell to what was left of my waves as I pulled it on over my head.

"Feel secure?" Cary asked. "Nod your head." I did and felt the helmet slide slightly forward. "This'll help," he said. He took a step closer to me, then paused. "May I?"

"Sure," I said, enjoying my up-close view as he leaned forward and pulled the strap under my chin tighter. His brow was furrowed in concentration, and his eyelashes were so long they were practically casting shadows on his cheeks. I knew that there was enough going on tonight that I shouldn't have been paying attention to things like how attractive this guy was, but . . . I mean, I was only human.

"Better?"

I nodded, hoping none of my recent thoughts were readable on my face, and my helmet stayed put. "Perfect." I looked at the scooter. "Now what?"

Cary showed me where I'd sit behind him, and told me to be sure to keep my leg away from the tailpipe—that it got really hot, and you didn't feel it sometimes until you'd gotten a serious burn.

I tried to remember all of this as Cary got onto the bike, and then I climbed on behind him. I was grateful that the skirt of my dress was so twirly, because it meant that climbing onto the back of the scooter wasn't a problem. I didn't know what I would have done if I'd been wearing a tighter skirt—ride sidesaddle and hope for the best?

I settled myself on the bike, and then put my feet on the little tilted rests that seemed to be there for that purpose. I held on to the bar behind me and evaluated the situation. There was some space between us—it wasn't like I had my legs wrapped around him or anything. But . . . we were *very* close together, and I tried to sit as far back on the bike as possible. A second later, I shifted forward a little, worried about falling off the back and getting hit by a taxi.

I felt a sudden urge to check the time—I was finding myself tonight, for the first time ever, wishing that I had a watch. I couldn't let myself get too distracted here. I had to focus on making sure I got to the play. I was about to ask Cary to double-check the alarm settings, when he took the key and turned the engine on.

"If you need to hold on to me, you can," he said over the sound of the engine, turning his head to look at me. "I mean," he added quickly, "if you feel comfortable. Just . . . whatever works best."

"Thanks," I said, giving him a quick smile and tightening my hands on the back bar.

"Ready?" he asked.

"Ready."

Cary revved the motor, pulled out into traffic—and we were off.

At first, my heart was hammering as I was sure, in every moment, that we were about to die a horrible death and be talked about gravely on NY1. We were *in* the traffic in a way I'd never experienced in a car. We zoomed around taxis and squeezed past cars to wait at stoplights.

Then, when the light turned green, we took off again with a force that sent me backward each time.

Cary suddenly braked hard to avoid a car swerving out into traffic, and I nearly lost my balance. For one heart-stopping second, I thought I was about to fall off the bike. A volley of insults from all around us followed; the driver yelled back, giving as good as he got. My pulse was racing triple-time, even as I righted myself on the seat and told myself that it was fine, that I was safe. But the problem with holding on to the bar behind me was that it threw my weight backward—so that I was already partway to losing my balance whenever the bike swerved or stopped suddenly. And after that close call, I didn't want to hold on to the bar anymore. All of which meant I was going to have to hold on to Cary.

Any reservations I might have had about this—because it was significantly more than just flirting with someone in a bodega—went away when compared with the fact that I'd just come pretty close to falling into New York traffic. So as Cary slowed for the stoplight turning yellow at Forty-Ninth Street, I took one hand off the back bar and grabbed onto the fabric of his brown leather jacket. I was trying not to hold on to him—even though he'd said it was fine—but figured that holding on to his coat was a good compromise. I reached around with my other hand to grab his coat on the other side—just as the light turned green and the scooter jolted forward. I instinctively stopped holding the fabric of his coat and gripped onto him, holding either side of his waist.

And I didn't even have time to worry if this was okay or get embarrassed, because it was clear after just a few minutes how much better it was. I was able to lean forward slightly and move with Cary when he leaned to the side when taking a turn, finding the rhythm of moving with him.

It let me relax a little bit—and then I was able to actually enjoy it, and take it all in. The cold air rushed around us, and the lights blurred as Cary sped down the city streets. I turned my head and looked at it all—*New York*—flying past me. People hurrying down the street bundled up, yellow taxis in front and behind and all around us, doormen in long coats huddled under awnings, stomping their feet and rubbing their gloved hands together. I was breathing in exhaust, yes, but also wafts of scents from the shawarma and pretzel carts on the corners, and the bite in the November air that had always meant *snow*.

I closed my eyes for a moment and felt the wind on my face as we flew down the street. I wasn't entirely sure how I'd gotten here—how this was what my Friday night had turned into, riding on a scooter driven by a cute boy, in New York City, wearing my favorite dress. But for the moment, with the honk of the horns and the rush of the wind, the pretzel scent in the air and with Cary to hold on to, I wasn't thinking about anything except right now.

All too soon, though, Cary was starting to slow the scooter down, and a moment later was steering it into a makeshift spot between two cars. When the bike had stopped, I got off carefully, making sure to avoid the tailpipe.

I looked around. We were on East Fifty-Seventh Street, halfway down the block.

"Take that from you?" Cary asked, and I handed him my helmet, trying my best to fluff up my hair, but do it subtly. "How'd you do? Not too bad, right?"

I laughed. "It was fun! I mean, a tiny bit scary. I only confronted my mortality like three times. But mostly fun."

"Good." The jazzy guitar sounded again, and he pulled out the phone. "Maybe that's my uncle," he said, then looked at the screen and groaned. "Nope. Paradise Cruises."

"Where are they calling from this time?"

"Kauai." He declined the call and put his phone back into his pocket, then twirled his keys around his finger—but they went rogue, and spun away, landing near my feet.

I reached down to grab them for him, but instead of bending my knees, I did what I always did when I had to pick something up—I bent forward from the waist, so that my nose almost hit my shin, then straightened up again. All dancers did this—it was like a little bonus stretch.

Cary just stared at me as I dropped the keys into his palm. "Impressive."

I shrugged. "Former dancer."

"Former?" I nodded, not wanting to go into it. "And now you act."

"I do." Suddenly, anxiety about making it to the play on time flooded back in. "We're still good on time, right?"

Cary pulled out his phone and turned it so I could see the time. "More than. Want me to set a second alarm?" I could tell he was kidding, but it actually didn't sound like a bad idea to me. I was about to suggest it when his phone rang again. "Same number as before," he said, shaking his head. "They're being persistent tonight."

"Maybe block that number?"

"Good call." He pressed a button on his phone and the ringing stopped. He dropped his phone back into his pocket and tipped his head toward the nearest storefront. "So that's where I work."

I looked at it, and my eyes widened. MAVERICK CLEANERS was written on the awning in a font that looked familiar. There were little wings on the side of it, like the *Top Gun* logo. . . .

I turned back to Cary, suddenly putting it together—why his outfit had been ringing a bell all night. "No. Way."

Cary grinned and unzipped his jacket—and I could see that he was wearing a white T-shirt with his jeans, with a pair of aviators tucked over the top, to complete the look with the brown bomber jacket. "Yeah. The owner came over to the States in the eighties and got very into Tom Cruise movies. But this one was his favorite."

"So he makes everyone dress like off-duty fighter pilots?"

"What do you mean?" Cary asked, his eyes wide and innocent. "This is just what I like to wear. What's wrong with it?"

For a moment, I believed him—but then he broke, and started laughing. "You almost got me."

"He thinks that it helps to have a gimmick," Cary said with a shrug.

"I mean," I said, gesturing to his outfit, "*I* will certainly never forget this. So it's working on me."

Cary laughed and held the door for Maverick Cleaners open for me, and I stepped inside to a small, overheated space. "Welcome," a woman behind the counter, who looked like she was in her thirties, said before she saw Cary.

"You made it," she said, shaking her head and looking up at the clock on the wall. It was shaped like a man's dress shirt, with two tails of a tie making up the clock's arms. She raised an eyebrow at me. "You got laundry to drop off, doll?"

"No," I said, then took a breath, trying to think how to explain what exactly I was doing there.

"That's my friend Kat," Cary said, and I smiled involuntarily, even though I had a feeling he'd just called me that because saying *girl I just met tonight because she got locked out of my uncle's apartment building and who I bought bodega snacks for* was pretty inefficient. "She's going to help me out."

"Is it because you're finding it too much to . . . carry?" the woman asked, then cracked herself up.

"Never heard that before," Cary said cheerfully, clearly lying.

"I'll get the deliveries," she said, getting up and walking toward the back.

As the woman walked away, I let myself really take in the place. The Maverick theme was not, I was thrilled to note, just confined to the name and the outfits the employees were required to wear. There was a large sign on the wall that read WHEN YOU FEEL THE NEED . . . THE NEED FOR SPEED-Y DRY CLEANING! There was a box by the door with wire hangers piled high in it that read HIGHWAY TO THE HANGER ZONE (RECYCLING). A sign behind the register advertised ICEMAN COLD STORAGE for furs, and on the register was a handwritten note that read *Don't write checks that your bank can't cash*. But best of all was the small TV up in the corner that was playing—and this shouldn't have surprised me—*Top Gun*.

"This place is amazing," I said, looking around. I was pretty sure the beach volleyball scene was coming up, and I was hoping we'd be here long enough to see it.

"It's not so bad," Cary said, looking around himself. "And it works out with my schedule, since most people want their stuff delivered in the evenings. Especially if they don't have a doorman—they want to make sure it's a time when they'll be home."

"Okay," the woman said, returning from the back, now sounding out of breath as she hauled two huge bags with her. They were square, almost like oversized duffels, with tags stapled to the outside. "Here you go." She then pushed a button and the dry cleaning, on motorized racks behind her, started to spin. It stopped, and she pulled off three separate plastic-wrapped bags, each with a number of hangers in them twist-tied together, also with tags stapled to the front of the plastic.

"Do you take all this on the bike?" I asked, looking at the duffels and the dry cleaning, wondering how Cary could possibly drive the scooter and hold everything at the same time.

"Something much cooler than that," Cary said as the woman behind the counter handed over what looked almost like a folded-up stroller. Cary unfolded it, and I saw it was a wheeled cart. He gave it a spin. "See?"

"*Much* cooler," I agreed.

"Leon Russo called, wanted to make sure we were bringing his soon," she said, flipping though some papers on the desk. "Apparently he's got a date tonight." She arched an eyebrow.

"Gotcha," Cary said. "We'll go there first." He stacked the bags in the cart, picked up the dry cleaning, and smiled at me. "Ready to go?"

I nodded and walked out the door he held open for me. "So it looks like I'm your wingman." Cary groaned, which I took as a compliment. He started pulling the cart behind him while also carrying the dry cleaning—which seemed like a lot for one person to do. "You're going to let me help, right?"

"Sure," he said, giving me a quick smile. "Absolutely."

Cary wouldn't let me help.

He told me that he did this all the time by himself, so he was used to it. But I felt incredibly guilty as I walked along next to him, eating the snacks that he'd bought me, while he pushed the cart.

After a few stops, I was starting to get the hang of it. In a doorman building, we just left the laundry or dry cleaning at the desk in the lobby. In a walk-up, we buzzed, and when the door was opened for us, we went right to their doors, leaving the cart behind on the ground floor. Cary kept trying to get me to wait in the lobbies of the walk-ups, but I was having much too much fun peeking into these New York apartments. There was the couple we could hear screaming at each other as we got close to the door, but who were then perfectly pleasant as they picked up their laundry and wished us a good night—and then went back to screaming the second the door had closed. The apartment that had vinyl records stacked everywhere; the apartment that had three cats that came to the door along with their owner, sitting on the doorstep at his feet and looking up at us with big green eyes like they were all assessing our job performance. And if I hadn't gone with him, I wouldn't have found out to my shock that Mr. Russo—he of the hot date—had to be pushing ninety.

"Chip?" I asked Cary now, as we walked down the street toward our fourth building. I figured that if he wouldn't let me help, I could at least offer some snacks.

"Thanks," he said, shifting the dry cleaning to his other arm and taking some Doritos. "That's really nice of you."

"Well, you did pay for them." He laughed. "You can have anything else you want too," I said, holding out the bag, then remembered what Pete in the bodega had said. "Well—except for the peanut M&Ms, I guess."

"Yeah, I'll give those a miss."

"Is it a bad allergy?" I asked, as Cary tipped his head toward Sixty-Third Street and we both turned down it, my feet falling into step with his. "Do you need me to take the bag away?"

"I'm fine when things are, you know, sealed in packaging. It's just when they're out and about that things turn deadly."

"*Deadly?*" Cary nodded. "Jeez. So Mr. Peanut isn't a friendly cartoon mascot to you. He's, like, a serial killer."

Cary turned to me and gave me a smile that was wide-open, like I'd just surprised him. "Exactly," he said with a laugh. "Other people see an anthropomorphic peanut; I see evil in a top hat. Fun fact—"

"About Mr. Peanut?" I raised my eyebrows.

Cary laughed. "I'm full of them."

"You're full of something," I parried back, then wondered a second later if I'd gone too far, but he just rolled his eyes good-naturedly and continued on.

"Mr. Peanut was actually designed in a contest by an eleven-year-old kid. He earned five dollars for it."

"*Five?*"

"Well, five dollars went a lot further in 1906. But then Planters paid his way through college and he became a doctor."

"That is a fact," I said. "I'm not so sure about the 'fun' part. But my brother would be very impressed—he loves stuff like that."

"A man of excellent taste."

"He's ten," I pointed out, and Cary laughed. I noticed he seemed to do this easily, with no hesitation. I liked it. "What's with the interest in Mr. Peanut?" I paused. "There's a sentence I've never said before."

Cary laughed again. "You always want to be well versed in the things that could kill you. Here we are." He'd stopped in front of a building with a lobby and pulled the door open for me. There hadn't been a doorman outside, but there was one behind the desk just inside, wearing a military-style long coat with gold braid on the shoulders. "Hey, Wes," Cary said, approaching the desk.

The doorman—Wes—smiled when he saw him. "Was wondering if I'd see you tonight."

"Well, wonder no more," Cary said with a grin. He squinted down at the paper that listed all the drop-offs and pickups. "Tonight it's dry cleaning for Three C, laundry for our friends in the penthouse, and a pickup for Eleven A."

"Gotcha," Wes said, already dialing the phone as Cary started setting things down on the desk and sorting through bundles. "How's the movie going?"

My head whipped over to him. "Movie?"

He gave me a quick, embarrassed smile, but before I could ask him for more information, Wes was talking to us, lowering the phone slightly. "I can take the dry cleaning and I have the pickup here, but the penthouse would prefer you bring it up right away. They don't want to wait until I can go off the desk."

"*Oh.*" Cary exchanged a look with Wes. "I take it . . ."

"Yep," Wes said with a nod. His eyes wandered to me and he raised an eyebrow. "Is she . . ."

"She's helping," Cary said quickly as he took one of the bundles out of the big black bag—until tonight, I had no idea laundry was delivered to people in cubes—and left the rest down by the desk. "Be right back."

Cary nodded toward the elevators at the other end of the lobby, and we walked toward them. I could see a Christmas tree in the corner—at least ten feet tall—but it wasn't decorated yet, and I hoped it wasn't real, since it was still early November and I didn't see a real tree hanging on for another six weeks.

"Okay," I said as Cary pressed the up arrow. "I have so many questions."

"Fire when ready."

"What movie was he talking about?"

Cary cleared his throat and looked at the numbers lighting up above the elevator, letting us know where it was. "It's nothing. It's stupid."

"Do you act too?" My voice rose in excitement. "You should have said something—"

"God, no." Cary shook his head. He set the bag of laundry at his feet. "I'm . . ." He looked at me for a moment, like he was making a decision. "Well—what I really want to do is make animated movies."

"Wow," I said, impressed. "That's really cool."

He gave an embarrassed shrug and looked up at the elevator lights again. "I mean—it's not a movie yet. Not even close. But I've been working on storyboards, and one night when I was here, someone took about an hour to get their dry cleaning together for me to pick up, and Wes saw me sketching. . . ."

"What's it about? Your movie, I mean."

"It's an adaptation," he said, looking back at me, the tips of his ears slightly red. "Of 'Bartleby, the Scrivener.' It's a short story by Herman Melville. Do you know it?"

I shook my head. I'd never read any Melville. My dad carted around an old copy of *Moby-Dick* on our lake vacation every year, always promising that this would be the year he read it, but my mother and

I had decided that this was just because he liked telling people that finishing it was his white whale. "What's it about?"

"It's about this guy—"

"Bartleby?"

"I thought you hadn't read it."

I rolled my eyes at that, and Cary grinned and continued. "Anyway, he's a scrivener—he writes documents. And then one day he stops. When his boss and the other clerks ask him why, he just says 'I would prefer not to.'"

"I would prefer not to?" I echoed.

"Yeah. And so he refuses to work, and then refuses to leave the office, always just telling people he'd prefer not to. And eventually he's thrown in jail, and won't eat—because he'd prefer not to—and then eventually dies of starvation."

"So it's a musical?" I asked, deadpan.

"I know," he said, shaking his head. "Kind of a weird choice for animation."

"Is this for a class?" As soon as the words left my mouth, I realized, all at once, just how much I didn't know about this person. We'd ridden the streets of New York together, and it was easy to banter with him, but we'd skipped right over the foundational details. I'd assumed he was about my age, maybe a little older, but I wasn't sure if he was in high school still, or in college. He'd been wearing an NYU sweatshirt when he'd first opened the super's door, but I wasn't sure if this meant anything.

There was a *ding*, and the elevator doors slid open, and a woman dragging a reluctant toddler by the hand struggled out the door. Cary picked up the bag and stepped into the elevator, holding his arm across the door for me, and I followed. He pressed PH and the doors slid shut.

"Not for a class," he said, picking up the thread of the conversation again. "I graduated last spring and got into NYU, but I deferred for a year to try and earn some money. It turns out one of the most expensive schools in America is actually not cheap?" he asked this in a faux-amazed voice, and I laughed, because I could tell he wanted me to. "My aunt and uncle can't really afford to help much, and I don't want to be completely buried under debt my whole life, so I just wanted to try and make as much as I could."

I was about to ask where his parents were, why he lived with his aunt and uncle, but something in his tone—the finality of it—stopped me. "Hence the multiple jobs."

"Hence!" He raised an impressed eyebrow at me. "But yeah."

"Six of them, right?" Cary nodded. "So what are the rest? I know about watering plants and helping your uncle. And delivering dry cleaning and laundry dressed like Tom Cruise."

Cary laughed. "I also scan IDs at the New School Library," he said. "And tutor two kids from Allen-Stevenson for the SAT. But their scores are actually getting worse, so I might need to start giving that money back."

I counted in my head and realized that only took us to five. I took a breath to ask what his sixth job was when the elevator stopped and the doors slid open on floor ten. But there was nobody there, and after another second, they slid shut and we continued upward.

"So you're . . . a senior? In Connecticut?" he asked.

"Yeah," I said, even though I was still confused. "But wait, if this movie isn't for a class . . ."

"I'm just doing it," he said with a shrug. "The way I figure, you wait around for permission, you never stop waiting, right?"

"Right," I murmured, like this was normal, and not a revolutionary idea to me—that you could just *make a thing*. That if you wanted to do something creative, you could just do it. It had never even occurred to me to do something on my own, or outside the theater department. "That's really cool," I said, giving him a smile. "Good luck with it."

"Thanks," he said. He smiled back, and our eyes met, and neither of us looked away. I took a breath to say something when the elevator stopped again, and a guy wearing the same uniform as the doorman downstairs was standing there with a cart stacked with suitcases. He waved us off. "I'll get the next one."

"No, it's okay," Cary said, holding his arm across the elevator doors and motioning him in. "We can fit."

I wasn't exactly sure about that, but after some maneuvering, both the guy and the luggage cart were inside—and Cary and I were standing very, very close to each other at the back of the elevator.

Our hands were just centimeters away from each other, and if it hadn't been for the guy riding with us, I might have accidentally-on-purpose brushed my hand with his. . . .

"Whoa!" Cary reached forward to steady one of the suitcases, which had started listing to the side, about to topple off.

"Oh, jeez," the guy said—he was on the other side of the elevator, and blocked by the cart.

"I've got it," Cary assured him cheerfully. "I'll just hold it."

"Thanks," he said, sounding grateful.

I looked over at Cary. His hand was now holding on to the suitcase, which meant he'd taken a step even closer to me and his hand was just above my shoulder. It was almost like his arm was around me; like he was doing the doorframe lean, but with suitcases.

He grinned at me. "Hi."

I smiled back at him. I could see that his eyelashes curled up slightly; that he had the faintest scattering of freckles across his nose. "Hi."

The elevator stopped at the twenty-fourth floor, and there was reorganizing as we helped the suitcase guy get both carts out before we started rising up again. Even though we now had the whole elevator to ourselves, we were still standing close together, much closer than we actually needed to, which was giving me excited, swoopy butterflies in my stomach. But before anything could happen, the elevator stopped—and the doors slid open at the penthouse.

"Okay," Cary said, stepping off first and putting his arm across the elevator again until I got out. It looked like we'd arrived in a little private hallway—there was only one door ahead of us. "This one might be a little . . . weird."

"What do you mean?" I asked, figuring that this explained the look that he and Wes had exchanged down in the lobby.

"You'll see," he said, as he knocked on the door.

"You sure you don't want to put the aviators on?" I asked. I could still see them looped over the top of Cary's white shirt.

"It's night."

"Still."

"And indoors."

"Even so." I gestured down to my still-zipped navy coat. "Is it okay that I'm dressed like this? And not like Kelly McGillis?"

"It might be more concerning if you were, actually."

The door opened, revealing a harassed-looking woman in her twenties, dressed all in black with an earpiece in. "Maverick Cleaners," Cary said, holding up the bag.

"Oh, thank god, come in," she said, swiping down at the iPad she was carrying. "We have no napkins or towels left—it was going to be a disaster. . . ."

Cary followed her through the apartment, and I trailed behind him, trying to take in everything. I'd never been in a penthouse before. This almost could have been a hotel—the rooms looked pristine and matching, no personal touches anywhere—and it was huge. It wasn't until we were almost to the kitchen that I stopped short.

In what was probably supposed to be the living or dining room, a poker table had been set up. The room was filled—waiters walked around pouring drinks, there was a dealer at the head—and every seat at the table was full. I realized with a shock that I recognized a lot of the players. There was one of the Yankees, a singer who was a judge on a singing show, an actor who'd been in a bunch of action movies about ten years ago . . . and was that the *mayor*?

"Kat," Cary hissed, and I turned my focus away from the room and hurried to join him. He was in the kitchen, taking out what I could see now were linens and towels from the black bag.

"Thanks so much," the woman said, still looking stressed. "Tonight's been a disaster, and it really needs to go right."

"So it's . . . high stakes?" I asked, my expression innocent. Cary bit his bottom lip like he was trying not to laugh and shot me a look. The woman, however, just nodded.

"Yeah," she said as she took the napkins from Cary and hustled out. "Thanks a lot! Water in the fridge if you want it."

When she left, I widened my eyes at Cary. "That's an . . ." I nodded toward the other room, then mouthed, *Underground poker game.*

"Not really underground," Cary said, like he was thinking the matter over. "We're in the penthouse." He headed out, taking the empty black bag with him, and I followed, not quite able to resist one last peek at the poker table, where someone I was pretty sure I'd seen on *Shark Tank* was angrily throwing down his cards. For just a moment, I thought about asking the mayor if she had the contact number for her employee Flora . . . but then immediately decided against it.

It wasn't until we were back in the elevator and heading down to the lobby that I felt like I could speak at a normal volume again. "*Oh my god!*" I said, turning to Cary, who laughed. "That was very exciting."

"This job has its moments. I'm just glad you're not bored. I know this isn't a very exciting way to spend your night."

"Are you kidding?" I shook my head. Teri would be so impressed when I told her about the celebrities I'd just seen. I couldn't wait to tell Stevie. . . .

A second later, reality brought me up short—like running full speed into a brick wall.

Stevie.

She had no idea any of this was happening. Would I even be able to tell her about this, about riding around New York with Cary, my arms clasped around his waist? And where was she right now? Had she already dropped Brad off and gotten her stuff? Was she halfway home by now—or maybe even back at Teri's? Was she thinking about me at all, wondering if I was okay? Or had she totally forgotten about me the second the B train had pulled out of the station?

"You okay?" Cary's eyes were on me, his expression worried.

"I'm good," I assured him, trying to shake it off. "We're okay on time, right?"

"More than," he said. "But if you want to leave . . ."

"No way," I said as the elevator dinged and the doors slid open. "Let's keep going."

I knocked on the door and looked at Cary. We were in another walk-up, this one on Sixty-Seventh. "Maverick Cleaners," I called. Cary gave me tiny golf claps. *Nicely done,* he mouthed.

The door was flung open, and a woman in her thirties was standing there, wearing a black dress and a fur stole. "And who are *you* claiming to be?" she asked, arching an eyebrow, looking from me to Cary.

"Maverick . . . Cleaners?" I repeated, wondering if I hadn't said it loud enough the first time.

"Right, totally," she said with a wink. "*Cleaners.* Sure. So what can you tell me about the disappearance of Murgatroyd?"

"The . . . who?" I asked.

"Nothing," a guy said, hurrying up behind her. He was wearing a suit, and a monocle on a chain. The monocle bounced out when he reached us, and he put it back. "They're just dropping off the laundry, Diya."

"Uh-huh," she said, giving us a look like we were in on the joke. "Sure. *Laundry.* Clearly they have information, unless"—she drew in a sharp breath—"they're also suspects!" Her eyes darted from me to Cary. "This changes *everything.*"

I glanced at Cary. "I don't understand."

"We're doing a murder mystery night," the guy explained to us as his monocle bounced out again. He'd opened the door a little wider, and I could see that there was a group of people, all dressed up, standing around in little clusters with drinks, and what appeared to be a dead body on the floor, lying in a pool of blood.

"That would explain the corpse," Cary said, sounding relieved. He handed over the dry cleaning. "Laundry will be ready Monday."

"Thanks so much."

"Actually?" The corpse sat up and looked toward us. Someone had done what looked like a very realistic bullet hole in the center of her forehead. "Can you see if they can have it by tomorrow?"

"I'll ask," Cary called.

She gave him a cheerful thumbs-up, then lay down again, her eyes going glassy and head lolling to the side.

"Thanks a lot," monocle guy said. He started to close the door.

"But he *has* to be part of this," I heard Diya say as the door closed. "Who delivers laundry at night dressed like a fighter pilot?"

"It's not an unreasonable question," I pointed out, and Cary laughed.

The last building included an apartment with a silent DJ, everyone dancing to music only they could hear; a studio in which a man slipped Cary a twenty if he could wreck his husband's sweater because he hated it and it was causing them to get into fights; and an apartment in which four children were running around and screaming and their parents, who looked like zombies, all the fight taken out of them, listlessly took their clothes from Cary and shuffled back inside. I'd shuddered as that door had closed. Why would you have four children if you lived in Manhattan? Or for that matter, period?

While we walked back to Maverick Cleaners, Cary texted his uncle for an update, but they were still stuck in Pennsylvania, and clearly not coming home anytime soon. Cary returned the cart and dropped off the laundry he'd picked up, and when I saw what part of the movie was playing, I averted my eyes from the TV before I had to see Goose's death.

"So what now?" I asked him, as we stood on the sidewalk by his bike.

"Now I go to the West Side location and do this all over again," he said with a laugh. "But I can give you a ride over if you want—you said you had to be over on Tenth, right?" I nodded. "And we're still good on time," he said with a smile, like he'd just anticipated the question I'd been about to ask.

"Great," I said, realizing how glad I was the timing was working out. I wasn't quite ready to say goodbye to Cary, not yet.

"It shouldn't take that long to get to the West Side," Cary said as he unlocked the bike's compartment and pulled out the helmets. "I think the fastest way will be to cut through the park."

"**S**o I think we should cut through the park," Mateo told me after we'd been riding on the subway for a few stops.

"Oh," I said, glancing down at my feet and trying not to wince. "You . . . do?" The pain in my feet had only gotten worse on the walk from Columbia to the subway, my feet hurting with every step I took, like I was in the book version of *The Little Mermaid.* I had been praying that we'd just take the subway right to the Upper East Side and that there would be very little walking—or at least a cab—to get us there.

"Yeah," he said, looking up from his phone. "Otherwise, we're basically going to have to backtrack to get one of the shuttles to cross to the other side of town, then go back up again—much easier this way."

"Uh-huh," I said, trying to look excited by this possibility and not like I was in extreme amounts of pain.

"And plus," he said, reaching out to ruffle Brad's fur. The dog was sitting on his lap, as he had done for most of this subway ride, in which he'd basically become the mayor of the 1 train. He was perched there, looking around, and everyone who passed through stopped to give him some attention, including a very tough-looking guy in construction clothes. "Fluffy!" he'd yelped, pointing to Brad, who waved his front paws in response. "This way the Senator gets to go for a walk."

"The Senator?" I asked, feeling like I'd missed something.

"Senator Bradford B. Higginbottom," Mateo said, pulling Brad into the crook of his arm and scratching his belly.

"Is that . . . his real name?"

"I *wish*. No, it's just what I call him. He's the junior senator from North Dakota with big plans." As he spoke, he waved Brad's paws around like he was gesticulating. "And when he's barking a lot, I call it filibustering." I raised my eyebrows, and Mateo laughed. "It's one of those things you do with a dog, I guess. Margaux does this whole thing about how he's a talent agent in Hollywood."

I nodded and looked down at my lap. The nicer and funnier he was, the more retroactively ashamed I was about all the dinners when I barely deigned to talk to him. "Thank you for this," I said, after taking a big breath and making myself say it. "For helping me. It's really—really nice of you. You didn't have to. And I feel like I've ruined your night."

He stopped making the dog's paws move and settled him back into the crook of his arm. "You have to stop apologizing," he said firmly. "This is all Mallory's fault, and you never should have been pulled into any of it."

"But still. I'm sure that you had better things to do—"

"And *especially* after Stephen cancelled your birthday dinner, to have this happen tonight . . . the last thing I was going to do was leave you to work it out alone." As we'd walked to the subway, I'd filled Mateo in—skipping over the fight with Kat, but bringing him up to speed on everything else. "We'll get this sorted out," he said with such confidence that I couldn't help but believe him. He nodded toward the subway doors. "This is our stop."

We got off at Eighty-Sixth Street, and I limped off the train, following behind Mateo and trying not to be too obvious about the fact that I was maybe dying. "You okay?" he asked, turning to look at me as he zipped up his motorcycle jacket.

"Fine," I said automatically, even though I was very much not fine.

"You sure?"

"Uh-huh," I said brightly, and in that moment in which I was lying my face off, I suddenly missed Kat so much it took my breath away. She would have seen right through me—taken one look at my face and known the truth—and then not given up until she'd fixed the situation. She would have insisted we stop and buy Band-Aids, or flip-flops, and she would have bought a pair for herself, too, so I wouldn't be alone and embarrassed. I never wanted to make a fuss; Kat never minded making a fuss, especially if it was to help me. What was she doing now? Where was she in the city? Was she okay?

I followed Mateo up the stairs and out of the subway station, then blinked, surprised that the park was right there, just across the street. "God knows what Margaux is doing on the Upper East Side," he said, shaking his head as he pressed the button for the light to change. He set Brad down on the ground, and he immediately started straining against his leash, darting back and forth, trying to sniff three things at once. "It's usually impossible to get her out of Brooklyn."

"That's where she lives?"

Mateo nodded. "Dumbo. There's the light." He started to cross the street as I steeled myself to start walking again. "Stephanie?" he asked, seeing I wasn't with him.

"Yeah," I said, hurrying to join him and trying to ignore my current inner monologue of *gahhhhhhhhhhh*. "It's actually Stevie." I had reached my quota of Stephanies for the night. The only person who had ever called me that was my grandmother, give or take the occasional substitute teacher.

"Oh," he said, holding on to the leash as Brad lunged forward and we made it across the street, and Mateo started walking toward the park entrance. I knew there were streets that cut through the park for cars, but I'd always loved that most of it was just for people. And even though it was night—and cold—the park was bustling, with bikers and runners in cold-weather gear, people pushing strollers, hot dog and pretzel vendors just outside the park entrance. "Sorry about that."

"No big deal."

"While we're doing this," he said, "it's actually Matty. I mean, that's what my friends and family call me."

"Oh," I said, embarrassed that I'd been calling him the wrong name all this time. "Got it. Sorry." I held out my hand. I knew I didn't deserve a fresh start, but I was hoping he'd give me one. "Nice to meet you, Matty."

He smiled and we shook. "It's a pleasure, Stevie." He nodded ahead of him. "This way."

I'd never walked through the park at night before. My dad lived right on Central Park West—just a handful of blocks down from where we'd entered—but it wasn't like I'd spent a ton of time there. And even though it was night—and chilly—out, the park was still crowded. There were lots of people walking dogs; people passing through, on a mission, carrying briefcases or purses; other people wandering along, more aimlessly. There were parents pushing strollers, and lots of runners. The path we were on was pedestrian only, which was a good thing, considering Brad was running in every direction, barking at every dog he passed, but always with his curved tail wagging, like he was just saying hi. For the first time since I'd been in charge of him, it felt like Brad wasn't somewhere he didn't understand and wasn't wanted—he was in his element, with things to sniff and dogs to bark at and tree trunks to mark. It even seemed like he was happier—he was walking jauntily, his tail curved up high, practically prancing along.

I was surprised by how quickly the rest of the city disappeared. We hadn't been walking that long before the noise of the traffic and the lights of the buildings were swallowed up and things were darker, and quieter.

It was very peaceful—or it would have been, if my feet hadn't been about to go on strike.

"It's only going to take about ten minutes to get across," Matty said, looking over at me, then frowning. "You sure you're okay?"

"Super!" I said, trying not to sound like I was going to cry. If a pedicab, or a horse-drawn carriage, or just someone with a bike, had come by at that particular moment, I would have lunged at it and offered all I had (nineteen dollars. And a Pomeranian.) if they would take me across the park. "Let's go," I said, making myself smile. It was just ten minutes. I could handle that.

Five minutes later, I wasn't sure if I could handle it. I limped to the side of the path and rested my hand on a fence post, seriously considering just sitting down on the ground. THE GREAT LAWN, read a nearby sign, and I looked over at a dark expanse of meadow. "I just wanted to . . . look at this."

I knew that I should probably keep going—that every time I stopped it would only get harder to start up again—but I just had to take a break. Brad trotted over and started sniffing around my feet, and I wondered if dogs could smell blood. They had to be able to, right? Bloodhounds had to be named that for a reason.

He flopped down on the ground, then rolled on his back and shot me a look, clearly indicating that a belly rub was in order. Glad for any excuse that would mean I didn't have to keep on walking, I bent down and gave his belly a scratch.

I heard a *hiss* on the pavement but didn't turn to look until Matty said, his voice casual and unconcerned, "Oh, look. Rollerblades. Haven't seen those in a while."

"What?" I looked around, and saw, my stomach dropping, that a man in sweats and a short puffy coat was rollerblading right past us, eyes fixed ahead and arms doing a weird slalom-y motion. "Matty—" I started as Brad rolled over and then jumped to his feet, eyes tracking the rollerblader. A moment later, though, the guy passed out of sight, and I breathed a sigh of relief and turned back to Brad.

Which was why I didn't see them coming.

The sound was like a wave, the same rasping sound on the pavement—but so much louder. I turned in horror to see what had to be fifty roller-bladers, all—rolling? blading?—toward us in a huge group. Brad's black eyes went wide and he started shaking from head to tail, practically vibrating.

"Wow," Matty said, shaking his head as he pulled out his phone. "It's like it's 1997 or something. I have to take a picture. Archie's gonna love this—"

As he adjusted his phone, his hand holding Brad's leash slackened, and even though I staggered to my feet to reach for it, it was too late.

"No—" I started. But it was no use. Brad darted out toward the rollerbladers, his leash slipped out of Matty's hands—and he was gone.

CHAPTER 16

Kat

I'd never been through the park at night.

I held on tightly to Cary, my arms now wrapped around and clasped in front of him. Which honestly seemed like better scooter safety and allowed me to get closer to him as an ancillary benefit. As we drove, I turned my head to look at everything as it zoomed past around us—cars and night runners and a band playing somewhere, faintly, the music carried on the breeze and then fading out again.

The traffic slowed as we passed through a tunnel, and Cary braked the bike and brought one foot down to the ground to steady it. A cab pulled up next to us, and I could see a couple in the back, both of them scrolling through their phones.

"Brad!" I heard someone yell. "Come back here!" The voice sounded nearby, panicked—and familiar? I sat up straight, looking around.

"Bradford Higginbottom!" another voice yelled—a guy's voice. I slumped back down again, realizing it was stupid to have hoped. But I had thought maybe—for just a second—

"Hang on!" Cary called as the traffic started moving again and the scooter jolted forward. I used the excuse to tighten my arms around him as we drove, and I just tried to take it all in while I could, but all too soon, Cary was exiting the park on West Seventy-Second Street, and hung a right. He turned down Seventy-Third Street and parked the bike between two cars. I pulled off my helmet—praying my hair still looked somewhat decent—and looked around.

Sure enough, across the street, there was an awning and logo that matched the one I'd seen on the East Side—but this one read MAVER-ICK CLEANERS WEST. Cary locked up both our helmets and adjusted his messenger bag. "We're okay on time, right?"

"We are," he said, pulling out his phone. "An hour and a half."

"Great," I said, even as I felt a stab of disappointment. Suddenly, our time together—which had felt so expansive—was counting down. It was like I could practically feel the clock ticking.

"I had a thought," Cary said, twirling his keys again, despite what had happened the last time. He raised an eyebrow at me. "Are you hungry?"

"I am," I admitted. "Is there a place around here we could grab a slice?"

"Yes," he said. But he tilted his head to the side, like he was thinking about something. "Or . . . have you spent a lot of time on the Upper West Side?"

"Just, like, going to the Natural History Museum," I said. "Or Lincoln Center." Now that I was in the city, walking around in it, seeing little side streets and residential buildings and pockets, I was realizing how limited my previous trips into the city had been. We'd come in to do one thing, maybe have a meal, then go back home again. I'd never just let New York unfold.

"In that case," Cary said, smiling at me, "there's somewhere we have to go."

"No hundreds," said the guy behind the counter at Gray's Papaya, looking at me like I was crazy.

"I did try and tell you," Cary said as he pulled out his own wallet.

"Yeah," I said with a shrug as I looked around the tiny hot dog restaurant, which was one block over from Maverick Cleaners West. I was pretty sure I'd seen it in a Nora Ephron movie but had never actually been inside myself. When we'd walked in, the letters on the side of the building had been lit up in red neon, and this, coupled with the fact that I was about to get something to eat—to say nothing of the fact that Cary was promising me it was the best hot dog in Manhattan—had given me a jolt of happiness.

There were people standing and eating by the windows, where there was a counter, and brightly colored signs everywhere, advertising the different kinds of fruit drinks you could order. There were paper fruits hanging from the ceiling—apples and pineapples and bananas and oranges dangling over our heads. I'd gone with the same as Cary, a hot dog and a drink. I'd chosen papaya—it seemed like the thing to do—and Cary had gotten pineapple. I was secretly adding up all the money he'd spent on food for me tonight, so that I could Venmo him as soon as I got my hands back on my phone.

"Thanks so much," I said as I took my hot dog and drink away from the register to the area with extra condiments and napkins. He went right for the mustard dispenser, while I walked up to the ketchup, which is the only acceptable condiment to put on a hot dog. Everyone knows that.

"Ketchup?" he asked, raising an eyebrow at me.

"Mustard?" I replied, raising one right back at him.

"Yep."

There was a silence between us, and then I shrugged. "So, this has been fun," I said, pretending to leave.

Cary laughed and nodded at my hot dog. "What do you think?"

I took a bite, then widened my eyes at him. It might just have been because I'd had nothing to eat since lunch other than two bags of Doritos, but it was the best hot dog I'd ever had. "Oh my god."

"Right?" he asked happily, taking a bite of his. "I usually stop here either before or after work."

"Which work? I mean," I said, swallowing, "you've got a lot of jobs to choose from."

"It's true," he said with a grin. "But I meant Maverick."

"Well, I'm glad that after this you'll be done for the night."

He shook his head. "You'd think! But no. I have another job later tonight, but I'll get a little break first."

"Your sixth job?" He nodded. "What is that?" I asked, remembering that I still didn't know. Cary took a breath to answer just as a woman, juggling four hot dogs and two little kids, walked up behind us.

"You done with the ketchup?" she asked, looking aggrieved, and I nodded and stepped out of the way.

"Sorry about that," I said. Like we'd discussed it ahead of time, we both headed out and started walking down the street, finishing our hot dogs in companionable silence. When I was done, and had thrown out the little paper tray it had come in, I tried my papaya drink—cold and sweet and exactly what I wanted right then. "How's the pineapple?" I asked, glancing over at Cary.

"Excellent," he said, with an affirmative nod. "You'll have to try it next time."

I nodded, even though I had no idea the next time I'd be in the city—much less with enough time to wander up to the Upper West Side and get a hot dog. But it was a nice thought. "Absolutely."

"So what's this play about?" he asked me, after we'd gone into Maverick Cleaners West and Cary had picked up a large black duffel of laundry—since there was only one, it meant he didn't need a cart this time. "The one we're making sure you get to on time?"

"I don't actually know." I took a last sip of my papaya drink and tossed it into a nearby trash can. "But my drama teacher wrote it. And we were supposed to find out casting for our winter play this afternoon, but . . . he's rethinking something." The second the words were out, I felt an anxious twist in my stomach. "So I thought if I showed up at his play, showed him how committed I am . . ."

Cary laughed. "A plan! A stratagem. I love it. What's the play you're waiting on the casting for?"

"*King Lear*," I said. Just talking about the play—even saying its name—was bringing all my anxiety from this afternoon back to me. Just how much I wanted it. How much was hanging in the balance, all to be decided by Mr. Campbell.

"Is that the one with the storm?"

"Yes," I said, then paused. "Well—I mean, there's a storm in *The Tempest*, too. And the Scottish play. And *Winter's Tale*. And *Twelfth Night*, actually, come to think of it."

Cary rolled his eyes. "C'mon, *William*." I laughed. "Does Stevie do theater too?"

"Yeah," I said, and flashed back against my will to the subway platform, Stevie telling me she was going to throw all of it—everything we'd done together—away. "She's amazing. But she says she's done after this year, which doesn't make any sense to me. I love it."

"What do you love about it?" Cary asked. When I looked over at him, he shrugged. "It's just that I have no performing talent whatsoever. The last time I tried was fourth grade, when I was Linus in *You're a Good Man, Charlie Brown*." He leaned a little closer to me, like he was sharing a secret. "I was *very* bad."

I laughed. We'd done some numbers from it for our musical revue, sophomore year. "A book report on *Peter Rabbit*."

Cary smiled, like I'd surprised him. "Yes! God, I haven't thought about that in years." He shook his head. "Sorry if that's a rude question. I'm just curious."

I thought about it as we walked down the street, Cary adjusting the bag on his shoulder, and I somehow knew that he would give me enough time and space to answer this question, one I'd never had to put into words, exactly.

Unbidden, a flood of images and memories flashed through my head. The first cast meeting of every show—everyone sitting around with their new scripts, more high energy than usual. The way you could practically feel the excitement for the adventure that was just about to start and relief that the auditions were over, the play had been cast, and we could finally begin. Everyone laughing, knowing that over the next two months we'd be seeing a *lot* of each other.

Sitting in the back of the theater, wrapped in my big cardigan, watching a rehearsal for *A Doll's House* as Stevie and Erik went over a scene again and again, tweaking it slightly, trying to make it perfect—trying to do something that felt true.

Standing backstage before the play started, how dark it always was back there—the glow tape never seemed to be quite bright enough—heart hammering, sensing the audience waiting on the other side of the curtain, the rustling of the programs, and the way I could always tell my dad was there from the way he'd clear his throat.

The ghost light at the edge of the stage, always, like it was keeping watch.

The rustle of long skirts and the clicking of the heels of character shoes, trying to keep quiet if you had to cross around backstage, the way everyone was transformed in our first dress rehearsal, a little more of the magic unfolding.

The feeling that came in rehearsals when everything started to click, started to work. The first run-through when we were off book, not even allowed to hold scripts in our back pockets, always about to break into laughter, and the terrified looks we'd all give each other, the feeling that we were all in it together.

The way Teri and Stevie and I would run lines in the greenroom—how we knew everyone else's by the time we got to dress, and how the three of us could do the whole play in twenty minutes flat, then run it again.

The sound of the orchestra tuning up before the musical.

The monologue I got to give at the very end of *Noises Off*, when my character had finally had enough and was letting everyone know it—listening to the audience laughter build and build, riding the wave of it.

The superstitions, the rituals. Warm-ups and routines that we all had to do, and in a particular order, every time. *What a to-do to die today at a minute or two to two; a thing distinctly hard to say but harder still to do.*

The tech weekends when we basically lived at the theater, all of us hanging out in the hallway, everyone coming with lattes and donuts in the morning. Homework and card games to pass the time as the lights were tweaked, cue by cue, the way we'd get a lunch break and would bring back pizza or Rinaldi's and eat it sitting on the floor, sprawled in a circle. The inside jokes and routines from every show, the way you could never even really explain them to someone who wasn't part of it.

The way we'd all hold hands in a circle before opening night.

The feeling I had when we got our first laugh, the way we always stepped on it at first—not because we weren't ready, but because of the heady surprise of it, that something that had only existed with us was now out in the world.

The way that it felt like you were *part* of something—that you'd been selected, that you were special. That Mr. Campbell had seen something in you, chosen you, and let you be included in this.

And most of all, the way that I'd gotten to do all of it with my best friend. That Stevie had been there, with me, at every show, as we rose up from nameless, lineless people in the background to the leads of the productions and how we'd done it together.

I looked over at Cary and realized I had no way to try and tell him all of this. "It's been my whole life," I finally said slowly, finding the words one by one. "The last four years. It's just the best—you get to make something with your friends, and put it in front of an audience, and then do it again. It makes everything else . . ." I paused, trying to think about how to put it. "Everything else just doesn't measure up. It's like summer camp, all year round. It's the only place you want to be."

"Do you want to do it in college, too?"

I nodded—because of course I did. This was what all the fights with my parents had been about. I thought back to the one we'd had earlier today—had it just been today?—screaming at them in the kitchen about how *unfair* it was that they wouldn't let me apply to the colleges I wanted. And I suddenly felt utterly ashamed of myself as I walked next to Cary, currently working six jobs to try and defray the cost of NYU. Like it had back in the lobby, it was hitting me, somewhere deep in the center of my chest, that I'd never even understood until right now what a privilege that was. To have never even considered in anything but the most superficial way what it was like for almost everyone else. It was as though the bubble I hadn't even realized I'd been in was slowly cracking open to let in the light.

"Do you know where you're going?" Cary asked.

I shook my head. "There's some conservatories I want to apply to; I'm still narrowing it down. But I know it's what I want to do." But even as I spoke, it hit me, for the first time, that all these people I'd done theater with all these years—Stevie, Mr. Campbell, all the other thespians—wouldn't be there. This was obvious—of *course* they wouldn't—but it was like in that moment, it was the first time I'd considered that a college acting program wouldn't just be the Stanwich High program, but bigger and with more swearing. I wouldn't be doing this with all my friends next year. It would be something totally different, with all new people.

Which was okay.

It was fine.

It just hadn't really occurred to me until right then.

"I'm impressed," Cary said, smiling at me. "And I hope you get this part you want. I assume it's King Lear?"

"Actually, it's the storm."

Cary laughed just as the jazzy guitar sounded again. He stepped to the side of the street, closer to the buildings, and I joined him, careful to avoid the open doors of what seemed to be a sidewalk cellar—there were stairs but a steep drop and what looked like a storeroom below. Wasn't this super dangerous? Did New Yorkers just instinctively know to avoid these?

"It's my uncle," Cary said, looking relieved as he answered the phone. "Hi, Uncle G!" he said, taking one more step closer to the building. "Tell me something good." But it didn't seem like this happened—his face fell a second later, and he mostly just nodded and said variations of *okay* and *sure* until he hung up.

"I take it he's not back?"

"No," Cary said. "They finally got the car to a garage near Allentown, but now, of course, the garage is closed."

"So they're living there in Allentown?" I kept my face very straight, and Cary shook his head.

"You did not just say that."

I laughed. "What?" I took a breath, about to tell him all about Stevie's dad and his Billy Joel obsession and Stevie always putting his songs on her mixes, but I stopped myself—then realized what I was doing. I wasn't even going to share stories about Stevie anymore? How had this all fallen apart so fast? My anger was ebbing away, and now it was just making me sad.

"I think the Allentown of it all means my uncle isn't going to be back tonight to let Stevie in," Cary said, his brows furrowing.

"I bet she got a key from her stepbrother," I said. "I'm sure it's fine." We started walking down the street again, falling into step together. "It's nice that you can live with him. Your uncle, I mean." When I was a kid, all I had wanted was to live with my aunt Linda on her ranch in Jackson Hole, with horses and dogs. It had always seemed like the perfect arrangement—there would still be an adult, but one who wouldn't be as strict as your parents. Plus all the dogs.

Cary nodded and dropped his phone into his pocket. "It is," he said, speaking a little more slowly than usual, like he didn't like what he was about to say and wanted to delay it as long as possible. "My mom took off when I was little, and my dad died three years ago. So I moved here from Pittsburgh to live with them. They really stepped up."

"Oh my god," I said, my heart somewhere in my throat. A moment later, I shook my head at myself, angrily, since this was not the correct response. "I mean, I'm so sorry, Cary. I'm so sorry for your loss."

He gave me a sad smile. "Thanks, Kat." He stopped, slung his messenger bag around, pulled out his black sketchbook, and started flipping through the pages. "He had a heart attack on a job—he was a mover—and it was quick, at least. No pain or anything." He stopped flipping and turned the sketchbook toward me.

On the page was a drawing of a man. Just from this one picture, I could immediately see how talented Cary was. The drawing was in a cartoon style—but there was so much personality coming through that it seemed almost photo-real. The man looked like Cary, but older, and with a mustache. He was laughing, his head thrown back, one fist pounding on the table. "That's my dad," Cary said, smiling at the picture. "How I like to remember him."

I nodded, swallowing the lump that had formed in my throat. "It's really lovely," I said, my voice coming out crackly.

"Thanks," he said quietly. He looked at the drawing for just a moment longer, then closed the sketchbook, and after a moment, we started walking down the street again. Cary looked down at his phone, like he was checking the time, and I realized as long as we were okay on time, I didn't want to know just how much time was left. I wanted to keep hitting the snooze button on tonight, extending our night together. "Is Stevie going to meet you at the play?"

I shook my head, but just for a second, I let myself see the *Sliding Doors* version of tonight—the way I'd imagined it would be. The two of us, bashing around New York together, eating giant slices of pizza you had to fold, taking selfies with an unbroken phone. Watching Mr. Campbell's show sitting next to each other, then getting to talk about it afterward at Josephine's, going over all our favorite moments as we kept an eye out for celebrities so we could tell Teri.

But if I'd had that version of tonight with Stevie, I wouldn't have had this version with Cary. And if I was going to keep all of this—the bodega and the scooter rides and the penthouse poker games—I had to give something up to get it. And for reasons I didn't even understand, Dara Chapman suddenly flashed into my head. I wondered if she'd felt something similar, sitting in the audience and watching us act without her, the path you can't un-take.

"No," I finally said, trying to focus. "I'm pretty sure Stevie's back in Connecticut by now. And even if she was still in the city, I don't have any way of meeting up with her...." A second later, though, something hit me, and I smiled.

"What?" Cary asked, and I glanced over to see him looking at me.

"Well," I said, shrugging one shoulder, "we actually *did* make a plan, earlier in the night. That if anything happened—if we got separated—we'd meet at Grand Central at eleven-eleven."

"A very good time."

"Why, thank you."

He nodded at the building just ahead of us. "Here we are."

It was the first commercial building we'd been in all night—which meant we could just walk in, not having to deal with doormen or buzzing residents' apartments.

We climbed a flight of stairs—Cary still refusing to let me help him—and I saw, at the top, that there were two businesses on this floor. Cary headed toward the one on the left. SWEATYOGA, a sign on the door proclaimed. I followed him but saw the door next to it had FREEDOM OF MOVEMENT etched into it, along with a stylized drawing of a girl doing a turn—a dance studio.

We stepped into the yoga studio, and it was suddenly much warmer. I didn't think it was just the contrast from being outside, it felt like the heat had been cranked up. Cary immediately unzipped his bomber jacket, and I did the same with mine.

"Hey," the guy behind the desk said, smiling at Cary, just as the phone rang. "Sorry, just a second."

I pulled off my coat, draped it over my arm, and picked my hair up off my neck. I looked over to see Cary looking at me. I worried that I'd gotten something on my dress and not realized it, but when he looked away a second later, slightly flushed, I suddenly realized that in all our interactions tonight, I'd always been wearing a long coat. I tried to hide my smile as I shook out some of the wrinkles from my skirt, glad that I was wearing one of my best dresses, that Teri had done my makeup for me.

"Sorry," the front desk guy said, hanging up the phone again. "I'll take—" The phone rang again. "Argh," he said. "Just a sec . . ."

"Want me to just bring them into the studio?" Cary asked, and the guy's shoulders slumped with relief.

"Would you?" he asked, as he picked up the phone. "That would be amazing. Thanks so much. SweatYOGA," he said, answering the call.

Cary nodded for me to follow, and we navigated our way around the people standing around in the hallway with their mats, presumably waiting for a class to start. They looked like anyone going to a yoga class, just wearing less clothes than the yoga classes I'd gone to back home. But since this was clearly some kind of hot yoga, I could understand it.

"It's this one," Cary said, opening the door to a studio. He stepped inside, and I followed. I immediately kicked off my ankle boots, then a second later, realized what I was doing. But in all my years dancing, it had been drilled into me, for more than half my life—you *never* enter a studio with street shoes on.

I decided to leave them by the door—I could just put them back on when I left. I took a step into the studio and looked around—wooden floors, mirrors, mat set up at the front of the room, cubbies filled with yoga blocks and props, a small wooden incense burner perfuming the whole space. Cary hadn't hit the lights, but with the moonlight and streetlights shining through the windows, there was more than enough light to see.

"It'll just be a second," Cary said. He opened the Maverick bag and started pulling out a stack of white towels from it. I was about to offer to help him when I heard music wafting in. At first I thought it was music from another yoga class, but after a moment, I realized I knew it. I knew it better, in fact, than almost any other piece of music. After all, I'd heard it for months every year, over and over again, for more than a decade—*The Nutcracker Suite*.

I was baffled by why this was happening until I remembered the dance studio that was also in this building—I must have been hearing it through the walls.

I'd been in *The Nutcracker* every year since I started dancing, working my way from Candy Cane to Mouse to Party Scene Girl and finally Clara, the lead, which I'd danced for two years in a row. I knew this music like I knew nothing else. And what's more, I could hear my steps in them, hear Miss Felicity, the head of my dance school, count-ing them out—*and one and two and give your hand and five and six and then we turn. . . .* I hadn't realized I'd still know them, that they'd been there this whole time. That note meant a pas de bourrée. That one meant a relevé, two jumps and a pirouette. . . .

"This is impressive."

I turned to look at Cary—I hadn't realized I'd started to move. I was just half doing the steps, mostly marking them. "It's *The Nutcracker*," I explained, nodding to where the music was coming from. "I did it every year. I guess I still know my steps."

"I guess so," said Cary, sounding awed. "I know you said something about being a dancer, but I didn't think . . ."

"No," I said, even though as I said it I stepped back into a wide, Balanchine fifth and did a pirouette. It was rusty, but I landed it. I turned to face Cary. "I used to be. But . . ."

"But what?"

"I wasn't good enough," I said bluntly, wondering why this still hurt after four years. "I wasn't going to be able to do it professionally. So I . . . quit." Hearing this out loud, I remembered what Stevie had said to me on the subway platform. That it was always all or nothing with me. And in this case, it had been true—when I couldn't dance at the highest level, I had thrown myself into the next thing. Into theater.

"You still seem really good," Cary said. "Do you miss it?"

Even two hours ago I would have laughed this off, said absolutely not, and meant it. But now I was suddenly thinking about what Cary had said about grape soda and kickball, back in the bodega. About pushing away things we loved when we were younger, for no reason. And the idea that maybe you didn't have to.

"Yeah," I said, hearing the surprise in my voice. "I do."

There was a crescendo in the music—the moment that signaled my solo, and without even knowing I was going to, I was bending backward, sweeping my arm overhead, and starting to dance it full-out.

The room spun all around me as I moved across it, taking up space, and as I danced—as I jumped and turned and balanced on one leg, as I gave myself over to it, I felt the freedom I'd only ever really felt while dancing, the moment when you're not even thinking about the steps—you're just moving. I did a double pirouette and a quick jump. I could hear the steps in my head—*extend your hand and yes I will . . .*

I came to a stop in B plus, one leg tucked behind the other, my arm extended.

"What?" Cary asked, after a moment, taking a step over to me. "Why did you stop? That was great."

"It's—" I was catching my breath and coming back to myself, back to the moment. I knew I should probably be embarrassed, to be dancing in my socks in a yoga studio, but I wasn't, somehow. "That was when the pas de deux started—when my partner came in." I lowered my arm.

"What did he do?" Cary asked. He walked slowly across the studio to me, his eyes on mine.

"Not that much," I said, not looking away. My heart was pounding, and I knew it wasn't just from the jumps. "A turn and then a lift."

"Want me to try?" He closed the distance between us and held out his hand to me, one eyebrow raised slightly.

I placed my hand in his, our fingers fitting together, his thumb rubbing a slow circle on my palm, sending a shower of sparks exploding through me. "So it's just a turn," I said as Cary raised his arm and I spun under it, then extended my leg into an arabesque, feeling his hand gripping mine, steady, supporting me. "And then—a lift that turns . . ."

He put his hands on either side of my waist and lifted me up, and began to walk slowly in a circle, like he had done this a thousand times before, a natural *Nutcracker* prince. And I caught a glimpse of us in the mirror, Cary in his white T-shirt and jeans, looking like something out of an eighties dream, lifting me high in this studio in Manhattan— dancing in the dark.

When we'd come back to where we started, he lowered me down slowly, inch by inch, his hands sliding up my waist until they stopped at my rib cage. "Like that?"

I was still on my toes, taller than him, and I lowered myself down until I was standing on the ground, and we were now the same height.

We were very close together—sharing a dance space, just a breath apart. "That was good."

"I'm glad."

"Yeah." I knew we were saying things, but I wasn't really aware of what they were and I knew they didn't matter. What mattered was that his arms were tightening around me, and that excited, nervous butterflies had started zooming around in my stomach. His hazel eyes were locked on mine, and his hands were still spanning my rib cage, and I was sure he could feel my heart pounding hard underneath.

He leaned closer, and I leaned forward too. My eyes fluttered closed. . . .

BEEP. BEEP. BEEP.

I froze, then opened my eyes and looked around, worried the building had caught fire—it seemed loud enough.

"It's the alarm," Cary said, pulling his phone out of his pocket and silencing it. "For the play."

"Right." I blinked at him. We were still standing so close—I could have reached out my hand and traced his jawline, tangled my fingers in his hair, without even extending my arm. But the moment was slipping away—it was like trying to hold on to water. *"Right,"* I said again, taking a step back. Things were coming into focus again, the fuzzy edges sharpening. "The play. Of course."

"Yeah," Cary said, although he didn't move. Feeling like I had to break the spell, I walked over to the door and concentrated on pulling my boots back on. Cary unloaded the rest of the towels, placed them in an empty cubby, then walked over to join me.

"I should get going," I said, pulling on my coat, trying to get myself to focus. I'd been so concerned about getting to Mr. Campbell's play on time all night; I shouldn't be disappointed that the alarm we'd set to get me there on time had gone off.

"Or you could stay." I looked over at Cary. He'd pulled his brown leather jacket on, and he rocked back on his heels and stuck his hands in his pockets.

"What?"

"I have to keep doing deliveries, but I'll be done in an hour tops, and my next job doesn't start until eleven thirty. We could . . . hang out? Go see a movie. Or cross the bridge to Brooklyn and get the best cheesecake in the whole world. Or the Whitney is open late. Or we could find some music . . . or just walk around. . . ." He gave me a hopeful, nervous smile.

I could practically see it, this New York night he was describing. Walking around with Cary, riding on his scooter, ducking into coffee shops or diners when it got too cold, talking and exploring the city . . .

I shook my head, trying to stop myself before I went too far down this path, however nice it seemed. I was here to see this play. I'd fought with Stevie about this play. I'd come too far to just give up at the last minute. I had to do this—too much was on the line. "I have to see this show."

He eyes were searching mine. "Are you sure?"

I swallowed hard and made myself nod. "Yes."

Hurt passed over his face for just a moment, and then it was gone. He gave me a smile that didn't meet his eyes. "Right," he said. "Of course! So we should get you there on time."

We didn't talk much as we walked back to the scooter, parked on Seventy-Third Street.

Cary got on first, and I took my place behind him, but I put my arms around him for a second, holding him, breathing him in, knowing that our time together was almost over. Cary covered my hand in his, and we both just stayed like that for a moment until he let go of my hand—it now felt much too cold—and started the bike.

The drive seemed to take no time at all, and before I wanted it to, the bike was slowing down. Cary pulled it over to the side of the street, and I looked up and saw that Fifty-First Street was blocked to traffic. He turned and looked back at me. "Tenth is one block over," he said, pointing. "But we can go around if you want. We can go back up to Fifty-Third, then cut down—"

"No. Thank you, though," I said, getting off the bike carefully, avoiding the tailpipe like it was second nature now. I took off my helmet, and Cary cut the engine and stepped off the bike as well. "I can just walk—it'll probably be faster."

Cary took the helmet back from me and rested it on the seat. We looked at each other for just a moment, and it was like all the things we weren't saying were filling up the space between us and making it crackle, like static electricity, the charge you could feel when you got close to it.

"So," I started. I didn't want to say goodbye to him—I didn't want this to end—but I was now also very aware that I needed to get to Tenth Avenue. I hadn't come this far to arrive at Mr. Campbell's play late.

"Here," Cary said. He dug through his messenger bag, and then held out a twenty and a ten to me. "I can't leave you running around the city with a bill no one will break."

"That's really nice of you," I said, taking a step back. "But you already bought me dinner, and all those snacks. . . ."

"The snacks might have been with an ulterior motive," he said. "Maybe I'm just trying to slowly get peanut products off the shelves, where they won't keep coming after me." I smiled. "But seriously," he said, holding out the money to me. "You can pay me back another time. The . . . next time I see you." He said this in an offhand way that let me know just how brave he'd been to say it.

After a moment of silent deliberation, I took the money. Because what if people really wouldn't take this hundred? How was I supposed to buy a train ticket home? "Thank you," I said, folding the bills and pocketing them. "I will pay you back."

I looked at him for a moment longer—at his pushed-back hair, his kind face, his collar slightly askew. I smiled, knowing that there wasn't anything left to do but say goodbye. "Well—it was really nice to meet you, Cary."

He smiled back at me. "You too, Kat."

Knowing that if I didn't leave then, I just might not do it, I gave him a nod and made myself walk away. The light had just turned, so I was able to cross the street with the crowd, and once I'd gotten to the other side, I looked back and saw him, still by his scooter, making sure I made it okay. I lifted my hand in a small wave, and he gave me one back.

I turned around and started walking with purpose down Fifty-First Street, telling myself that it was ridiculous to feel like crying. This was what I'd wanted to do all night—and now I was doing it.

I pulled the hood of my coat up against the wind, which seemed to be picking up. I was trying to concentrate on Mr. Campbell, and the play, and what I should say to him afterward, but my thoughts kept coming back and back, to Cary and his expression when I told him I had to go, the way it had felt with his arms around me, how he'd smiled the tiniest bit before he'd closed his eyes and leaned in to kiss me—

"Kat?" I stopped in my tracks, then spun around, already smiling. Cary would be there like before, out of breath, having run to catch up with me—

But standing there, holding three pizza boxes in his arms, and looking very confused to see me, was Beckett Hughes.

CHAPTER 17
Stevie

Brad!" *I screamed as I* ran alongside the inexplicable group of rollerbladers. My pulse was pounding in my throat, and though my feet still hurt, they'd just been pushed so far down the priority list at the moment, it was like I was barely aware of them. I turned in a circle, desperately searching for any sign of a tiny, fluffy dog. "Come back here!" I yelled, my voice breaking.

"Yeah?" One of the bladers slowed and did a little hop out of the group onto the grass. "I'm Brad."

"Not you," I said as I hurried away. He shrugged and joined the group again. "BRAD!"

"He's up ahead," a woman said cheerfully to me as she bladed past.

"Not him," I said impatiently, picking up my pace. I tried to look across them to the other side of the path, where Matty was. "Anything?" I yelled.

"No," he said, and I caught glimpses of his beanied head in between the bladers. "Bradford Higginbottom!" he yelled.

The final, straggling rollerblader moved on with the group, and it was just Matty and me looking at each other across the path lit by streetlights, his horrified expression reflecting exactly how I felt. "What if we can't find him?" I whispered, the thought making my stomach clench. The park seemed suddenly so vast, and so dangerous . . . there were animals in the park, weren't there? Wasn't there a *zoo*?

"We'll find him," Matty said, his voice determined. He nodded down the path. "We know he went this way. Brad!"

"BRAD!" I yelled, hurrying alongside Matty, searching desperately for any glimpse of his white-and-tan fur. "C'mere, boy!" I turned fully in a circle, my thoughts starting to spiral out of control. This was all my fault. I never should have come into the city tonight—and if I had just stayed home, where I belonged, Brad would be safely in his apartment, not running around, lost, scared. . . .

"Stevie," Matty said, relief in his voice. He nodded down the line of benches, where I could see an older woman sitting on a bench, Brad cuddled in her lap.

"Oh my god," I said, starting to run again, Matty falling into step next to me. We reached the woman—she had Rollerblades on and a tracksuit, and Brad was getting hair all over her, but she didn't seem to mind.

"Hi," Matty said, sounding out of breath as he reached her first. "I see you found our dog."

"He found me," she said with a smile, giving him a scratch behind the ears. "He ran into us on our first loop."

"I didn't realize," Matty said, shaking his head, "that there was a Central Park night rollerblading club."

"There is," she said cheerfully as she tightened her buckles. "Twice a month, rain or shine. You want to join?"

"Uh—maybe," Matty said, but I could tell he was just trying to be polite to the woman who'd rescued Brad. And then a moment later, I realized that I could tell these things about him now. When had that happened?

"We're always looking for people who can roll with us," she said, and then laughed at her own joke. "We're in a fight about names at the moment. We used to be Strawberry Wheels Forever. Then it was Corporate Bladers. Now we're Bladers of the Lost Park. . . ."

"I'll find you," Matty assured her.

"Thank you so much," I said gratefully.

"No problem," she said. She set Brad down on the pavement, then stood up, holding the leash out to Matty—but she lost her balance, one of her Rollerblades shooting out behind her.

"Oh my god!" I lunged forward to catch her and so did Matty, and we managed to steady her before she fell. "Are you okay?"

"Yes," she said, straightening her helmet. "Thank you."

I looked around in alarm as I suddenly realized what was missing. "Where's Brad?"

Matty looked around too, his expression panicked. "There," he said, pointing up the road, where Brad was joyfully running, leash dragging on the ground behind him.

We took off running at the same moment, both of us yelling his name.

"Brad!" I called, trying to make my voice sound authoritative despite the fact that I'd just met him tonight. "Come here!"

"Senator, you turn around *right now*," Matty yelled, doing a much better job of being commanding than I was.

Maybe Brad heard in his voice that Matty was serious, because he stopped and turned to look at us. "Good," I said as we started moving toward him. "Just stay—" But as soon as we got nearly close enough to grab his leash, Brad took off again, weaving around people and bikers and strollers and joggers.

"I think he thinks it's a game," Matty said as we chased after him—and I narrowly avoided plowing into a couple walking with their arms looped around each other.

"Yeah," I said, slightly out of breath. As long as I could see Brad, though, I was feeling less panicky. And Matty was right—Brad only seemed to be running a little ways ahead of us, then waiting for us to reach some unspecified point, and then taking off again. He had a big doggie smile on his face—he clearly thought this was an *excellent* game.

Brad raced up to a truly gigantic St. Bernard being walked by a middle-aged guy with a beard. Brad's tail was wagging wildly, and I hoped maybe he'd be distracted enough by a new friend that we could grab him, but as soon as we got close enough, he gave chase again.

"Your dog needs to be on a leash," the bearded guy said, frowning at us over his glasses.

"He is on a leash," Matty called over his shoulder as we ran after Brad. "We're just not holding it!"

It seemed like Brad was starting to slow down—which was a good thing, because I was getting a serious stitch in my side—when he turned and raced toward a gray stone building. "We can grab him in the castle!" Matty yelled over his shoulder.

"The what?" I called back, then stopped short as I registered what was ahead of me—a structure with turrets and a flag flying from a tall spire, like we'd happened to wander into a fairy tale in the middle of New York. I could see just the back of Matty's beanie as he took the stairs two at a time, and I hustled after him, trying to take it all in. How had I not known there was a castle in the middle of Central Park? Shouldn't it be something people *mentioned* occasionally?

I followed Matty up the stairs. This led into a big, open courtyard, with two pagoda-y roofs on either end. I looked around but didn't see Matty—or Brad—anywhere, so I figured they must have gone inside. There was a narrow, curving stone staircase with a railing to hold on to, and I took the stairs up, hoping that I hadn't missed them out in the courtyard, and that Brad had actually gone in here—that we weren't losing track of him to the point where we might not find him again. But I was trying not to think about that as I came to the top of the staircase and just stared.

I had stepped into a Renaissance dream—arched windows and informational signs in a big, open room. Apparently, this was Belve-dere Castle. There were posters on the wall about the Birds of Central

Park, but I was more concerned about the Brads of Central Park at the moment—and he was nowhere to be seen.

The room opened out onto a wide terrace. People were dotted around it, taking selfies or pictures of the view, and I could see why. From this vantage point, you could see the pond below and the skyline in the distance and Central Park, rolling on for as far as you could see in between.

"Stevie!" I heard Matty shout. His voice sounded muffled—and above me. "Up here!"

I realized that they must be one more level up—I could see from this terrace that there was one level higher. It was with relief that I hurried up another flight of stairs. There was nowhere else to go after this, so we were finally going to get Brad.

I made it to the top and almost crashed into Matty, who was standing in the doorway that led out to another terrace. This one was smaller than the one below it, but it also had a little pagoda-type covering, and absolutely stunning views.

"What?" I asked. "Where's—" But then Matty pointed ahead, onto the terrace, and gave me the *shhh* gesture.

There were two people, a guy and a girl, both of whom looked like they were in their thirties, both carrying bags from Shake Shack. And Brad was standing a few feet beyond the doorway, out of Matty's reach. But I didn't understand why we were waiting here, or why Matty didn't just grab him. I was about to ask this when the guy started talking.

"I wanted to do everything just like on our first date," he said. The girl smiled at him, a little quizzically. "Burgers from Shake Shack, then a walk through the park . . ."

"Our first date was in June," the girl pointed out with a laugh. "It made more sense then."

"I know, but the thing is . . ."

"Matty," I said, shaking my head, "what's—"

But that was when the guy dropped to his knee. He set down his Shake Shack bag and pulled a ring box out of his coat pocket. "Hannah," he said, holding out the box to her, "I love you so much. . . ."

It was then that I noticed that Brad's nose was twitching, and he was zeroing in on the bag with the burgers in it. *"Brad,"* I hissed as quietly as I could, trying to get him to come to me.

"I can't imagine my life without you," the guy was saying as the girl sobbed, managing to look both shocked and joyful.

"Come here," Matty shout-whispered, edging out a step. But Brad just looked at us and started slinking toward the bag, his eyes on the prize. Matty gave me a look that clearly said *oh crap*.

"Will you do me the honor," the guy asked, his voice shaking, his eyes closed, "of being my wife?"

Brad dived for the burgers.

"No!" I snapped.

Brad froze, and the guy's eyes flew open, his expression crestfallen. "No?"

"What?" the girl said, glaring at me. "I didn't say that."

"You did," the guy said, wobbling a little on one knee. "I heard you. Is this because of Keeley?"

"Um," I said, taking a step forward and scooping up Brad, who I could tell was about to lunge at the burgers again. My face was radiating heat; I knew it was bright red. "That was me. So sorry. Really. My—the dog was about to eat your burger, so . . ."

They both glared at me, and I backed away, wanting to get out of this situation as quickly as possible. "But . . . um . . . congratulations! That's so exciting, and yay love. . . ." I practically ran toward the stairs, but I could hear the girl say sharply, "Keeley? What do you mean, *Keeley*, Brian?"

Matty led the way ahead of me as we went down two flights of stairs as fast as we could. I was holding on to Brad tightly, his leash wrapped twice around my hand. When we made it down to the main level, we turned to each other and I clapped my hand over my mouth, hysterical laughter bubbling in the back of my throat. "*Oh* my god."

"My thoughts exactly," Matty said, shaking his head with a guffaw. He looked up toward the highest tower, with the turret—it looked like Brian and his possibly not-fiancée were in the middle of a pretty intense argument. He turned to Brad and held his face in his hands. "No more of that! No more running away and wrecking once-in-a-lifetime moments!" Brad panted happily at him.

"I'm not sure it would have worked out," I said. My heartbeat was only just now returning to a normal level. We had Brad back, and we no longer had to run, both of which were good things. "I mean, what do you think *was* going on with Keeley?"

Matty laughed and glanced down at his phone, then pointed out where we were supposed to go. I kept Brad held firmly in my arms. I wasn't about to put him down and risk him getting away again. He was just going to have to be along for the ride. Not that he seemed to mind—he was looking around from this new vantage point, his nose quivering as he sniffed, occasionally taking the opportunity to lick my face. And once the panic about losing him had fully died out, as if on cue, my feet started screaming at me again.

"How did you know he was going to propose?" I asked, trying not to limp. "You stopped me from going in, but the proposal hadn't even started."

"I worked at Mama's Fish House for a summer," he said with a shrug. "*Everyone* proposes there at sunset. You learn to read the signs. . . . Seriously, what's wrong with your feet?"

I looked from him down at myself and the weird lurching, hopping gait I'd taken on, and realized there was probably no point in pretending anymore. You reach a point with physical pain where it's so bad your sense of dignity goes out the window.

"My shoes are just . . . a little bit painful," I said, in what might have been the understatement of the century. "I might have a blister." *Or five*, I added silently to myself.

"Why didn't you say something?" he asked, looking baffled. "We could have stopped, or taken a car. . . ."

"It was fine," I lied. "I didn't want to bother you."

"But you're in pain."

Hearing it like that—like it was so obvious—made my face get hot. Why hadn't I just told him what I was feeling? Why had I been too afraid to tell him what was going on? As we rounded a bend in the park, though, I realized I knew my answer: because I didn't do that.

Because I *never* did.

"I think we should be getting close," Matty said, glancing down at his phone, and then frowning as he looked ahead. "But that doesn't make any sense, because . . ." He stopped and stepped to the side of the path, and I joined him, running my hand over Brad's floof.

"What?" I asked, looking ahead. Through the trees, I could see a large white building, lit up against the darkness. "This is where we're meeting her?" I asked, stunned. It wasn't—it couldn't be . . .

"Yep," Matty said, shaking his head with a laugh and walking forward.

"But . . . ," I said, hurrying to catch up, still not understanding, as we walked toward the large white building in front of us.

Also known as the Metropolitan Museum of Art.

I'd been to the Met a lot over the years. With my mother, mostly, either on trips into New York specifically to go museuming, or when we were in town to see a show and she just wanted to pop in. She'd also bring me along sometimes for exclusive preview events—one of her perks as the Pearce curator. My grandmother had loved the Frick the best, and my mother preferred the Whitney or the Guggenheim (in New York, that is—her favorite museum anywhere was Crystal Bridges in Arkansas). But although I had a soft spot for MoMA and I loved going to the Neue Galerie to see Klimt's *Woman in Gold* (and eat their café's apple strudel), my favorite museum had always, always been the Met.

There was something about the sweep of it, how epic the collection was. All the centuries and schools and time periods it encompassed in one single building. I'd been there more times than I could count—but until now, I'd never been there at night.

As we walked up to the museum, I smiled as we passed a poster for an upcoming show. *The Early Art of Hugo LaSalle: From Pittsburgh, with Love* was written in a font that was meant to look like graffiti. It wasn't coming to the Met until next month, but I'd heard all about it. My mom had lent them several paintings from the Pearce's collection for it. And apparently, there would even be a section of it devoted to the mystery of *New York Night* number three.

The poster for the show was a blown-up Polaroid of a young-looking Hugo LaSalle. He was standing in front of a small house, an overstuffed suitcase on the steps next to him. In the background, you could see a white moving truck with CARUSO & TASSO painted on it in bright blue letters.

I looked at the image for a moment longer before hobbling faster to catch up with Matty. Something was ringing a faint bell, like this was familiar in some way to me, but I couldn't put my finger on it. Maybe I'd seen this picture before, in one of the many LaSalle books around our house, and just hadn't remembered?

We climbed the stairs to the front entrance—the museum was closed for visitors, but there were still people sitting on the steps, though the fountains on either side had been turned off for the night. I tried not to gape as we walked up to the entrance, but it was hard—it was all lit up, light spilling out from inside the building and lights outside, the white marble columns framing the long red banners that read THE MET, just in case you weren't quite sure you were at the right massive art museum.

Matty had texted Margaux that we were there, and we were brought inside by the security guards and her assistant, a guy named Zephyr who was in his twenties and seemed extremely put-upon.

"Come with me," he said with an irritated sigh, after we'd gone through the metal detector and pulled off our coats. "Margaux did not tell me she was having guests. Like I need more things to handle . . ."

"I don't think we'll be here long," Matty assured him as we stepped into the Great Hall. He looked up, just like I did, and my jaw dropped.

We were practically alone, in my favorite museum, at night. The information desk was empty, and the usual throngs of people were just gone. The wooden benches were empty, the seated pharaoh statue was keeping watch over nobody. I looked up at the vaulted ceilings and skylights, at the vases of flowers, at the darkened members' desk and closed coat check, at all the marble everywhere.

It was like something out of a dream I hadn't even had yet.

"What is *that*?" Zephyr asked, stopping short and frowning at Brad, who gave him a doggie smile.

"That's . . . Brad," I said after a moment.

"Margaux knows about him," Matty added.

"I don't think the *security*," Zephyr mouthed this last word, "is going to let you have a dog in the museum."

"He's an emotional support animal," Matty and I said at the same time, and then I had to bite my lip hard to keep from laughing.

Zephyr shook his head, clearly irritated with both of us, and led the way forward, up the staircase that led to the galleries. I wished he wasn't walking so fast—I wanted to take everything in.

There was a gallery I'd always loved on the first floor that had a lot of gems and jewelry, and I wondered suddenly if there was any way I could break off and just check it out without looking like I was planning a heist. I would have loved to wander through without crowds of people pressing up behind me for a better look. . . .

"This is really something," Matty said, climbing the stairs, and I followed, not as embarrassed by my halting gait now that he knew the reason why and I no longer had to try and hide it.

"I know," I said, looking around, as we walked up the wide, empty marble staircase. If Kat was here, she would have pulled me into doing the dance we'd done on the stairs in *Anything Goes* our sophomore year, I just knew it.

Where was Kat right now? Had she been able to get around okay? Was she regretting the things she'd said to me, like I was regretting what I'd said to her?

We reached the top of the stairs, the huge *Triumph of Marius* looming large ahead of us. Zephyr zipped us through the gallery—there were security guards in every gallery, and one that seemed to be especially assigned to us walking behind me—and I was just trying to see as much as I could, because when was this going to happen again? I wasn't even sure why it was happening now, so there was no way I'd ever be able to re-create it.

We were walking fast, down the hallway that always had photography exhibits displayed, and I wanted to stop, and look at everything I could, but Zephyr was practically running, and I was just doing my best to keep up. I heard Matty ask Zephyr a question about the shoot as we hung a right, and then we were in the part of the museum I knew best, because it had gallery after gallery of impressionists—my favorite.

I was about to ask what Margaux was doing here—styling or shooting—just as we came to a stop in front of a gallery that, unlike the others, was not empty. In the middle of all the Renoirs and Manets and Monets and van Goghs, there was a photo shoot going on. Dressed in what looked vaguely like a school uniform, but was undoubtedly designer, was a model I recognized immediately, as she'd been on magazine covers and national campaigns and seemed to date a roving collection of sad-faced drummers—Kaya, no last name necessary. She was perched on what looked like an instrument case, and sitting next to her was a guy so gorgeous he could only also be a model, resting his elbows on a violin case on his lap and gazing at the camera. There was a photographer circling them, the camera clicking, and lights and round silver discs to bounce light everywhere.

It was a *photo shoot* at the *Met*, and somehow I was there for it. It was so outside my normal Friday night—so beyond what I'd thought tonight would be—that for a moment I just pulled Brad closer to me, drinking it all in, not entirely sure how I'd ended up here.

"Okay, hold," the photographer said, lowering her camera and squinting into the viewfinder. She walked over to where a table had been set up by one of the benches—and a Picasso—with laptops on it, and people were sitting around it, peering at the screens. The models immediately relaxed, and Kaya said something that made the guy laugh. There was something in their clothes and props that looked . . . familiar somehow? Even though I wasn't sure how that was possible.

"Matty?" We both looked over, and from the other side of the room, a brunette stepped forward—Margaux. A second later, she was running over to us in a topknotted blur. She launched herself at Matty, giving him a bear hug, then stepped back and looked at me, smiling in a wide-open way. "Stephanie!" she said. "And Brad, my darling!" She cuddled his face, and Brad turned his head to the side, like he was telling her where she should really be scratching him. "You're here! This is so great."

"It's Stevie," Matty corrected, nodding at me, and Margaux smiled even wider.

"Love it," she said, reaching up and smoothing my hair back. "It suits you." Margaux was a few inches shorter than Matty. She was willowy, with big, dark eyes and a scattering of freckles across her nose. She had perfect blunt bangs, the ones that I knew Kat had been going for but hadn't ever quite achieved. And as usual, she was dressed like a search result for *cool beautiful girl vintage* had just achieved sentience and come to life. And it didn't seem contrived on her either. You actually felt like she'd be dressing this way even if it wasn't in fashion. And that the stuff she wore wasn't from Anthropologie, but had been most likely found in some market in Chefchaouen, which I hadn't even known was a place, let alone a stunningly beautiful one, until I'd seen her there on Instagram last month.

She was wearing a whisper-thin patterned dress, gold flats with a buckle, like a very stylish pilgrim, and had stacks of metal and woven bracelets going up both wrists.

"You might have mentioned you were sending us to the Met," Matty said, arching an eyebrow at her.

Margaux frowned. "I thought I did." She shook her head. "Sorry, today has been crazy. This shoot, then organizing invites for this little get-together I'm throwing tonight . . ."

"This is amazing," I said, finally finding my voice. I gestured to it all—models, clothes, lights, priceless art. "Really truly."

Margaux beamed at me. "You like it?" she asked, her big eyes fixed on mine. "Because it was all my concept, and I had to fight for it in, like, every meeting for the last three months. . . ."

"What's the concept?" Matty asked.

"It's my spin on *From the Mixed-Up Files*," Margaux said, and something clicked into place, like a puzzle piece.

"Yes!" I said, without realizing I was going to. "Sorry—I've been wondering why this all seemed so familiar."

"What's *Mixed-Up Files*?" Matty asked, looking from me to Margaux.

She rolled her eyes at him. "I'll get you a copy. It's a classic. This brother and sister run away to the Met."

"They come in on the train from Connecticut," I said slowly, remembering. I'd always loved that because so few books took place in my state, let alone in suburban commuter towns like ours. "They take the train in together and then have adventures in New York."

"Yes!" Margaux grinned at me. "See, Stevie gets it."

"Margaux?" Zephyr was suddenly back, his tone now a lot more polite. He gestured at the guards in blazers by the doors. "They say the dog is a problem."

"Brad?" she asked, scooping him up from me in one movement, smoothing his fluff down, and kissing him on the head. "He's part of the shoot. Didn't I say? Tell them to take it up with Anna if there's still an issue." Zephyr nodded, then hurried away.

"He's part of the shoot?" Matty raised a skeptical eyebrow.

"Well, maybe he is now," Margaux said, scratching under his chin. "I'm Bradley LePom," she said in an old-timey accent, waving Brad's arm around. "Stick with me, kid. I'm gonna make you a star!" I bit my lip, trying not to laugh, and Margaux shrugged. "It works better if you picture him with a tiny cigar." She smiled at both of us, then tipped her head to the side. "Not that I'm not happy to see you both, but remind me why you're here?"

"You said you had Mallory's keys," Matty prompted. "Stevie got locked out, with Brad. . . ."

Margaux snapped her fingers. "Right! Come with me." She led us out of the gallery and into the area that normally was just the space with a gift shop and bathrooms, water fountains and benches, but had been taken over as a kind of staging area. There were racks and racks of clothes, a curtained-off changing area, hair and makeup stations, a table with drinks and food. It was very impressive, and I was a little bit stunned that Margaux had been the one to make all this happen—that this all stemmed from her idea.

She tucked Brad in the crook of one arm, then picked up a big, soft-looking leather bag with the other. She dug around in it, then emerged triumphantly with a set of keys, an *M* key chain attached to them. She handed them to Matty with a flourish.

"Oh, wow," I said, letting out a long breath. Was this long, strange night finally coming to an end? She could give me the key, I could head back to Mallory's, return the dog, finally get my stuff, and go home. Which was, after all, what I wanted to do.

Right?

"Margs," Matty said, turning the keys over in his hand, "these are *my* keys."

"What?" I asked, all my happy, relieved feelings suddenly crashing down to earth.

"Really?" she asked, taking them back and turning them over. "Huh. I guess I should have labeled them or something." Matty closed his eyes for a moment, like he was summoning patience. "What?" Margaux asked with a shrug. "Blame Mom for naming us all with the same letter." She cuddled Brad's face. "Who's my good boy? Who's my happy dog?"

"So you don't have Mallory's keys," Matty said, in a tone I'd heard Joy use with her, like trying to pin down a butterfly. "Not even at home?"

"No," Margaux said, then paused, like she was remembering something. "You know, I think I *did* have them, but I gave them to Mom. She wanted a set of all of ours, just in case we had an emergency." She looked at us and smiled. "Which is kind of what this is! So good planning on Mom's part, huh?"

"You couldn't have told us this before?" Matty asked.

"Ms. Lampitoc?" A girl wearing overalls, but somehow making them look incredibly chic, approached her timidly. "We're getting questions about the next look. . . ."

"Right," Margaux said, and it was like everything that was dreamy and fuzzy about her fell away. She handed Brad to Matty, then headed over to the farthest rack of clothes, motioning for us to follow. "Look, just call Mom," she said, already flipping through the rack as I hobbled up. "And . . ." She stopped and frowned at me. "What's wrong with your feet?"

"Oh," I said. Matty shot me an *I told you so* look. "I—um—don't think I broke my shoes in enough."

Margaux winced in sympathy. "I have *been there*," she said. "This one time I was in Tulum, and I forgot where I parked my bike . . . or maybe someone stole it." She paused and tilted her head to the side, like this possibility had never occurred to her before. "Huh." She grabbed a long, silky slip dress in red, and then what looked like basically the same dress in champagne, and handed them to the girl in overalls. "Options for Eight A," she said. "There's alternatives if it's clashing with the painting. Let me know."

"Absolutely," the girl said, taking the dresses carefully.

"I'm going to call Mom," Matty said, walking a few steps down the hallway.

"Tell her to come by," Margaux called over her shoulder. "The more the merrier!" The girl in overalls visibly paled when she said this, but Margaux didn't seem to notice. "Come on," she said to me. She paused by the food table and picked out a small bag of regular Ruffles from the basket. "Here," she said, handing it to me with a smile. I took them, a little baffled. "Oh," Margaux said, frowning. "Sorry—I just thought you might be hungry and remembered you liked them. From that time when we were getting snacks at the deli by the apartment?"

I nodded, pressing my lips together, my thoughts spinning.

I had a theory—even though I'd never told anyone, not even Kat—that love was about paying attention. It's the one thing you can't buy or fake or make up for at the last minute. So the things that meant the most to me were the little details that told you someone had been paying attention, memorizing your random preferences, letting you know they cared. It was why it mattered to me when I met my mom for breakfast near the Pearce and she had my favorite scramble waiting for me, just the way I liked it. Why when Kat ordered my drink perfectly at Starbucks, it always made me smile. When Teri brought me a bag of sour peach slices, it was more than just bringing me a snack. It was saying, I see you. I *know* you. Have some candy.

I had just never thought that Margaux would have been one of those people, and I was suddenly ashamed of myself. "Thank you," I said, pulling open the bag. "Want one?"

"Always," Margaux said with a grin. She took a chip, then slung an arm around my shoulder and steered me toward the curtained area. "Let's get you fixed up."

Five minutes later, I was feeling better than I had dreamed was possible. I'd taken off my shoes—and Margaux and the wardrobe assistants behind the curtain had let out gasps of sympathy at the blistery, bloody mess that my feet had become. But even though I knew I should be embarrassed, it was actually just such a relief to get my shoes off and have the pain stop that I didn't really care my feet were horrifying fancy fashion people.

Margaux had jumped into action, getting first aid supplies from the kits she explained came to every shoot with them—Neosporin, Band-Aids, moleskin pads to put over the Band-Aids so they wouldn't rub. It reminded me of when Kat had shown me her dance bag—which she was still holding on to despite the fact that she wasn't still dancing, not that she seemed to like me to point that out.

Once my feet were patched up, Margaux had eyeballed them and procured a pair of flat leather boots for me to wear, made by a designer whose name I recognized but whose shoes I'd never actually seen in person. I tried to protest, but Margaux steamrolled me, giving me a pair of cashmere socks to wear with them, telling me to treat my feet gently for the rest of the night and assuring me they'd look great with my jumpsuit.

She gave me a canvas bag for my terrible heels, even though I was tempted to tell her to just throw them away, and when I'd pulled on the new boots, she stepped back to admire her handiwork. "I think they look awesome."

I nodded and tried to give her a smile, but then had to look away, blinking hard.

She was being so *nice* to me. So was Matty—coming all the way over here with me, trying to help me out. I had never given them any reason to be so kind, I knew with a kind of creeping shame. I had three siblings, and I'd been pushing them away for a year. And where had it gotten me?

Suddenly, I felt so small. Petty and jealous and young.

You stand in your own way. I'd been so furious at Kat when she'd said it. But she was right—this was just one more piece of proof. I could have had a year of inside jokes and text threads and known Brad's secret identities and all about the Raptor. I could have had a year with my family, new and different and unexpected as it was.

But I was here now. And maybe that was enough to start?

"Thank you so much," I said to Margaux. I didn't know how to apologize, to explain all this to her. "I just," I started, my voice choked. "I'm really . . ."

"Oh, no," Margaux said, swooping in to hug me. "Oh, honey. I know, those things can really hurt. But it'll be okay."

"Yeah," I said, running my hand over my face and giving her a watery smile. "I hope so."

"Margaux?" One of the people I had seen at the table with the laptops stuck his head around the curtain. "You're needed."

"Right," she said, all business again, turning to follow him. She glanced back at me and winked. "See you out there."

I hurried after her—I didn't want to give anyone the opportunity to ask what, exactly, I was doing with what I was sure were prohibitively expensive boots. In the hallway, I could see Matty leaning against the wall by a water fountain, one knee bent, talking on the phone, Brad flopped down at his feet. I walked over to join him just as he hung up.

I looked at his expression, trying to see if he'd gotten good news or bad. All at once, it was like whatever spell had been cast by the museum and Margaux was broken, and I was back to reality, focusing on what I had to do. I had to try and get back into Mallory's apartment, and drop off the dog. . . .

Matty smiled at me and held up his phone. "My mom *assures* me the keys are in her office."

"Oh," I said, hope flaring in my chest again, even though I wasn't entirely sure what this meant.

"And if she says they're there, they are. We can trust her. Not like Margaux." He said this last part for Margaux's benefit. She was breezing past, carrying a romper that was supercute, trailed by Zephyr, who was engrossed in his phone.

"Talking about me as usual, I see," she said as she put the romper on a rack. "What did Mom say?"

"She left the keys at her office. She's gone for the night, but she told the guard at the front desk I'll be coming to get them."

"You don't have to do that," I said, shaking my head. I was suddenly aware of just how long Matty had spent with me, when it clearly hadn't been on his agenda. He still had Ukrainian food to eat on the Lower East Side. "I don't want to hijack your whole night."

"Excuse me, his whole night will start at eleven, when my little soiree begins," Margaux said firmly. "He has no night before that."

"Oh, I don't?"

Margaux rolled her eyes and shoved his arm. "You are coming, right? And you, too, Stevie?"

"Coming where?" I asked, just trying to keep up.

"We're having a few people over to the apartment," Margaux said. "I'll text you the address. Things'll be getting started after eleven."

"She broke her phone," Matty reminded Margaux. "I'll write down the address for her on the way to Mom's office."

"I can go by myself," I said. It was my dad's office too, after all—that was how he and Joy had met in the first place—so it wasn't like I was unfamiliar with it. And I realized, with a jolt of happiness, that I could go and see my dad. Even if he was working, I could swing by and say hi. He was going to see that I'd been here from the credit card charge, after all. And even if he was super busy, I could at least get a few minutes with him.

"But the guard is expecting *me*," Matty pointed out. "They're not going to let you into her office without permission."

"You do look untrustworthy," Margaux agreed as she flipped through the racks.

I took a breath to try and convince Matty I could go it alone, but then just let it out when I realized I had nothing to say. My best chance for getting back into Mallory's apartment was to get the keys from Joy's office—which meant I'd have to inconvenience Matty a little bit longer. "Okay," I finally said.

Matty gave me a smile, then picked up Brad so that he was tucked into the crook of his arm. "Say bye, Senator," he said, making Brad's paw wave.

"Actually," Margaux said as she took him back from Matty, looking at the dog appraisingly. "Can I keep him? I really think that I might be able to use him in one of the setups later."

"Really?" I asked. Relief coursed through me, like I'd just taken a cool drink on a hot day. This suddenly seemed the ideal solution, not leaving Brad alone in a dark apartment. The dog wouldn't be by himself, and he'd be with someone who knew and clearly loved him, and who he seemed happy to be with. After having spent all this time with Brad, I was now realizing that this circumstance was the only way I would ever have given him up.

"Do you want to stay with your auntie Margaux?" she asked Brad, as she kissed him on top of his head.

"It won't be a problem with the museum?" I asked.

Margaux shrugged. "If it is, Zephyr can just take him outside until the shoot is over."

"I can what now?" Zephyr asked, not sounding particularly thrilled about this.

"Just as long as Mallory knows that she might not be getting him back," she said, running her hand over his ears like I knew he liked.

"I'm not sure Allison would go for that."

I looked between them, wondering what I'd missed. "Allison?"

"Margaux's girlfriend," Matty said.

Margaux shook her head. "Fiancée."

"Oh my gosh," I said. I was suddenly realizing just how much I didn't know, about either of them, really. But hopefully I'd get the chance to fix that. It seemed like it. "That's great—congr—"

"Since when?" Matty asked, his voice skeptical.

"Well, *technically* she hasn't asked me. But she's going to eventually, and this way it's just a nice subliminal reminder for her." I laughed, and Margaux grinned at me. "But you'll have to meet her, okay, Stevie? Tonight! Or come over and we can all have brunch or something. I can't cook *at all*."

I smiled at her. Suddenly a whole new world—a whole new way to be with my siblings—felt like it was opening up before me. That maybe—unbelievably—it wasn't too late to start over. "Sounds like a plan."

Zephyr's phone beeped and he looked up. "They need the fountain look."

"Right," she said, then pulled me into a tight hug. "See you later?"

I nodded, even though there was no way I would still be in the city three hours from now. And then I looked down at Brad, still in her arms, and realized with a pang that I had to say goodbye to him, too. Even though the problem was being solved—and I knew things would be easier, now that I didn't have a tiny Pomeranian with me—it also suddenly seemed like they would be a lot less fun.

"Bye, buddy," I said, giving him a scratch behind the ears. "Behave yourself, okay?" He panted happily at me, and then nudged my hand, letting me know that he didn't like that I'd stopped, and he'd prefer if I continued petting him. I gave him one more pat, then made myself take a step away.

"Ready?" Matty asked me, and I nodded. Margaux waved at us and made Brad wave too, and then she disappeared back into the gallery.

Matty and I started retracing our steps through the empty, quiet museum. I tried to memorize it all, well aware this was a once-in-a-lifetime opportunity, just trying to appreciate it while I could.

When we reached the grand staircase again, Matty turned to me as he zipped up his jacket. "Next stop midtown?" he asked. "Glamorous, exciting midtown?"

I laughed and pulled my own jacket on. "Let's do it."

Meanwhile, somewhere in upstate New York . . .

THEY DROVE.

They drove on the darkened highway, the exits flashing by, past the gas stations and rest stops.

Parker fell asleep on Teri a few minutes into the drive, curling up against her with her thumb in her mouth. Gilroy glanced over, and something in his expression softened. He shrugged out of his suit jacket and handed it to Teri. Teri draped it over Parker, who sleepily snuggled down into it. Teri gave Gilroy a thank-you smile, but he'd already gone back to focusing on the drive ahead.

After an hour and a half passed, Teri was getting nervous and the kids were getting restless. She had thought *north* meant maybe New Haven or Danbury. Not wherever they currently were, in New York State. And just doing the time math was getting worrisome, because they would also have to drive *back* to Stanwich.

"Can you tell us spy stories?" Daryl asked, leaning as far forward as his seat belt would allow. "Can I see your badge?"

"Afraid not," Gilroy said, shaking his head. "Don't have it on me."

"Why not?" Chris asked, also leaning forward. "I thought CIA agents were always supposed to carry their badges, no matter what."

Some expression Teri couldn't make out passed over Gilroy's face. It was gone just as quickly. "That is true," he said. "But since I was deep undercover, I couldn't risk it being found."

"Oh." Daryl nodded. "That makes sense."

There was a moment of silence in the car. Then Chris shrieked loudly enough that Gilroy jumped, and the car swerved. Parker, not bothered by any of this, continued to snore. "What?" Teri asked, looking toward the back.

"He's on my side," Chris yelled, shoving her brother, who shoved back.

"Am not!"

"Are so!"

"This reminds me of my brother," Gilroy said, and it was like everyone in the car quieted to hear him. "We fought all the time when we were kids. And when we were adults . . ." His voice hardened. "My father thought he should be the one to take over the family business. Even though I was more suited for it and more experienced. And how are you supposed to react when you're passed over like that?"

His words hung in the car. "Well, but it all worked out, right? Because then you joined the CIA. . . ." Teri's voice trailed off.

"Right," Gilroy said. "It worked out in the end." Teri was about to ask how much farther it was they were going, when Gilroy slowed the car down and signaled. "We're here."

Teri looked around. "We are?" She'd never thought about where spies stashed their go bags, but she hadn't expected it to be a rest stop off the highway. This was not the kind she'd stopped at on road trips, big travel plazas with an Auntie Anne's and a Starbucks inside.

This was small, just bathrooms, vending machines, a few flickering lights. It was also deserted. Only one other car in the parking lot.

Teri gave Chris and Daryl all the cash and change she had on her so they could pick out their snacks. They piled out of the car, and Teri handed Gilroy back his suit jacket. She started to join the kids at the vending machine. But then she noticed Gilroy hadn't moved. "You okay?" she asked.

"Fine," Gilroy said, sounding like he was talking himself into something. "Just preparing myself. After all, this is what I trained for. At Quantico." He nodded toward the woods. "I'll just be over there."

Teri was surprised he was going into the woods, but after a moment, it made sense. He probably had stashed his stuff somewhere nobody would ever look twice at. And this rest stop certainly fit that description. "Could you leave the keys?" Teri asked, as she shivered. "I think it's going to be too cold for the kids to wait outside."

Gilroy looked at her and hesitated, a pause stretching on for what Teri thought was a simple request—for a car that wasn't even his. "Oh, sure," he finally said, tossing them to her. "I'll be back soon." He walked around the back of the rest stop, then disappeared from view.

Teri watched him go. Something was bothering her, something in the back of her mind. But she couldn't put her finger on what. . . .

The kids returned, laden with snacks. Parker handed her an open bag of Fritos, and she took it, picking out a chip slowly. Her mind spun. "What's Quantico?" she finally asked.

"It's the FBI training school," Chris said immediately.

"Not the CIA?"

"That's *Langley*," Daryl said patiently.

Parker gave her a pitying smile.

Teri felt a cold sensation in her stomach. "Get in the car," she said. "Keep the doors locked."

The kids didn't argue—maybe something in her expression let them know she was serious. She deputized Chris to be in charge, then headed to where Gilroy had gone, shivering in the November cold.

She'd expected him to be in the woods beyond the rest stop, maybe digging his go bag up. She hadn't expected to hear him talking to someone.

There was a man standing next to him. He was dressed in dark clothing, a head shorter than Gilroy. "These kids think you're in the CIA?" he laughed.

Teri quickly ducked behind the nearest tree.

"I had to do something," Gilroy said. His voice sounded different now—rougher edged, with an accent creeping in around the edges. "I had to get them out of there and get them on my side or they would have phoned the police. And I couldn't have that, not when we're so close to pulling this off."

"And what will you do with them now?"

"I'll take care of them." There was a chilling finality in this answer. Teri forced herself to keep breathing. She wished she hadn't listened to quite so many true-crime podcasts.

"So to business. You have them?" the other man asked.

"Obviously. You have what I want?"

"Show me the ice first."

"Right here," Gilroy said. Then there was a long pause. "I swear they were right here. . . ."

Teri ran. For once in her life, she didn't need to ask someone what she should do.

She ran around the back of the rest stop, back across the parking lot, beeping open the yellow car as she went. She threw herself into the front seat—all the kids were in the back—and started the car with shaking hands.

"What's going on?" Chris asked.

"Where's Gilroy?" Daryl added.

Teri moved the seat up and pulled out of the parking lot as Gilroy ran toward them, fury in his eyes, the other man at his heels.

"Who's that?" Chris asked.

"Put your seat belts on," Teri said. She stepped on the gas as she aimed the car toward the highway, as fast as it would go. She gripped the steering wheel tightly and glanced back at the kids in the rearview mirror. "We're getting out of here."

Beckett?" *I asked, even though* of course it was him. I was just trying to make sense of it. "What are you doing here?"

"I could ask you the same question," he said, taking a step to the side so we wouldn't be in the middle of the sidewalk, and I followed. "Where's Stevie?"

"Oh," I said, stalling as I played with the toggles on my coat. I knew this wasn't going to be like with Cary, where I could just pretend that Stevie and I had gone our separate ways, and not expect any follow-ups. "It's . . . we . . ." I took a shaky breath. "We had a big fight and then we got separated, and I waited and waited but she never came back for me. . . . She just left me behind in the subway." Tears stung my eyes as I finally said these words out loud.

"Wow," Beckett said slowly, rocking back on his heels, adjusting the stack of pizzas in his arms. I noticed now that he was more dressed up than he had been at school, in dark pants and a blue button-down, an open black peacoat over them. For just a minute, like right now, it was like I could see past all my annoyance and anger at him, and there he was—the guy I'd been truly friends with for a year. "But—why were you even with her? I thought she was going into the city to have dinner with her dad."

I shook my head. "Her dad cancelled," I said. Beckett rolled his eyes, like he wasn't surprised by this. "He had to work. So we were going to take the reservation, but then . . ."

"Wait, how are you guys still separated?" Beckett said, frowning. "Why didn't you just call her?"

Just like that, I remembered that Beckett was from the Before Times, a world where everyone had a cell phone and could receive things like calls and texts. "I left my phone back in Stanwich," I said. "And . . . I broke Stevie's phone." I hadn't planned on saying this, but the second the words left my mouth, I knew they were the truth. Why had I been pretending otherwise? Who did that help? I had been taking her phone all night, not even really asking. I'd grabbed for it and sent it flying—this was on me.. "It was my fault. And that kicked off our fight. She left me behind and ended up with Brad. . . ."

"Brad?" Beckett's eyebrows flew up, and there was a touch of jealousy in his voice.

"Mallory's Pomeranian," I explained, but judging by the expression on Beckett's face, this hadn't cleared anything up.

"God." Beckett shook his head, his eyes wide. "You've been having quite a night."

"You can say that again."

"You've been having quite a night." He said it with the exact same intonation, and even though I didn't want to, I smiled. This was the kind of dorky humor I remembered. Before everything had changed.

"What are you doing here?" I asked, looking around. "I thought you were going to your parents' play."

He lifted up the pizzas in his arms. "Just picking some dinner up for the crew. It'll be intermission by the time I'm back. Best pies around."

"Sure," I said. "Well, see you." I gave him a nod and a tight smile and then started to walk away, being as curt with him as I always was. I hadn't gotten more than a few steps, though, before I flashed back to what Stevie had said on the subway—the revelation that the truth of their breakup was not what I'd thought it was, that there was more than an outside chance I'd been a jerk to Beckett for no reason all school year.

I tried to remember the details of when Stevie had shown up at my door in floods of tears. Had she ever actually *told* me that Beckett had dumped her? I didn't think so now—but she'd let me believe it, and let me go on believing it. If that was the case, it was the biggest lie of omission ever.

I turned around and walked back—Beckett was still standing there with his pizzas. "I—actually," I started, then shook my head. I knew I had to be getting to Mr. Campbell's play, but I also didn't want to let any more time go by before fixing this, if I really was in the wrong, like I was afraid I was. "Stevie said something to me earlier. About how you weren't actually to blame for your breakup?" Beckett looked down at the stack of boxes in his arms, not meeting my eye. "I guess I just assumed . . ."

"You know Stevie," Beckett said with a shrug and a sad smile. "She doesn't like to have the hard conversations."

"Yeah," I said, my head spinning. I knew that about Stevie—of *course* I knew it—but I hadn't thought that this had extended to *me*, to not telling me basic truths. "But I'm really sorry." I winced, thinking back to the last few months, how cold I'd been to him, how dismissive. "I thought I was defending my friend. What actually happened?"

Beckett took a breath, like he was going to say something, then shook his head. "If Stevie hasn't told you, I don't think it's my place to."

I nodded. That was fair. And that, I realized, was what Beckett had always been. He was a good guy—he hadn't even called me on the fact that I'd been an asshole to him for months when he wasn't in the wrong. "I should really get going," I said, knowing that I should probably have already been inside the theater by now. I started to walk down the street, and Beckett fell into step next to me.

"Where are you going?"

"Mr. Campbell wrote and directed a play and it's premiering tonight. On Fifty-First."

"But what about Stevie's dinner?"

"What about it?" I asked, turning to him, surprised by the question. "I mean, I don't think she's going to be there. Before we got separated, she said she was going home."

Beckett shook his head. "She wouldn't have left you there. Something must have happened."

For the first time, I let myself consider this possibility, and all its ramifications. "I waited for her," I said, but with less conviction now. "I waited for a really long time. . . ."

"She wouldn't have just left you behind," Beckett insisted. He stopped walking and I stopped too. "This is *Stevie* we're talking about."

"But . . ." I tried to get my head around this. What if something had happened and she had gone back and found that *I* wasn't there? It was all a lot to try and process, at the very moment I had no time to process it. "I'm supposed to go see this play," I said faintly.

"You know she might be waiting for you at Josephine's. She might be sitting there all alone," Beckett said, his eyebrows furrowing.

I swallowed hard at the thought of it. But I'd come too far and gone through too much to back down now. And if this could do it—if I could guarantee I'd get Cordelia—I had to do it.

Didn't I?

For just a moment, I thought about it—about changing direction, going down to the Village instead, being there at Josephine's for Stevie. And we could have dinner together after all, and . . .

I shook my head, trying to stop this fantasy scene from playing out. The probability was, even if she hadn't gone right away, by now she was probably back in Stanwich. And then I'd just be alone at a restaurant I couldn't afford, having missed my chance to impress Mr. Campbell. And then all of this would have been for nothing.

"I have to go," I said again, trying to sound sure about this but utterly failing.

"Okay," he said. He nodded down to his pizzas. "I should go too."

I gave him a small smile. I hoped that maybe—when we were both back in our regular lives—things might be a little better between us now. "I'll see you back home?"

He gave me a half smile. "See you there."

I turned my back on him and started walking fast down Fifty-First Street, my thoughts in a jumble. Had I totally messed up everything tonight? Wrecked it like I'd wrecked my friendship with Beckett? I tried to see tonight from Stevie's perspective. I break her phone—and don't even apologize—and then when she comes back, I'm gone. Was that what had happened? Or was it something else, some other possibility I wasn't considering?

I looked around and saw the Echo Theater up ahead. There wasn't a brightly lit marquee like Broadway. The sign out front was small, and the theater was down a set of steps, in a basement. I knew I should go in—knew that I was already cutting this much too close. But the thought of Stevie, sitting alone at her birthday dinner and hoping I'd be there, was too much for me to take. Could I actually sit through this play, knowing she might be there?

I suddenly remembered the original plan for tonight, and that there was a way to do both.

I could see the play—I was here, after all—but I'd leave at intermission. It would give me enough time to get to Josephine's in case Stevie was waiting there. Because if there was a chance she was there, I couldn't leave her there alone. I couldn't do that to her. And I didn't want to.

I'd leave a note for Mr. Campbell telling him how much I liked it—because of course I would—and then I'd go. And I might not get as much credit as I would have if I'd gotten to stay afterward and talk to him, but it was better than nothing, and it had to help somewhat.

Buoyed by this plan, I took the steps to the theater two at a time. Outside the door was a framed poster I'd seen on the website, and

I thrilled a little as I saw the words *A new play by Brett Campbell* in orange type across the bottom.

I pulled open the door and stepped inside. I'd assumed there would be a box office, that it would look more like the Broadway theaters I was used to, but there was only a small lobby. A bathroom, a threadbare couch, a refreshment stand with paper cups selling wine and sodas. There was a guy behind a card table with a cash box in front of him.

I crossed my fingers that it wasn't sold out as I approached. There were a few people milling around the lobby, but not many—the rest must be inside already.

"Hi," I said, as the guy looked up from his phone. "Are there still tickets for tonight's performance?"

"Um. Yeah," he said. "Fifteen."

"Okay," I said, reaching into my coat, deciding to try one last time. "Can you . . . break a hundred?"

"No," he said flatly, looking at me like I was crazy. "I can't."

"Okay," I said, silently thanking Cary as I pulled out his twenty and handed it over. The guy handed me a five, then pushed a photocopied program—black and white—at me. "Do I . . . get a ticket?" I asked, feeling stupid that I didn't know how this worked.

"Just sit anywhere," the guy said, gesturing toward the theater. He gave a short, humorless laugh. "There's plenty of seats."

"Oh," I said. I wasn't sure what I'd expected, but it wasn't any of this. I told myself that maybe this was like edgy independent theater or something. Like how *Rent* started off-off-Broadway and just grew a huge following, and *Hamilton* started scrappy and small at the Public. "Okay." I walked through the door and blinked.

It was a very small theater—maybe even smaller than our blackbox theater back home. There were sections of seats, a narrow aisle between them, and a small stage without a curtain. Maybe it was the fact that we were in a basement, but I couldn't help feeling a little bit claustrophobic, like the walls were pressing in on me as I took a seat on the aisle, in the middle.

The guy had been telling the truth—this was *not* a very full house. There were only a handful of people in the audience, and what made it worse was that everyone was spread out. If everyone could have grouped together, maybe it would have seemed fuller?

I chose a seat on the aisle, took off my coat, and flipped through the program. My eyes widened as I saw that the play was written by, directed by, and *starring* Brett Campbell. I hadn't realized I was going to see Mr. Campbell act. He directed all our productions, of course, and we all knew that he was writing a novel, and he'd told us how a play of his had won some big award a few years ago. But acting? Aside from the old commercials I'd found online, I'd never seen Mr. Campbell perform.

I had just started to read the description—it took place in South Florida, in 1995—when the lights dimmed. I closed my program and smiled. I was going to get to see, finally, one of Mr. Campbell's productions. I'd have to take mental notes so I could tell Stevie all about it—the better to speculate wildly about what might happen in the second act.

The lights came up, and I settled back in my seat to watch the first half of the play.

CHAPTER 19
Stevie

*T*he law offices of *Genereux*, Meyers, Ennis & Young were in a medium-size building in midtown. I had been here a lot when I was younger—back when I was thrilled to spend time, while my dad was working, in a conference room with a stack of papers, coloring diligently and telling anyone who passed by about the important work that I was doing. When I'd outgrown my coloring phase and moved into middle school, I'd still liked to go to the office—even just doing my homework while I waited for my dad felt somehow exciting. There was something about working in wood-paneled offices, with shelves and shelves of uniform law books all surrounding me, that made doing English or social studies homework seem somehow elevated.

But as we approached the building, and Matty pulled the door open for me, it was hitting me that it had been a while since I'd been there. The lobby was the same as ever—fairly stark, white marble, and a guard behind a desk reading the *Post*.

"Hi," Matty said, giving a winning smile. "I'm here to pick up something from my mom's office. Joy Lampitoc?" The guard just raised an eyebrow at him but didn't say anything. "She said she would call," Matty said after a pause, glancing at me, his expression clearly saying *ruh-roh*. My stomach clenched. Were we, now that we were on the verge of finally getting the keys, going to be stymied at the very last minute?

"Lemme check on that," the guard said, closing the paper and turning away from us as he picked up the phone.

"Welcoming place," Matty said quietly to me.

"Yeah," I said, silently praying that this would all be resolved, and soon. Whatever her flaws, Joy really did seem on top of things—so hopefully this was just a failure to communicate. "I hope I don't have to go through this every day this spring."

Matty frowned at me. "Why would you?"

"Oh—I'm applying for an internship here," I said, standing up a little straighter as I said it.

"Oh?" His expression hadn't become less confused at this explanation.

I nodded. "It would be great to have on my CV. I'm hoping to get into Northwestern, prelaw. Double major in history and political science, then straight to Harvard Law."

Matty looked taken aback by this. "Wow. That's—quite a plan."

"Thanks," I said, giving him a smile, even though I wasn't sure he entirely meant it as a compliment.

"Northwestern, then Harvard for law school," he said slowly. "Isn't that the same thing Stephen did?"

I flexed my toes in my unfamiliar boots and crossed my arms. This was hitting a little too close to what Kat had said in the subway. "Yeah," I said, not liking at all the defensive tone that was coming into my voice. "So?"

"Nothing," he said, holding both hands up. "You just impressed me with your acting tonight. With the Raptor," he added, "not when you were trying to pretend your feet didn't hurt. That was just awful."

I laughed. "Shut up," I said, then immediately wondered if I shouldn't have. Had I just crossed some line?

But Matty just smiled. "You shut up," he said. "It was *bad*."

"What are you studying?" I asked, realizing belatedly—and ashamedly—that I didn't know, because I had never asked. "At Columbia?"

"I'm not sure," he said with a shrug. "I mean," he added, when he must have seen my expression, "I know what classes I'm taking. But I'm not sure to what end yet." He rocked back on his heels. "I want to cast as wide a net as possible—to see what I like. So I'm doing marketing and art history and medieval literature and psychology."

"Wow. That makes—no logical sense at all."

Matty grinned. "Exactly."

"Okay," the guard said, hanging up the phone and facing us again. "Go on up. Seventeenth floor."

"Cheers," Matty said. The guard buzzed open the automatic turnstile security entrance thing and we walked up to the elevator, which was waiting in the lobby. Matty pressed the button for floor seventeen, and then just as the doors started to close, I pressed the button for thirty-eight.

"I'm going go and say hi to my dad," I said. "He's working late, so he'll still be in the office." In the back of my mind, I was secretly hoping that once I was there, he'd realize that he could, in fact, take the hour or so off and come have dinner with me. It wouldn't need to be something fancy like Josephine's. Or I could even pick something up and bring it back to the office, and we could eat together. After what a stressful night it had been, the thought of getting to still have a win— getting to have dinner with my father after all—was too appealing to ignore. I was hoping that he wouldn't be *too* mad about me coming in without permission. I could catch him up on my night—or an edited version of it. Somehow, I knew that he'd like that I'd spent time with Matty and Margaux.

The doors slid open on floor seventeen. "Meet you down in the lobby in ten?" Matty asked as he stepped out.

I nodded as the doors started to slide closed. "See you soon." I figured that if my dad was free to take some time to hang out, I could just run down and get the key from Matty.

When the doors opened on floor thirty-eight, I stepped out, looking around. Even though it was a Friday night, the office was far from deserted. These kinds of hours were one of the things my parents had fought about, even though they tried to keep it from me. As if I wasn't sitting on the top of the stairs, or in the bathroom with the vent that led to their bedroom, straining for every word. As if I couldn't sense that something was wrong. It was a slap in the face, honestly, that they'd tried to keep me in the dark for so long even when we all knew it wasn't working, a horrible farce with stilted lines that we were all performing at the dinner table and on holidays. It was like they were saying they thought so little of me—what I could pick up on, what I could understand. When they finally came out and told me, on vacation in a rented vacation condo in Colorado, there was a big part of it that was a relief. That at least we didn't have to go on pretending any longer.

But they'd argued a *lot* about the hours he worked. My dad telling my mom that he was a partner in a New York firm, that it was an hour for him to come back and forth from Stanwich each day, and if he'd missed dinner with us anyway, it was just easiest to stay in the city so that he could keep working. My mom protesting that he was missing everything, missing things with me, and I'd had to grip my legs hard so I wouldn't jump up, burst in, and promise that he wasn't missing anything, that I was fine, that there was no point in fighting. And it was the worst kind of fight to overhear, since it was the kind that went around and around in circles, the facts of the case never changing. My dad's work was in the city; my mom's was in town. She couldn't change that and neither could he. All they could do, it seemed, was have the same argument over and over again, sometimes dressed up in different clothes, but always the same thing underneath. Until, finally, they'd decided that they'd rather not have it at all anymore. And they'd both walked away.

As I walked into the office, I stopped short—shocked by how

different it looked. The color scheme was different, the font on the sign with the partners' names had been changed, and all the décor was new. Had it really been that long since I'd been here? I knew everything had gotten busier in the last few years—school, rehearsals, my dad's work . . . but I wouldn't have thought it had been that long.

I was hoping his office would be in the same place—back in the corner suite, with windows that looked out onto Fifty-Third. As I got closer, I could practically see it in my mind—what it had always looked like when he worked late on something. And even though it had been a while, I knew what to expect, because it never changed—all the lights in his office blazing, the opera he always played when he needed to keep his energy up. The scattered Coke cans spread out over his desk, the candy bars he would pretend that someone else had left there for some reason he couldn't explain. I felt myself smile as I got closer. He was going to be so surprised to see me. And it had gotten almost impossible to surprise him, now that we didn't live in the same house together, and everything always had to be so scheduled.

As I rounded the corner, I saw his assistant, Carla, looking frazzled, sitting behind her desk, the one just outside my dad's office. She had three stacks of paper in front of her, and she was pulling pages from each of them and sorting them together. "Hello," I said quietly, trying not to disturb her and make her lose track of whatever it was she was doing. But even so, she jumped and looked up at me, her annoyed expression turning confused for just a moment before she smiled.

"Stevie?" she asked, standing up. She shook her head. "Look at you! All grown up."

"Oh," I said, giving her a smile back. I never knew what to say to that. *Thank you?* "It's so good to see you again."

"Likewise. It's been too long," she said, giving my hand a pat.

"I was just going to say hello to my dad," I said as I started to head around her desk.

"Oh, I'm sorry hon," Carla said, sitting back down and glaring at the piles of paper. "He's gone already, I'm afraid."

I paused, blinking at her for a moment. "Gone?" I took a step around the corner and there, sure enough, was my dad's office. But it was dark and quiet, the desk clean—no piles of paper, no soda cans, no *Turandot*. But maybe he was working at home, back in his apartment—

"Yeah, he took off around seven. Said he was going to have dinner with Joy."

I staggered back a step. It felt like someone had just slapped me. "He did?" I finally managed.

"He'll be sorry to have missed you." Carla was back to sorting the papers, not looking up at me. "So are you in the city with friends? Seeing a show or something?"

I swallowed hard. I could feel my eyes brimming with hot tears, and my chest was tightening. It was getting harder to breathe. "Yeah," I said with a tremendous effort that took absolutely every bit of my acting ability. "Yeah, something like that. Good to see you again, Carla."

"You too, hon. Take care," she called.

I turned to walk back to the elevators, my chin quivering wildly, out of control, the way it only ever did when I was crying for real, not stage tears. I kept my eyes on the dark-patterned carpet, trying to keep it together. I just needed to make it down the hall to the elevator. Then I just needed to make it down the elevator. It was how you eat a whale, after all.

But this technique was no longer working, as the reality of the situation crashed over me like a forty-foot wave. My dad had bailed on my birthday dinner. He'd lied to me about it, then gone to have dinner with Joy instead. And the worst part of it was that, deep down, I wasn't actually as shocked by this as I should have been. It had been obvious for years now—that my dad had had other priorities. He had moved on, and I wasn't nearly as important to him as his new family.

I pressed the button for the lobby through a haze of tears, then just prayed for the doors to close without anyone else getting on. I truly felt like I couldn't endure this ride with a cheerful paralegal, no matter how well-meaning. As the doors finally, blessedly closed, I let myself fall apart, sobbing into my hands—big, ugly, openmouthed sobs, the kind that I would never have done onstage.

It was like all my excuses and rationalizations were collapsing before my eyes like a house of cards. This had been going on for *years* now. And I had just let it, happy to take crumbs, never asking for what I wanted or telling my dad how I felt. Because what if I did, what if I told him that I missed him and that he should have come to my play— and it backfired? I barely got to see him as it was, and that was without me getting mad at him.

But, a tiny voice in my head, one that sounded a lot like Kat's, whispered. *Would that really be worse than what you're feeling right now?*

I didn't have an answer for that, but when the elevator passed the eleventh floor, I tried to compose myself. I wiped off my face, took one long, big breath, held it, and then let it out for twice as long.

I'd learned to do this sophomore year, during *A Doll's House*, when, as Nora, I needed to get super emotional and then pretend to be super composed. And it was the same thing now. I could pull this back. I could shake this off. I could walk through the lobby and Matty would never know that anything was wrong.

The elevator doors opened and I stepped out. Matty was standing by the guard's desk, but the second he saw me, his whole expression changed. "Oh my god, what's wrong?"

"Nothing," I said, making myself smile wide at him. His brows were furrowed, and judging by his expression, I had a feeling I was blotchy and puffy—not to mention that what was left of my eye makeup was probably all over my face. "Just allergies, I think."

"Okay," Matty said, clearly not buying this. "Was your dad there?"

"Gone for the night," I said, trying to skim lightly over the words, like skipping a stone over the surface of the water. "His assistant said he was working from home." I didn't want Matty to ask any questions about why he wasn't there—I didn't think I could take it if his expression suddenly turned either pitying or angry on my behalf. "Any luck?"

He grinned at me and held up a set of keys on a leather key chain. "Got 'em."

"No way," I said, just looking at him for a moment before taking them. There had been enough blind alleys tonight that a piece of me had just resigned myself to the fact that I'd never get into Mallory's apartment again. That I'd somehow have to arrange with someone to get my purse later, because the place had suddenly turned as inaccessible as Fort Knox. "Thanks so much," I said, gripping onto the keys as tightly as I'd ever held anything. "I can't believe we got them."

"I'm making, like, eight copies of Mallory's keys whenever she gets back," Matty said. "Because knowing her, with a door like that, this is absolutely going to happen again."

"I can just leave these in the apartment when I go, right?"

"Or maybe with the super? That way she can get them when she comes home. I can text her and let her know that's where they'll be."

"The super," I echoed. I suddenly flashed to Cary, and his sweet smile, and how he hadn't been able to stop looking at Kat. "Can I use your phone again?" I called I CRUISE one more time, and like before, it went right to voice mail. I left yet another message, telling him that I'd gotten a spare set of keys anyway, and he didn't need to bother his uncle.

I handed Matty back his phone. "I don't know how you've been getting around all night without one," he said.

"It hasn't been that bad," I said, almost meaning it.

He smiled at me, checked the time on his phone. "I'd go with you to Mallory's, but . . ."

"You have to go back to the USSR." Matty laughed. "I get it. Say hi to Alyssa and Archie. Thanks for coming all the way over here with me, and for—everything tonight."

"You want to come?"

"It sounds fun, but I think I'm just going to go get my stuff."

"Understandable."

We looked at each other for a moment, like before in his dorm—but this time without the awkward pressure of expectations. Before, there was someone I hadn't known. And now? It was Matty. Somehow, unexpectedly, and against all odds—my brother.

I reached out and gave him a hug, and he gave me one back, picking me up off my feet for a second before putting me down again. "Bye," I said. "Thanks again for everything."

"This isn't *goodbye*," Matty said, shaking his head like the notion was ridiculous. "You're coming to Margaux's later, right? Hang on—let me get you the address." He pulled a receipt out of his wallet, borrowed a pencil from the guard, and scribbled down Margaux's address for me. I took the folded paper and stuck it in my coat pocket. "I'll see you there?"

I just smiled. "Bye, Matty. I'll see you soon."

He grinned back, then pushed open the door, wincing slightly against the cold, putting his head down against it as he fell into step with the thinned-out Midtown crowd.

A second later, I stepped outside myself and looked around. I was twenty blocks away from Mallory's apartment. I could walk there, even though it really was getting colder. There were cabs with lights on flying by, and I realized all of a sudden that I could take one. I had my nineteen dollars in cash, but I no longer had to hoard it, because the rest of my money and my emergency credit card—along with our train tickets and my keys—were at Mallory's, and now I could get back in there. And even if nineteen dollars wasn't enough to get me twenty blocks, it would be enough to get me close.

And that was what I should do.

It made sense. It was what I'd been trying to do all night, after all. Get back to Mallory's. Get my things. No longer be broke and stranded in New York.

And yet . . .

Knowing full well this was a bad idea, I walked to the curb and put my hand up when I saw a yellow cab, the SUV kind, with its white light on. It pulled over, and I got in, slamming the door behind me and taking my nineteen dollars in cash out of my pocket, prepared to watch the meter closely and stop the cab at around fifteen, so I'd have enough for the tip and for all the extra charges I'd never understood but that were always added on.

"Where to?" the cabbie asked, meeting my eyes in the rearview mirror. I looked at the clock on the TV screen playing Taxi TV. It was nine—which meant I could still make it.

And so, I leaned forward and said, "Josephine's. In the Village."

TERI PULLED INTO THE PARKING LOT OF THE BORDERLINE. IT wouldn't have been her first choice—a roadhouse off the highway, a wooden-framed building with neon beer signs in the windows—but she needed a break, had to go to the bathroom, was starving, and her phone was dead. So the roadhouse it was.

She'd been driving for nearly two hours, and most of it blind. As she'd pulled away from the rest stop, all she was thinking about was throwing Gilroy and the other man off their trail. She'd changed highways and interstates at random, just trying to make sure they couldn't be followed. And when she felt sure they'd lost the trail, she'd pulled over and reached for her phone, to try and get directions that would take them home.

All she got was a text message from Ryan Camper, telling her they were over.

Then her phone died.

And while she was pretty sure she was headed the right way, she figured it wouldn't hurt to check. She steered the car into a parking spot, killed the engine, and looked at the kids sleeping in the back-seat.

"Are we home?" Daryl asked as he stretched.

Parker looked around, at the neon signs. She shook her head at her brother.

"Not yet," Teri said. "Quick food and bathroom break. Let's go." As she ushered the kids inside, Teri couldn't help thinking that if this was what it was always like to babysit, it was no wonder Kat had wanted to retire.

The Borderline was a big space, a bar at one end, booths and tables, and an area with a pool table and pinball machines. It was crowded, and loud. It was Friday night, after all.

Teri took the girls into the bathroom after Daryl promised he wouldn't wander off. And after they were done and everyone's hands were washed, she felt like she could finally breathe a little.

Teri saw that Parker's overall straps had gotten crossed in front. She knelt down to help, straightening them. As she did, she brushed against a bulge in the front of Parker's overall pocket. "What's that?" The toddler's eyes went wide and she clamped her hands over it.

"Hand it over," Chris commanded with big-sister authority. Parker sighed, unsnapped the pocket, and handed a small black velvet bag to Teri.

"What is this?" It was heavier than she expected. She pulled it open and blinked in the sudden glare. She was looking at a bag of diamonds that sparkled back at her. "Where . . . did you get these?" Teri asked, feeling faint.

"Whoa," Chris said, leaning down to look as well.

Parker folded her arms and stuck her lip out. So she *was* a magpie after all. "Did you take this from Gilroy's jacket?" Teri asked. Her mouth felt dry.

Parker nodded, with a *what're you gonna do?* shrug.

"You have to stop that," Chris said. "Seriously. I'll tell Mom and Dad."

"Well, we'll see," Teri said quickly. The list of the things the Stones didn't need to know about was large, and ever-expanding, and now included things like their toddler stealing several million in diamonds.

The bathroom door swung open and an older woman walked to the mirror, frowning at her bangs. Teri dropped the bag of diamonds into her purse. "Sorry," Teri said to the woman, deciding to use this opportunity to get some information. "Can you tell me . . . where we are?"

"The Borderline." The woman didn't glance away from her own reflection.

"Right. But—the border of what, exactly? Connecticut?"

The woman looked away from the mirror, then threw back her head and laughed—which was not the reaction Teri had been hoping for. "This is Clayton, New York, honey. On the border of Canada."

"Why are we in Canada?" Chris asked.

"We're not. We're just . . . next to Canada." Teri was reeling. How had this happened?

"And what about the . . ." Chris nodded at the bag of diamonds, then mouthed *bag of diamonds*. "Isn't Gilroy going to come looking for them?"

"I don't think he could have followed us," Teri said, with more confidence than she felt. "Let's find your brother and get some directions."

Daryl was standing by the pool table, looking fascinated. "Can I play, Teri?" he asked as they approached. "It's a C-note buy in with an escalator, double if you run the table."

"I don't know what that means." Teri tried to steer him away.

"Want a translation?"

Teri turned around, frowning at whoever just spoke—but her frown disappeared when she saw him. The boy standing across from her looked around her age. He was tall, with broad shoulders and bright aquamarine eyes. He had a nervous smile, and sandy hair underneath a green baseball cap that read ALBERTA'S GOODS. "Oh," Teri said, smiling. "That's okay."

"Want to stake me?" Daryl asked. "I'll give you a cut."

The guy laughed. "Thanks," he said. "But I'm working, so I probably shouldn't."

"Working as what?" Chris asked.

"I work for my dad's company, delivering supplies. I'm Dustin, by the way. Dustin Alberta."

Teri tried not to swoon at the wonderfulness of this name—streets ahead of *Ryan*. Daryl introduced himself and his sisters. Dustin shook Parker's offered hand gravely, like he was meeting the mayor. "I'm Teri," Teri said, holding her free hand out. "The babysitter."

"Nice to meet you," Dustin said, shaking her hand. The second they touched, her pulse started racing. "Aren't you guys kind of up past your bedtime?"

"It's a long story," Teri said.

"I think it just got longer," Chris said, her voice low, her eyes worried. Teri looked—and saw that Gilroy was standing by the door, scanning the room.

Teri turned away, trying to think what to do. "Okay, we need to find a back entrance or something."

"Everything okay?" Dustin asked, taking a step closer.

"We have to go," Teri said. Her heart was beating double-time. She knew how dangerous Gilroy was. He had a gun, after all. And was willing to lie to children about being a federal employee. "Chris, can you go to the window and see if you can see our car? Slowly."

Chris nodded, walked to the window, and then returned, looking scared. "There was a guy sitting on the hood. Dressed in black."

"He's with Gilroy," Teri said. It was like the walls were closing in. "How are we supposed to get out now?"

"Leave it to me." Dustin's voice was so assured that Teri felt she could trust him. "Come on," he said, as he headed across the room. "I know a back way."

They followed Dustin, Teri keeping a firm grip on Parker, her eyes on the ground. They were nearly to the door when the yell rang out.

"Not so fast, rugrats!" Gilroy yelled. He was hurrying over to them, his face twisted into an ugly expression.

Teri grabbed Daryl and took a shaky breath. She locked eyes with all the kids. *"Run."*

CHAPTER 20

Stevie

The cab's meter was steadily ticking up—and so was my anger.

After my brief cry in the elevator, I was done with sadness. As the ride down to the Village continued, I could feel myself stewing, my resentment building up. *Fine* was the refrain echoing in my mind.

My dad cancelled my birthday dinner with only a few hours' notice? *Fine.*

He lied to me about it and went to dinner with Joy instead? *Fine.*

But that didn't mean I had to take it like I always did. There was a reservation, and a credit card at a restaurant waiting for me. So *fine*. I was going to go and use it and buy the most expensive dinner I possibly could and charge it to his card, and if my dad had a problem with it, he'd actually have to talk to me. He'd actually have to ask me what was going on, see how I was feeling. . . .

I bit my lip hard, because tears were waiting in the wings, in hair and makeup, listening for their cue, ready to jump on at a moment's notice. I took a deep breath and forced them back to the greenroom. I was in control. I was okay. And I didn't have to take this anymore.

The rational part of my brain whispered that this wasn't the best way to handle things—and, really, wouldn't it be better to just go home? But I was done listening to that part. I was always the responsible one, and Kat got to make the big mistakes. Well, not tonight. Tonight I was going just act, for once, and not always be the person cleaning up the messes.

As the cab sped down Sixth Avenue, I looked out the window and caught my reflection in the window. Smudged eye makeup, puffy eyes, hair flying every which way. Not great. And not the way I wanted to show up at the hottest restaurant in New York, even if I was mostly going there for revenge. I pulled my hair up into a knot and used some tinted lip balm I'd found in my inside coat pocket, figuring it was better than nothing.

I glanced at the meter, relieved to see that we were still at ten dollars—still within the realm of what I could afford. I hoped it would be enough to get me close. Even though I felt like I could probably ask people for directions safely—because what were the odds of getting mugged twice in one night? Probably not *that* high, surely?—I'd prefer to be as close to the restaurant as possible.

"All right," the cabdriver said, slowing down. I looked around and saw that we'd pulled to the side of the street. And there, in front of me, was Josephine's. There was no sign—just a small engraved plaque. It was a converted carriage house that I recognized from the paparazzi pictures I'd seen, flashes lighting up whatever celebrity was just trying to make it outside.

"Thanks," I said, handing the driver the fare plus tip. I glanced at the time—9:20. I was even early. I pulled the door open and stepped inside. It had a cozy, old-fashioned feeling, with two fireplaces, dark wood, and décor that made it seem like you'd wandered into a tavern.

"Hi," I said to the hostess standing behind a little podium. "Um—reservation for Sinclair?"

"Sinclair," she said, stretching out the word as she looked down at her iPad. "Ah! Yes, I see it. And we have a card on file for the bill with instructions, lovely. . . ." She frowned down at the iPad for another second, and then glanced up at me with a smile. "It looks like the other party is already here. You can follow me."

Before I even knew what was happening, my coat was being shucked off and whisked away and I was presented with a claim ticket. The hostess turned and started walking briskly through the dining room, and I followed, trying to figure out where my coat had gone, and also, what she was talking about. The other party? I knew it wasn't my dad. And I'd told Matty about the dinner, but none of the details, so it couldn't be him or Margaux. . . .

It was Kat. It had to be.

Relief and happiness rushed though me, all at once. Kat had come through for me after all—I would get to see her, and we'd be together, the balance of the universe restored. She'd remembered the reservation and had taken the chance that I would be here too. It was like I hadn't let myself feel the depth of how much how much I'd missed her all night until now. No doubt she was just ahead, sitting at our table, looking around eagerly and taking mental notes to share with Teri. Of *course* she would be there. And I could tell her about my dad—about what he'd done. . . .

"And here we are," the hostess said, rounding a corner and stopping at a table.

I stared ahead of me, caught off guard. Because Kat wasn't there.

But Beckett was.

PART FOUR
9:25 p.m.–11:11 p.m.

Lloyd: That's farce. That's the theater. That's life.
Belinda: Oh God, Lloyd, you're so deep.
—Michael Frayn, Noises Off

Meanwhile, in Brockville (Ontario) (Canada) . . .

SITTING ON THE COUNTER OF ALBERTA'S GOODS, TERI TURNED HER bottle of water in her hands. She tried to count how many laws she'd broken over the course of the night. She'd brought minors across state lines. Accidentally stolen diamonds. Driven a rental car she hadn't rented. Not to mention illegally crossed a border.

Dustin had brought them all to his father's store. It was the safest place he could think of. This meant, however, that they were now in Canada—which was certainly not where she'd intended to be tonight.

The store was dark and quiet—they'd closed at seven. Dustin explained they were mostly a wholesaler, but they kept a store in front of the warehouse. There were refrigerator cases, shelves of groceries and snacks, and most appealing to Chris and Daryl, a small arcade in the corner.

Dustin had given the kids handfuls of tokens and they'd run off to play. Teri had plugged in her phone to charge, then settled the sleeping Parker onto a few big bags of rice, creating a makeshift bed for her.

And then it was just the two of them, sitting next to each other on the counter.

"Some night, eh?" Dustin asked.

Teri nodded, with a short laugh. "I can't thank you enough for all the help. But I don't want to get you in trouble."

"What was I supposed to do, leave you there?" He shook his head. "I couldn't leave behind the prettiest girl I'd ever seen—" Dustin stopped short, his face turning red. "I mean . . . I was worried about the kids. That's all."

Teri blushed. "Well, I think we're just lucky we ran into you."

"Maybe I'm the lucky one."

Teri looked into his dazzling eyes and her heart beat hard—but for the first time all night, not because something was going terribly wrong. Because something was going right. "I really should figure out a plan," she said, even as she felt a force, like gravity, drawing her closer to Dustin.

"A plan," he echoed, his eyes fixed on hers, the space between them growing smaller and smaller. "We should totally get one of those."

Teri smiled and he brushed her hair back gently. In that moment, it felt like maybe everything tonight—all of it—had happened so that she could be right here, with this boy. And maybe nothing else mattered. She tilted her head to the side, and so did he. They were just a breath apart. She closed her eyes—

BAM BAM BAM!

They both jumped—someone was pounding on the front door. Teri gasped. She squinted through the darkness, thankful the door was locked.

"We're closed," Dustin called as he slid off the counter.

The figure outside paused—then kicked the door so hard wood went flying, and the door came off its hinges.

The figure stepped through what remained of the door. He was tall, mid-thirties, Black, wearing a suit. He glanced back at the mess he'd made and shrugged. "Sorry. I didn't have time to wait around."

"Who are you?" Teri demanded, trying her best to sound brave.

The man reached into his pocket and pulled out a badge, flipping it open. "Damon Gilroy," he said, snapping it closed again. "CIA."

Beckett?" *I asked. I mean,* obviously it was him. But what was he *doing* here? "What are you doing here?"

"Please enjoy your Josephine's experience," the hostess said warmly, clearly choosing to ignore whatever was happening right now, and then hurrying away.

"Hi," Beckett said, standing up slightly and giving me a nervous smile. Our table was a small, circular booth, covered in soft, cracked brown leather. I slid in next to him and he sat down too. I just looked at him for a moment, trying to understand this. "I wasn't sure if you'd be here."

"You weren't sure that *I'd* be here?"

"Well, Kat thought you'd gone back to Stanwich," he said with a shrug. As though this was a normal conversation to be having. Like he always passed along messages from Kat and surprised me in five-star restaurants.

"Kat?" I echoed. Now that she wasn't the person waiting for me at the table, the absence of her was hitting me all over again. It suddenly seemed crazy to think that she would have been here—she'd obviously gone to the play like she'd planned.

"Hi." A smiling, redheaded waiter had appeared in front of us. Like all the waitstaff, he was wearing a denim shirt and black pants, but whereas some of the servers just seemed like maybe they happened to wear this in off the street, something about him suggested this was more like a uniform, a costume he wasn't quite comfortable with just yet. "I'm Todd, and I'll be your waiter tonight. I've just finished my training, but I want you to know you'll be in very good hands. There's no question I can't answer."

I turned to Todd. The vengeance that had brought me down to the Village was suddenly coming back full force. "What's the most expensive nonalcoholic drink you have?"

Todd opened his mouth, then closed it again, and blinked at me. "I—don't think I can answer that question," he said, deflating a little. "Let me just . . . check on that for you." He hurried away.

"*What?*" Beckett asked, staring at me, a smile starting to play around the corner of his mouth.

"Don't worry about it," I said, waving it off. Though it now occurred to me that if there were two of us, we might be able to do more damage. Lobster and steaks and truffles on everything. I didn't exactly like lobster, I wasn't exactly sure what truffles were, and when we'd been together, Beckett had been going through a vegetarian phase, but *who cared?* I could give it all to Todd or something. "What do you mean, Kat said?"

"I ran into her," Beckett said, playing with his silverware, turning the knife and fork over, then crossing them. It was funny, the details about someone you used to know so well that could then get fuzzy and fade away. I'd forgotten, until this moment, how there was some small part of him that always had to be in motion. "On Fifty-First."

"Huh." What was on Fifty-First Street? What had she been doing all night? And since when was she hanging out with Beckett?

"Yeah," he said. "She told me your dad bailed on dinner. And she said that she broke your phone, and you guys got separated—"

"Kat said *she* broke my phone?" I interrupted, dumbfounded. This might have been the biggest revelation of the last few minutes. The whole time I'd known her, nothing was *ever* Kat's fault.

"Yeah, she said she was waiting and waiting for you on the subway platform. She thought you'd left her behind, but I said it had to be a misunderstanding. . . ."

I sat back against the booth. So Kat *hadn't* just taken the opportunity to leave as soon as I'd gotten on the train without her—and she certainly hadn't missed the train on purpose. While I'd been dealing with muggers with fake knives, she'd thought I'd gone on without her. She'd been waiting for me, thinking I'd been the one to leave *her* behind.

So it had all been a misunderstanding—on both our parts. It gave me some hope in terms of us fixing things. I knew we were going to have work to do—we'd have to deal with everything we said during our fight—but things no longer felt quite so dire. There was a tiny bit of light at the end of the tunnel.

Before I could tell Beckett any of this, Todd came hustling back to the table, his face slightly red. "Okay," he said, giving us a nervous smile. "So it seems like the most expensive drinks are our smoothies and juices. However, they're not on the dinner menu. I spoke to Chef to see if she'd make an exception, but—"

"That's okay," I said, shaking my head. I looked at Beckett and smiled, for what felt like the first time in a while. "He'll take a Roy Rogers." Beckett rolled his eyes at me, but smiled. On one of our first dates, he'd ordered this, and I'd had no idea what he was talking about, until he explained to me that he'd been drinking them since he was little. His older sister, Emily, would always order a Shirley Temple, and though he liked them, his six-year-old masculine pride meant he couldn't abide a pink drink. So a waitress had brought him a Roy Rogers—Coke, grenadine, way too many maraschino cherries—and from that moment he was hooked.

"Oh," Todd said, looking a little bit thrown by this reversal. "So no smoothies. And you want a Roy . . ." His voice faded out, a question in it somewhere, and Beckett and I nodded. "Sorry . . . but can I see your ID?"

I stared at Todd. "What for?"

"Seriously," Beckett said, his voice firm. "I get them all the time. I've been getting them since I was a little kid. It's not a big deal." Todd looked from me to Beckett, swallowed hard, then scribbled something on his server pad. "And for you?" he asked me. "Do you want a . . . Roy?"

"She'll take an iced tea," Beckett said slowly, looking at me. "Less ice than normal, but with a lemon squeezed in. Mint if you have it."

Todd hurried away, looking stressed, but I just looked at Beckett—thinking about Kat and my Starbucks and Margaux and Ruffles and now Beckett, who still knew my drink even after how I'd treated him, even after all this time. "You remembered," I said, my voice a little strangled.

"You too."

"You think I'm going to forget your cowboy drink order?" I shook my head. "Never." I looked at him across the table. I was used to seeing Beckett in school, or working in the shop, scattered with a faint layer of sawdust. He didn't look like that now. He was wearing a button-down, in a blue that brought out his eyes, the sleeves rolled up over his forearms. His dark blond hair, which turned curly if he let it grow, was as usual cut short.

I was suddenly flashing back to the last time we'd sat across a table and shared a meal together—just the two of us, not cast and tech crew splitting a pizza before a dress rehearsal. It had been late August, the week before school started again. At the Boxcar Cantina, where I'd broken his heart, and mine, all in one fell swoop.

We were halfway through our meal—enchiladas for me, a huge burrito for him, queso to share—when he'd taken my hand and told me, his voice shaking with nervousness and emotion, that he loved me.

I'd just sat there, my heart pounding, but not with happiness or excitement. Without warning, everything in me was screaming *danger danger danger*. And even though a part of me—a big part—wanted to say it back, because I loved him, of course I did . . . I couldn't do it.

Suddenly, everything that had happened with my parents—the fall-out, the riptide I'd been caught in the middle of—was looming in front of me, there in a booth at my favorite Mexican restaurant. And so even though I knew I was lying, that I was burning down something beautiful, I'd pulled my hand back from his and watched his face fall.

There really is no coming back from that—and we both knew it. When Beckett had said, as the mostly full dishes were cleared by a confused-looking waitress, "So I guess . . . that's it?" I'd just nodded, knowing that as soon as I spoke, I'd start crying and I might not ever stop. And that had been the end.

And then I hadn't even been brave enough to tell Kat what really happened—that we'd broken up because I was scared. Because, like always, I didn't tell people how I actually felt. Because I'd rather walk on bleeding feet than tell someone I was in pain. Because I was willing to let someone I loved slip away because I wasn't brave enough to tell them I loved them, too.

"Why are you trying to order the most expensive thing on the menu?" Beckett asked, bringing me back to the present. He was smiling, but I could hear the real confusion behind this question.

"Well," I said, taking a deep breath, anger starting to bubble up again. It wasn't that it was an unfamiliar feeling. What was unfamiliar was that I wasn't pushing it down, pretending it wasn't happening. "I found out my dad cancelled on me tonight so that he could have dinner with Joy." Hurt shot through me again just speaking these words. "And he lied to me about it. So I said, screw it. Revenge via credit card charges." I tried to sound defiant and rebellious, but I could hear that this sounded petty—and small. But I wasn't about to back down now.

"I mean, normally ordering a ton of food we don't have to pay for would be great," Beckett said with a quick smile, there for just a moment but then disappearing again. "But I'm not sure . . ."

"Well, it's what I'm doing," I said, sitting up straight, hearing the defensive note creep into my voice. I looked around for a menu, to see what the most expensive item they sold here was, but we didn't have any. "You can leave if you want, but that's what I'm doing."

"I don't want to leave," Beckett said, his voice quieter, leaning toward me. "I was just going to say—remember how I told you I ran away when my parents were starting to tech *From the Blue*?" he asked, referring to their play about Edison and Tesla.

"What about it?"

"All I was trying to do was get their attention. But there are better ways to do it."

"I'm not trying to get his attention! I just . . ."

Beckett raised an eyebrow. "Really?" I raised one right back at him, folding my arms across my chest. "Are you still applying to Northwestern? Still want to do prelaw?"

I stared at him. "What . . . does that have to do with anything?"

He gave me a look that let me know that he'd once known everything about me, and what's more, hadn't forgotten it all in the last few months. "Stevie."

I looked down at the table, my thoughts churning. This was what Kat had said during our fight, what Matty had implied in the lobby. I couldn't dismiss it—because deep down I knew it was true. I'd known for a while now that the easiest way to get my dad's attention was to bring up Northwestern, talk to him about going to law school after college, same as him. And then I'd said it enough that it had started to feel true. But was it? Was any of that what I actually wanted?

And why was this the first time I was really asking myself this?

"Well," I finally said, "maybe we can just get the moderately expensive things?"

Beckett laughed and it felt like the air cleared a little, that things became not quite so serious, at least for a little while. "Sounds good."

But my thoughts were still racing, and circling around what, until now, I hadn't wanted to face. But I'd known it was there. It was there every time Kat made an offhand remark about how I should think about doing theater in college, and in the expression on Matty's face tonight when I told him about the internship. I could see it with my mother's frustration that I seemed so locked in. It wasn't new. What was new was that I didn't think I'd be able to deny it any longer.

"Okay!" Todd said, hustling up, carrying two drinks. He set an iced tea with lemon and mint, paper straw, in front of me. I'd expected to see something similar for Beckett, just with cherries instead of a lemon wedge. But instead, he set a martini glass in front of Beckett. It was filled with a dark orange liquid, and there was a twist of orange and a cherry stabbed through with a stick and resting across the top. "Here are your drinks," Todd said. "Iced tea and, um, Roy . . . Are you ready to order?" He looked at our table and seemed to deflate even more. "Menus. Right. Be back in a jiff." He hurried off, and I could hear him mutter under his breath, "Get it *together*, Todd!"

"What is that?" I asked, picking up my glass and taking a drink.

"Maybe this is how they make them here?" Beckett asked, picking up his martini glass carefully, with both hands. "They're usually not this color, though. . . ." He took a big drink, then coughed. "*Not* a Roy Rogers," he said, shaking his head, sounding hoarse. "Like, that is extremely alcoholic. And—not very good."

"What?" I asked, reaching for it and taking a sip. I immediately gagged. "Ugh," I said, pushing it back toward him and taking a long sip of my iced tea as a chaser. "Is that scotch?"

Beckett shrugged. "I don't know—maybe?"

"I think it is," I said with a shudder. At a house party sophomore year, Kat and I had gotten bored and decided to try all the different liquors in the liquor cabinet, so we'd know what they all tasted like. Needless to say, this didn't last particularly long, was a terrible idea, and was also the reason that Kat couldn't go near peach schnapps and even the smell of brandy made me gag. But one sip of the scotch had been enough to let me know I had no interest in having more. "Why would they bring that to you?"

"It's probably a mistake," Beckett said, pushing it away.

"Wait," I said, suddenly remembering why Beckett was even in the city. "How was the play? How are previews going?"

"Well," Beckett said, taking a breath. "There's this one part in the first act that's a little—" He stopped and I noticed that we were being descended upon. A woman in a collared shirt and blazer was approaching. "Hi?" Beckett asked.

"Hello," the woman said in a soft voice, bending down so that she was more at our level. "I'm the manager here at Josephine's."

"Hi," I said, looking from her to Beckett, who seemed as confused as I was. Maybe there was a problem with my dad's card or something?

"May I ask how old you both are?" she asked, looking from me to Beckett.

Suddenly, I got nervous that I wasn't supposed to be there—that we were about to be kicked out. That we were clearly suburban teenagers, and everyone could tell, and we weren't welcome there.

But a second later, I remembered I was eighteen now (in my defense, I'd only been eighteen for a week) and had just as much right to be here as anyone. "I'm eighteen," I said, making myself sit up straighter, starting to channel whoever I'd been when I'd been lying to the Raptor about needing an emotional support animal. *She* wouldn't have taken any guff. "Why?"

"And you?" she asked, turning to Beckett, a note of desperation in her voice, though she was still speaking quietly.

"Seventeen," Beckett said, frowning. "Why?"

"And neither of you are members of the press? Or law enforcement?"

"No," we both said together, exchanging a look. What was *happening* here?

"Just a moment," she said, and hustled away.

"This is getting weird," Beckett said. He took another sip of his drink, then coughed again. "Well, that didn't get any better. But on the bright side, I think I'm drunk now."

"So wait," I said, trying to focus. "What were you saying about the play?"

Beckett started to answer, just as the manager came back again, now flanked by two other servers. Bringing up the rear, and looking mortified, was Todd.

"I'm so sorry," she said as one of the people who'd come with her whisked the martini glass away and replaced it with what actually looked like the drink Beckett had ordered. "One of our . . . waitstaff," she said, turning for a moment to glare at Todd, "mixed up a Roy Rogers and a Rob Roy. And as an apology, and in the hope that you won't mention this to the press or the police or . . . the liquor board . . ." Even in the restaurant's dim lighting, I could see her grow paler. "We'd like to cover your meal, of course, and we're going to be sending over some complimentary appetizers. With our apologies."

I exchanged an incredulous look with Beckett. Just how bad *was* it to serve alcohol to minors? It was probably a good thing that Kat wasn't here. She would have milked this for absolutely all it was worth. "We won't tell anyone," I assured her, and Beckett shook his head.

This woman looked so relieved that her whole posture seemed to change. "Oh, good," she said, nodding a few too many times. "That's— wonderful. Here is my card," she said, taking a creamy piece of card stock and sliding it across the table. "If you would like to visit us another night, please just call and I'll make it happen. And my apologies again. Todd?" she snapped, raising her voice just slightly, and he stepped forward. "Do you have anything to say?"

"Um, sorry," Todd said, looking sincerely miserable. "But they both have Roy in the name, so . . ."

"Thanks, Todd," she said crisply, and he slunk away.

"There is your Roy Rogers," she said to Beckett, gesturing at the drink in front of him. "I'm sorry, again." She gave us a smile, then backed away quickly, the other serious people trailing behind her.

We waited until they had left before I stopped fighting my urge to laugh. "Oh my god."

"Do you think we should have mentioned to her that we still don't have menus?" Beckett asked, taking a sip of his replacement drink. "*Much* better. Sorry your plan to spend all your dad's money was foiled."

I shook my head in mock annoyance. "Everyone wants to buy us dinner tonight, it seems."

"Yeah, I have no compunction about charging the *restaurant* a lot of money," Beckett said with a grin. "Should we push the boat out?"

I smiled back. "Let's." I looked at him for a moment, then took a breath, feeling like it was finally time to talk about the elephant in the room, the one who'd been patiently biding his time in the corner, just waiting for us to finally talk about him. "Why did you come here tonight?" I wasn't sure what I wanted the answer to be. It felt like we were somehow balanced, precariously, on a turning point.

Beckett looked down at his hands, turning the silverware over again. "Because you're my friend," he said, finally looking right at me. "And I didn't want you to be here alone."

I smiled at him, even though it hurt. I could see that he hadn't come because he was trying to get back together, and I saw in his eyes that he no longer had those feelings for me. It was over. If I'd been brave enough back in August, maybe we wouldn't be here. But we were. And I was lucky enough to have him as a friend.

I slid a little closer, until I was right next to him, closer than I'd been in months. Close enough to see how his teeth were just slightly crooked, the birthmark by his ear. I reached out slowly and touched his cheek, knowing it was the last time I'd be able to do it.

I stretched forward and kissed him—a last kiss.

He kissed me back, but I could tell it was the same kind of kiss for him. This wasn't a kiss that was leading to anything. It was a goodbye.

I pulled back and smiled at him. "Thanks for coming tonight."

"Anytime."

"Okay, here we are with your appetizers." The people who'd flanked the manager were back, and were setting out more food than made any sense out on the table—oysters on the half shell and truffle mac and cheese and bruschetta and what looked like some kind of slider. Todd wasn't with them, and I wondered if he'd been exiled away from our table for the night. "We'll be back with the rest," the man setting the sliders down murmured, before backing away.

"The *rest*?" I asked, incredulous.

"We still don't have menus," Beckett called after them, but they were already gone. He shook his head, then turned to me. "Stevie? What do you want?"

I looked at the food—which smelled amazing and was reminding me just how long ago it had been that I'd eaten anything. But as I looked at it, I realized that the answer wasn't anywhere on this table. I hadn't been brave enough to tell Beckett the truth when I needed to, and I didn't want to make the same mistake again. "I want to go talk to my dad," I said slowly, feeling how true it was as I spoke the words.

"Oh," Beckett said, macaroni serving spoon halfway to his plate. He set it down and looked at me. "I meant, like, food-wise."

I laughed. "I know. But—I think I need to talk to him. I think I should have talked to him a long time ago." Beckett nodded, and I knew that whatever I wanted to do—leave him behind with enough food for four, or sit here and hash out the pros and cons—he'd be fine with. And the thought of leaving right then, heading straight to the

Upper West Side, was appealing. But so was the smell of the mac and cheese. I'd waited so long to come here, and all we'd done was get beverages and accidentally cause the restaurant to commit a misdemeanor. "Although maybe," I said, pulling the slider plate toward me, "I'll just have a little bit of this first." Beckett smiled and held out the macaroni spoon to me, and I took it happily.

But when I'd eaten this—free, apparently!—meal, there was only one place I wanted to go.

I was going to talk to my dad. And we were finally going to tell the truth.

CHAPTER 22

Kat

*I*t wasn't until the middle of the second scene that I realized I was in trouble.

Navel Gazing was a play about five college friends who reunite in a Florida beach town after one of their group dies in mysterious circumstances. When an actress came onstage who looked familiar, I flipped through my program, squinting in the darkness to read her bio, trying to figure out what I knew her from.

But I never got to the cast bios, because there, printed on the title page, were the words that sent my heart thudding: *Navel Gazing will be performed without an intermission.*

I stared down at the program, trying not to panic. My whole plan had been built around there being an intermission. How was I supposed to leave and get downtown if there was no intermission? How was this going to work?

I tried to concentrate on the play—I didn't want to miss anything big in case Mr. Campbell wanted to discuss it back home—just hoping that it would be short. Most of the plays I'd seen without intermission were ninety minutes, max. But not all of them. I suddenly remembered watching *Fun Home* with a sippy cup of soda, not realizing until the lights went down that it was over two hours, with no intermission and no reentry. Stupid theater in the round.

But! This was not in the round, and it also wasn't a musical, so surely it wouldn't be longer than ninety minutes. I sat back to watch, all but certain that it would be over soon enough that I could still make it to

Josephine's—and possibly even with enough time to tell Mr. Campbell how good the show was before leaving.

But the more I watched, the more I realized I wouldn't actually be able to tell Mr. Campbell that without lying. Because the play was not good. *At all.*

I spent the first few scenes rationalizing that this was all deliberate, these were choices that were being made, that there would be a payoff for the actors being out of synch with each other, the tone being just a little off. As I sat in my seat, I told myself that surely, it would get better.

It didn't.

Everyone always seemed to be screaming or stating exactly what their feelings were. The jokes didn't land, even though the actors seemed to expect them to, holding a beat too long for laughter that really wasn't coming. And though I was trying not to, I couldn't help but think about what Mr. Campbell would have told us if we'd been putting on a performance like that. Everything was too big, directed toward the audience, nothing internal . . . and maybe, I figured, desperately trying to rationalize, that this had been intended for a larger space. That maybe everything wouldn't have been so overdone if the space had been bigger and they wouldn't have had to indicate so much?

But it just . . . wasn't working, which I didn't understand. This was *Mr. Campbell.* His taste was sacrosanct. He knew *everything* about theater. And if he'd just been acting in someone else's production, or directing a play someone else wrote, I could have put it down to other people's decisions . . . but this was all him. So what did it mean that it was almost unwatchable?

And it just kept *not ending.* I'd never in my life wanted a watch so badly. I had no idea how much time was passing, but when it seemed like at least an hour had passed—and the play really didn't appear to be winding down, since everyone was talking about the police inspector who was going to come investigate the death, and that would be a weird thing to end a play on—it became clear to me that I was just going to have to go.

I knew it wasn't ideal, but I figured I could always write Mr. Campbell an email later and tell him I came to see the play, but I had to leave early, since I had to be somewhere at nine thirty. I slowly gathered up my coat—every crinkle of the fabric sounded like a cannon blast. I wished the theater wasn't so small. The lights started to dim on a scene change, and I knew this was my moment.

I got up and hustled toward the back, ducking low—and crashed into an actor walking down the aisle. I kept my balance, but barely, stumbling back a step. The lights came up a second later and I saw, my stomach plunging, that the person I'd crashed into was Mr. Campbell.

His eyes widened in surprise and recognition and I stepped to the side—but he moved to the same side. I moved to the opposite side, just as he did the same. It was probably only a few seconds but it felt like ages, a terrible dance we were doing, until finally he walked around me and strode down the rest of the aisle and onto the stage, announcing himself as the police inspector everyone had been talking about.

I hesitated for only a moment before I took a seat again, my heart slamming against my ribs, wishing more than anything I could just undo the last thirty seconds. Because even if I'd waited just a little longer, I might have been able to leave. But now? Now that Mr. Campbell had seen me? I had to stay. I had to stay to the end or it would be worse than if I'd never come here at all.

My only desperate thought was that maybe it would end sooner than I thought. Maybe, just maybe, there was still a way out of this.

But the play just continued. Not getting any better, somehow getting worse—it was revealed that the character who'd spent the whole time sitting in the back of the room and not talking to anyone was, in fact, the ghost of the man who'd died. (Since the character's name was

Bank Quo, I really should have picked up on this sooner.) There was a second murder, but then that character showed up as the judge at the end—and I couldn't tell if they'd run out of actors, or if it was supposed to be a metaphor.

But by that point, I didn't care. All I could think about, with every minute ticking by, was that while I was trapped there, watching this bad play, Stevie might be sitting alone at a restaurant.

When it finally ended—it certainly felt like we were pushing beyond two hours—the cast filed out for bows. As the lights went up, I realized with a shock that I had not been the only person who had wanted to leave—there were now more cast members than people in the audience, which made me feel embarrassed, even though I wasn't sure for who.

The second the applause petered out—there hadn't been that much to begin with—I grabbed my coat and bolted for the exit. I could still get down to the Village. I'd be late, but I could still make it. I could show Stevie that I wanted to be there for her; I could explain about trying to leave and bumping into Mr. Campbell. If we could talk about it, it could become something funny as opposed to what it was now, something stressful that was twisting my stomach into knots.

I was already mentally planning out the email I'd write Mr. Campbell, telling him I had to catch a train but it was a great show—something friendly and kind and inoffensive and totally untrue.

I was halfway to the door when I heard my name. "Kat?" I turned around and there was Mr. Campbell walking toward me. He'd changed out of his last costume and was wearing regular clothes—but the kind we never saw him wear. At school, Mr. Campbell was always in button-downs, occasionally a golf shirt if we were rehearsing on a weekend. But now he was wearing jeans that were skinny, and a little too tight. He had a white T-shirt on with a low V, and a scarf looped around his neck. It was a look that one of the Chrises could have pulled off—*maybe*—but on Mr. Campbell it was just kind of embarrassing.

"Hi," I said, giving him a bright smile, wishing I'd moved a little faster. I would have been out the door, walking down Fifty-First Street right now, eyes peeled for a cab. "I hope it's okay I'm here."

"Well," he said, shaking his head with a chuckle, "I had a feeling one of you kids would show up one of these days. What's done is done. I wish you would have asked me first, though." He raised an eyebrow at me and I just stared at him for a moment. Was he saying I was in *trouble*?

"I'm so sorry," I said, and then a second later, it was like I could hear myself echoed back. Why was I apologizing? "So I should—"

"I really was," he said, talking over me, "surprised to see you. And attempting to leave early, no less." He was smiling, but I could tell there was a steeliness underneath his words.

"Oh—no," I lied. "I was just . . . going to the bathroom . . ."

"Listen, I have to debrief with the stage manager and then do notes, but stick around for a moment, would you? I'd love to get your thoughts."

"I—" I took a big breath and half a step toward the door. "I actually have to—"

"Great," he said, giving me a nod and striding away, leaving me standing in the lobby, holding my coat. The rest of the audience—such as it was—was streaming out around me, walking through the exit door and up the stairs to the street, and in that moment I desperately wished I was one of them.

This was all I had wanted —to have a moment to talk to Mr. Campbell, to show him my commitment, to do everything I could to make sure I would get cast as Cordelia. Only a few hours ago, the idea that Mr. Campbell wanted my thoughts would have been the best thing ever. But now . . .

I looked at the door one last time, but I knew I wasn't going to walk through it. Just like I knew I had to watch the rest of the play after he'd seen me, I now had to stay. I couldn't leave once he was expecting me to be waiting for him.

I walked back toward the entrance to the theater, trying to tell myself that Stevie might have gone home hours ago. That maybe she wasn't there alone, and I wasn't letting her down a second time. . . .

The door to the theater was propped open and I peered inside. The cast was sitting on the stage, slumped over their phones.

When we got notes after our performances, we were always laughing and talking, giddy with postshow adrenaline, inside jokes flying fast and free. It was the time when we felt the most like a unit, a team. We'd done a thing together and now the jitters and nerves were behind us—we could just relax and have fun.

But nobody on the stage was even talking to each other.

I saw two actors coming up the aisle and hurried away from the door, pretending to be interested in a framed playbill for *Burn This*.

"He's gonna be pissed," the guy who'd played the first murdered man said to the girl who'd played the main character's ex-wife as they walked through the lobby, both pulling on their jackets.

"I really don't care," she said, lifting her hair up out of her collar. "If he wants us to stay and get his crappy notes on his even crappier play, he needs to actually pay us."

"You have a point," the guy said, holding the exit door for her, letting a gust of cold air blow into the theater before it slammed shut again.

It was shocking to hear anyone talk about Mr. Campbell that way—but I also couldn't blame them. The show had been *so bad* and none of this made sense, and I just wanted to leave . . . which was, unfortunately, the one thing I couldn't do. I took a seat on one of the folding chairs in the lobby, knowing there was nothing to do but wait.

Twenty minutes later—I knew because there was a crooked wall clock in the lobby—Mr. Campbell came out of the theater, his scarf trailing behind him. He smiled when he saw me, then grabbed the folding chair next to me, turning it around to sit backward in it. "The work of a director is never done," he said with a chuckle, and I laughed—not because it was funny but because, I realized, I was supposed to.

"I actually can't stay too long," I said, starting to edge off my seat. "This was just—so fun, but it's getting late, and I have to get a train—"

"But I haven't even heard what you thought of the play! I'd love to get your review." He gave me a smile and folded his arms, nodding for me to commence.

I took a deep breath—I knew exactly what I was supposed to do here. Like it was a character I was playing, I knew what was expected. For me to be gushing and over-the-top; complimentary and awed. Wide-eyed and dazzled.

It was like I could practically see the script flashing in front of me, and there was only one option as to how to play this. It was the same thing, I realized, when he was directing us. You could state an opinion, maybe argue a point or two, but in the end, you were going to play the role how *he* wanted you to play it. And if you fought against it, you didn't get cast next time. Everyone knew it without anyone having to spell it out.

But tonight, this was a gear that I couldn't quite find. The play had been *so* bad, and seeing it had made me miss getting to Stevie. And in light of those things, I couldn't be the Kat who would have lied through her teeth and gushed over it. She suddenly felt like a whole other person. But the longer I wrestled with this, the longer my silence stretched on, which I knew was only making things worse. "It, um," I said, trying desperately to think of something that wouldn't involve me either telling the truth or lying, which was—not surprisingly—a difficult needle to thread. "It reminded me of that really old movie? *The Big Chill*? Have you seen it?"

"I've seen *The Big Chill*," he said, starting to sound annoyed. "And I'm not sure I'd call it *really* old, but . . ." He stopped and shook his head.

The theater door opened and one of the actresses stuck her head out. "Are we cut?" she asked. "Bob needs to get his ferry."

"In a minute!" Mr. Campbell snapped. She rolled her eyes before disappearing and letting the door swing closed. He turned to me, his smile looking very fixed, and I had the distinct feeling that I was suddenly on thin ice. "Kat," he said, raising an eyebrow and folding his arms again. "Did you have any thoughts about the play—about my work—that you want to share?" He looked at me expectantly.

I nodded, trying to prepare myself to do this, to tell him what he wanted to hear. But all at once, the line from *King Lear*—the one that I'd loved right from the very first read—flashed into my head. *I cannot heave my heart into my mouth.* Cordelia couldn't fawn on cue. And neither, it seemed, when it came down to it, could I.

"I just . . . ," I started. I didn't want to be cruel—there was no need to be. But I also wasn't going to lie. And suddenly, in that moment, I was very aware that I shouldn't be asked to. "Maybe it just wasn't for me," I finally said, and Mr. Campbell flushed red, all the way up to his hairline. "Since it's really about adult themes," I continued, trying to stick to the facts as much as possible. "I'm probably not the audience for it."

Mr. Campbell just looked at me for a moment, then shook his head. "No, you're probably not," he said, his voice colder than he'd ever used with me. "There's a reason I don't tell you kids about this."

"Right," I said, giving him a quick smile and preparing to go. "So I should—"

"I mean," he said, with a short laugh, "why am I even asking your opinion anyway? Like you know *anything* about theater? You're a child. And I'm sorry if it wasn't up to your lofty standards, Katrina. But I should have known better than to ask."

I drew in a sharp breath. "I . . . ," I said, and was horrified to hear that my voice was wobbling. "I didn't—"

"Brett!" The actress was back, looking more aggrieved than ever. "Bob needs to *go*—"

"I'll be there in a minute! For fuck's sake!" he yelled. There was silence in the lobby that seemed to expand and reverberate, and I had no idea where I was supposed to be looking.

The actress shook her head and disappeared again, and I stood up. It was not that I'd never heard a teacher swear—we'd studied Mamet, after all—but this was different. This was making me feel like I was seeing a side of this person that I was never supposed to.

"I should go," I whispered, hating that my voice was breaking. Hating that I'd come here at all.

"Yeah," Mr. Campbell said, running his hand through his hair, clearly trying to get himself back under control, his voice dripping with contempt. "You should."

I backed away toward the exit, pushed my way outside, then hurried up the stairs and out into the New York night. It was disorienting—after what had just happened, and the terrible play, to suddenly be back in the bustle of it all.

Tears were stinging my eyes, and I brushed my hand across my face as I walked to the curb.

It was now clear to me that at every turn tonight, I'd done absolutely everything wrong. Cary had wanted to hang out with me, and I'd chosen the play instead of him. I could have gone to the Village and tried to make things right with Stevie, but I'd stayed. And now it was too late—even if she was still at Josephine's, me showing up this late would make everything worse. Which meant I'd missed my chance to try and make things right with her. I had put everything on the line—and for what? For *that* play? It would have been better if I'd never come here at all. I'd wrecked absolutely everything that mattered to me.

Through my haze of tears, I saw a cab coming. I put out my arm, and thankfully it saw me and pulled over.

I got into the backseat and pressed my lips together hard, trying to get my tears under control. I couldn't stop thinking about the contempt on Mr. Campbell's face. About the way those actors hadn't seemed to like each other at all—and how they'd talked about him. About how wrong I'd been about so much . . .

"Where to?" the cabbie asked. I was about to say Grand Central. There was no point in staying in the city any longer—I'd wrecked everything here so thoroughly. I knew I should go there and catch a train.

But suddenly the thought of all that was just too much, and I found myself starting to cry for real, pressing my hand over my eyes. More than anything, in that moment, I just wanted to go home. "Hon," the driver said, a little louder. "I need an address."

"Right," I said, blinking as I realized I could give him one. I dug in the pockets of my coat with shaking hands and pulled out the address that Grady's babysitter had given me. I knew this would lead to me being in trouble, but right now, I no longer cared. "Um—18 Ninth Avenue."

"Got it," the cabbie said, swinging into traffic. He looked in the rear-view mirror, and his eyes met mine for a second before they returned to the road. "What's there?"

I took a big, shaky breath before I answered. "My parents."

The problem with doormen was that they completely ruined the element of surprise. After we'd attacked the appetizers—and Beckett and I realized that the way to get truly great service was to almost cause the establishment to lose their liquor license—I'd headed out. Beckett had offered to go with me for moral support. But I knew that this conversation with my dad was long in coming. And I had to do it myself.

I did find myself wishing, though, as I collected my puffer from the coat check, that I could talk to Kat about all this. Not only because I needed, finally, to tell her the truth. But also because she was always there when important things happened. I always talked them through with her. I wasn't mad anymore; now I was just wishing she was with me, and feeling that something was very off because she was not.

I'd taken a cab to the Upper West Side—Beckett had lent me twenty dollars. I'd promised to Venmo him as soon as I could, but he just gestured to the truffle mac and cheese incredulously and told me we were even.

My dad and Joy lived at Mayfair Towers, an apartment building on Central Park West, right next to the famed Dakota. The doorman on duty had called up to my dad, and from what I could tell of the one-sided conversation, my dad was surprised to hear that I was there, but he must have agreed to let me up, because the doorman put the phone down and nodded at me.

"Twenty-four C," he said, and I wanted to tell him that I knew—

that I'd been there before, that this was my *dad*—but instead, I just thanked him and walked to the elevators with my heart hammering.

I stepped off the elevator on the twenty-fourth floor and paused for a moment in the hallway—carpet, light fixtures every few feet, a table with a mirror right in front of the elevator. Was I really going to be able to do this?

There was a piece of me that was still telling me not to rock the boat. I didn't have to, after all. Not tonight. I could just tell my dad I was in the neighborhood, that I wanted to stop by and tell him hello, and leave it at that. . . .

But I *didn't want to*. Standing there in the hallway, I was aware that this was what I always did. I made things easier for people. I smoothed things over. I kept everything inside until I felt like I was going to explode. And where had it gotten me?

I was just tired of this—of not even letting *myself* feel what I was feeling, needing to push everything away.

I was done living my life that way. I'd been almost-mugged tonight and made friends with college students and taken care of a dog and been to a fancy photo shoot and could have shut down Manhattan's hottest restaurant. I needed to say what I felt. I needed to take up some space.

It was time.

I glanced at my reflection in the hallway mirror, trying to prepare myself. I knew this was going to be more than a little scary—going against everything I'd done up until now, against the way I'd grown up. But it was going to be better this way, I somehow knew. Harder—but in the long run, better.

I exhaled and made myself keep walking down the hall until I got to the apartment at the end, 24C. I knocked, and a second later, the door swung open and there was my dad.

He looked the same as ever, his gray hair carefully parted. Everyone said I looked like my mom, so it was always a little startling when I saw my dad and remembered that I took after him much more—his nose, his ears. And I recognized his expression as one I'd seen on my own face—equal parts happy and guarded. He was wearing dress pants and a black cashmere sweater I didn't recognize. "Hi, pumpkin," he said, using what had always been my nickname. "What's going on?" He leaned out into the hall and looked around. "Is . . . your mother here?"

"No," I said, pushing past him into the apartment. It was so strange for me to see things that had been in our house in Connecticut, part of our lives there, in this two-bedroom on the twenty-fourth floor in Manhattan. Like it was one of those circle-what's-out-of-place puzzles.

"Stephen?" Joy called, coming down the hallway. It looked like she was still wearing her work outfit—a suit with a skirt, all in black. Though she had, I noticed, swapped out her work shoes for a pair of fuzzy slippers, also black. As ever, she looked almost preternaturally composed—her sharp silver bob didn't have a hair out of place. Her eyebrows raised when she saw me. "Stevie, hi," she said, giving me a nod and coming to stand next to my father. "Is everything . . . all right?"

It was like they were both willing me to tell them that things were fine. That this was just an unexpected social visit, but nothing was *really* wrong. Nothing that anyone had to have their night wrecked over. And the part of me that was used to being obliging wanted to go along with it. But I made myself push back. "No," I said, swallowing hard and looking right at my dad. "I need to talk to you."

"I'm going to make some tea," Joy said, demonstrating an excellent grasp of reading the room. She rested her hand on my dad's back for a moment, then beat a hasty retreat into the kitchen.

"Stevie, what is going on?" my dad asked, closing the door and locking it automatically. He never used to do that in Connecticut—you didn't need to lock your doors in Stanwich. I wondered how long it had taken him to get in the habit of doing this in Manhattan. "Where is your mother?"

"She didn't come in," I said, walking down the hallway into the apartment. I had a feeling that if I stayed too near the door, I'd be tempted to just flee when things got hard, and I wanted to take away that possibility.

"You . . . came in by yourself?"

"I came in with Kat."

My dad looked around, as though maybe she was about to materialize. "Then where is Kat?"

"I don't know, actually. We got separated. I haven't seen her for hours."

"Honey," my dad said, walking into the small living room and sitting down on the couch. He shook his head and I noticed in that moment just how tired he looked, his face more lined than I remembered it. Seeing how it was after ten, was probably about to get ready for bed, and having his teenage daughter show up and not be forthcoming probably hadn't been on his agenda tonight. He ran his hand over his face, and his new wedding ring—platinum, not gold—flashed in the lamplight at me for just a moment. "I don't understand."

"Me neither." I took my coat off and set the bag with my heels down at my feet. Not only was I getting hot, but I wanted to let him know I wasn't planning on going anytime soon. I was going to stay here and say what I'd come to say. I sat on the chair across from him and dug my nails into my palms.

I could hear my cue, even though it was a script I'd never seen before. But I could feel that it was coming, knew that at any moment the real scene would begin. And you weren't allowed to avoid a fight scene in a play; I wasn't going to let myself do it here, in this living room, where even though the audience was smaller, the stakes were so much higher.

I took a breath—it was already coming out shaky and I hadn't even started yet. This did not seem like a great beginning.

"Mom had plans with Aunt Eliza tonight, so she couldn't come with me when you cancelled dinner." I had to pause for just a second after saying it, before I could make myself go on. I looked at his face, trying to see if he would flinch or give anything away, but I couldn't see anything. "So Kat and I thought we'd come in and take the reservation."

"Uh-huh." My dad gave me a knowing look. "And did your mother know that you were coming into the city?"

"No," I said, feeling like this was the least of what I was concerned with right now.

"Stephanie Sinclair," my dad said, his voice getting louder and lower, always the first sign I was In Trouble. Normally, this would have scared me, but right now it just made me angrier. He thought that he could still play the father in charge after everything? After what he'd done? "Are you saying—"

"Dad!" I snapped, "let me fucking talk!" I could practically feel him drawing back in surprise. I never raised my voice, especially not to him, and I *never* swore. I was very aware that I was about to wade into uncharted waters and drag him in with me. I closed my eyes for just a second, trying to get my courage up.

Why was this so scary?

I opened my eyes and made myself keep going. "So. Matty and I had to go to the office to get the keys to Mallory's apartment because I got locked out—"

"Wait," my dad said, holding up a hand, sounding baffled. "What do Mateo and Mallory have to do with this?"

"And then," I said, talking over him, knowing that if I stopped for even a second, I'd lose my nerve entirely, "I thought while I was at the law firm I'd go up to your office and say hi. Because you told me you'd be working late." I made myself look right at him. My lower lip started to quiver as I thought about how excited I'd been to see him, how sure that I knew what I would see, because there was no way my father would have lied to me, not about something that important. "But Carla told me the truth—that you weren't working late. You'd left *hours* ago. So you could have dinner with Joy." I was speaking faster now, my voice rising. "And that's how I found out that you lied to me, and that you cancelled my birthday dinner—" My voice broke and I stopped and took a deep breath, trying to get myself together.

My dad shook his head. "Stevie, wait a second. I know you're upset," he said, jumping in when I started to say something. "But listen to me. Around seven tonight, after I spoke to you, we received orders from the judge to remand all the files. There had been an issue with the chain of evidence. So I *had* been working late—until I was legally compelled to stop."

"You—were?"

"And since I assumed you would be coming in with your mother, I didn't think it would be a good idea—or fair to her—to tell you that since I was now free, we would go to dinner instead. So Joy and I went out to eat, because I didn't think that I could have dinner with you any longer."

"Oh."

"I wouldn't have lied to you," my dad said, a half laugh in his voice somewhere, and I could tell how much he wanted to get this conversation back on ground we were both more comfortable with. "But I can understand why you would have been upset by that, honey. Of course I do." He smiled at me, and it was like I could see the door that I was supposed to walk through. The one that let this go, that let us go back to who we'd always been to each other.

But I couldn't do it. I'd come too far tonight to back down now.

"But I believed it," I said, my voice shaky. I looked up at him and saw my dad frown. "When Carla told me. I was upset because I believed it. Because I believed that was something you would do. What does that say?" I could feel hot tears building up, but I just had to keep going—I knew that much. "I just feel," I began, then had to stop and take a breath as the first tears started to hit my cheeks. "That I'm not—that important to you." My dad was shaking his head, about to jump in, but I held my hand up, just like he'd done. "I never see you anymore, but you see Matty and Margaux all the time, and you never come to see me and I tell you it's fine but it's not fine. And you didn't come to see me in my last—last play. And I miss you." Tears were pouring out over my cheeks, and I wiped them away and made myself keep going. "And I'm going to go to college next year and I don't know how often we'll get to see each other and I . . ." It was getting hard to speak, but I took a ragged breath and made myself finish this out. "I just feel like I'm always the last thing on your list. And I hate it."

I swallowed hard and looked up and saw that my dad's eyes were red, that he was looking away and clenching his fist tight as a muscle pulsed in his jaw. "Stevie," he said, his voice crackly. He walked over to me and hugged me tight. I hugged him back, and there was something about this—about being hugged by my dad, which had always meant that things would be okay, somehow—that made me cry even harder, right onto his cashmere sweater, which couldn't have been very good for it.

"I'm so sorry, honey," my dad said, his voice trembling as he ran his hand over my hair. "That I made you feel that way—I'm so, so sorry. I'm going to do better, okay? I promise."

I nodded, and the tears were just falling now; I couldn't stop them if I wanted to. I knew that somewhere, Joy was in the kitchen pretending to make tea, and that we had lots more stuff to figure out. But it felt like—in that moment—we had taken our very first steps toward doing just that.

I *stared out the window* as the cab came to a stop. "Are we here?"

"Yep," the cabdriver said, "18 Ninth Avenue. Gansevoort Hotel." I stared at it, at this huge building, its purple neon columns bright against the night, wondering if I should laugh or cry. This hotel—the place that Stevie and I had talked about when we first came in—was where my parents had been all along.

I paid the driver, mentally thanking Cary for his cash, then walked up to the entrance to the hotel, hoping that it wouldn't be too hard to find wherever this engagement party was. And I was well aware that I was going to be in big, big trouble. But you reach a point where you just want your parents.

I was tired of being scared and being by myself and having to navigate New York City without a phone. I didn't want to think about how I'd hurt my best friend and made a huge mistake when I'd chosen myself over her. I didn't want to see the people who I'd believed in suddenly turn on me and reveal their true selves. I didn't want any of it anymore. It had seemed like such a fun, adult adventure when Stevie and I had headed into the city, but clearly I wasn't able to handle it.

I wanted my mom and dad. I wanted to go home.

And the thought of being able to get into my parents' car and have my dad drive us home over the bridge, heated seats on and NPR playing softly in the background, getting to fall asleep in the backseat, knowing that someone else was navigating and getting me home—all at once, nothing sounded better than that. I was just done. Goodbye to all this.

I walked up to the door, which was pulled open by a doorman in an overcoat, who looked at me a little questioningly. But I just gave him a nod and raised my chin. I was going to act like I belonged, and hopefully it would work.

I looked around the lobby. There were purple chandeliers and lots of white marble surfaces and very high ceilings. There was a check-in desk, and chairs grouped around a fireplace, a mostly filled bar, and a number of truly gorgeous people just kind of lounging around the lobby. Had the hotel hired them to be there? Or did they just appear in New York hotels on Friday nights?

I looked around, wondering who I was supposed to ask. I had thought there might be a sign, or something directing me to the engagement party. I realized a moment later that I didn't even know who it was for. My mom's colleague Sarah's daughter, I knew that much, but that did not seem to be a huge amount to go on, especially if I was trying to pretend I was friends with the couple, and invited. Was I supposed to say I was there for the party of "daughter of Sarah" like we were in biblical times? As a last resort, I figured I could always throw a fit at the check-in desk, tell them I was alone in New York and demand they contact my parents. It would be embarrassing, but I was nearing the point where I no longer cared.

I noticed a woman, all in black, sitting behind a desk, who looked like someone I could ask. The whole lighting scheme of the hotel seemed to be set to *dim*, so maybe it wasn't that surprising it took me a minute to spot her. "Hi," I said, walking up to her, trying to look like I knew what I was talking about and wasn't grasping wildly at straws. "The engagement party is . . . ?"

She looked at me for a moment, like she was assessing something, then gestured down the hallway. "Second event room," she said, then added, "Invitations checked at the door."

"Wonderful!" I said, and patted my pocket, like I was indicating that was where mine was. She just raised an eyebrow at me, and I hurried down the hall where she'd pointed. The hall led to another room that also seemed lobby-like, though smaller, with another fireplace, an elevator guarded by a guy wearing an earpiece and carrying a clipboard, and little groupings of armchairs. So that . . . you could rest before getting on the elevator? In case your walk from the other hallway had been too taxing?

I didn't know where the event rooms were, but they couldn't have been far; this was New York, after all, and real estate was at a premium. I was looking around, trying to figure out if I should ask the intimidating guy with his clipboard, just as the elevator doors opened.

And Amy Curry walked out.

I froze where I was standing and gaped at her. It was truly jarring—this girl, who I'd read so much about in magazines, and seen on the big screen, whose pictures in our theater lobby I'd stared at until I had them memorized—suddenly, here she was, in front of me, an actual person.

And of course it made sense—her movie's after-party was here tonight. But I'd never thought I would actually *see* her, just standing here in the lobby, not going out though some special celebrity exit. She was with her boyfriend—I recognized him from red carpet pictures and blurry paparazzi shots. They took a step away from the elevator, walking toward the armchairs, discussing something. I realized it was probably a good thing, in that moment, that I didn't have my phone. Because I wasn't sure that I would have been able to stop myself from taking pictures, or FaceTiming Teri and walking past a lot, faux-casually, so that she could see Amy in the background. She was even prettier in person, her bright red hair a little more auburn than the last pictures I'd seen, and flowing in soft waves down her back. She was wearing a short, long-sleeved dress, blue-and-white stripe, but when she moved, you could see the stripes were sequins. She had paired this with tall, flat white boots, and the whole effect was somehow both modern and sixties and I wanted to try and re-create it immediately. Her boyfriend was tall and blond and broad-shouldered. He was wearing a suit and a collared shirt with a blue gingham pattern on it, no tie.

I thought I was being subtle about looking, but apparently not, because the guy said something to Amy, and then they both looked at me.

My eyes went wide and I took a step backward. What was I supposed to do? Apologize for staring? Pretend that I'd been looking at someone else? Amy Curry gave me a smile and a half nod, like she was saying it was okay, and I gave her a relieved smile back.

And then, in that moment, I realized that I didn't have anything to lose. I was going to be grounded for the foreseeable future anyway; I might as well embarrass myself in front of a movie star. I took a deep breath and hurried up to them before I could realize that I was about to make a huge mistake and stop myself. "Um—Ms. Curry?" I asked, when I was still standing a few feet away. Nobody liked having their personal space invaded, and I was sure this was doubly true for famous people. "I'm so sorry to bother you—both of you. I just wanted to say that I'm a huge, huge fan."

She smiled at that, and she was even more gorgeous up close, her teeth impossibly white. Her eye makeup was smoky and iridescent— how was that possible?—with liner that winged out so precisely I figured there must have been a protractor involved. "Thank you so much," she said. "That's really nice of you."

"I actually go to Stanwich High—it's where you went? For a year?" The second I said this, I regretted it. People generally didn't need to be reminded of their biography. "Which you know," I said, my face getting hot. "And I just wanted to say that—the fact that you were in the theater department too, and you made it, makes me feel like . . . like . . ." I lost my train of thought, and most of my words then, and just finished with a helpless shrug. How did famous people have conversations? Did every interaction break down like this when the person they were talking to realized they were famous and ceased to have the ability to construct sentences?

"Stanwich!" Amy exclaimed. "That's amazing." She whacked the arm of her boyfriend—his attention had been wandering, and he'd been looking around the room. "Luce, she goes to my old high school."

"In California?" he asked, in a honeyed Southern accent that was a little bit startling to hear in the middle of New York City.

"No, in Connecticut," she said, and rolled her eyes at me with a smile, like we were in on this together, like we were sharing a joke. I was about to explode with happiness. How was this *happening*?

"Oh well, that's cool," he said, giving me a quick smile that seemed friendly, just distracted. "Small world, huh?"

"And you said you do theater too?" she asked sounding genuinely interested. Interested! In *me*!

I nodded. "Yeah, it's pretty much all I do. Under Mr. Campbell." She frowned, like she was trying to place the name. "He . . . runs the theater department?" I prompted, speaking slowly. But surely she knew that—if she'd been keeping in contact with him and asking him for notes on audition tapes?

"Oh god, that guy," she said, rolling her eyes. "Man. I haven't thought about him in years. Is he still such a douche?"

I just stared at her for a second, my thoughts whirling. It probably should have been obvious to me before tonight, but clearly Mr. Campbell was a liar, pretending to be in touch with Amy when he wasn't, for the purpose of impressing his students. And also, that this was a spot-on description of Mr. Campbell, even though I hadn't let myself see it until half an hour ago.

"Why was he a douche?" Amy's boyfriend asked.

"I mean," Amy said, running her hand through her hair. That was when I noticed a *truly* massive diamond on her left hand, winking at me in the low light. "He was just a director, you know the type. But worse, because he didn't actually have any power and was taking it out on the kids by playing all these weird mind games. And it's like, you get enough of that in the real world. You shouldn't have it in high school. But maybe he's changed?" She looked at me with a kind smile, giving me an out if I wanted to take it.

"No," I said slowly. A lot of things were suddenly starting to come into sharp relief. The way he'd keep us on edge, always jockeying for his attention. The way we were constantly required to prove our loyalty. All the dues you had to pay, and sometimes even that wasn't enough. The vindictiveness if you stepped out of line. All the behavior that we'd just accepted—to hear someone name it and point out that it wasn't okay was making me see things clearly, for the first time in four years. "No, he's . . . the same still."

Amy shook her head. "Well, it seems like you have a good perspective on it, at any rate, which was more than I did. I'm Amy, by the way," she said, holding out her hand to me, and then laughing. "Which you know! But it always feels weird not to introduce myself."

"I'm Kat," I said, still not quite able to believe it was happening as we shook hands. I couldn't help but wish that this hotel was more like the White House, or Disneyland, with photographers around to take a picture of your handshake moment.

"Lucien Armstrong," her boyfriend—fiancé, apparently?—said, shaking hands with me too. His hand was massive, and practically closed over mine, and I saw he was wearing a thick gold class ring with a blue stone in the center. Maybe he'd been feeling left out and wanted a ring as large as his fiancée's.

"Are you here for an event or something?" Amy asked, looking around.

"No, I was just . . . um . . . ," I said, then paused. All at once, I was no longer so sure that I actually wanted to find my parents after all. Which now meant that I'd gone, quite quickly, from trying to find them to hoping they didn't see me, like I'd just rapidly switched sides in hide-and-seek.

"Well," she said, after it became clear to all of us that I was apparently ending that sentence there. "We were here for a party, but it was kind of . . ."

"It was on the roof!" Lucien jumped in, sounding horrified. "In November! It's gonna snow!"

"It's not going to snow," Amy said, smiling as she shook her head. "He's from Kentucky."

"What does that have to do with anything?" he asked, sounding so comically offended that I laughed.

"So we're going to find something else to do," she said, patting his arm. "Something less . . . Hollywood."

"What about that loft party?" he asked, rocking back on his heels. "The one that producer was talking about? It sounded so cool."

"The one in Dumbo?" she asked. He nodded. "We didn't get an invite, honey. You had to be notified where to wait for a pay phone to ring, and then when you answered you'd get a password, too . . . apparently, it's a whole thing."

I looked between them, my mind suddenly racing, pieces of a puzzle snapping together. I flashed back to the message I'd heard on the pay phone, and the uber-hip couple behind me who'd been waiting for something. Had I accidentally gotten their invite? It couldn't be . . . but then again, what else *could* it be?

"I think . . . ," I started. There was a pen lying on a side table, and I picked it up and pulled the piece of paper with the Gansevoort's address out of my pocket. I closed my eyes and tried to remember, not caring for the moment if the movie star and her fiancé thought I was being weird.

I tried to pull it up—the woman's voice, its low timbre . . . what exactly had she said? *Elephant*, I wrote, starting with what I was sure about. *Pilgrim. 113. Alaska? Daedalus??*

I turned to look at Amy and Lucien, who both had slightly frozen, concerned looks on their faces. "I think I got one of those invites." I held out the paper to them, then immediately felt embarrassed about my scrawly handwriting. They were probably used to getting fancy invitations on beautiful stationery.

"You did?" Amy asked, sounding surprised.

"I answered the wrong pay phone," I said, and she laughed.

"What is this?" Lucien asked, frowning at the paper. "Elephant—is this at the zoo?"

"No, it's Dumbo," Amy said.

"Then what's Pilgrim?" I asked, bending over to look at it too.

Amy snapped her fingers. "Plymouth Street," she said. "Has to be. And Alaska . . . maybe it means Anchorage Place? I'm pretty sure it intersects with Plymouth. And 113 must be the address."

"You're welcome to use it." The second I offered this, I very much hoped that this *was* actually a party, and not like a front for black-market organ harvesters, or anything.

Amy shook her head and pulled out her phone. The case was a picture of two dogs squinting in the sun, one little, one massive. "I'll take a picture of it," she said, snapping one, and then handing the paper back to me. "In case you want to go too."

"Wait," Lucien said, looking alarmed. "We're just . . . going to Brooklyn? Just like that?"

"You were the one who wanted to go," Amy reminded him with a laugh. "I trust Kat. It'll be an adventure."

I tried not to smile as wide as I was feeling when Amy said that, but I don't think I pulled it off, and she gave me a tiny wink.

"Can we get something to eat, though, first?" Lucien asked, slinging his arm around her.

"Okay, we'll get food." Amy laughed and turned to me, just as her phone rang, her ringtone an old Elvis song. Her face lit up as she looked at it. She held the phone up to Lucien, who nodded. "I have to take this," she said to me with a smile. "But it was so nice to meet you, Kat." She turned and walked farther away, then answered the call by shrieking joyfully into the phone. "Agh! Hi hi hi! We finally get to talk! I miss you!"

Lucien smiled at me, shaking his head. "Her best friend," he explained. "They're usually on the phone for two hours minimum. So I don't think I'm getting any food." He suddenly brightened. "Do you think you can get room service delivered even if you don't have a room?"

I shrugged. I was still watching Amy, who looked lit up from the inside, smiling and then letting out a guffaw of laughter that practically had her bent double. Her best friend . . . all at once, I realized that I wasn't out of options. I still had one more thing to try, one more chance to take.

"So," Lucien said, and I tried to focus back on him. "Are you staying around here, or . . . ?"

"No," I said, making a decision. And one that meant that I needed to get out of here, and fast, before I was accidentally seen by my parents. "I have to go to Grand Central. I'm meeting a friend."

The car pulled to a stop in front of the apartment building in Murray Hill. "This it?" the driver asked, turning around to look at me, and I nodded. My dad had insisted on getting me a car service to take me home to Connecticut. I'd used them sometimes with him, or when my mom and I went to the airport, but I'd never been in one before, just me. The driver looked like he was in his mid-twenties, and cute, with dark hair sharply parted. He was wearing a suit and seemed to be taking his job very seriously. He'd already called me *ma'am* three times, and the drive hadn't been all that long.

"Yeah," I said, unbuckling my seat belt and reaching for the door handle. "You're—it's okay for you to wait, right?"

"Of course, ma'am," he said easily. "Take as much time as you need."

I nodded at him. "Okay, I'll be right back." I opened the car door, then stepped out onto Thirty-Seventh Street, looking up at Mallory's brownstone.

After my dad and I had talked, he'd gone into his room for about ten minutes, while Joy poured me a glass of mint tea and showed me pictures from their most recent antiquing trip and I pretended to be interested in Vermont. Joy was never going to be my favorite person, but maybe she didn't have to be. She was horrified when she learned what Mallory had done, and had left her daughter a voice mail that made me resolve never to get on her bad side. But I knew that she was also getting mad on my behalf, which secretly made me feel good.

When my dad came back, he was holding his calendar, and his eyes were red, something neither of us mentioned as we sat down with our schedules and figured it out—specific times that we could spend together. I told him I didn't mind if some of our time was with Matty or Margaux (or Mallory, too, though this was less appealing to me. Though I did want to see Brad again, and if that was how it had to happen, I could accept those terms), but I wanted some time with just him—and it seemed he wanted the same thing.

It took a little bit of negotiating, but soon the two of us had worked out our schedules for the next few months—the ironclad dates we would see each other, when my dad would come to Connecticut, when I would take the train into New York. He told me that his first priority was a do-over of my birthday dinner, and that was when I'd been able to tell him, like it was no big deal, that I knew the general manager at Josephine's. I slid her card across to him, mentioning casually that I could get a reservation whenever we wanted, and was rewarded when my dad's eyebrows flew up. Before I could explain, Joy yawned behind her hand, which was when we both realized that it was already ten thirty.

I had just assumed I'd get a train home from Grand Central, but my dad refused. "I don't want you walking around Grand Central alone this late," he'd said, already reaching for his phone. "It's dangerous, and your mother would never forgive me." I didn't argue, sensing this would *not* be the time to tell him I'd been through an attempted mugging earlier that night. In the end, we'd reached an agreement: I wouldn't tell my mom he'd missed my birthday dinner, and he wouldn't tell her that I'd come into the city without permission. We shook on it, and something in my dad's expression let me know that he secretly liked the idea of the two of us having a thing we weren't going to tell my mother about. And a condition of these terms was that I'd take a car back to Stanwich.

He went down with me to wait for the car, and as we stepped off the elevator and into the lobby, I saw that it was snowing.

"Dad," I said, pointing outside. I walked up to the front windows of Mayfair Towers and looked at the snow. I'd been through enough winters to know that this version of the snow—when a soft blanket was covering things, everything looking pristine, before snowplows and boots and dogs—was not going to last long. But for the moment, suddenly, it was magical. "Want to go out and see the snow?"

Something softened in his face as I said it. *Let's go see the snow,* he'd been saying to me since I was little, and seeing the snow was a very big deal. And then when I'd gotten older, it was treated as a joke, but we still did it. Like we had to joke about it, to pretend we didn't care, even when the exact opposite was true. And we'd go walking in the snow, just the two of us. One of those things that doesn't make sense to anyone else, something that's hard to describe the importance of, but when it's no longer there, it's almost unbearable, like the world is a few degrees off its axis. And since the divorce—since we weren't in the same house anymore—that had been the end of looking at the snow.

Until now. Until tonight.

My dad didn't even have a coat, just his black cashmere sweater, but we went out anyway, through the revolving door and onto Seventy-Second Street. I looked up, enjoying the feeling of vertigo that always set in when you were looking up into a snowstorm, like maybe the snow wasn't falling down, maybe you were rising up to meet it. We passed the Dakota and nodded seriously at the outside doorman, whose top hat was starting to get a dusting. We walked around the corner onto Central Park West, and my dad showed me the gargoyle heads on the fencing of the Dakota that extended all the way to the subway stop on the corner. I scooped some snow off the head of one of the gargoyles and let it melt between my palms. We were faux-debating the pros and cons of going into the park to see the snow (I wanted to go because it was right there; he wisely pointed out that we didn't have our sleds) when my dad saw the town car make the turn onto Seventy-Second, pull up in front of Mayfair Towers and put its hazards on.

"I think that's your ride, kid."

"Yeah."

My dad confirmed the destinations with the driver—Mallory's apartment in Murray Hill, then the train station parking lot in Stanwich, Connecticut—and turned to me. "I'm so sorry about tonight."

"I know," I said, giving him a smile. "Me too. About the yelling, I mean."

"Don't forget the swearing."

"I thought you'd be proud. I mean, I had to learn it somewhere." My dad threw back his head and laughed one of his barking laughs.

"We're okay?" he asked, and I nodded.

"We're okay." I wasn't sure, but I was hopeful that we might be better than okay. That we couldn't keep what we were doing, some version of our dynamic that no longer worked with two houses, two states, two families. That maybe we'd started something new tonight. And we'd just have to see how it went from here.

"I just . . . , he said, then shook his head. "I feel like there's so much I want to fix, and make up to you, and—"

"Dad," I said, raising an eyebrow, "how do you eat a whale?"

He gave me a smile that went wobbly around the edges. "One bite at a time." He pulled me into a hug, ruffling my hair the way he'd always done. "Love you, pumpkin."

I closed my eyes for just a second, freezing the moment, then pulled back. "Love you, too."

"And now I should go back in. It's normal not to feel your feet, right?"

I laughed and got into the car. The driver had kept it running, heat on, and in that moment, I wasn't sure I'd ever experienced anything as nice before. I rolled down the window and saw that even though it was still snowing, my dad was standing on the sidewalk, smiling at me.

"Ready to go?" the driver asked.

"All set," I said, and buckled my seat belt. He put the car in gear, signaled, and drove forward. I raised a hand in a wave, and my dad did the same, and I turned and saw him, standing in the snow without a coat, watching to make sure that I was okay.

The drive to Murray Hill hadn't taken that long. The snow wasn't deep enough that it was causing problems yet, but you could practically feel the city readying for it, with snowplows trundling past—not plowing snow yet, but clearly getting ready. I took the steps down to the building carefully, holding on to the railing—my new designer boots didn't have a ton of tread—and let myself in.

The five flights hadn't gotten any shorter, but not wearing heels did help. I knocked before entering. I didn't want to scare Flora, in case she was back. I wasn't sure what *working late* meant if you had a job in the mayor's office.

But when nobody answered, I unlocked the door, stepped inside, and looked around—it didn't seem like there was anyone else here. I hurried over to the counter, and there it was, waiting for me—my purse. I picked it up and just held it for a moment, beyond relieved. I double-checked everything inside was accounted for—it was—and then just looked at it a moment.

What would have happened if I'd had the presence of mind to grab it when we chased after Brad? What would this night have been like?

I closed the door carefully behind me and took the five flights down to the lobby, relieved to see that the super's door was still a little bit cracked open, since it was eleven, and getting a little late to be knocking on doors. But even so, I tried to knock softly, holding on to the doorknob so the whole thing wouldn't go flying open. "Cary?" I called quietly.

I didn't hear anything—and I was about to knock again when the door swung open, and there was Cary, in black pants and a white button-down, his hair parted and combed, like he was about to go somewhere fancy.

"Stevie!" he said, with a surprised, happy smile. "Hi!"

I held up the leather key chain. "I found keys," I said, shaking my head with a short laugh. "Finally."

"That's great," Cary said. "I'm so relieved. You got in and got your stuff?"

"I did. I hope you haven't been calling my phone. It kind of . . . got run over."

He nodded. "Kat told me."

"Kat?" I echoed. How had Kat and Cary been in communication?

"Yeah, we ran into each other at a bodega," he said. I raised an eyebrow. He said "bodega" the way other people might have said "top of the Empire State Building" or "bank of the Seine," like it was the most romantic place imaginable. He was crushing on Kat, that much was apparent.

"So you guys . . . hung out?"

Cary shrugged, his face getting flushed. "For little bit. She helped me with my job."

I nodded, just trying to get my head around this, and all the adventures we'd both had, independent of the other, neither of us knowing the full story.

"Wait," Cary said, suddenly sounding alarmed. "Where's Brad?"

"He's fine," I assured him, and he visibly relaxed. "But if you could tell Flora that he's with her sister? Mallory's sister," I clarified. "Just so she won't worry."

"Of course."

"And here's the other set," I said, handing the keys back to him. "For when Mallory needs to get back in."

"Got it," he said, taking them from me. "Thanks." He looked at me for a moment, like he was considering something, then nodded, like he'd made a decision. "I have to get going to work, but would you—if I gave you something to give to Kat, would you pass it along for me?"

I took a breath to tell him that I wasn't sure where Kat and I were, what would happen when we finally saw each other again, and that I might not be the best person to be serving as a go-between. But I saw the nervousness and hope on his face and knew there was only one answer. "Of course."

"Oh, thank you," he said, giving me a happy, relieved smile. "I didn't want—I mean, I just wasn't sure when—anyway. I'll just be a second. You're welcome to come in," he said, opening the door wider and disappearing inside.

I stepped inside a small, scrupulously clean apartment, most of the lights on low. I could see a door right across from the entryway, and as Cary pushed his way inside, it swung wider. "Are your aunt and uncle . . . ," I started, and Cary poked his head out of the room he'd disappeared into.

"Still stuck in Pennsylvania," he said, shaking his head. "They're going to be there until tomorrow at least. My uncle feels so bad about the key thing. He keeps apologizing. . . ."

Cary kept talking, but his voice faded to background noise, because I'd seen something the moment his door had swung wide.

It was like how you can see just the side of someone's face for a fraction of a moment and recognize them. How a second of a song or movie clip is enough to recall the whole thing. How a blur in your peripheral vision is enough to make you jump back from the curb and avoid the bike barreling toward you.

This was like that. It was seeing something I'd been searching for my entire life, even if I didn't know what exactly it would look like. It was familiar and unfamiliar, and even though it was just a flash, a moment, I knew it.

And so I walked up to Cary's room and pushed the door open,

startling him—he'd been hunched over his desk, writing something. But I didn't care if I was being rude, because that half second had been enough to let me know I was right.

I had always thought that *New York Night* number three would be in blue. But it wasn't. It was golden.

Hanging on the wall in front of me was Hugo LaSalle's lost painting. It was right there.

I'd found it.

"Hi," Cary said, sounding surprised. "Sorry—I'm almost done. If you need to go, I can hurry. . . ."

I didn't respond, just walked closer to the painting. I didn't think it was a fake. Nobody had ever seen this before, so how would it be? But it was also just obvious this was a LaSalle. The size, the brushwork, the signature in the corner with a crown over his first name—it all fit. In all the speculation about what was in this painting, I'd never guessed this—that the third canvas in the series shifted perspective slightly. The skyline was still there, but we were now more with the people on the ground. Couples holding hands. People walking dogs. Parents and children. Friends. Dwarfed by but also somehow a part of the New York skyline.

It was beautiful.

"Oh—yeah," Cary said, smiling as he came to stand next to me. "Nice, right? My dad was on a moving job for this guy, transporting his stuff from Pittsburgh to New York, and he gave him this. My dad used to joke that next time, he was going to ask for a cash tip. He would always say it was the only time he'd ever been paid in art. My uncle didn't want me to hang it in here and damage the walls, but I don't know . . . I just liked the colors."

It was all coming together, like puzzle pieces snapping into place. That was why I'd recognized the name on the moving truck—it was Cary's. Which meant, against all odds, that the mover story about the painting had been true—but I supposed one of them had to be. I let out a long, shaky breath, then sat down on the perfectly made bed with its plaid comforter. "Cary," I said.

"Yeah?" He looked at me, now clearly a little bit concerned. I wondered if I should ask him to sit down too. It was like I finally understood why, in plays and movies, people are always being told to sit before getting big news.

"That painting," I said, pointing to it, "is a Hugo LaSalle."

Cary frowned, like he was trying to place something. "The . . . artist?" he asked, then shook his head. "Nah," he said. "It was just some guy in a studio in Pittsburgh."

"It's a LaSalle," I said. "It's his famous lost painting. I know because my family's been trying to find it for twenty years."

Cary looked at me, then at the painting, like he was trying to figure out if this was just some very elaborate and not-that-funny prank. "No," he said, a little faintly, and I could understand it—the instinct to hang on as tightly as we can to the world we understand before it all goes topsy-turvy.

"Yes," I said, on the verge of breaking into hysterical laughter. All the searching, all the years looking for it, and it had been in an apartment in Murray Hill, owned by a teenager who just liked the colors. From all I knew about LaSalle, he would have absolutely loved this. "It is. I'd heard the mover story, but nobody ever knew if it was true."

"But," Cary said, sounding more scared than anything else. I understood it. When your life's about to change, even with all good things, it's jarring. But you have to go through it to get to the stuff on the other side. "Hugo LaSalle . . . I mean, he's *famous*."

"I know," I said, not able to stop myself from smiling now as I stared at it. It didn't seem like Cary was going to have a problem paying for college—or much else—for a while. "Listen, you should absolutely do whatever you want. But I know my mom would love to have the chance to make an offer for her museum. She's been looking for this for so long."

Cary sank down on the bed next to me, looking a great deal paler than he'd been just a few moments before. "Are you sure?" he whispered.

I nodded. "Yeah," I said. We both looked at the painting in silence, and in that moment, it stopped being something hung on a bedroom wall. If you squinted, you could see it in a gallery, on the wall of a museum, a small white plaque next to it, as people grouped around and looked at it with their heads tilted to the side.

Cary shook his head. "Holy shit."

I burst out laughing. Because what else could you say? I smiled at him. "My thoughts exactly."

I'd been worried that I'd been too long—that maybe the driver would have left, or called my dad and told him that I'd disappeared. But the town car was still waiting, hazards on, wipers going against the snow. I let myself in before he had to get out in the cold, and just as I closed the door, I saw Cary also hurrying out of the building, carrying a helmet, looking like a man on a mission. I hoped it was to his job and not a late-night art appraiser—I wanted my mom to have a chance to at least bid—but he had the right to do whatever he wanted.

"Sorry," I said, putting on my seat belt. Then I tucked the folded note that Cary had written for Kat carefully into my clutch.

"Not a problem," the driver said, giving me a smile.

"I'm Stevie, by the way." It felt like our interaction had been going on far too long to continue without introductions. I was also regretting that town cars didn't have the drivers' names displayed like taxis did.

"Leo," he said with a nod. "Ready to head to Connecticut? You warm enough back there?"

"Just fine," I said, settling back in my seat. "Thank you."

The car pulled out, and I looked out the window at the falling snow, at the people bundled up against it, at the way it seemed to be making New York even more magical. I was still trying to sort through what had just happened. You somehow expect decades-long mysteries to be solved painstakingly over time, not discovered by random accident because a cute boy has a crush on your best friend. And yet . . .

I leaned back against the soft leather of the seat. It was undoubtedly a much more comfortable way to get from New York to Connecticut than Metro-North. But I couldn't help feeling this wasn't how I was supposed to end the night. I was supposed to be riding with Kat on the uncomfortable seats, nudging her to move her feet every time the conductor passed so we wouldn't get kicked off.

I looked at the clock on the radio, which was turned to some kind of soothing jazz station. Would Kat be at Grand Central, at the clock, waiting for me at 11:11?

I looked fixedly out the window and told myself firmly that she wasn't going to be there, that she'd gone home long ago.

But what if she hadn't?

Meanwhile, back in Canada . . .

AMONG THE MANY THINGS TERI HAD LEARNED THAT NIGHT WAS THAT it wasn't too hard to overpower and tie up someone claiming to be a CIA agent. It especially helped to have five people working together, even if three of them were on the small side.

When they'd secured the man to a chair with jumper cables and socks with Justin Trudeau's face on them, they all stepped back to admire their handiwork.

"You can't do this," the man growled, struggling against his bonds.

"I think we just did," said Chris. Daryl gave her a high five.

"I'm a CIA officer!"

"We've heard that before," Teri said. "We heard it tonight, in fact. And we also heard of someone claiming to be Damon Gilroy. So you'll understand if we're not about to believe you."

The man frowned. "What do you mean? Someone else is claiming to be Damon Gilroy?"

"Don't play dumb." Teri was getting annoyed. She might have

been hoodwinked by one fake CIA agent tonight, but she wasn't about to be tricked by two. *Fool me once,* like her mother always said. Just not usually about something like this.

"I think this is just a ruse to get the diamonds," Chris said.

Parker nodded knowingly.

"Diamonds?" the man asked. "What are you talking about?"

Teri exchanged a look with Dustin. "If you're not after the diamonds, what are you doing here?"

The man struggled against his bonds again. "I do not have time for this!"

"You think we *do*?" Teri was incredulous. "You know how long ago they were supposed to be in bed?"

"Teri," Daryl hissed. "You're embarrassing us in front of the hostage."

"Fine," the man said, slumping in his seat. "I'll talk." He took a breath and told them how he'd been embedded for the last year with the Hermitagi, the Bulgarian mob. How he'd risen through the ranks and convinced the boss's son, Dimitri, to turn evidence. It had taken months to set up. But just when he thought he was in the clear, he'd been made. Thrown into a car. The car stopped for gas—Dimitri was suddenly gone—there was a fight and he managed to get away. He looked up at the kids expectantly.

Parker rolled her eyes.

"Yeah, this is sounding very familiar," Teri said, shaking her head. She told him the details from the *other* Gilroy's story—and how they'd escaped and gone on the run. "So forgive us if we don't believe you."

"Yeah," Chris added, crossing her arms over her chest.

"But that means . . . ," the man said, frowning. He looked like he was putting something together. "Then Dimitri . . . so he could . . . it makes sense, but . . ."

Teri looked at him closely. She'd seen a lot of bad acting over the years. She knew what it looked like when someone was spinning. That didn't seem like what was happening here. "But what?" she asked, keeping her eyes on him.

"But this means Dimitri had a plan I wasn't aware of. And he outed me as a way to get free himself—then used my backstory when it became necessary to convince you."

"Why would he have done that?" Dustin asked, looking like he was trying to keep up.

"He's always been passed over for his brother. Never the favorite. It was this weakness I exploited to get him to turn."

"That's what he said in the car, right?" Chris turned to Teri. "About his brother? What does this mean?"

"Can you prove it?" Teri asked. "Can you prove you're who you say you are?"

"I have my badge—"

"Not enough," Chris and Daryl said together.

The man frowned. "I couldn't have too much on me—undercover, of course. But I have a locked file on my phone. It's in my pocket." Dustin got the phone, used the man's face to unlock it, then found the folder and keyed in the password—1234. "I know." The man hung his head. "I need to change it."

"You work for the CIA." Chris sounded appalled.

Parker shook her head, clearly disappointed.

Dustin held out the unlocked phone and they all gathered around it. They saw pictures of the man in a suit and tie, posing with other people dressed the same way, badge on a lanyard on his neck. A shot of him waving as he walked into the White House. In the desert, in a golf shirt and khakis, pointing to something. Playing bass onstage— he explained he was in a band called the Redacted Documents, and they played covers with some of the words missing.

"These could be faked," Teri said as she scrolled through them.

"No." Daryl pointed to the picture of the man outside the White House. "See these shadows? That's hard to fake. They're uniform all around, and there's no blurring on the edges. It's nearly impossible to get that kind of color bleed on a fake."

"Impressive," the man said.

Daryl grinned at Teri. "Told you I was good at Photoshop."

"So this is real?" Teri asked slowly, horror slowly dawning. "And we just . . . tied up a CIA agent?"

"It's okay," the man said, shaking his head. "After what you've been through tonight, it's understandable you're not too trusting."

"But how did you even find us?" Teri asked as everyone else started to untie the man—the Real Gilroy.

"I wasn't looking for you. I managed to get a tracker into Dimitri's arm. I've been tracking *him*."

Teri froze. "But if you were tracking him, and your tracker led you here, that means . . ."

"It means he's near," he confirmed grimly.

The sound of clapping made Teri turn around. There was Fake Gilroy, walking through the kicked-in door. "Well done," he said, smirking. "Bravo."

"Dimitri," Real Gilroy said, straining against the ties they hadn't fully released him from.

"Ah, my old friend the CIA officer," Fake Gilroy—Dimitri—said. "Gang's all here." He looked around, then paused at Dustin. "You, I don't know."

Dustin held out his hand. "Hi there. Dustin Alberta."

"What are you doing?" Chris hissed at him.

"Sorry." Dustin looked abashed. "We're a polite people."

"I suppose you told them everything." Dimitri was sneering, but Teri could see real fear behind his eyes—this situation spinning out of his control.

"Everything but why you did it." Real Gilroy's expression was calm, but Teri could see that he was working fast to try and free himself from their ties. She took a step closer, to help, but Dimitri drew his gun and turned it on her.

"Stay where you are," he ordered. "And it's not a mystery, Damon. I had an opportunity to punish the family that never appreciated me and expose a CIA agent. I took it."

"Who was the guy at the rest stop?" Teri asked. She still didn't understand what the diamonds had to do with any of this.

"I'm joining a new organization. Somewhere my talents will be appreciated. And there was a price for entry."

"You're joining the Knights of Darkness?" Real Gilroy asked. He sounded stunned. "Albanian mafia," he explained. "They prefer payment in diamonds."

"Well done," Dimitri said. "You figured it out. Too bad you're not going to be able to tell anyone." He leveled his gun at Real Gilroy and smiled at Teri. "So considerate of you to tie him up for me. Really saved me some trouble."

"Kids," Real Gilroy said, his voice relaxed and steady. "I want you to think about my password, okay? Say it to yourselves when I tell you, then run."

"I don't think so," Dimitri snapped. "That pint-sized thief stole my diamonds and I'm getting them back."

"One problem." Real Gilroy's voice was as calm as ever, but Teri could see that he'd gotten one of his hands free. While he was speaking deliberately and slowly, his hands were working furiously. It was some of the best acting she had ever seen. "There are six of us, and one of you."

"What—" Dimitri started.

"Now!" Real Gilroy yelled. Teri remembered his password, counted to four, then grabbed Parker and Chris, and saw Dustin grab Daryl.

They sprinted past Dimitri, who was whirling around, trying to figure out what was happening.

They made it through the door, and Teri looked back just in time to see Real Gilroy rip his arms free.

And then, a second later, to see Dimitri shoot him, right in the chest.

"*Grand Central,*" *the cabdriver said,* pulling up behind the taxi line. "Cash or credit?"

"Cash," I said, digging in my pocket for what was left of the thirty dollars Cary had given me. It turned out that taking cabs from the theater district down to the Gansevoort, then back up to Grand Central, added up. I started to count it out, then hesitated. "If I give you a truly excellent tip, can you break a hundred?"

The cabdriver turned around, like he was considering it. "Twenty-five percent and done."

"Great," I said, feeling relief flood through me. Now I wouldn't have to worry—I would have more than enough to get a train ticket and get a taxi back to Teri's, just in case Stevie wasn't going to be there waiting for me.

I didn't know if she was going to be there. I was hoping she would be. But either way, I had to go and see.

The driver handed me back my change, minus his tip, and I knocked on the glass partition. "Pleasure doing business."

"Receipt?"

"No, I'm good," I said, opening the door. "Have a good night."

"You too," he said, already pressing a button on his meter to clear my fare away and get ready for the next person he was going to pick up. I looked at it for just a second—not at zero, but at two-fifty, because New York—and felt, in that moment, just how many different stories there were in this city. He'd go off and pick someone else up, someone else either having the best or worst night of their life—or possibly both, like mine had been—or just a night, barely thought of again, one of thousands that all blended together. "You good?" he asked, startling me out of these thoughts.

"Uh-huh," I said, sliding out and slamming the door behind me. I stepped out into the cold night air, and the snow that was gently falling. The cab pulled back out into traffic, and a moment later I couldn't even tell it apart any longer, one cab mixing in with dozens. I was a little early, so I paused outside on the sidewalk and looked up. It was snowing, after all, and I was in New York City. You couldn't not take a moment to appreciate it.

But you can only stand for so long in the snow before it stops being cinematic and starts being cold. I turned to walk over to the doors when I saw something out of the corner of my eye. It was a guy getting off a scooter, taking off his helmet, and looking around. I couldn't see his face, but I knew that I knew him. And who else would be wearing a brown leather jacket? "Cary?"

He turned around, and surprise and nervousness seemed to be mingling equally on his face. "Hi," he said, setting his helmet on his seat and then starting to walk over to me. Then, a second later, he turned back and locked the helmet in the back compartment. He ran his hands through his hair as he walked up to me, and I could see he had changed his jeans for dark pants. The snow was falling on his jacket, on his hair.

"What are you doing here?" I asked. And my first, incandescent thought was that he was somehow there for me. But then a second later I told myself this was ridiculous. He was probably here to catch a train, or meet someone.

"I was hoping to see you," he said, and I couldn't quite stop myself from smiling, my heart swelling in my chest like a balloon, threatening to lift me off my feet. "Before you went back home. I just wanted . . . to talk to you."

"But how did you know I'd be here?"

"You told me," he said, giving me a smile. "Eleven-eleven, remember?"

"*Excuse* me." I turned and saw a guy in a business suit, standing behind me, looking aggrieved. There was lots of space to walk around us on the sidewalk, but he seemed to want to walk just where we were. Cary and I both took a step off to the side, his hand on my elbow so lightly, just guiding me a little, and like before, the touch sent a *zing* through me all the way to my toes.

"And then when I saw Stevie," he continued, once we were out of the way of people who wanted to pass by on the street, "it reminded me—"

"Wait, when did you see Stevie?"

"She came by the building," he said. "She finally got the keys and got into Mallory's apartment."

"Oh," I said, letting out a sigh of relief. "That's great."

"So," he said, looking away and running a hand through his hair again. "This might be a little awkward, but . . ." He took a breath and looked at me expectantly, and suddenly I realized why he was here, and it wasn't to pick up where we'd left off in the dance studio.

"Oh," I said, reaching into my pocket. "You want your money back! God, of course. I'm so sorry . . ."

"No!" Cary said, his face flushing red. "That's not why I came, Kat. I didn't need the money back. In fact . . ." His brow furrowed, like he was trying to get his head around something. Then he shrugged. "Never mind. That's—a long story. It's been kind of a crazy night."

I burst out laughing at that as everything that had happened tonight flashed through my head, a highlight reel of subway separations, pay phone riddles and scooter rides, hot dogs and dancing in the dark, of plays and realizations, movie stars and taxis. And that it had ended up with me, here, talking to a cute boy on the doorstep of Grand Central while snow swirled around us. "You can say that again."

He took a step closer to me and I looked directly into his dark eyes. "But the best part of it all was—I got to meet you."

"Oh," I said, my smile taking over my whole face.

"And, um," he said, looking down at the sidewalk for a second, taking a breath. "I know that you live in Connecticut, and I'm here, but they're not that far away, and—"

I didn't let him finish. I gathered all my courage, and stepped forward, and kissed him.

I broke away, and he looked at me, then smiled and took a step closer, tracing his hand over my jawline, letting it linger there for just a moment. And then he was leaning toward me and I was leaning toward him, and then we were kissing for real.

And *oh my god*.

Everything else got blacked out for just a moment, there on the sidewalk—the other people, the faint sound of sirens, all of it. It was just me and Cary and my hands in his hair and his arms around me. I could feel him breathe—I could feel his heart beat faster as his arms tightened around me so that, for just a second, my feet left the ground.

He set me down and we broke apart, but still stood close, looking at each other, as the snow fell all around us, on his cheeks, on his eyelashes. "Well," he said, smiling wide at me.

"Yeah," I said, trying not to smile back but failing miserably. And why not? We'd just made out in front of Grand Central—there didn't seem to be any point in trying to play it cool. "Wait," I said, suddenly panicked. How long had we just been kissing? It could have been a minute. It could have been a blissful hour—though if that was the case, I might have started to lose feeling in my feet. "What time is it?"

Cary pulled his phone out of his pocket. "11:08."

"I should go," I said, glancing toward the building. I didn't want to. I wanted to spend several more minutes—or days or weeks—kissing him. But if Stevie was there, I had to be there too.

"Yeah," Cary said, smiling at me, looking a little dazed. He gave me one quick kiss, then stepped back, toward his bike. "I have to go too, actually. I'm late for work. You know my number, right?"

"I Cruise!" I called, and he laughed.

"You got it." We just smiled at each other for a moment, New Yorkers passing between us, and then I waved at him quickly and made myself turn away. I looked back before I pulled the door open, and froze the picture in my mind—Cary, standing by his scooter in the snow, smiling wide, waving back at me. I gave him a nod, then pulled open the door and hurried into Grand Central, trying not to skip.

I picked up my pace as I hustled toward the main area. For once, I didn't want to be late. I wanted to be right on time to meet Stevie.

Because she was going to be there, I told myself as I hurried toward the clock, half running.

Wasn't she?

CHAPTER 27

Stevie

The taxi line outside Grand Central was deserted. I passed it as I hurried toward the door and pulled it open. I glanced at my watch, then started to walk faster.

Past the entrance to the subway, past the closed bakery, making the left turn before Hudson News, still open. Grand Central wasn't bustling the way that it had been late this afternoon, when it had been peak commuting time. There were a few people walking next to me, and one guy leaning against the wall outside the room of Metro-North ticket kiosks, yawning as he looked at his phone. Even the central area was more deserted, which meant it was easier to see the clock right there in the center.

I looked up at the clock just as the minute hand ticked over to 11:11.

My heart hammering, I started to walk around the clock, which was big enough that you couldn't see the other side of it. And though I couldn't see Kat, that didn't mean she wasn't there.

Had I been crazy to think that she would be here? That she was sorry too, that she'd missed me tonight as much as I'd missed her?

And when I was starting to lose hope, when my stomach was starting to plunge with disappointment that maybe I'd been wrong about this, when I was on the opposite side of the clock from where I'd started, I stopped short.

There was a girl in a long navy coat. She was tall, with fine blond hair. Her back was to me and she was shifting her weight from foot to foot and I could tell, without even looking at her face, that she was nervous.

And for once in her life, she was early.

I wanted to run up and hug her, but Grand Central Station, late at night, is not the best place to do that, and there was no need to give my best friend a heart attack, not when I'd just found her again. "Kat," I called, and she spun around. Surprise and happiness passed over her face one by one, erasing the worry that had been there.

"Oh my god!" she yelled, and ran toward me, pulling me into a tight hug.

I hugged her back, laughing even though I didn't know why. I felt like I could finally let out a breath I'd been holding all night. "Hi, frond."

"Hey, frand," she said, and I could feel her laughing as she pulled back from me. "You came!"

"Of course," I said, smiling at her, on the verge of crying—which was ridiculous, since I'd spent far too much time doing that tonight already. "So did you."

"Our contingency plan!" She was smiling wide, like she was as happy to see me as I was to see her.

We had shown up for each other. I knew we had a lot to catch up on and things we needed to say, but for the moment, that was enough. More than enough.

"I'm so sorry, Stevie." Kat's words were tumbling out like she couldn't say them fast enough. "I never should have lied to you about the play. I never should have chosen the play over you, and I'm sorry about the phone, and everything I said. I didn't mean it, any of it—"

"I'm sorry too," I said. And then we were hugging again, and Kat was wiping her nose and none of the people passing through Grand Central even gave us a second glance.

We broke apart and Kat's eyes widened as she looked at me. She frowned. "Did you kiss someone?" I pressed my lips together, trying to flatten out my smile, and she grabbed my arm. "I knew it!" she said. "I can tell! Who?"

"*You* kissed someone," I said, pointing at her, and she clapped her hand over her mouth like she was trying to hide the evidence, and even without being able to see it, I could tell she was smiling.

"Okay, I have to hear everything," she said, glancing down at my feet, then up at me, "including where you got these boots, because I love them, but first we need to figure out what train we're taking. Should we get the eleven-twenty and do our debrief there?"

I smiled and shook my head. "We've got a ride," I said, enjoying her shocked expression. "Follow me."

"This is fancy," Kat said, raising an impressed eyebrow at me as we both got into the backseat of the town car. We'd gone outside; I had thought it made sense for us to be out there to see if we could see Leo circling, and if not, I'd just ask to borrow someone's cell phone and call him—he'd given me his card. Kat had seemed shocked that I'd be willing to do that, but I'd explained that after someone tries to mug you for your phone, having someone tell you no doesn't really carry the same weight. "What!" she'd yelled, and I'd laughed even as I scanned the street, looking for the town car. I was just happy about everything right now—that I had all these stories to tell her that she hadn't heard. I needed to tell her about my dad, and finally tell her the truth about Beckett, safe in the knowledge that when I did, I would get to hear her reacting in the way that only she could.

I couldn't wait to hear her stories too. It was like we'd been on two separate adventures and were finally back together in the tavern, spreading out our maps and showing off our treasures. I had just walked up to a middle-aged woman trying to hail a cab—Kat's jaw had dropped open when she'd seen me do this, and I was secretly very pleased with this reaction—when I'd seen Leo.

"There," I said to Kat, and I'd waved at him and we'd both piled in.

"Evening," Leo said, glancing back at Kat. "You're going to Stanwich too?"

"Yes," I said as I buckled my seat belt. "Same stop."

"Hi, I'm Kat," Kat said, leaning forward. Leo gave her a bemused smile.

"Leo," he said. "Nice to meet you." He hit the button to stop the hazards and shifted the car into drive. "Next stop Connecticut."

"Or," Kat said. She arched an eyebrow and looked at me, then pulled a wrinkled piece of paper out of her pocket. "Anyone up for going to a party?"

PART FIVE
11:11 p.m.–3:00 a.m.

Soul mates aren't just lovers, you know.
—*Ryn Weaver, "Traveling Song"*

PART FIVE

ERI RAN THROUGH THE WOODS, AS FAST AS SHE COULD. SHE WAS holding Parker and gripping onto Chris with her other hand, stumble-running over leaves and tree branches. They'd fled out the broken door into the woods behind the store.

Teri was breathing hard, her thoughts going round and round in terrible circles. *Real Gilroy is dead it's all my fault oh my god I just saw someone get killed what are we going to do?*

"Dustin," she gasped, looking behind her as she ran, "are you okay?"

"I'm fine," came the breathless reply. "I've got Daryl."

Teri felt branches snag her hair but ran on. She had no plan except *run* and *get away* and *go.*

"Ow!" Teri was thrown off-balance. She stopped and saw Chris had fallen. "You okay?" She set Parker down.

"I just tripped on a tree root," Chris said. "I'm fine."

Dustin and Daryl caught up with them, both red-faced. Teri helped

Chris to her feet. They'd arrived at a clearing—trees made way for open sky above them. The moon shining down meant she could see everyone. They all looked as scared as she felt.

"I'm so sorry, you guys." Teri hung her head. "Tonight has been crazy. But I'm going to get us out of it and home safe. I promise."

"Wait." Dustin's brow was furrowed as he looked around. "Where's Parker?"

"She's right here." They all whirled around. Dimitri was holding the toddler. Parker's expression was angry, not frightened, which was the only thing preventing Teri from having a panic attack. He made a *tsk* sound. "You're not doing a great job tonight, are you, Teri?"

"Hey!" Dustin started to run toward him, but Dimitri aimed the gun in his direction and Dustin stopped short.

"Watch yourself, dillweed," Dimitri said. His voice was cold and menacing.

"Give her back." Teri glared at Dimitri with all the hatred she currently felt.

"Give me my diamonds and I will."

Teri looked at him, trying to see if he meant it. But what choice did she have but to comply? "Okay," she said, taking a step forward. "Set her down and I'll give you the diamonds. And then we're done, right?"

Dimitri smirked. "That's cute. Now let's do this nice and easy. . . ."

Teri looked at Parker, who grinned back at her. Then she bit down hard on Dimitri's hand. He yelled and dropped her. Teri rushed over, worried she was hurt, but Parker jumped to her feet and glared up at him.

"Watch yourself, dillweed!" she yelled, then kicked him in both shins before running back to Teri.

"Since when does she speak?" Dustin asked.

"I guess she really was waiting until she had something to say," said Chris.

"Hey!" Dimitri fired his gun in the air. They all froze and looked at him, the five of them stepping closer together. "I'm done messing around with you kids. I want my diamonds, now." He glared at Teri. "You're done, babysitter. You've got nowhere left to go."

Teri looked around and realized he was right. He was the mobster with the gun; they were three kids, their ill-qualified babysitter, and a cute Canadian boy. They didn't stand a chance. "Okay." Teri reached into her bag. "You win."

At that moment, light streamed in from all around them. Ten SUVs were ringing them—and they'd all turned on their headlights at once. "FBI!" someone yelled. "Drop the weapon and step away from the children!"

A sound from the sky made everyone look up—a helicopter was circling, a spotlight pointing down at them. "CIA!" came a voice projected through a speaker. "Hands where we can see them!"

The sound of hooves made Teri turn around. At least ten officers in red uniforms, on horseback, had just ridden up. "Royal Canadian Mounted Police!" one of them yelled. "Please get down on the ground, if it's not too much trouble."

Teri looked around—at the agent arresting Dimitri, at the cavalry that had shown up just in time—and started to cry with relief. This long night, full of misadventures—at last, it was finally over.

Twenty minutes later, Teri had turned over the stolen diamonds and given her statement, and everyone had been checked by the medics. The kids were meeting the Mounties' horses, and they all seemed thrilled about it. She tried to tell herself that she should be happy, that things had worked out. Dimitri was going to jail for a long time, the kids were safe, and she no longer was the one making the decisions. And yet . . .

"Hey." She looked over and saw Dustin walking toward her. "You okay?"

"Yeah," Teri said, nodding. "I just wish . . ."

"Hey, babysitter." She and Dustin turned around—and there was Real Gilroy walking toward them, smiling and very much alive.

"What?" Teri's jaw dropped. "How—"

Real Gilroy tapped his chest. "Bulletproof vest. I knew getting Dimitri to think I was dead was my best chance of getting my backup in place. Sorry if I scared you."

"No," Teri said, smiling wide, even though she felt like she was also about to cry with relief. "I'm so glad you're okay."

"Sorry about the door," Real Gilroy said, holding out his hand to Dustin to shake. "We're fixing it now."

"I appreciate it," Dustin said. "And my dad will too."

Real Gilroy tapped his watch. "It's getting late. We should get you kids home."

"Right." Just like that, the reality of the situation—which had been pushed from Teri's mind as she'd focused on more pressing things, like not getting shot—hit her. She was going to be in *so* much trouble. "I guess I have to face the music."

Real Gilroy cleared his throat. "Actually . . . it would be better if nobody knew any of this happened. National security."

"But we can't drive all the way back to Connecticut before the Stones get home. I left the rental car behind. . . ."

Real Gilroy just smiled. "We'll sort it out. Ready to go in five?" Teri nodded and he walked away, pulling out a walkie-talkie as he went.

She turned to Dustin and took him in. His sweet smile. His baseball cap. His kind eyes. She could practically feel the unspoken things between them. "Um," she finally said. "Maybe I could get your number? In case I'm ever . . . in Canada?"

Dustin brightened. "Yes! That's a great idea. . . ."

They exchanged phones to swap numbers. When she handed back his phone, she realized that this night—the one she'd wanted to be over—was suddenly ending much too fast. She looked up at him. She'd been brave tonight. She'd dealt with a fake spy and stolen a rental car and tied up a CIA agent. She could do this.

And before she could talk herself out of it, she took a deep breath, stepped closer, stretched up on her toes, and kissed Dustin Alberta.

Dustin kissed her back, pulling her close, and all time stopped as they kissed, there in that Canadian clearing, the moon bright above them.

"*Ew.*" They broke apart and Teri saw all three Stone children staring at them. Chris covered Parker's eyes. Daryl looked disgusted. "That was gross."

"Dillweed!" Parker exclaimed. She beamed at her linguistic prowess.

"We need to get her another word," Chris said.

"Dillweed," Parker repeated firmly.

Teri laughed and picked Parker up, then looked at all three of the kids. "Come on, guys," she said. "Let's go home."

xplain to me one more time how you got this invitation," Stevie said as we all got out of the town car—me, Stevie, and Leo the driver. When I'd suggested the party, he'd said that he could wait for us, but Stevie and I had both been emphatic that we weren't going to let that happen—and surely he had other people to drive?

"Not until an airport pickup in Hartfield at three a.m.," he'd explained. "I was just going to wait in a diner or something after I dropped you off."

That was when Stevie, using her most reasonable voice, had pointed out that he had to be in Connecticut at three a.m. anyway. So why not kill the time at a loft party instead of a diner? After a moment of silent deliberation, he'd seen the logic in that, and now the three of us were all walking across the cobblestone streets together, Leo in his suit looking extremely sharp.

"This is so cool," I said, head tipped back as I looked at the snow falling, at the bridge that seemed so enormous, at the views of the water. I wasn't sure I'd ever been to Dumbo before, but I'd immediately recognized it, from movies and TV, a dream of New York made real.

The ride to Brooklyn hadn't been that long, but we'd tried to get it all in—Mr. Campbell and Stevie's dad, Beckett and Cary. We'd had to get into movie stars and stepsiblings, bad theater and Pomeranians, botched proposals and underground poker games, muggers and free meals in expensive restaurants. I wanted to hear everything about Stevie's talk with her dad, and she wanted me to explain the note that Cary had given her for me.

I'd smiled when I'd seen it. It was a drawing, in the same style as his Bartleby illustrations. It was of the two of us, riding on his scooter down a New York street, my arms spread wide, a big smile on my face, Cary leaning forward over the handlebars like a racer.

"Explain this part," Stevie had said, tapping on the figure riding on a scooter next to us. It was a peanut dressed in the Grim Reaper's robes, bony hand reaching out for Cary, peanut brittle scythe over his shoulder (did peanuts have shoulders?).

"It's a long story," I'd said, laughing as I carefully folded it and put it in my coat pocket.

"Oh!" Stevie said. "I forgot to tell you—I think Cary's a millionaire now?"

"What!" I said, and Stevie laughed, and Leo turned down the radio to hear the story. And so when we arrived, even though we hadn't gotten through everything we still had to say, I knew there would be time for it. Hours and days and years, because Stevie and I were back. We were going to be okay.

"All right," I said, looking around at the buildings, looking for a number. "I think . . . there!" I spotted 113 and walked forward, to where the intercom was. There seemed to be only four names listed, though, which seemed strange, since the building was so big. Four of them were just regular names, but one of them had a piece of tape over it, with *PARTY* scrawled on it in Sharpie. I smiled and pressed the intercom button.

"Password," a voice said in low tones, stretching the word out.

So cool, I mouthed to Stevie. Leo looked fairly impassive, like he was always going out to parties in lofts that required passwords. And who knows, maybe he was. "Daedalus," I said confidently, giving Stevie a smile.

"That password has already been used," the voice said. "Goodbye."

"What?" I said, turning to face Stevie and Leo. But a second later,

I realized why. "This must mean Amy Curry used my invite!" I said excitedly. "She's probably in there! How cool is that?"

"Well—but now we can't get into the party, right?" Leo asked. His voice was surprisingly deep, and he seemed to speak every word he said carefully, like he was considering all of them. It was a very reassuring trait, especially in someone who was driving you at night across state lines in the snow.

"That voice . . . ," Stevie said. She narrowed her eyes, the way she did when she was thinking. Then she shook her head. "It can't be."

"What can't be?" I asked.

"No," Stevie said, shaking her head. "No, no, no . . ." She reached into her coat pocket and pulled out a folded piece of paper. She smoothed it out, and there, written on it in an untidy scrawl, was *113 Anchorage and Plymouth, Dumbo.*

"Whoa," I said, staring at her. "That was like a magic trick."

"Seriously," Leo agreed, looking impressed.

"How do you have the address of the party?"

But Stevie just bent forward, laughing, and I started laughing too, because it was what I always did when she was laughing, even though I didn't know what was funny. "It's Margaux's apartment," she said, straightening up, pulling herself together. "We're at Margaux's party." Stevie pressed the intercom button again.

"Password," the voice intoned, even deeper now. I had a feeling whoever was doing this was having fun with the cloak-and-dagger part of things.

"Hi—Margaux?" Stevie asked, leaning closer to the speaker. "It's Stevie. I'm here, and we—"

"Stevie!" The voice came through the intercom in a happy yell, all low portentous tones gone. "You came! Oh yay!"

"I'm here with my friends," Stevie said, glancing back at us. "Kat Thompson and, um, Leo. Is that okay?"

"Of course! Come on up!" The buzzer sounded and Stevie pulled the door open. She led the way inside, up the elevator—and into the most incredible party I'd ever been at.

The huge open loft space was packed with people—all different ages, an eclectic mix—although it seemed pretty clear that Stevie and I were the youngest ones there. Well, unless you counted the baby that a very tall, glamorous woman had strapped to her in a sling.

It was also immediately apparent that it was not just the *little get-together* Stevie had been promised. There was a DJ spinning in the corner, a full bar, and huge windows that showed views of the city and the water and the snow. There was a piece of me that was desperate to have my phone so that I could have taken pictures and posted and documented everything. But there was another piece of me that actually didn't mind just having this experience without having to box it up for other people to see and comment on.

As soon as we walked in, Stevie was tackle-hugged by a gorgeous girl in a flowing caftan who I guessed correctly was Margaux. And shortly after meeting her, I got to meet Matty, who also seemed thrilled that Stevie had shown up. I was introduced to Matty's friends, who greeted Stevie like a long-lost pal. The British friend started telling me a story about how Stevie had been brilliant when she'd cried to scare a raptor—which I didn't understand, but figured it might be some kind of British slang. I'd been about to ask him to clarify when something truly shocking happened. A tiny fluffy dog came barreling out of the hallway and jumped into Stevie's arms.

And rather than running away, or extricating herself, Stevie pulled the dog close. And when she turned to me, her face alight, I saw that it was Brad. He didn't seem quite as pleased to see me, or interested in leaving Stevie's arms, but that was fine, because she didn't seem particularly interested in giving him up.

Margaux clearly had a lot to do, and was being pulled in forty different directions, but she still took both of us in hand, linking her arms through ours as she gave us a quick tour of the party, pointing out the people she wanted us to be sure to meet: Jackson, her bagel man; Louisa, who owned a conceptual art gallery; James Domingos, who wrote the sudoku puzzles for the *Times*—we could recognize him because his shirt read *Eat my Shortz*.

"Now," she said, pointing out a table with snacks, "please eat! Mingle! Passed apps coming around soon . . . and Stevie, come with me. I need you to meet Allison, and before all her terrible finance friends arrive and you get the wrong impression."

She steered Stevie away, and I looked around to make sure Leo was okay, but it soon became very clear he didn't need any help. He was in the corner with a bottle of water, talking to Kaya, a model I'd seen in countless ads.

I smiled and had just started to investigate my snack options when someone said quietly behind me, "Of all the lofts in all of Dumbo . . ."

I whirled around, not able to believe it—but there was Cary, dressed in a white shirt and black pants and a bow tie. He was holding a tray of canapés, and he was grinning at me. "What are you doing here?" I shrieked happily, not even bothering to mask my delight.

He gestured at his silver tray. "Sixth job!"

"Oh my god." I started to laugh.

"So," he said gravely, holding out the tray to me. "Miss, do you see anything you'd like?"

"Uh-huh," I said, and I stepped forward and kissed him. He kissed me back, holding the tray deftly to the side and then dipping me backward slightly with one arm.

After that, what had been the best party of my life suddenly became even more fun. Cary had to work, of course—though maybe not for much longer if what Stevie had said in the car was true—but he always swung by me first with trays, lingering as long as he could, and he told me he was negotiating to try and be the first one cut.

Stevie and I navigated the party together, occasionally breaking apart to talk to people, but always finding our way back together again. Not because we couldn't be apart—the night we'd had had proved that we could. But because we wanted to be together, which somehow made it that much better.

We even got to chat a little more with Amy, which, I decided, would never stop being amazing. She thanked me for the invite, and I just took a moment to relish it—the movie star thanking *me* for getting her into a party. "Lucien's in heaven," she said, pointing across the loft to where he was talking to an older woman, gesturing big as he talked. "That's the head landscaper for the Botanical Garden—he's been obsessed with her for years. I'm never getting him out of here." Stevie and I took the opportunity to ask her all about acting, and her dogs, and what the supercute guy in the Ghost Robot movies was really like.

Matty wandered over at that point—he had big opinions on that franchise, it turned out. He started to ask Amy a question as a girl with a tray of champagne glasses approached. We all took one, and I was very grateful that nobody felt the need to point out that three of us were underage. If someone had, it might have broken the spell that seemed to have been conjured in the loft—where none of the normal lines that held people apart mattered. And maybe that was why Margaux had this party—and that was why everyone wanted to come.

"So what are you studying at Columbia?" Amy asked Matty once we'd moved on from haunted robots, and robot ghosts (both were present in the GR universe, and were almost always at odds). He reeled off a truly impressive course load, even if I couldn't seem to figure out what any of the subjects had to do with each other, or what he was going to do with any of it. I was about to ask something along those lines when Amy sighed and took a sip of champagne. "God, that sounds fun," she said, shaking her head. "School. I think it's the reason Lucien has two master's degrees. He says it's just because he has an irrepressible love for binders, but . . ." She laughed.

"So how did you guys meet?" Matty asked, and Amy just smiled.

"That's a whole other story," she said. "We certainly don't have time for it now. But I've gotta say, I think you're doing college right. I went in LA, and so I was auditioning a lot when I was in school, really focused on the industry right out of the gate. I kind of wish I would have done what you're doing—expanded things a little. Taken some chances."

"I think it worked out okay," Matty said, and Amy laughed.

Toward the end of the night, Stevie and I had found ourselves up by one of the windows, Brad curled, sleeping, in her arms, and snoring occasionally. Both of us were looking out at the lights of Manhattan across the water, at the snow that had almost totally stopped falling. "I'm really sorry about the subway," I said, after a moment of comfortable silence, punctured only by Brad's snuffling breath. Somehow, it was easier to say this without looking directly at Stevie, but knowing she was right there. "I did wait for a while, and then I just figured you weren't coming back. I should have stayed—I shouldn't have doubted you."

"I'm sorry too," Stevie said.

"It wasn't your fault you got mugged!"

"But the phone was an accident. I knew you wouldn't do that on purpose, and I shouldn't have reacted that way."

"I'm still sorry."

"Me too," she said. "And I should have told you the truth about Beckett." She turned to face me, and I did the same.

"Are we good?" It felt like we were—in the rush of finding each other again, in all that we had to catch up on, things felt like they used to. But I knew that we had to talk about this before we could really, truly move on.

She smiled at me. "We're good."

I turned to look at the loft. It was close to two a.m., and nobody was showing any signs of flagging. People had started dancing—Matty and his friends, Amy and Lucien, Leo and Kaya the model, who were dancing *very* close indeed. A pizza guy had just staggered in the door, his arms piled with what had to be twenty pies. Brad's nose twitched, and he sat up, straining to get down. Stevie set him on the ground, and he immediately ran for the pizza guy, yipping and running circles around his legs. I saw Cary emerge from the crowd, bow tie untied around his neck. He caught my eye and smiled at me, beckoning me forward to the dance floor.

I looked at Stevie—my best friend. "So, same thing next Friday?"

Stevie laughed, and then without looking at me, bumped me with her hip. I bumped her back, and then, like we'd discussed it ahead of time, we both walked forward to rejoin the party.

Meanwhile, back in Connecticut . . .

TERI HADN'T UNDERSTOOD HOW REAL GILROY WAS SO CALM—OR how they were possibly going to get home before the Stones.

That was before she realized they'd be traveling by helicopter.

As they flew home with the kids, Real Gilroy, and two other agents in what everyone seemed to call "the bird," Real Gilroy had pulled strings and gotten everything into place.

He had found the Stones' event, and then located their car, currently heading home on I-95. An officer had been dispatched to pull them over for an expired registration, and while it was being inspected, puncture a hole in their tire. All of which meant they wouldn't be getting home for a while. Real Gilroy had also arranged it so that someone would pick up the yellow car outside the Borderline and return it, and Mr. Stone received an email telling him Hertz had picked up the car from his house with a valet service that didn't actually exist.

Teri checked on the kids, but all were occupied. Chris was looking out the window, Parker was sleeping, and Daryl was playing on Teri's phone.

Real Gilroy hung up his phone and looked across the chopper at her. "All set," he said. He nodded. "Brace yourself."

The helicopter touched down in the Stone backyard and they all jumped off, ducking low to keep clear of the propellers.

The kids headed inside with the other agents. Real Gilroy had told her that they were going to do a sweep of the house, make sure there wasn't anything suspicious. Teri started to follow, but Real Gilroy shook his head. "Teri, hang back a minute, would you?"

Teri paused. "Everything okay?"

"Just wanted to talk to you about something." Real Gilroy rocked back on his heels and looked at her with a rare, wry smile. "You did well tonight. There are agents who've been in the field for years who couldn't have handled themselves as well. And with three kids, to boot."

"Oh." Teri felt a spark of pride ignite in her chest. "Um—thank you."

"We're always looking for talented people." He pulled out a business card and handed it to her. "And your theater background would be an asset. Actors are some of our best."

"How did you know I did theater?" A second later, Teri shook her head. "Right, because you can know everything and there's no privacy. That's cool."

"Think about it," Real Gilroy said. "You could have a bright future."

Teri nodded. Her head was spinning—but in a good way. "I will. I promise."

The two agents who'd done the sweep of the house came out. "All clear," the male agent said.

"We'll be off then. Take care," Real Gilroy said.

"You too," Teri said, giving him a wave. She watched as all three agents ran across the yard to the chopper, and a moment later, it started up again, the sound of the blades cutting through the quiet suburban night. The helicopter rose straight into the air, above the trees, up and up and up. Teri watched until it banked left and then headed out of sight. A moment later, the sound was gone and the leaves settled back down . . . like it had never been there at all.

The guesthouse was quiet and dark when she got home—Kat and Stevie still in New York, even though it was close to three. The Stones had come back an hour after she'd gotten the kids to bed, furious about their car trouble and so apologetic about the time that they'd paid her double the rate. Teri showed them the pictures that it turned out Daryl had Photoshopped on the chopper ride home. They showed an evening with the kids, her, and Kat—watching movies, playing board games, everything ordinary and wholesome.

Teri had used the lateness as a reason to explain Kat's absence—that she had a curfew she'd had to go home for. As the Stones walked her to the door, Bobbie Stone asked her if she'd had a good night. And she'd taken only a tiny pause before smiling and telling them that she had.

Teri stepped inside the guesthouse. She placed her shoes by the door—you could tell she'd been running through the woods; they were filthy—and looked around. Then she walked over and flopped down on the couch. There were all the snacks laid out for when she thought she'd have a very different kind of evening ahead of her. It was a little crazy, just how much could change over the course of a night. She curled up on the couch. She figured she'd start one of the movies while she waited for Kat and Stevie to come home. Then she could hear all about their night, even if she was legally forbidden from telling them about hers.

She'd just turned on the TV when her phone beeped with a series of texts.

Dustin Alberta

Hi Teri—hope you got home okay.

Look, I know we just met, and maybe this is too much.

But I didn't want to play any games—just wanted to tell you how I feel. I really like you.

And I was just wondering . . .

How do you feel about long-distance relationships?

Teri, reading this, smiled wide. She took a deep breath and started to text Dustin back.

Suddenly, despite the night she'd just had, she was no longer the slightest bit tired.

CHAPTER 29

Stevie

Shh," I said to Kat as we stood outside the door to Teri's guesthouse, Kat stamping her feet in the snow. It looked like it had actually snowed a little less here—which had been a relief, usually it was the opposite—just a dusting that I had a feeling would be gone by the morning.

"I didn't say anything!" she said, looking offended.

"It was a preemptive *shh*," I said. I bit my lip hard because I was on the verge of giggling, and Kat's outraged expression wasn't doing anything to quell it. The night—morning?—had taken on a punchy, fever-dream quality, with nothing seeming quite real anymore.

"You're the one who's laughing," she pointed out, though I could see that she was starting to laugh too—her voice was getting tighter, and higher, the sound of a laugh bubbling underneath somewhere.

"I'm not," I said, lowering my voice and trying to get the corners of my mouth to turn down. Kat burst out laughing and she got me too, both of us giggling and trying to stay upright.

"What are we even laughing about?" she laugh-whispered when we'd composed ourselves slightly.

"No idea," I said, taking a breath and trying to stop the last giggles, the ones that kept escaping, like hiccups. I had a feeling a piece of it was just that we wanted to celebrate that we could do this again—that we could laugh, that things were okay, that we were back together, that we'd gotten through, in the end, everything the night had thrown at us.

We'd crossed though the looking glass and had a night that I knew nobody would believe, and even though we were back in the real world again, it felt maybe like we could take some of the magic with us. Like maybe our ordinary lives wouldn't seem so ordinary, now that we'd hung out with movie stars and discovered fortunes hiding in plain sight; now that we'd found the answers had been in our pocket all along; now that we'd faced our dragons and slain them—or at least, in my case, come to a better and more communicative understanding with them.

But maybe, I realized as I started to turn the doorknob slowly, not wanting to wake up Teri or set off any alarms, our lives weren't so ordinary after all. Maybe the regular life you take for granted becomes unspeakably precious once it's not yours anymore. When Amy and I had found ourselves together in a corner of the loft, she'd asked me about the theater department, and whether I was going to act in college.

"I . . . don't know," I said, trying out every word carefully. I was in unchartered territory, now that I no longer had the easy answer. It was suddenly like the world was a whole lot wider than I'd realized. And it meant that I no longer had a plan . . . but maybe that was okay. "Maybe?" I finally said. "I'm still deciding, I guess."

"Just enjoy it," she'd said, smiling at her fiancé, who came over bearing a drink for her. "Before it all matters so much. Before it's how you pay the rent. There's something so wonderful about that."

I'd nodded like I understood what she was talking about, and she just smiled at me. "Have *fun*," she'd said, before giving me a quick hug (!!) and disappearing back into the crowd.

Now, I turned to Kat on the landing of the guesthouse, to make sure we were somewhat in control. She gave me a thumbs-up and I smiled back at her.

My best friend. I was never going to stop being happy to see her.

I pushed the door open slowly, and after Kat followed me in, closed it just as slowly and turned the lock. Since it was after three in the morning, I'd expected that Teri would have been in bed ages ago, but the TV was on, showing the changing screen saver—the Golden Gate Bridge, Hong Kong, a wide-open plain—and in the glow of it, I could see that she was stretched out on the couch, fast asleep. There were empty snack wrappers spread all around, and Kat's phone in the center of the coffee table, just where we'd left it.

I was about to point it out to Kat but found myself hesitating. It had not been fun to be so without our phones tonight—very inconvenient, undoubtedly scary, and incredibly frustrating. But even though I wasn't going to make a habit of it, there had been some good things about it too. I'd had to be in the moment, not able to duck out when things got too real or uncomfortable. And on the ride home, even when Kat and I weren't talking—looking out the window or just sitting in comfortable silence—we'd both been *there*. We hadn't been comparing experiences, watching someone else's night. We'd been too busy living our own.

Kat smiled at Teri, fast asleep, then grabbed a blanket off the other couch and draped it over her.

I reached for the remote, figuring that Teri might sleep better without the TV light flashing all night. As I did, I must have woken the TV up—because there was Teri's Netflix queue, showing us how she'd spent her night.

"Jeez," Kat whispered as she looked at it. She turned to me in the glow of the TV light, her eyes wide. "Did she watch all these movies tonight? She's gonna have crazy nightmares."

I looked at the screen—*Adventures in Babysitting*, *The Bourne Identity*, *Midnight Run*. "She looks like she's okay," I said, and we both glanced down at her. Teri was still in her clothes for some reason, with a brown streak across her forehead that looked like dirt, her hair tangled at the ends. "What is that?"

Kat peered closer, then shrugged. "Maybe she did a mask or something."

"Hey," I said, picking up Kat's phone and holding it out to her. One night was one thing, but it wasn't like we were going to live like it was 1992 again. And who would want to? But as she reached out and took it, I was suddenly, surprisingly glad that there were no pictures of tonight—no stories, no narration, no shaping the night for other people to see it. No proof at all. We'd just have to remember.

She took it from me and held it close. "Thank god," she said, and I laughed. She went to unlock it, then stopped, her hand hovering over the screen.

"Something wrong?"

Kat looked up at me, hesitated for a moment, then handed her phone to me. "Here."

"What?" I asked, not understanding. "You need me to unlock it?"

"No," she said, holding it out to me. "You should take it. I know you've backed your phone up recently—"

"Yesterday. Why you don't ever back your phone up is beyond me—"

"So you can just transfer everything over. Move your number over, the whole thing. Here." She stretched it out farther to me, and after hesitating a moment, I took it.

"You don't have to do this."

Kat shook her head. "I *do*," she said, her voice rising. Teri stirred in her sleep, muttering something that sounded like *helicopter*, and Kat and I both took a step away from the couch. "I do," she said again, more quietly. "It was my fault your phone got broken. I have to take responsibility for once. This was my fault. So take the phone."

I took it from her and turned it over in my hands once. I knew it was a largely symbolic gesture at the moment—it was still Kat's phone, after all, with her numbers and texts and all her information, and lots of technical Genius Bar things had to be done before it was mine—but that didn't mean I didn't appreciate it. "Thanks, Kat."

Kat smiled at me, but halfway through it turned into a gigantic yawn. "God, I'm tired."

"Really? Why would that be?"

She laughed and headed back toward the guest room we'd be sharing.

The screen saver was back on the TV again, and as I watched, the ocean view transformed into a panorama of New York City at night. I looked at it for a moment—the impossible buildings, the bright lights, the millions of stories. I smiled, and looked at it for one moment more before I pointed the remote at the TV and turned it off.

PART SIX
Saturday

CASEY

And you can see, not that much happened here tonight. Nothing that you can point to. But we can all feel it. One world ended and another began.

RYLA

Plus, there was the whole Robot uprising.

CASEY

Right, that too.

—*Dave Stuart,* Ghost Robot 5: Ghost in the Machine

CHAPTER 30

Kat

Tell me again," I said as I curled up on the couch and looked at Teri. She was positively glowing, her whole face alight. I was not quite so happy or well-rested, but that might have been because I'd gotten about five hours' sleep. As soon as Stevie was awake and ready, I was going to suggest a Starbucks run. I needed it injected directly into my veins. I yawned behind my hand and tried to get myself to focus, then grabbed a handful of the gummy candy on the coffee table. "You and Ryan Camper broke up?"

Teri rolled her eyes. "Ugh, *yes*. He was way too possessive and jealous. And there was no trust there! Dustin is so much better. I can already tell."

"Dustin, your new boyfriend," I said, trying to keep up.

"Yes," Teri said, beaming. "He's so sweet and so cute and so nice and super polite—which makes sense. I mean, he is Canadian."

"Uh-huh," I said, trying to keep my face very still. "And this all happened . . . last night?"

"It was a *really* eventful night."

I smiled at that as I bit down on a sour gummy peach. Breakfast was the most important meal of the day, after all. "So—" I started, just as the guest bedroom door opened and Stevie came out in her pajamas, her hair up in a messy bun. "Morning."

"Hi," she said around a yawn, and came to sit next to me on the couch. "Have you guys been up long?"

"Not that long," I said, moving over to make room for her. I met her eyes and widened mine slightly. "Teri was just telling me all about her new boyfriend."

"Oh," Stevie said, looking from me to Teri and back again. "No more . . . Ryan Camper?"

"Nope," Teri said, with a wide, *I have a crush on someone* smile taking over her face. "Dustin is so much better than stupid Ryan."

"Dustin lives in Canada," I said, glancing at Stevie again and trying to keep my face from betraying anything.

"Your . . . boyfriend who lives in Canada!" Stevie said, smiling at Teri and then shooting me a fleeting look that was gone in the blink of an eye. But I knew exactly what she'd been saying with it—that this was getting *ridiculous*. Teri had seen *Avenue Q* too—how did she not hear this?

"Yeah," Teri said, hugging a pillow to her chest. "Dustin Alberta."

I bit the inside of my lip hard enough that tears came to my eyes. *"Hrm,"* I said, nodding a few too many times. "That's great, Teri."

"I'm really happy if you're happy," Stevie said, and I could tell that she meant it.

Teri beamed at us both. "Thanks, guys." She reached forward for the candy again. "So how was your night? How was Josephine's? Did you see any celebrities?"

Stevie and I looked at each other, and I started laughing. *"Well,"* I began as Stevie shook her head.

"I want to tell it! Oh my god, Teri, so it started at Grand Central—"

I frowned. "Grand Central? Why are you starting it there?"

"With Mallory."

"I mean, you *could* start it there, but I wouldn't."

"See, this is why I wanted to tell it."

"No! I am. So—"

Teri's phone beeped with a text, and I heard mine beep as well—though technically it was now Stevie's phone—from back in the guest bedroom. Teri grabbed her phone from where it was resting on the couch next to her. As she looked at it, her whole expression changed. "Guys," she said, her eyes still on her phone.

"What?" Stevie asked. "What is it?"

Teri lowered her phone and swallowed hard. "The list is up."

Stevie and I drove in silence to the school. Most of the snow had melted overnight—there were just patches of it here and there. Teri had taken her own car, and we'd lost sight of her almost immediately, due to Stevie's geriatric driving style. For once, though, I didn't mind it. I was tempted, as Stevie passed by the entrance ramps for I-95, to tell her to just turn onto the highway. We'd drive north, pass New Haven, and finally try Mystic Pizza. Or south, back into the city. We could pick up bagels on the way, go to Columbia and find Matty and his friends. Or see if Cary was working a shift at Maverick. We could go to Dumbo and get Brad from Margaux, take him on a walk down by the water. We could stay in the not-knowingness a little bit longer.

"Eric didn't say anything," Stevie said again, even though we'd been saying variations of this to each other ever since the texts on the group thread had come through. He was the one who'd spotted the list when he'd been on a bike ride this morning. But he hadn't included a picture of it, or any takes on the casting, just the information that it was up. No exclamation points, no emojis. And then the thread had gone quiet as everyone had jumped into their cars and sped over to the theater.

"What do you think that means?" I asked. A day ago, this would have been all-consuming. I would have been desperately trying to get any information that I could, and would have been playing out all kinds of scenarios, and trying to get Stevie to drive faster, to get there sooner. I would have been convinced that this casting, this part, this theater department, was the only thing that mattered—it was all everything had been leading up to. And now?

Now I wasn't so sure.

"I guess we'll find out," she said, her voice quiet. Maybe she was also trying to grapple with the fact that on the surface, nothing had changed since yesterday. But absolutely everything felt different.

The school was deserted—not that surprising, since it was nine o'clock on a Saturday. Stevie parked in the senior parking lot, and we headed over together to the theater building. I could see the group crowded around the door, everyone looking at one piece of paper.

The list was up.

As we got closer, Stevie reached down and grabbed my hand, gave it a squeeze. I smiled without looking at her and squeezed her hand back.

The crowd around the list was most of the senior thespians. I was sure that word would soon trickle out to everyone else, but for right now, it was just us. Somehow, a list had gotten printed out and taped to the door, so either Mr. Campbell had been here to do it or he'd emailed the list and gotten someone else to do it for him. But he wasn't anywhere that I could see, and I was very grateful for that at the moment.

It felt like the walk to the double doors had never been so long, and I was trying to tell myself that whatever it was had already been decided. There was nothing that could be done about it except for me to cross from not knowing into knowing. Teri was standing right in front of the paper, and as I got close, I tapped her shoulder. She turned, and when she saw it was me, her eyes widened and she took a step back. I could feel her—and most of the other seniors—watching us as Stevie and I stepped up to read the list.

It was already covered in blue and black pen signatures of people indicating they were accepting their parts. The black letters on the white page swam in my vision for a second as I tried to make them make sense. Jayson had gotten Lear, as we'd all known he would . . . Erik was Gloucester and Eric was Kent . . .

. . . and Stevie was Cordelia.

I drew in a breath without knowing I was going to, forcing myself to keep reading. Teri was Regan, Emery was Goneril . . . I scanned down the page, looking for my name, faster and faster, and there at the bottom, after the list of the ensemble and understudies:

Kat, please see me about assistant directing.

"Oh my god," Stevie breathed. Her hand was over her mouth, and I turned around to see that all the other seniors were staring at me, with looks ranging from baffled to pitying to horrified, or some combination of all three. I could see just how shaken everyone was by this— this was *not* supposed to happen in a world they understood.

And in that moment, I knew, without a shadow of a doubt, that this was payback. If I'd been able to lie last night—if I'd been willing to say the right things—I would have been looking at a list with *Cordelia* across from my name.

"Kat," Teri whispered, and I could see there were tears in her eyes. "I don't . . ."

"He's such an asshole." I turned to see that Stevie was looking angrier than I'd ever seen her. She was practically shaking with fury. "He's such a *fucking* asshole."

"Who?" Aminah asked nervously, looking around, like we were being bugged. "Mr. Campbell?"

"I never even read for Cordelia!" Stevie exploded. "The only reason he cast me was to mess with Kat, to hurt her. . . ."

"Why would he want to do that?" Erik asked, sounding baffled.

Everyone looked at me, and I could tell that they were all waiting for something. Some explanation, something to put this in context, something that would let them know that there was still order in the world as they understood it. Because, I realized as I looked at the list, at my name on the bottom like an afterthought, they still thought that the emperor was a great guy, wearing a really nice suit.

I let my eyes roam over the paper one last time and felt a pang—not a huge one, but it was there. The kind you get whenever you say goodbye.

And then—because there was no other reaction, really—I threw my head back and laughed.

"Kat?" Stevie asked. I could hear in her voice that she clearly thought my disappointment had caused some kind of psychological break.

"I'm fine," I said, shaking my head, trying to get control of myself. But I was, I realized. I was *fine*. And what's more—I was free. "Really, I'm good," I assured my best friend, looking right into her eyes so that she would know I meant it. "Anyone have a pen?"

Jayson handed me his, and I took a breath and stepped forward. There, at the bottom of the list, right next to my name, I carefully wrote, *I would prefer not to*.

I took a step back and smiled as I looked at it, then handed Jayson his pen. "Thanks," I said, and he nodded, still staring at me like he wasn't sure who I was or what was happening.

I headed toward Stevie's car, and she fell into step next to me. I glanced back at all the other seniors, most of whom were still looking gobsmacked. I had a feeling that as soon as we drove away, the speculation would begin—and I had no doubt a new group thread, but this one without me, was already being put together. "Congratulations," I said as we both got into Nikola. Stevie paused, hand hovering near the ignition, and gave me an anguished look. "I mean it."

"I didn't want it. You know that—"

"Of course I do. But he didn't give it to you just to mess with me."

"Partially, at least."

"Well, maybe a tiny bit. But you're going to be great. You're going to be *so* good. And I'm going to be cheering you on."

Stevie nodded, and looked at me for a moment, then smiled.

I smiled back at her. It was going to be okay. We would make it okay.

Stevie started the car and I folded my legs up underneath me. "Breakfast?" she asked.

"Oh god, yes. I'll text Teri and see if she wants to meet us at the diner."

"And just what are you going to text her on?"

I laughed. "Can I borrow *your* phone?"

"Thank you," she said. "I mean, it's been my phone for a whole five hours, so . . ." As she talked, Stevie pulled out of the parking lot, and I made sure to look straight ahead, so as not to be tempted to look in the rearview mirror and see what was behind me.

Because after all, there was coffee and a diner breakfast in my near future. I had a brand-new crush, I had to decide what I was going to do now that I wouldn't be in this play, not to mention that I needed to talk to my parents about why I needed another phone, And beyond that—I would just have to figure it out as I went. Like Stevie always said, I had to eat the whale one bite at a time.

I finished texting Teri just as Stevie pulled into the diner parking lot. She immediately responded that she'd be right there. "We good?" Stevie asked.

I smiled at her. "We're great," I said, unbuckling my seat belt, already dreaming of pancakes. "Let's go."

PART SEVEN
February

Think where man's glory most begins and ends,
And say my glory was I had such friends.
—*William Butler Yeats*

Ten minutes to places!" The assistant stage manager, a sophomore named Greta, stuck her head into the green room and
looked around.

"Ten minutes, thank you," we all chorused. She nodded and hurried
away.

"How are you feeling?" Teri asked, grabbing my arm and, as usual on
opening nights, looking a little bit green.

"I'm feeling great," I said, as calmly as possible. We'd all learned,
over the last four years, that if you displayed even a hint of nervousness, Teri was liable to forget her first few lines. But if everyone was
calm and collected, she got past her early jitters and was able to shake
them off entirely by her second scene. "You're going to be fine."

Teri nodded and adjusted the collar of her skirt suit. Mr. Campbell
had decided on a modern-day setting of *King Lear*. In this version,
King Lear was actually the CEO of LearCorp, and the play was about
the company being broken up, hostile takeovers, everyone in business
attire.

Despite a rocky start, the show had really come together. I'd loved
playing Cordelia, and I couldn't wait for everyone to finally see it.
I looked around for Kat, out of habit, and then realized what I was
doing.

Of all the changes in the last few months, that had been the hardest
to get used to. I kept expecting her to be there—at the read-through,
at rehearsals, at the tech. All of us were aware that we were missing

one of our regular people. But between her and Dara Chapman both absent—and the fact that they were both doing great, even without being in the production—it was almost like it was giving other people permission to think about the possibility of not doing every single play. Of stepping away occasionally. Nothing had happened yet, but there were rumbles. I'd heard Erik talk about training to do a half-marathon instead of the musical, and Jayson hadn't told Mr. Campbell yet, but I knew he was thinking about going on his history class's trip to Greece, which would mean he couldn't be in the improv show.

It wasn't huge, but there were little cracks, and I knew my best friend had been the one to make them.

I paced around the greenroom, running my first line in my head, even though I knew this script backward and forward. I'd even used my monologue for my two conservatory auditions. In the end, I'd decided to cast a wide net. Northwestern, yes, but also USC and College of the West and Bates, Vanderbilt and Colgate, Scripps and Tulane, Columbia and NYU. Now that I wasn't following my dad's exact plan, I'd decided I might as well have as many possibilities as I could.

Though I hadn't started to narrow them down, more and more I was liking the idea of staying closer to home. I was just getting to know my siblings, after all, and even though it had only been a few months, things were undeniably better with my dad. And even though I knew this wouldn't stop if I was at school in Los Angeles or Evanston or Nashville, I didn't have a huge need to get out of town. I decided that I'd just see how I was feeling when the acceptances—or rejections—started to roll in.

I needed to take a minute, just to get centered, so I stepped out of the greenroom and into the hallway. I walked slowly up and down, rolling my shoulders back and taking deep breaths. I was always fine once the show had started and all this anticipatory energy burned off. It was just in this moment before that it helped to get out of my own head.

I stopped in front of a poster that had been hung up. *The Scriveners*, it read. *An Original Works Festival. Short plays written, directed, and starring Stanwich High School students.*

I smiled as I looked at it. It had all been a fight—even getting this poster hung up in the hallway had been what my dad would call a knock-down, drag-out—but Kat had done it, in the end. And I was so proud of her for pulling it off.

The festival wasn't until next month, but getting it off the ground had been the biggest challenge of all. Mr. Campbell had not taken kindly to the idea of someone coming in and putting on a show that he wasn't in charge of and hadn't sanctioned—especially not when it was being spearheaded by Kat, who he'd been pointedly ignoring ever since she turned down assistant directing. It was essentially the cut direct, something I'd read about in old novels but had never seen someone employ in real life, or modern day. But through lots of fights, she'd prevailed. I was acting in three of the plays, and was directing one. I knew it was going to be a huge success.

And even though it was still very hard for me to do, I was trying not to think too far ahead. Right now, the furthest out I wanted to plan was this summer—and *someone* had to plan it, since everyone had very different ideas, and none of them were compatible. My mom wanted me to come with her on a gallery tour of the Catskills—she'd been acquiring a lot recently. I was pretty sure it had something to do with finally getting *New York Night* number three, now hung in the spot that had been reserved for it all those years, completing the series. After she'd gotten it, she'd starting acquiring for the Pearce in a different way. It was like she was less locked into what my grandmother would have chosen. She was even thinking about getting a separate space, or a different wing, for emerging artists. She was still figuring it out, but it had been a revelation to me that no matter how old you get, it's hard to shake your parents' expectations.

Matty was making big plans for what he was calling the Sinclair/Lampitoc Sibling Summer (Winter) Friendship Fun Tour. He was determined that we should all go to Australia and New Zealand—possibly Fiji, too—and the rest of us had a suspicion it was just because he liked how absurd it sounded.

And as for me, I'd been looking into internships and assistant positions for me and Kat, something we could do together our last summer before college. The Williamstown Theatre Festival had a great one, and Amy thought she might be able to get us PA jobs on her upcoming film. There were some summer stock theaters in Pennsylvania and Tennessee and Ohio . . . we didn't have to make any decisions yet, but it was fun, for the moment, to just look at all the opportunities and know we had options for a truly epic summer.

I turned away from the poster and saw Beckett walking down the hallway toward me, dressed all in tech crew black. I gave him a smile, and he gave me one back.

"Hey," I said, and he raised his eyebrows at me.

"Ready?" he asked.

"As I'll ever be." Things between us had been different since we got back from New York. A few weeks into *Lear* rehearsals, Beckett had started dating the junior running the sound board. We were still friends—I knew we'd always be friends—but what we were doing now felt more balanced, somehow. Healthier.

Beckett smiled at me. "You'll be great," he said. "Break a leg."

"And you, *don't* break one." He laughed, and gave me a nod before hurrying off.

Greta passed him as she half ran up the hallway, clutching her clipboard, looking around. "Places! That is places, people."

I nodded. "Places, thank you."

Greta stuck her head into the greenroom and announced places, and I decided to beat the rush as I headed off toward the wings. I stood in the dark, and smoothed down my costume, and took a deep breath.

I was ready.

CHAPTER 32

Kat

As I stood in the lobby of the theater, I realized that it was my first time on the other side.

I had dressed up for opening night, of course, and there was a seat saved for me in the auditorium. But as I walked into the building with the rest of the parents and friends coming to see the first performance of *King Lear*, I realized that it was my very first time there as just an audience member. On the other side of the curtain, not running around getting ready or preparing or putting out fires. Just someone there to see a play, one face among many in the audience.

I nodded at the sophomore selling refreshments and she gave me a quick nod back before looking from side to side, like she was making sure she should have done that. I didn't blame her—Mr. Campbell still had a lot of power in the department, and I was basically persona non grata these days.

I shucked off my coat as I walked inside, well aware that everyone else was waiting for me, and at least three people were probably rolling their eyes at each other about my tardiness. But I'd driven my own car over because I'd thought it might take me a minute, just to process it all.

Even though turning down assistant directing had been the right thing to do, that didn't mean it hadn't been difficult. The day rehearsals started, I waved goodbye to Stevie and saw everyone—all my friends—heading over to the theater together, off on some grand adventure I wouldn't be part of. It had hit me harder than I realized it would, and I'd gotten in my car to go home, but hadn't even made it half a mile before I'd pulled over to the side of the road and cried.

And Stevie did her best to try and keep me in the loop, but it wasn't easy—I still sat at lunch with everyone, but there were now inside jokes I didn't understand, which is just what happens when a group of people spends hours together every day. It was tough, but I understood it wasn't personal. And over time, it had gotten easier.

I'd also been keeping busy. I'd written two essays for the *Pilgrim*, our school paper, and had joined mock trial as an alternate at Dara Chapman's urging, because they always needed people who could act, and none of the people who did theater were ever free. I really liked it, even though law was something I'd never considered, despite the fact I liked acting and arguing, which seemed to be the two main requirements.

But the biggest thing of all was the original works festival. It had started as a small idea, as I'd been suddenly aware of all the people at the school who were interested in writing, or directing, or acting— but somehow weren't involved in the theater program. Maybe they wanted to do more than one thing. Maybe they'd never been cast and had eventually given up. But whatever the reason, there were a lot of talented kids and I had time on my hands. So I decided to try to get it started. I loved the idea—all short plays, student written, student directed, student acted. I'd known, of course, that Mr. Campbell was going to be against it. I'd just underestimated how much.

To say it had been a fight would be to do a disservice to the word "fight." We'd had a terrible meeting with the headmistress after Mr. Campbell had basically blacklisted it, proclaiming that if you participated in my festival, you would not be considered for casting next fall. The meeting had been beyond intense, with me calmly stating my points while Mr. Campbell screamed about the fact that he wasn't going to let his theater be used for amateur junk. The headmistress just arched an eyebrow and pointed out that it wasn't *his* theater—it was the school's.

In the end I'd prevailed. We would have a weekend in the theater in April, before musical rehearsals were in full swing. And nobody would be punished for auditioning. We'd been able to generate a lot of interest when we announced that Andrea and Scott Hughes were going to serve as playwriting mentors, and that Amy Curry, who would be in New York shooting a movie this spring, would also be helping out when she could. (Amazingly, we'd found the day after the party that she'd followed both me and Stevie on her private Instagram. We'd been able to transition that into emailing occasionally, but both of us were very careful not to bug her too much, hyperaware of *don't bother the movie star who for some reason is putting up with us.*)

But after all the fights to get it off the ground, the original works festival was *fun.* I was getting to write my own stuff, which I was loving, and getting to act and direct. It definitely wasn't as polished as the productions Mr. Campbell put on, but that was okay. I had ended up doing what my mother wanted me to do—changing the system. And I was just hoping it would turn out well and be able to continue even after I graduated, a small legacy that I could leave.

I hadn't auditioned for any conservatories after all (my parents were thrilled). I'd applied to mostly liberal arts schools with good theater programs. I wasn't sure what I wanted to do yet. Maybe I'd audition. Maybe I'd direct, or keep going with playwriting. Maybe I'd take a different kind of writing course or I'd discover I loved something I hadn't even considered yet—Russian literature or sports psychology or calculus (probably not calculus). But mostly, I wanted to try a lot of things. I wanted to see what there was to see.

The three tones sounded in the lobby—they meant that it was five minutes to showtime. I grabbed a program from the stack and started to head to my seat. As I crossed the lobby, I saw Mr. Campbell standing by the entrance, greeting the parents he knew, ushering people in. I met his eye and he looked pointedly away.

"Hi, Mr. Campbell," I said cheerfully as I got closer. He continued to look right past me, but I was not about to just take that. *"Hi, Mr. Campbell,"* I said, louder this time. I saw the parents around me notice—that a teacher was ignoring a student.

He must have noticed too, because he finally turned to me and gave me a curt nod. "Katrina." He strode away and I allowed myself a small smile. Getting an opportunity to prove that you were more mature than your teacher who was almost forty had been an unexpected silver lining in all the events that had transpired. Because of everything that had happened, it was hard for me sometimes to even remember how I used to think about Mr. Campbell—the pedestal I'd put him up on. And while I was glad things had turned out like they had, occasionally I missed that kind of clarity. It's always easier to believe someone is perfect and never wrong. Easier—but never true.

I hurried down the aisle, looking around for my group, rising up on my toes to try and see better. I'd started taking dance classes again—just two a week. I was slowly getting back into ballet shape, but I'd also been trying modern and occasionally jazz. I was having fun with it. It had taken me a while, but after I stepped away from the theater program, I'd started to remember a lot of other things I'd loved and had pushed aside—like dance. And I'd come to realize that just because I wasn't going to do it professionally didn't mean I had to cut it out of my life entirely. And my modern class was in the city—which was a bonus, because that was where my boyfriend lived.

"Hi," I said, finally seeing him and giving him a smile as I took the seat on the end. "Sorry."

"No problem," Cary said, helping me drape my coat over my chair, and then giving me a quick kiss.

"Gross," Grady said from Cary's other side.

I made a face at my brother as I settled into my seat. The one thing that turned my brother from a middle-aged man back into a ten-year-old was any public display of affection. But Cary and Grady had gotten along right from the beginning—Cary dropped a few of his fun facts and my brother was won over. "You won't always think it's gross," my dad assured him from his other side. He glanced at his watch pointedly. "Cutting it close."

"But I made it," I said, and my mother leaned over from my dad's other side and caught my eye. I knew she was silently asking if I was okay. I nodded and she gave me a small smile.

"While we were waiting for you, I was able to lock down some more research dates with Cary," my dad said. I gave Cary a look, and he just shrugged happily.

After he sold the painting to the Pearce, my dad had done a follow-up story, and then an entire profile. It had turned into a huge news moment. Everyone loved the hook—the unrecognized painting, the millions just hanging on a wall, the chance by which it was discovered. He was now considering a book, about unexpected discoveries of all different kinds, and as a result was spending a lot of time with my boyfriend. But they got along great, which I loved, even as I pretended to be annoyed.

My mom had taken him under her wing and introduced him to financial people, who set up trusts and funds and all kinds of things to protect him and his sudden windfall and keep most of it tied up in investments. But college—and any grad school—would be more than covered. And his aunt and uncle had retired and moved upstate to a house Cary bought for them. We'd gone to visit last week; his uncle still took credit for setting this all in motion when his car broke down in Pennsylvania, but Cary had just looked at me and smiled. Both of us knew that if anyone deserved credit . . . it was Brad.

Cary reached over and took my hand. We were just having fun—seeing where it went, neither of us making any long-term plans. Teri and her boyfriend, Dustin Alberta, were also apparently still going strong, though we had yet to meet him.

I looked down the row, liking what I saw. Stevie's dad had come in early from the city and had claimed the seats for us as soon as the doors had opened. Which had been a good call, since we took up the whole row—Stevie's dad, Joy, Stevie's mom, Margaux, Margaux's now-wife Allison (they'd eloped last month), Matty, my mom, my dad, Grady, and Cary.

It was a motley group, but it was one I was happy to be among.

"You okay?" Cary whispered to me. I looked over at him and smiled.

"Yeah," I said as I squeezed his hand. "I'm great." The lights dimmed, and Cary squeezed my hand back. I heard Matty's laugh and then a hush fell, and I settled back into my seat.

The show was about to begin.